REDEMPTION

Text copyright ©2012 by Susannah Sandlin
All rights reserved.
Printed in the United States of America.

Published by Montlake Romance
P.O. Box 400818
Las Vegas, NV 89140

ISBN-13: 9781612183541
ISBN-10: 1612183549

REDEMPTION
THE PENTON LEGACY

BOOK ONE

SUSANNAH SANDLIN

Dedication

To the people of Chambers County, Alabama, whose beautiful towns and countryside I borrowed for this book.

❊ PROLOGUE ❊

November, New York City

Matthias Ludlam watched the smoke drift toward his study ceiling, fumes from burning photo chemicals stinging his eyes. In an ashtray on the desk, the image of his son William, taken last week, curled into blackened edges as the fire took hold.

Finally, he knew where the boy had gone. Now he had to teach him where he belonged...and to whom.

"Does he know you spotted him?" Matthias rubbed his eyes and focused on the human lounging in the armchair across the desk. Roger Hobb worked for the Vampire Tribunal as a private eye, and his specialty was tracking down vamps whose acts endangered their society. But this wasn't an official job, and Matthias needed discretion.

"'Course not," Hobb drawled. "I know my job. It's why the Tribunal pays me."

viii | SUSANNAH SANDLIN

The Tribunal pays you because you're cheap, expendable, and too stupid to be afraid of your employers. "Then you won't have any problem going in with an enforcer and extracting my son. Use any means necessary short of staking him. Bring him to me."

William wouldn't like it but after a few months without feeding or women, he'd be forced to fall in line. His son liked his luxuries.

Hobb took a sip of Matthias's best whiskey, then another. "It, uh...it won't be that easy, Mr. Ludlam. Sir."

Matthias finished his own glass and leaned forward, elbows on his desk, his gold signet ring making a loud crack as it hit the wood. "Why not? You said William doesn't know we've found him." He ticked through Hobb's body language: tightly set shoulders, shaky hands, sweat beaded on his forehead. The man reeked of fear. *Bloody hell. What now?*

Hobb cleared his throat, straightened his spine, and handed Matthias a manila folder from his briefcase. "Helluva lot more going on in Penton than just a place for William to hide. Thought about takin' it to the Tribunal but figured since your boy was involved...you'd be, uh, grateful, if you know what I mean."

"If I'm not grateful, you'll know it." Written on the tab: Penton, Alabama. *How much could possibly be going on in the middle of bumfuck nowhere?* Sighing, Matthias leaned back in his chair and flipped open the folder.

On top was an eight-by-ten close-up of a man he had no trouble recognizing: handsome, dark haired, icy blue eyes brimming with arrogance. "Aidan Murphy? That's who Will is with?" He'd heard Murphy had moved from Atlanta and settled somewhere in the sticks. What a total waste of a master vampire—strong-willed and fearless, but rejecting every overture the Tribunal had made to get him involved in the vampire power structure. Murphy had never been openly defiant, though. "I still don't see the problem."

Hobb stood up and held his hands toward the fireplace, where a low flame crackled. New York winters were cold, and this one had gotten off to a brutal start. "Murphy's got a big scathe, Mr. Ludlam. And every vampire in Penton, near as I can tell, is blood-bonded to him or one of his lieutenants." He paused. "Including your son."

Anger, cold and hard, seeped through Matthias's bones. Bad enough William had rejected his birthright after he'd turned the boy vampire and groomed him for a future of wealth and power. Now he'd bonded himself to a rogue Irish peasant?

Matthias shoved the photo of Murphy aside and froze when he saw the one underneath it. No mistaking this man. His size, scowl, and tattoos were distinctive, even though the photo had been shot from a distance. "Mirren Kincaid has been dead for years—what does he have to do with this?"

"H—he's alive. The Slayer's alive, and he's bonded to Aidan Murphy too. There's at least twenty-five of them in that scathe, near as I can tell." Matthias fixed him with a glare, and Hobb talked faster. "They're isolated in that little town. Everybody who lives there seems to be either a vampire bonded to Murphy or a human bonded to one of his vampires. At least a hundred, all told. Maybe more. I couldn't get close enough for a count. Had to spread around a lot of money to find out this much."

Matthias's mind raced through the ramifications. "Shut up and let me think. Have another whiskey."

The sounds of a decanter being unstopped, ice clinking in a crystal glass, liquid pouring. The noises were usually comforting, but with this news, nothing would ease the chill that spread through Matthias as he rose from the desk and stared out the study window at the snowflakes settling on the bare branches and slushy sidewalks illuminated by the streetlights.

The average scathe was four or five vampires strong—and Murphy had bonded more than twenty-five? That wasn't a scathe; it was an army. With his son and the Tribunal's most lethal enforcer paying fealty to him, Murphy could be powerful enough to defeat the Tribunal if he wanted to.

And if they had bonded humans with them...

Matthias rubbed his hand over his stomach, flatter now than it had been a year ago when a worldwide pandemic vaccine had resulted in an unexpected change in human blood chemistry. Tens of thousands of humans had died from the virus itself, reducing the vampire food supply. Then came the goddamned vaccine.

The blood of a vaccinated human was lethal to vampires.

Vampires were starving, and they were getting desperate. All of the Tribunal's attempts to counteract the vaccine's effects had failed. Even human blood banks were tainted and unreliable. Yet Aidan Murphy had a town full of apparently unvaccinated humans bonded to him so no other vampires could feed from them? Bloody outrageous.

He turned back to Hobb. "You think it's possible to infiltrate Murphy's scathe, break it up from within?"

Hobb swallowed so hard that Matthias could hear him across the room. "No, sir. The guy I paid for the info only talked 'cause Murphy wouldn't let him move to Penton—says he interviews everyone personally and if he don't want you, you don't live there. They're real organized."

Murphy had friends on the Tribunal, so taking this to the full council wouldn't yield quick results: technically, he hadn't broken vampire law. So far.

Matthias returned to his desk, looking again at the photos. An idea came to him, brilliant in its simplicity. "Murphy's older brother, Owen. He still alive?"

Hobb's eyebrows bunched. "He's supposed to be executed next week."

Matthias smiled. "Get him here. I'm about to make Owen Murphy the offer of a lifetime."

✳CHAPTER 1✳

Never tick off a starving vampire. Aidan Murphy guided his BMW along the dark-as-midnight country road with his left hand and shook the makeshift bandage—a bar napkin—off his right. The puncture wounds had healed.

What a waste of time. Since the pandemic vaccine had made human blood poisonous to his kind, he'd held dozens of meetings like the one he'd just left, interviewing prospective scathe members for Penton, a tiny ghost town on the edge of nowhere that he'd bought up after life became dangerous for his scathe's unvaccinated humans. A place where his people and their human familiars could live in peace.

Aidan had founded Penton on the idea that humans were the equals of vampires. Respect them for keeping you alive, he preached. Treat them as family. Don't act like monsters. But vampires were growing desperate. Hungry predators suddenly considered his quiet Alabama community of vampires and bonded, unvaccinated humans to be the vampire equivalent of a midnight buffet in the Garden of Eden.

And he usually told them the same thing: Sorry, but foxhole converts never keep the faith. One of the SOBs hadn't liked his answer tonight and took a plug out of his hand. Like that was going to convince him the guy would fit in.

Aidan!

At the shock of the voice echoing through his head, he jammed a foot on the brake, simultaneously trying to control the car and listen to the frantic mental SOS. His tires squealed when he jerked the steering wheel into the skid, sending the car spinning across both lanes of the deserted blacktop. It finally jolted to a stop in a shallow ditch, nose-first.

His forehead cracked against the driver's-side window hard enough to spiderweb the glass and shoot stars across his vision, but the blood trickling its way down his temple barely registered.

Mark was in trouble.

Shit. What the hell had happened? The mental cry for help faded, taking the images with it: a blood-coated knife, a wet parking lot, a Dumpster, and his brother's name: *Owen.* Now he was alone in his head again, alone in his car listening to the tick-tick-tick of the cooling engine, an owl hooting in the thick woods next to the road, and the rustle of pine needles as a cold wind blew away the last of the January rain clouds.

Owen had attacked again, and not just anybody. Mark was his business partner, his friend, and the husband of Aidan's human familiar. They were his family, more than Owen had been in a long time. And he couldn't lose another family member.

Unconscious doesn't mean dead, idiot. Stop the pity party. Resting his head against the smooth leather seat, Aidan closed his eyes and unleashed his mind to search for Mark, sending psychic tendrils along the blood bonds that the humans and vampires of his scathe shared.

Finally, a spark. Mark's mental signal was no more than a faint pulse, but Aidan was able to get a fix on a location: the abandoned Quikmart outside Penton.

God. Damned. Owen.

Aidan gripped the wheel in frustration, and then pulled his fingers away before it cracked. He needed to tear something apart, to turn his rage at his psychotic brother into broken glass and twisted metal. But it would have to wait. First he had to reach Mark.

He shifted his car into neutral, wrenched the door open, and slid out, his boots sinking sole-deep in rusty clay. The rains had finally stopped after soaking the Southeast for the weeks since New Year's, and the night air washed over his skin, crisp and clear. A doe ran from the dense woods and paused to stare at him, lifting her nose to scent the breeze before bounding away. There were no other signs of life in rural Chambers County, Alabama, tonight, which was good. The last thing Aidan need-ed was an audience.

Mud sucked at his feet as he stepped back to view the car's position: nose in the muck, tail a couple of feet off the pave-ment. Pulling would be easier than pushing.

Aidan lifted the back end of the car, eased the wheels out of the mire, and dragged it onto the asphalt. Scrounging a couple of shop towels from his trunk, he wiped the blood off his face. The wound had already healed. Then he wiped mud off the headlights before tossing the towel aside.

After stomping the crud off his boots, he slid back into the car and turned the ignition, frowning when the Bimmer rattled and died on the first try.

He growled in frustration. "Start, or I swear to God I will send you back to Germany in pieces."

Another crank and the engine caught, sputtering and finally humming. He let the car idle a few seconds, slung mud off his tires, and sped south toward Penton.

Mark was OK—he had to be. Aidan couldn't bear to think about how losing his friend would change things. Between starving vampires wandering into town from urban areas like Birmingham and Atlanta since the pandemic and the attack on the town's doctor last month, people in Penton were already jumpy. And holy hell, but he couldn't imagine trying to tell his familiar that her husband had died.

No, Mark had to be alive, which meant Aidan needed to consider his options.

The nearest hospital was almost forty miles from Penton, and a 911 would prompt too many questions. Even if he took Mark in, how would it look: a man with fangs hauling a stabbing victim into a small-city ER? The local deputies would pin every unsolved crime in the last month on him, right before they threw him into Lee County lockup to fry at sunrise.

So a hospital was out, and thanks to Owen's attack last month, Penton no longer had a doctor. Which left one option, and it went against everything Aidan believed in.

A bitter laugh escaped him, echoing through the car. *What the hell is one more thing to feel guilty about?*

He snatched his cell phone off the center console and speed-dialed Mirren, his second-in-command. Normally he would contact him mentally, but Mirren also might be behind the wheel, and nobody would profit if both of them landed up to their fangs in a ditch.

Mirren answered on the second ring, his deep voice muffled. "What's up, A?"

"Mark's been attacked. He's by the old Quikmart south of town, and I'm about twenty miles out now. He's unconscious." Not dead. Not going there.

"Shite. Want me to get him?" Like Aidan, Mirren had been gone from Ireland for so long that it took stress or shock to evoke the brogue.

"No, I need you to drive up to LaFayette."

The crunch of boots on gravel crackled over the phone connection, followed by the slam of a truck door, the rumble of an engine, a screech of tires. Mirren's voice cut through his thoughts. "Know who did it? One of Owen's scathe?"

"Owen himself. He must've scented my bond on Mark." He kept his voice neutral, not wanting Mirren to know how badly this had rattled him. The big guy knew some of the history between Aidan and his brother, but not all of it. Nobody knew that story, and nobody would.

Aidan had avoided his brother for four centuries, moving across continents and finally settling in one of the smallest, most remote outposts imaginable. Until he'd run into Owen in Atlanta last month. His brother had called it a coincidence, that meeting, but Aidan knew his brother and knew that nothing happened by chance where Owen was concerned. It wasn't too long after that the town doctor was murdered, his throat slashed, the Gaelic word for "brother" carved into his chest, and his body left in the middle of Main Street.

Mirren muttered a curse, jarring Aidan back to the present. "What d'you need me to do in LaFayette?"

"The woman I hoped to recruit as the new doctor is coming into Penton for an interview tonight." And getting Krys

Harris to agree to a nighttime job interview had taken some tap-dancing.

"Yeah, so?"

"I'm going to flag her down and get her to help Mark—even enthrall her if I have to. Go to LaFayette and check her out of the hotel, get her luggage, take it to one of the sub-suites beneath the clinic. We can't let her leave Penton, not with Mark hurt and Owen on the attack. We've got to have a doctor."

Mirren was still on the line, but he hadn't responded. The car's tires screeched in protest as Aidan took a curve too fast, and the back end shimmied before the rubber settled onto the pavement. "You got an opinion, just say it."

"This has the makings of a grade-A cluster. Of all the stupid shit we could do, forcing this woman to stay in our town is capital Stupid."

Aidan's chuckle lacked humor; he couldn't argue with stupid. He hated what he was about to do. "This isn't a democracy, Mirren. Unless you're going to challenge me as master of this scathe, do it. Then get to the Quikmart with your truck—we'll need it for Mark."

Aidan ended the call and ripped off the headset. He tried to focus on the road, but couldn't exile the ghosts that rattled around inside him whenever his brother got within spitting distance. Owen had cost him everything that mattered once, and now it looked as if he was trying to destroy Penton. Which bloody well was not going to happen.

❈CHAPTER 2❈

Krystal Harris pulled to the shoulder of the two-lane road—
highway was too grand a word—and punched the button to
turn on the old green Corolla's dome light. She counted to five
before thwacking it with the heel of her palm, and a dim light
blinked as if considering her demand. It stayed on—this time.
The car was a dinosaur, but it was a paid-for dinosaur.

She dug a folded Alabama road map from beneath her briefcase on the passenger seat, smoothing the creases to make sure
she hadn't driven past Penton, which she suspected was no more
than a wide spot on a narrow road. She didn't want to get lost
out here in the boonies.

Yep, County Road 70. The highway to Penton just *looked*
like the express lane to nowhere.

A gust of wind rocked the car, sending icy air around the
loose door seals. Maybe the chill of this night was an omen
that she *should* take this job if they offered it, just so she could
buy a more respectable form of transportation. Still, doubts
nagged at her. What kind of clinic conducted a job interview at

nine p.m.? She should never have agreed to it, but the Penton Clinic administrator had waved big bucks in front of her huge college and med school debts, and she'd trotted after them like a donkey after a carrot.

"You had the goody-two-shoes idea of practicing rural medicine, plus you're already here," she chided herself, clicking off the overhead and pulling back onto the road. "And you've gotta admit, this is *rural*."

Another omen, and not a good one: she was talking to herself. Out loud.

A couple of miles later, her headlights illuminated a battered wooden sign covered in peeling paint: Welcome to Penton, Alabama. Founded 1890. Population 3,275.

Twenty years ago, maybe. Krys had done her Penton homework, and that was the boomtown population, when the mammoth East Alabama Mill still churned out threads and batting. It had wheezed its final belch a decade ago, and the town had suffered a slow death by attrition even before the pandemic. The most recent listing Krys found online estimated a population of three hundred. She was surprised they could afford to hire a doctor, much less pay a more-than-competitive wage.

But this was what she wanted, right? A place to practice medicine and be her own boss, to find a community where she could belong? After growing up in Birmingham—the wrong side of Birmingham—she hated the grime and crowds and noise of the city.

Lost in thought as she approached the outskirts of town, she thought she saw an animal in the road—a deer or a bear, maybe—God only knew what wildlife lived out here. But it was a man. He wore a long coat that flapped in the wind and was backlit by a lone streetlight in front of an abandoned convenience store. She'd have blown past him if he hadn't moved into the middle of the road when the glare of her headlights hit him like a spotlight.

He stood with his hands in his pockets, feet planted apart, watching calmly as she floored the brakes. The Corolla's old tires squealed, stinking up the air with the smell of hot rubber and stressed brakes.

Good Lord. Was he nuts?

She got the car stopped and took a deep breath, hands frozen to the wheel, her muscles jittery from the aftershock. The man walked around and tapped on her driver's side window, motioning for her to lower it. Krys's foot hovered over the accelerator, indecisive. Should she drive on and get the hell out of here?

No, by God, she should not. She'd at least lower the window enough to tell the jerk how close he'd come to ending his life as a hood ornament on a green Toyota Dinosaur.

He held up his empty hands in a gesture of peace. Right. Like he was going to hold up a sign that said Beware of Murderous Backwoods Whack Job.

She snaked her right hand to her purse in the passenger seat, wrapped cold fingers around the handle of a small pistol, and slipped it into the pocket of her suede jacket—after she was sure the man had seen it. The .38 Smith & Wesson snub-nose was her security blanket, and she knew how to use it.

His only reaction to the gun was a raised eyebrow. "I have a man injured here." His voice was deep and melodic, and he had a trace of an accent, as if he'd grown up not speaking English but had been around a few too many Southerners. "You the doctor coming to Penton for the interview?"

She lowered her window an inch and stared as he knelt next to the driver's side door, putting his face at eye level. And damned if it wasn't one of the most beautiful faces she'd seen since...maybe ever.

He'd pulled his dark hair into a short ponytail except for one wavy strand that had pulled loose and blew against his cheek. The streetlight cast enough illumination for her to see the dark lashes fringing blue eyes that reminded her not so much of summer skies or robin's eggs but of the richness of an arctic sea flowing over darker depths. They appeared to lighten as he studied her with an intensity that almost robbed her lungs of air. He had a strong jaw, full lips, and a slight cleft in his chin. If he was a serial killer, he was at least a pretty one.

He cleared his throat. "Are you Dr. Harris?"

Krys caught her breath. Good Lord, what was wrong with her? She'd been practically drooling through a half-open window as though he were Adonis personified. He could be Charles Manson's separated-at-birth, unidentical twin.

Except he knew her name. "Who are you?"

One side of Adonis's mouth twitched. "I'm Aidan Murphy. Please, my friend is unconscious." He jerked his head toward the parking lot to their right. Warped plywood covered most of the front windows of the square cinder-block building, the single light illuminating a dingy sign advertising Camels at twelve dollars a carton. The Quikmart appeared to have been closed for a long time.

A lump lay on the ground near the edge of the lot. Krys eyed Aidan Murphy a heartbeat longer, and shifted the Dinosaur into drive. She turned into the lot and parked between a silver compact car and what would probably have been a gorgeous black or midnight blue BMW if it hadn't been coated in mud.

Something had hit the driver's window with quite an impact—it looked like a strong gust of wind would crackle it into a zillion pieces.

She glanced in her rearview mirror at the man walking into the parking lot behind her and then at the motionless figure on the pavement. How dangerous could this be? Aidan Murphy was the Penton Clinic administrator she'd been scheduled to interview with, although he didn't look like any health-care admin she'd ever seen. Besides, she'd be damned if she let an injured man go untreated because she was a chicken.

Streams of icy air whipped around her as she exited the car, and the streetlight didn't quite reach the heavy shadows at the edges of the parking lot.

Aidan stopped a few feet away. Maybe he was afraid that if he got any closer she'd shoot him.

She slammed her car door. "Have you called nine-one-one? Where's the nearest hospital?" She'd bet there wasn't one within thirty miles.

He came a few steps closer. "Just look at him first." Aidan's expression was unreadable.

Shaking her head, she squatted beside the injured man and mentally ticked off what a fast glance could tell her in the dim light. Breathing was labored but steady. Abdominal injuries—maybe a stab wound plus some surface cuts, judging by the way his shirt had been ribboned and by the darker blood pooling at the bottom of his rib cage. Swelling and bruising on the temple. She placed her fingers over his carotid artery and closed her eyes to focus on his pulse. Fast but strong.

"You know his name?" She flicked her gaze up to Aidan and shivered at the keenness with which he watched her. It would be easy to stare into those eyes all night.

He blinked and took a step back. "His name's Mark Calvert."

Weird—Aidan looked almost fearful. Maybe he was freaked out by all the blood. Krys had seen grown men faint dead away at no more than a pinprick. She tapped the injured man on the cheek and repeated his name. A flutter of lashes, and then his glassy eyes opened, didn't quite focus, and closed again.

"Well, hell." Krys clambered to her feet, no easy task in a skirt, and brushed past Aidan on the way to her car. *The Hippocratic oath sure can be inconvenient.* She reached in the driver's door, grabbed the keys from the ignition, and walked around to open the trunk—no remote-controlled locks on the Dinosaur. She considered rolling the heavy suitcase that served as her medical kit over Aidan's foot as she passed him again. Would it have killed the oaf to put his muscles to use instead of watching her struggle while he lounged around with his hands stuffed in his pockets? She couldn't tell much about his build because of the long wool coat, but he was tall and broad-shouldered and if she hadn't been dead broke she'd have been willing to bet good money his body looked as fine as his face.

"What's your role in this, Mr. Murphy? You need to help me out here. Call an ambulance, then call the sheriff." If she lost the Penton job by being assertive, so be it. Aidan Murphy needed to know what he'd get by hiring her. She'd never be an administrator's puppet.

Aidan didn't move. "See how badly he's hurt first."

Krys dropped to her knees and cursed as the unmistakable tickle of a gravel-induced run raced up her pantyhose. Terrific.

She looked at the bloody man lying in front of her. And to think that fifteen minutes ago, she'd thought her biggest challenge was an evening job interview.

Aidan stared at the woman kneeling beside Mark. *Holy hell. Why didn't I feed earlier?* In hindsight, taking the meeting in LaGrange before feeding had been stupid. And now here he was, ogling an unvaccinated woman with legs a mile long, a husky bedroom voice, and a give-'em-hell attitude.

His lieutenant, Will Ludlam, who'd found Krystal Harris among the meager pickings of unvaccinated human doctors, said she'd be a perfect Penton recruit. She'd had an abusive childhood, Will said, and was a loner. She'd like the easy pace and security of life as a vampire familiar once she got used to the idea. She had a wide do-gooder streak, school debts up to her ears, and could be tempted with a good salary.

Will obviously was full of shit. Krystal Harris struck him as more lion than lamb. And she was pushing his buttons, big-time, which had to be the hunger talking because he didn't get mixed up with human women. Period. Wasn't going to happen.

Yet here he was with his hands jammed in his pockets because his fingers twitched with the urge to touch her. His damned fangs even ached.

She pulled a portable light stick from her kit and cracked it, surrounding them with a bright greenish glow. He moved a few steps closer, watching the red highlights that shone in the dark hair she'd pulled back in one of those twisty braids women liked.

"I don't hear you making phone calls." She lifted Mark's eyelids and shone a penlight in them. "Pupils reactive," she muttered. "Good."

She paused and looked up at Aidan, her dark eyes widening when she saw him. Shit. He was staring at her as if she were a fresh steak.

As quickly as her eyes widened, they narrowed in anger. "While you're contacting the sheriff and an ambulance—and, yes, that was another hint—I'll get Mark ready to transport to the hospital. We can reschedule our interview."

Well, that wasn't happening. No ambulance. No rescheduling. "I won't call an ambulance until you tell me—"

The rest of his response was interrupted by a spray of gravel as an oversize, souped-up monster of an SUV pulled into the lot and lurched to a stop directly behind Krys's beat-up car. Aidan smiled. Leave it to Mirren to make sure she couldn't drive away even if she wanted to.

Krys paused with sterile wipe in hand, gaping as Mirren climbed out of the Bronco and approached. At six foot eight, he had eight inches on Aidan and at least sixty pounds of muscle. Those crazy tattoos and a serious investment in black clothing added up to one sinister first impression, and Aidan watched to see her reaction.

Krys's gaze had frozen on Mirren. His second-in-command had that effect, even on other vampires.

"Dr. Harris, this is Mirren Kincaid. He's law enforcement for Penton, and he'll take care of any official reports that need to be filed. We'll take Mark to the Penton Clinic in the truck and you can treat him there. Then we'll have our interview." Aidan's gaze drifted to her mouth, which she'd clamped shut and tightened as he talked. Even angry and shooting storm clouds at both of them, she was getting to him. He hoped Mirren had fed so he wouldn't be in the same shape.

Krys arched an eyebrow at Mirren. "Nice to meet you, I think."

Mirren gave her a curt nod and assumed his normal expression, something between a sphinx and a turnip. Aidan stifled a laugh; Mirren considered that his friendly look.

Krystal turned her attention back to Mark, easing the lapels of his jacket away from his chest and gently cutting open what was left of his shirt. She tugged on vinyl gloves and pressed a couple of sterile wipes around the injuries. "The slashes across the abdomen are shallow—they're just messy," she said. "They're masking a stab wound here"—she pointed to his side—"but whoever did this was either talented or stupid. It doesn't look like it hit any organs, and that's not easy to do with a knife to the gut. His vitals are good."

She lifted the blood-soaked bandages off Mark's cuts and tossed them aside, pulling fresh ones from her kit.

The bloody bandages landed near Mirren's feet, and he stepped back with a hiss, crossing his arms over his chest and looking toward the cars.

Krys laughed. "Both of you are afraid of blood? I swear, men can be such babies."

Aidan exchanged a bemused glance with Mirren. She had no idea what being around all this blood—and her—was doing to him, and probably Mirren, too.

She shifted position to look more closely at Mark's head. "I don't like the look of this bruise on his temple—we need to get the bleeding under control and get him out of here. There are a couple of towels in my trunk. Would one of you get them?" She pulled her keys from her pocket and tossed them at Aidan. He grabbed them on instinct, not thinking to slow his reflexes.

She stared at him a moment, shook her head, and turned back to Mark.

Krys worked quickly once she had the towels, cleaning off the blood to see the wounds better, then sat back, frowning. "What does it mean?"

Damn. Aidan stared at the cuts. "No idea." Which wasn't true. The letters spelled out "food" in Gaelic—Owen's idea of a freaking joke.

"These are letters: *b-h-i-a*. They have to mean something." Krys cocked her head and frowned at Aidan. "You're lying about not knowing. In fact, you already have an idea who did this, don't you?"

"We'll damn sure find out." He couldn't take his eyes off Mark's chest—the cuts were deep enough to leave a scar. He'd wear "food" like a billboard the rest of his life. "Mirren, get the truck ready."

Krys blew out a breath of frustration. "Fine," she said. "I'll get him ready to take to the clinic so we can get him warmed up and I can get a better look at him. But if you aren't going to help, get out of the way. You're casting a shadow."

He took two short steps back, barking a quick laugh. "So feisty. I hadn't expected that."

She grumbled something he couldn't make out, although he thought he heard the word "asswipe."

Krys pressed the towels against Mark's abdomen with one hand and used the other to tilt his head gently to the side. "OK, let's get him somewhere warm. But he's not a small guy, so we need to be careful about lifting him—"

Good. They were in business. Aidan slid his hands under Mark's knees and shoulders and lifted him gently. He placed him in the Bronco's cargo area and looked back at Krys. "Want to ride with him, or with me, or follow us?" He wasn't sure he wanted her left alone to follow them, but he'd offer it up and hope she took one of the other options. He didn't want to enthrall her. Maybe he could get her to Penton voluntarily, at least until Mark was well. Then they could convince her to take the job.

Indecision warred on her face as she looked at her junk heap of a car. She slipped her hand into her coat pocket where she'd stashed her handgun, and Aidan felt a wash of admiration. She probably thought she could shoot them if they tried to hurt her. She had no idea it wouldn't even slow them down unless it was a lucky close-range shot to the head.

With a final look at Mirren, she seemed to reach a decision. "I'll ride with the patient." She hitched up her skirt enough to crawl into the back of the Bronco, giving Aidan a heart-stopping view of those long, long legs, and settled next to Mark, placing a firm hand on the towels covering his wounds.

Mirren retrieved her medical case and purse and set them next to her, then paused and stared at his hands, which had gotten covered in Mark's blood when he'd thrown the discarded bandages into the Dumpster.

Krys pulled a fresh wipe from her kit and held it out to him, but the blood had taken hold. Mirren swiped his tongue across one of his palms, closing his eyes for a moment and then fixing Krys with a slightly unfocused gaze.

Holy hell. The big guy's eyes had lightened to silver and he was about a half step from losing it.

"Hey." Aidan spoke sharply and squeezed his friend's shoulder hard enough to break bones in a human.

Mirren blinked at Krys. "Sorry, darlin'." He shook his head and stalked to the driver's side door, climbing in with a rumble of cursing.

Krys sat openmouthed for a moment before whispering, "Is he, uh, OK to ride with?" She looked about a half second shy of bolting.

Aidan gave her the most reassuring smile he could manage. "You'll be safe."

❊ CHAPTER 3 ❊

K rys stared out the side windows of the Bronco as Mirren pulled onto the two-lane road leading into Penton. They'd encountered a surprising amount of traffic in the downtown area. A lot of people on the streets, too.

She eyed them curiously, trying to imagine them as patients, colleagues, maybe even friends. She hadn't had a lot of those, and maybe being the only doctor in a small town would make it easier to settle in and become part of a community. She glanced at her big, silent chauffeur, who certainly didn't seem like friendship material. *Plus, he licked blood off his hands, and Aidan Murphy was giving off some intense vibes from that mouthwatering face of his. Don't forget the weirdness.*

At the main intersection, she looked out a side window at a massive black rectangle blocking the road that led west. "What's that?" she asked Mirren, not holding out much hope that he'd answer. He'd been sullen so far, not to mention being the size of a Macy's Thanksgiving Day Parade float.

"The old cotton mill," he said, his voice a deep, scratchy rumble. Like Aidan, he had a trace of an accent. Scottish, maybe? Irish? Something-ish.

"Is it being used for anything?"

"No."

Well, OK then. So much for conversation with Mirren Kincaid. She checked Mark again and settled back to finish the ride in silence.

The steady click of the truck's turn signal drew Krys's attention back to the issues at hand: a patient to treat, a semimute giant with questionable sanitary habits, and a man over whom she'd practically made a fool of herself. Aidan Murphy was too attractive to ever be interested in a plain Jane like her, and he might be too controlling to be the kind of boss she wanted—basically, one who'd leave her alone and let her run a clinic the way it needed to be run. She'd been controlled enough in her life.

She fought the urge to look out the back window of the Bronco's hatch, where she knew he was trailing them in his muddy car.

Mirren turned the Bronco in to a parking lot and stopped in front of the double doors of a one-story, midcentury, red-brick building with a sign out front: Penton Medical Clinic. She was surprised. She'd been expecting a small converted house or Quonset hut—this looked more like a hospital, which might even be an omen in Penton's favor.

Mark Calvert was one lucky guy. Krys applied the last bandage to his sutured abdomen and checked the CT scan of his head one final time on the wall-mounted light table. Minor concussion. He'd regained consciousness before drifting to sleep, and, as she'd suspected, the cuts were mostly messy. They'd hurt like hell and leave some ugly scars, but his life hadn't been in jeopardy.

No one—not even Mark's wife, Melissa, who turned out to have a year of nursing school and a level head once she'd gotten over the shock of seeing her husband carved like a turkey—had commented on the strange word carved into his flesh. Krys decided to stitch it up and forget it. Not her concern. Her job was to treat his wounds, not figure why someone had turned him into a greeting card with legs.

She also didn't comment on Mark's inner arm full of needle tracks, uncovered when she'd cut off the remains of his shirt. None recent, but at one time the man had had one heck of a drug problem. It might be her concern if she decided to stay here, but it wasn't now.

The inside of the Penton Clinic delighted her as much as the outside. Its equipment was state-of-the-art, better than Sumter Regional's, where she had completed her residency. She could do almost any procedure here. Why would a town this small have such good facilities, she wondered. That, plus the salary they were offering, meant Penton wasn't nearly as economically depressed as the rest of East Alabama and West Georgia.

Mark awoke while she was securing the last bandage, cracking open the blue eyes she'd glimpsed earlier. They were still glassy, but somebody was home this time.

"Where—?" His voice cracked, and Krys filled a plastic cup with water and offered him a sip through a straw. He tried to push himself into a sitting position, but slumped when he couldn't gather enough strength. Pressing his shoulders onto the bed, she punched the button to elevate his head and stuck the end of the bent straw into his mouth.

"I'm Dr. Krystal Harris, and you're at the Penton Clinic. You need to be still, not move around much for a few hours. You're going to be sore for a few days while you heal, but you'll fully recover. Do you remember what happened?"

He blinked at her, face creased in a frown. "You're already here? Where's Aidan?" He swallowed hard and gathered his words. "Gotta talk to Aidan."

Why the heck would he want to talk to the hospital administrator before he asked for his wife? "Let me get your wife." Krys opened the door and Melissa Calvert pushed past, followed by Aidan and Mirren, all so focused on Mark that they didn't give her a second glance. What did they think this was—a block party?

She assumed her best I'm-a-doctor-and-I'm-in-charge expression, the one she and every other resident had practiced since first-year med school. "Everybody but Melissa—out. Mark needs to rest tonight. You can talk to him tomorrow."

They ignored her, so she walked to the opposite side of the bed, glared at Aidan, and raised her voice: "Now."

Her brain stalled when he raised his gaze to meet hers. This was the first time she'd gotten a look at him in decent lighting, and it only confirmed her earlier impression. When God was handing out looks, Aidan Murphy had gotten a double dose. Dark hair with a hint of curl, light stubble, and a small scar on one cheek kept him from being too pretty. He'd ditched the black wool coat and wore a navy sweater that accentuated the blue eyes that were narrowing at her above a frown.

And he shouldn't be in this room. Her brain finally gave her libido a kick in the butt, and she found her voice. "I'm sorry, but you gentlemen need to take it outside and let Mark get some rest." That sounded about as authoritative as a Muppet.

Aidan stared at her for a couple of seconds longer before giving her a tight smile. "No problem, Dr. Harris. Come to the office when you're finished with Mark, and we'll talk about how to keep you here." He gestured to Mirren and the big man followed him into the hallway, the door closing behind them with a click.

He wanted to keep her here—did that mean he already knew he was going to offer her the job? What in the world was she going to tell him?

❋CHAPTER 4❋

From the shadowed alley beside Penton Hardware, Owen Murphy had a direct view of the clinic entrance. He smiled as a dark blue sedan whipped into the parking lot behind a big SUV.

"There you are, Brother."

Nice feckin' ride. Aidan had done well for himself. Of course, Saint Aidan would have done it the hard way, learning how to invest and play the stock markets. No way he'd stoop to enthralling rich humans to take what he wanted the way Owen would.

The man had no idea how to be a decent vampire, which was why he'd never be able to protect this little empire he'd created.

After sitting in the car for a few moments, Aidan climbed out, spoke to the driver of the SUV, and walked up the front steps of the clinic. His broad back in its fancy black coat made a tempting target. Owen raised his shotgun, caught Aidan in his sights, and whispered, "Bang." Too bad a bullet wouldn't get the job done.

"You gonna let him know you're here?" Anders moved alongside Owen, waiting like a dog for his master to bark out instructions. The *eejit's* ability to follow orders without overtaxing his brain had earned him the job as Owen's second-in-command.

But what a bloody nuisance. "Not yet. This has to be done right." *My life depends on it.*

He needed to make sure his message had arrived safely—tucked in the back of that SUV, he guessed. Owen lowered the shotgun and settled back to wait, resting against the side of the building. Its brick façade spread cold into his shoulder blades even through his coat.

"What if the human kicks it before he can tell your brother about the meeting?" Anders asked.

"Didn't cut him bad enough to kill him." Owen leaned his head back and took in the sprinkling of stars. Damned air was too heavy and humid here, even in the cold. Too quiet. Too dull. Perfect for his farm-boy brother, but not him. He missed the noise of Dublin, the music, the women. But he bet Aidan didn't. The fool tended a greenhouse full of plants in the dead of winter, for the love of all that was holy.

But Dublin, like most of Europe, was full of the hunger now, and from what Owen had seen in the last month, America wasn't far behind. Couldn't walk a block without tripping over starving vampires fighting over the same unvaccinated humans. Except for Aidan and his little u-frickin'-topia free of the pandemic vaccine. Whole vampire world went hungry while Aidan and his cronies drank like kings.

"Here we go." At the sound of the SUV door opening, Owen edged toward the mouth of the alley again. He frowned and stepped closer to the street for a better look as the driver climbed out. "Bloody hell. Wouldja look at that?"

Anders sidled alongside him and swore. "Only one vamp I ever heard of that big, but I thought the Slayer was dead. Maybe it's a human."

"No, it's him. I've seen the bastard before. Seems the rumors of Mirren Kincaid's death have been a wee bit exaggerated. He's a game-changer." Owen believed he could best his brother in a fight. Aidan might be physically stronger but he'd get tripped up following the rules. Not that bloody mercenary Kincaid. The Slayer had no rules. And if that damned Matthias Ludlam knew he was here and hadn't warned Owen...well, the price for killing Aidan just went higher.

"And there's my message." Owen grunted in satisfaction as Mirren pulled Aidan's human from the truck and carried him inside. A woman climbed out of the truck as well, and he studied her. Tall, slender. Maybe the Slayer's mate? She might be leverage. God knew Aidan wouldn't have taken another woman. Probably still flogging himself over his dead wife.

"Mission won and done. Let's go." Owen led Anders through the alley, taking a dark shortcut to the old mill village, a dead-end street lined with small houses originally intended to keep workers in debt to the Man while they inhaled cotton dust till their lungs collapsed. Now the houses sat abandoned, the woods behind them dense and the hills full of caves. All convenient hiding spots for the small scathe he'd pulled together after Matthias called, and the few humans they'd been able to scrape up for food.

"Pull a female out of the herd and bring her to the house," he said, turning left in the direction of the village. "I'm starving."

Anders nodded, taking a sharp right toward the mill and its dank, partially collapsed basement where their humans had been tethered since the previous night. Since Aidan bonded his humans, Owen's scathe couldn't feed from them. They'd had to provide their own, and it was a sorry lot—mostly junkies grabbed off the streets of Atlanta.

He continued to a small, white-framed house at the dead end of Cotton Street, digging a cell phone from his pocket and punching a number as soon as he'd slipped inside.

The voice answering the call didn't bother with a greeting. "Did you set it up?"

"A fine evening to you as well, Matthias," Owen said. "And how are things with our esteemed Tribunal leader? Relaxing over brandy and cigars, are you?"

"Shove the sarcasm, Murphy." Matthias's hard-edged Yank accent annoyed Owen more than the stale beer at most of Atlanta's so-called pubs. "You said you could get a meeting with Aidan. Did you?"

"I sent the invitation, and he'll bloody well answer," Owen said. "He's too much of an optimist not to. He'll try to convince me to go back to Dublin and leave him and his little town alone."

"And you're willing to end it?"

"You mean, will I kill him? What's wrong—don't want to get dirty by saying the words?" Owen swung the door open for Anders, who sauntered in gripping the arm of a young woman with dead eyes and a slack-jawed expression. Owen flicked his eyes over her body and nodded. Almost used up, that one, but she'd do.

Matthias snorted. "You get extra credit for getting Aidan out of commission for good, but first priority is to get that town of his shut down and his scathe broken up. He's getting too powerful." He paused for a moment, and then resumed in a softer voice. "And you know what's waiting for you if you don't."

Yeah, Owen knew. A date with the Tribunal's executioner. The current one. The guy might not make you suffer as long as the Slayer would have, but at the end of the day, your head would still be lying in a separate plot from your body.

Speaking of which. "So, Matthias, guess where your old friend the Slayer is spending his time these days?"

Ludlam snorted. "Saw Mirren Kincaid already, did you? We want him back in the fold so don't kill him unless you have to. As for you, we have others who can take you out if you don't perform."

"Oh, the job will be done, but your price just went up."

Owen flopped down in a threadbare plaid armchair that smelled of mildew and poverty, and pulled the woman to his lap, grabbing the scruff of her neck to turn her head toward him. Her eyes grew glassy, and she leaned into him, running a dirt-smudged hand between his thighs.

"You're a lucky bastard that my brother pisses me off even more than the Tribunal," Owen said, closing his eyes as the girl worked him through his jeans.

Matthias laughed, a brittle cackling sound. "Come on, Murphy, you're only doing this to save your own miserable life. You had half the cops in Dublin looking for the so-called Vampire Killer."

"It would have blown over." He grabbed the girl's hair to get her attention and shook his head when she began fumbling at his zipper. Not yet.

"You're reckless, Murphy. Lucky for you the Tribunal is split on this little social experiment of Aidan's." He paused, and Owen heard the clink of a glass. "Aidan has friends on the Tribunal, so remember—I'm not involved. No one on the Tribunal is involved. Don't forget that."

Owen walked to the window and looked out, jerking the shade into place as a dark sedan crawled down the street, paused in the cul-de-sac, then turned and slowly rolled the other way. Aidan had started patrols around the mill and village after the murder of the town doctor, which meant that most of Owen's people had to stay in the woods, living in the dark like beasts.

"Look, we don't have enough people for an all-out war, so I have to hit slow and strategic-like, especially with the Slayer in the picture," Owen said. "Besides, Penton has more than twice as many humans as vampires, and near as I can tell, every human is bonded directly or indirectly to Aidan. Once he's down, the rest of his people will run."

Another long silence. When Matthias spoke, his voice dropped a few decibels. "I can't send you fighters, but I can send a courier to Atlanta with a new weapon." He paused. "And if I ever hear you link it to me, there's nowhere you can hide. Understand?"

Owen grinned. "Must be a fine bit of stuff, that. Tomorrow night's kill is going to make me a free man."

✳ CHAPTER 5 ✳

"That woman's gonna be a handful." Mirren followed Aidan down the hospital corridor. "Not too late to change your mind about keeping her here."

"Yeah, it is." Aidan couldn't remember the last time he'd been this angry. First Doc and now Mark. He wasn't likely to be the last of Owen's victims. "Get someone to bring her car in and stash it."

Mirren grumbled something beneath his breath but headed out the front door when Aidan turned left toward the clinic office for a quick meeting with Will.

He slowed his pace, wishing he had time to feed before encountering Krystal Harris again. Because no way he'd have reacted this way to her if he hadn't been hungry and angry—skin heating, slow vampire heart speeding, every blood and sex urge igniting. She was pretty enough, sexy as hell, but he was acting like a besotted vampire who'd encountered a potential mate.

He'd never felt it before, and he didn't want to feel it now—especially about this woman. Not only was she human, but he'd spent the last two hours planning her abduction. How screwed up was that?

After all these years, he should know better than to get into an emotional situation around that much blood when he hadn't fed. *Idiot.*

Now that he'd met her, he hated what he was about to do even more, but the plan to keep her had to move forward. He'd worked hard to turn Penton into a place where his scathe and their human fams could live in peace, so he'd just have to suck it up—even if Krys Harris pushed all his buttons. Besides, she was responding to him as a man, not as a vampire. He'd seen desire turn to fear in a woman's eyes in the span of a heartbeat.

He needed to get a grip before she came in for her interview. And he needed to find out why Will had picked her.

Aidan unlocked the office door and flipped a switch that simultaneously turned on the three lamps scattered around the room. Their soft light cast dramatic shadows on the deep teal walls and cherry furnishings—and the head of spiky blond hair emerging through an opening in the far corner floor.

"About time you got here. How's Mark?" Will Ludlam pulled himself out of the hatch and slid the interlocking wooden panels back into place to cover the opening. He brushed imaginary dust off his pants legs before reclining on the sofa beneath the window and taking a not-so-subtle glance at his watch. Aidan chuckled; it was Will's way of saying that night was burning and he had more interesting things to do than to check the locks on a suite for an about-to-be-abducted human.

"Mark'll be fine. Owen hurt him enough to scar him, not kill him, so I'm guessing he sent a message. Haven't had a chance to get Mark alone yet, though."

Aidan sat behind a cherry desk roughly the size of a football field. Scathe members had been using the office as a general meeting place since the town's doctor had been murdered, but nobody had had the heart to move his furniture or take down the ugly-ass primitive oil paintings that dotted the walls.

He paused for a beat. "How sure are you about your research on Krystal Harris? She's a lot tougher than I expected." Tough didn't cover it.

Will straightened the shirt cuffs peeking out from beneath his jacket sleeves. "You asked for a human doctor who hadn't been vaccinated for the pandemic, and that's what I got you. She's perfect." He counted off points on his fingers. "She's unvaccinated, estranged from her family, no close friends, finishing a residency in general medicine, looking for a job in rural medicine. Probably meek as a kitten and homely as a toad."

"Wrong and wrong." *Holy hell.* Aidan rolled his head from side to side, cracking his neck. "Hard to believe no one will miss her."

Will looked at him sharply. "What's with you, man? You look rattled. But you and Mark and Melissa are tight. I get that. Something else going on?"

Rattled. Right. "So the doctor is—"

"She's perfect—believe me. I hacked into the friggin' personnel files of every human hospital in the Southeast looking for an unvaccinated doctor and she's the best I found. Besides, we have a bigger issue."

He didn't have enough problems between his homicidal brother and a soon-to-be-abducted doctor he wanted to wear like a glove? "What's wrong?"

"When I came into the office to check the locks on the suite door, the hatch wasn't covered and the panel was hanging open.

Whoever went down there last needs a serious reminder about security."

"Lucy, who else?" *Shit.* One of his best fighters had turned into a head case since Doc had been murdered. The pain of losing her human mate wouldn't dull any time soon, so the faster she learned to work through it, the better. Aidan knew that firsthand. "I'll talk to her. I know she's hurting, but she's really been screwing up."

"If you'd let me work security, she could take some time off."

Aidan stifled a sharp answer. They'd had this argument before. He wished Will could help them hunt Owen—they could use his muscle and smarts. But it was too risky. "You can't fight with us, not as long as there's any chance the Tribunal could be backing Owen. Last thing we want is your father declaring war on Penton to get to you. We have enough trouble without Matthias making us a personal project."

Anger and resignation fought on Will's features before he finally slumped back on the sofa. "Daddy dearest—screwing up my life one day at a time, unhappily ever after." He shook his head, and Aidan saw steeliness settle in his brown eyes. "Fine, then. When you figure out what you need me to do, I'm there."

"What's the status of the doctor's apartment?"

"I have a couple of our humans taking care of it," Will said. "As soon as you let me know for certain we're going to take her, I'll send our guys to Georgia, pack up her stuff and put it in storage, and then leave a month's rent and fake forwarding address in the landlord's mailbox. As far as our people are concerned, it's a normal move."

Aidan nodded, hating this idea more every minute. "What about her job at the hospital in Americus?"

"The chief of staff will receive a letter with her resigna—"

Will grew still and silent, his eyes trained on the hallway. They listened to the staccato sound of heels hitting the linoleum floor, gradually growing louder.

Aidan's senses shot into hyperdrive. He could smell the light fragrance of her perfume, and he shifted uncomfortably in his chair simply from the knowledge that she was coming toward them. He glanced at Will to see if he was having the same reaction; hoped he was. But Will looked toward the door with polite interest and nothing more. *Shit.*

A sharp knock and Krystal pushed the door open, pausing uncertainly. She blinked when she saw Aidan behind the desk, fought a grin, and burst into laughter—a rich, musical sound that contradicted the no-nonsense demeanor he'd seen earlier. It sent a jolt of heat right down to Aidan's gut.

"Sorry." She shook her head. "It's just weird seeing you behind a desk and trying to do a job interview after what's happened tonight."

Aidan took a deep breath. Time to try Plan A and charm her into staying voluntarily without freaking her out or letting his vampire crap get out of hand. "Let's just start over, although I don't have any doubts about your medical skills."

He introduced her to Will. "He's our IT guy. You have a problem—Will can solve it."

Will treated her to his best playboy smile. "Nice to meet you—I hear you got hijacked on the way into town."

One of these days, I'm going to have to slap the shit out of that smart-ass. "She was nice enough to stop and help Mark," Aidan said, giving Will a warning look.

Krys laughed. "Not like Mr. Murphy gave me much choice—it was either stop or turn him into roadkill."

Will grinned. "Roadkill? Oh, I'm going to like you." He looked at Aidan. "Hire the woman already, *Mr. Murphy.*"

Aidan shook his head. Will was such a pain in the ass. "Call me Aidan," he told Krys. "And say good-bye to Will. He has work to do."

"Bye, Will. Nice to meet you." Krys held out a hand for Will to shake.

He held it a few beats longer than necessary, and Aidan felt a long-dormant stirring in his gut. He was surprised to realize that he didn't want Will touching Krys. Since when did he get territorial over a virtual stranger?

He nodded at Will as his lieutenant paused on his way into the hall. Will didn't look any happier about taking Krys than he felt. His mental comment to Aidan was clear: *We're predatory assholes; might as well act like it.*

Once Will closed the door behind him, Aidan left his desk and approached Krys. "We got off to a bad start, Krystal, so I'll try a do-over. I'm Aidan Murphy." He held out his right hand, relishing the touch of her long, slim fingers.

Earlier, he'd been so focused on her scent and his own warped reaction that he hadn't realized how tall she was— maybe five foot nine without the heels. Long and rangy, with killer legs and dark auburn hair. Fair skin and a heart-shaped face would have given her a sweet look but for the sharp intelligence behind her dark brown eyes, which still held traces of laughter as she met his gaze.

"Call me Krys. I try to forget my parents named me after a fast-food hamburger."

Aidan laughed. "My business manager wants a Krystal's franchise in Penton, but I don't think we can support it. Tell me that's not really how you got your name."

She shrugged, and the small action drew his eyes to her neck, where he could sense the pulse beating fine and strong. He was struck with the urge to put his mouth there, to taste her. He should have told Will to find him a substitute feeder for tonight.

"Knowing my dad, anything's possible," she said wryly. "He always said I was conceived after a drunken trip to Krystal's where he ended up with food poisoning and a kid."

Aidan knew all about bad parents—despite his best intentions, he'd been one. He met her gaze again and held it for a few seconds, concentrating, waiting for her focus to waver. It took a few moments, but she finally blinked and looked down. Her willingness to make eye contract was a strength in the human world but would make her vulnerable to enthrallment if he had to do it. Quite the paradox.

Just like the fact that he was getting all hot over a woman whom he planned to treat like prey in order to save a town he'd built so the vampires who had bonded themselves to him wouldn't have to live like predators.

One big paradox.

———◦———

Good Lord. Krys couldn't believe the sparks and hormones flying around this room. On the way into Penton, she had assumed Aidan Murphy would be a little, old, retired country doctor with Irish ancestors, not an exotic-looking demigod in a sweater and jeans that played up his broad shoulders and slim hips. Things she shouldn't notice in a potential employer.

That trace of an accent could be Irish, but she'd had nothing else right. He also had an intensity in his odd-colored eyes, a way of looking at her that made her heart thump and her skin feel as if she'd spent an hour in the sun. She didn't react that way to men, especially men she wanted to work for. He probably had women lined up down the block, waiting for him to look their way. He sure wouldn't be interested in a flat-chested, geeky girl from the wrong side of Birmingham.

Get a grip, missy. You're here for a job, not a man.

OK. Right. And it was a ridiculous hour for a job interview. "Are you sure you want to do this tonight?" She placed her briefcase in one of the armchairs and sat in the other as Aidan again took the power seat across the desk. "We can reschedule later in the week. It's only a three-hour drive to Americus."

"You're here, so let's talk if you're not too tired." He smiled. "Thanks for helping out tonight. We don't have many emergencies, and Mark is a good friend."

Good friend, huh? Krys still wasn't sure why this guy was the first person Mark had asked for. Then something clicked. "He works for you, right? I didn't make the connection at first, but he's the one who made my travel arrangements. Got the hotel room for me in LaFayette."

Aidan nodded. "Right. Mark's my main go-to guy, handles all of my day-to-day business transactions."

Which brought them back to what a man like Aidan Murphy was doing running a small-town hospital. Krys eyed him with open curiosity. She might as well just ask him. If she was really going to consider living here, she needed to know the players, and Aidan Murphy dished out major-player vibes—not sexually, although there were plenty of those vibes, too, but in a leadership kind of way.

She studied him—neat, controlled, and except for the long hair, a better fit for the business corridors of downtown Atlanta than the wilds of rural Alabama. "You are what, exactly? No offense, but you look too young for a hospital admin. I've rarely seen one under sixty, and all these people treat you like a mob boss."

She paused, imagining massive Mirren Kincaid in a pin-stripe suit with a tommy gun, taking orders from the dark and dangerous local godfather. Then she smiled. "Not that I actually know any. You're not one, are you? A mob boss?"

Aidan smiled and leaned back in his chair. The change in his posture made Krys realize he'd been tense—the set of his shoulders had been tight. Guess his friend's attack had shaken them all up. Laughter took five years off his age. He couldn't be much over thirty. And when he laughed, a deep dimple creased his left cheek and made him even hotter. Like he needed any help with that.

"Not a mob boss," he said. "I don't own a machine gun, and there are no mobsters anywhere in my family—just a bunch of Irish farmers, although that's been a while." His look grew more serious. "So, Mark's really OK?"

Krys crossed her legs, stared in horror at the run in her hose, and uncrossed them again, tugging her skirt down to hide it. *Boy, way to make an impression, Krys—he'll think you're a total hick. Oh, wait. Job, not man.*

"Mark should be fine in a few days," she said. "Although he's going to have a scar in the shape of whatever that word is. Why would anyone carve him up like that?"

A flash of something—anger, maybe—flitted across his face before his expression settled into stony neutrality. "I have no idea."

She'd been right earlier. Definitely lying. She'd had a lifetime of reading her father's moods, and there were few expressions she couldn't interpret. He either knew that word or knew who had done it—and was royally pissed about it.

Still, not her problem. "Mark's lucky his attacker didn't know what he was doing. If the stab wound had been a few inches to the left, we'd be having a different conversation and your refusal to call an ambulance might have had serious consequences."

"Looks like we were lucky, then." Aidan flipped open a file folder on the desk. "Let's see. You grew up in Birmingham, went to Auburn, med school at Emory, residency at Sumter Regional. Why are you interested in Penton? Do you have family around here? You mentioned your father." He looked up at her, those odd eyes drilling holes in her as if mining for truths she might not tell him.

She shifted in her seat, laying her jacket in the adjacent chair alongside her briefcase. She bent quickly to catch the jacket as the Smith & Wesson in the pocket began pulling it toward the floor—she'd forgotten about the pistol. Thank God, the thing hadn't fallen out. In hindsight, she felt silly for flashing it at him earlier.

"No family," she said. "My mom is dead, and my father and I are not close." Heck, she hadn't seen the man since her mom's funeral six years ago when she was a junior in college. He'd made it clear that he expected her to drop out of school and move home to assume Mom's job as maid, cook, bartender, and emotional doormat. No, thanks.

"So what's the attraction to Penton?" He steepled his hands in front of him, elbows propped on the desk, and watched her with those icy blue eyes that somehow managed to smolder. *Smolder?* What kind of thought was that to have during a job interview?

"I wanted to do a few years of rural medicine after my residency. I like the idea of being my own boss, of getting to know my patients as people, of going somewhere I'm really needed." She laughed. "I sound like a real Pollyanna, don't I?"

He didn't need to know that after living under her dad's tyranny for seventeen years, she wouldn't hand over that much control to anyone ever again. If she had to live in the freakin' woods to be in charge of her own life, so be it.

They spent the next fifteen minutes walking through the clinic, two wings with four patient rooms to the right, three exam areas to the left. There were also two well-stocked supply rooms, a couple of offices, and a lab full of diagnostic equipment set up for X-rays and other imaging tests, which she'd seen earlier while treating Mark. Even a small blood bank stocked with O-neg. The setup beat anything Krys had seen outside a hospital.

"I'm really surprised at how up-to-date everything is." She stopped to examine a piece of ultrasound equipment.

"Our former doctor—the one whose job I'm about to offer you—made sure we had the best. He had a big equipment budget to use however he wanted. I'll offer the same thing to you. This would be your little kingdom here, to run however you like. Anything else you think we need, just say so."

Krys stared at him. He said all the right things, and he'd virtually offered her the job and what sounded like a carte blanche budget. Still, the whole encounter with Mirren Kincaid had been bizarre, even before he did the bloody-palm lick. Something struck her as *off* about Penton, and she'd learned to trust her instincts. She knew one person who could put her at ease, though.

"Did your former doctor retire? Is he still in town? I'd like to talk to him before I decide."

Aidan's face lost its animation as he motioned her back toward the office. "I wish he'd retired, but no. He died recently— a hunting accident. We all miss him."

Krys nodded. Seemed like every weekend in November and December at least one deer hunter was hauled into the Sumter County ER. Either they shot themselves or each other—too often with alcohol involved.

They reentered the office and took the same seats. Aidan closed the file folder and propped his arms on the desk, studying Krys so intently that she got fidgety. She glanced at her watch and saw it was almost one a.m.

Aidan caught her looking. "Sorry, I know it's late. Just a couple more things." Krys hoped she hadn't turned an unflattering shade of fuchsia. "I need to sell you on Penton. We have just under two hundred people and, as you saw, Doc made sure we have a well-equipped clinic. You'll find the salary generous enough to compete with bigger cities."

Krys blinked. There was small town, and then there was *really* small town. She'd been prepared for three hundred, but fewer than that? "Master of her own destiny" could easily devolve into "everybody knows your business." "How do people support themselves with the mill closed?"

Aidan leaned back in his chair. "Most people own small businesses, or have business interests or investments outside town. We all support our local economy. I think you'll find we have just about anything you'd need, a lot more than most of the larger towns around here, plus we're only a couple of hours from Atlanta."

Aidan stood and walked around to sit in the chair next to her, moving her things to the desktop—Krys let out a mental sigh of relief when the Smith & Wesson didn't tumble out of her jacket pocket and shoot him in the foot.

He turned the chair toward her and his knee brushed hers. They touched glances, and Krys caught her breath before shifting away from him.

Aidan blinked, seeming to lose his train of thought for a moment. "Uh, that's the sales pitch. How can I convince you to say yes?"

Krys looked at the floor, and then back at Aidan. She needed to give this a lot of thought, maybe make one of her side-by-side lists of pros and cons to see which side won—and she needed to factor in their chemistry, or whatever it was. If Aidan was her boss, he had to be her boss and not some guy she crushed on or did something stupid with. As tempting as that would definitely be.

"I promise I'll think about it, but I can't give you an answer tonight. Don't you want to ask me anything? I mean about my qualifications?"

He laughed softly and stood up. "You had a trial by fire tonight, yes? The job's yours if you want it. Could I convince you to hang around a couple of days, just to make sure Mark's OK? We'll pay you for your time, even if you decide not to take the job."

Krys stood as well. "Look, I'd just be taking advantage of you. Mark's going to be fine, and Melissa can watch for infection. I gave her a prescription for antibiotics just in case. Let me think about the offer for a few days and I'll call you at the end of the week. Will that work?"

Aidan's face tightened as he held out his right hand for her to shake. "If you're sure."

She grasped his hand, thinking she wouldn't mind seeing him again under different circumstances. Definitely wouldn't mind. But as a boss or something else?

She nodded noncommittally, and then remembered the Dinosaur. "I hate to ask, but can I get a ride back to my car? It's still at the convenience store where Mark was injured."

He didn't answer, but moved closer, still holding her hand.

How weird was that? She tried to pull her hand free, but he only tightened his fingers around hers. She frowned and tugged. "What are you doing?"

Strong fingers cupped her face and pulled her gaze up to his. She could drown in those pale eyes—and not in a bad way. Her muscles grew languorous, and, holy cow, if he wasn't the most beautiful man she'd ever seen. She wondered what his lips would feel like on hers.

"You'll never believe this, Krys, but I am sorry." His voice came from a few light years away as he led her to the sofa beneath the windows. She didn't remember sitting down, but she awoke as if from a brief nap to find him next to her, pushing up the sleeve of her blouse and piercing the big cephalic vein in her forearm with a syringe.

Oh no, that couldn't happen. "No drugs," she whispered—it was the only thought she could express from the fog of her mind. Except that he wasn't pushing anything into her vein with the needle. He was withdrawing blood.

She swallowed hard, trying to force her thick, useless tongue to work. "What...doing?"

He stroked her hair, and leaned over till his face was inches from hers. She had that crazy urge to kiss him again, and focused on his lips—the bottom one fuller than the top, firm and strong. A mouth made for kissing.

"Look at me, Krys," he said softly, and as she raised her eyes to his again, her awareness fuzzed around the edges. The room spun. She fought it, struggled to keep her thoughts clear, but eventually a wave of nothingness washed over her.

❊ CHAPTER 6 ❊

Three a.m. tomorrow night, behind the mill. That was the message Owen had sent with Mark, or at least it was all he'd been able to tell Melissa.

After a meeting with the lieutenants, a shower, and a quick surveillance drive around town, Aidan returned to the clinic. Mark was zombied on Vicodin, so Melissa's report had to do for now. Maybe he was naïve considering the brutality of Owen's attacks, but Aidan still hoped he could reason with his brother—even pay him off if he had to.

Except nothing involving Owen had ever been that simple.

Aidan and Melissa walked to the clinic office from Mark's room. Since he had a couple of hours to kill before sunrise, he might as well check in on Krys—she'd still be enthralled, so he wouldn't have to worry about her testing his control. He pulled aside the area rug and deftly moved the wooden pieces to release the hatch lock. "Shut this up after me." He looked back at Melissa. "When I leave, I'll go through the tunnel."

"Will do," Melissa said. "You coming back to talk to Mark? He might know more than he told me—I know you boys have your secrets. And you need to feed."

Aidan paused halfway through the hatch and met her smile. She'd been his human familiar—his feeder—for four years, and they'd become good friends, no benefits. Just the way he wanted it. "You know everything that goes on around here, Mel. Tell Mark I'll be there as soon as I can after rising, and don't worry about the feeding. I'll get a sub for a few days."

The hatch clicked shut above his head as he descended the ladder into the first lower level. They'd spent a year excavating another space beneath the existing basement, creating half a dozen subbasement suites with an elaborate ventilation system. A hidden escape tunnel branched off to lead to different spots in town, and a couple of the rooms, such as the one Krys was in, locked only from the outside. Sometimes guests in the vampire world couldn't be trusted.

Krys was their first…well, he couldn't exactly call her a guest, but *prisoner* made him sound like the predator he'd spent years pretending not to be. Guess desperation brought out the blackest part of a person's soul—if vampires had souls. He'd always believed so, but he couldn't put in much of an endorsement for it right now.

Krystal Harris definitely wouldn't when she woke up tomorrow and found herself drafted as Penton's newest citizen. Aidan grimaced as he crossed the basement storage area to reach the hidden hatch into the subbasement. His reaction to Krys tonight had been way off the normal chart, and he wasn't sure what to make of it. Sure, he was hungry and she was beautiful—but it wasn't as if he hadn't experienced either lust or hunger in the last four hundred years and controlled both of them. Krys Harris was just a new kind of test.

He'd had his mate, and she was dead because he'd failed her. He wasn't going down that road again.

The cool, damp air chilled his skin when he climbed down the ladder into the subbasement stairwell. The smell of cement and glue and wood remained fresh despite the ventilation system's work to keep the heated air flowing. He might need to light the propane fireplace to take the chill off the suite if Will hadn't done it.

Thick carpet blanketed the long corridor and ornate brass light sconces showed off Will's luxurious taste in furnishings. Left to Aidan or Mirren, the ambience would have been somewhere between storage room and hunting lodge—strictly function and comfort. But he could appreciate Will's sense of style.

He paused outside the door to Krys's suite, key halfway to the lock. He sensed her presence, her heartbeat, her soft breath, the scent of her skin as she moved about the room. Shit. How the hell was she awake so soon?

He'd had trouble keeping her enthralled upstairs. She'd started coming around when he tried to withdraw blood to test for the pandemic vaccine and he'd had to roll her mind a second time to put her under. There were stories of humans strong-willed enough to resist mental manipulation, but he'd never met one. Well, maybe until now.

Chickenshit bastard that he was, he'd expected her to sleep well past daybreak, have her initial freak-out, and then be calm enough to talk by the time he rose at dusk. Think again.

Maybe he should leave, go home to relax for a couple of hours before his daysleep, and just let things play out. She wasn't screaming, and he wasn't picking up signs of fear—no rapid heart rate, no quickened breath—so she obviously didn't realize she'd been locked in. Maybe he could find out what she thought had happened, salvage this mess somehow, and talk her into staying. Worth a try.

He knocked softly on the door to give her a heads-up, and then slid the key into the dead-bolt lock. The heavy wooden door swung silently inward, and Aidan stepped into the room.

The quilt over the king-size bed had been thrown back, and the bed was empty. The sound of water splashing from a faucet trickled in. What would she assume had happened? How could he explain...

Krys appeared in the bathroom doorway and stopped with a surprised yelp. "Oh my God—you almost gave me a heart attack."

Her nervous chuckle blossomed into that husky, throaty laugh he'd noticed before, the one that made him wonder what she'd sound like late at night, tangled in the sheets with his hands and mouth on her. The laugh wasn't all that drove his desire—she'd pulled off her business suit and wore a tiny red T-shirt and black panties that exposed a thin line of smooth skin between the lacy waistband and the hem of her top. She'd unbraided her dark auburn hair, and it fell in loose waves around her shoulders.

She was magnificent and unself-conscious and, holy hell, why hadn't he just gone home? His fangs and his cock were suddenly battling it out to see which one could ache with need the most, and the blast of desire that shot through him almost drove him to his knees.

She quit laughing and stared at him with a half smile. "Did I faint or something? I can't remember what happened, and this"—she looked around the suite—"this sure isn't the little hotel room in LaFayette." She tugged on the hem of the T-shirt. "I found this in the bathroom. Hope it's OK I took it."

"Ah, yeah." Aidan shook off the mental shock and tried to focus. How had she come out of the enthrallment so completely and so fast? She didn't even seem to have a post-enthrallment hangover.

He improvised. "You got light-headed, so I thought you could spend the night here in Penton—one of our guest rooms became available. Someone who stayed here earlier probably left the shirt." Someone as in careless, grieving Lucy, whose come-to-Aidan talk couldn't wait much longer. "I came back to check on you. How do you feel?"

Krys laughed again and leaned against the bathroom doorjamb. "A little woozy but maybe I went too long without eating. I guess low blood sugar caught up with me."

"I'll bring you something to eat," he said automatically. But not yet. Forget trying to talk her into staying while she was half-dressed and he was hungry. He needed to get her enthralled again before she realized this wasn't an ordinary hotel room and he wasn't the small-town hospital administrator she thought he was.

But damn, he didn't want to put her under. He wanted to wind his fingers through her hair, see if its shiny darkness felt as silky as it looked. He wanted to run his hands over every curve, taste her skin and her blood. He wanted to memorize her scent.

Her pulse quickened as if she sensed his thoughts. Such a tiny physical reaction, yet it almost undid his ability to stay in control of his raging instincts.

"Your eyes are amazing—I swear they change color," she said, searching his face but not settling on his gaze long enough for him to study her pupils. Didn't matter anyway—no way she was still buzzed. Fully enthralled meant unconscious. Lightly enthralled, people were functional sleepwalkers. They didn't stand there with bedroom laughs, tugging at the hems of little red shirts, ratcheting his hunger up until his damned body screamed for her. He hadn't reacted to a woman with such raw need since—well, since he'd been turned. Mated males acted this way. He didn't.

Aidan closed his eyes and regrouped. Enough already. He wasn't going to have this woman—not tonight, not ever, even if she was setting off every alarm in his food-sex control panel. Even if she wanted him, he might as well brand a big H on his forehead for "hypocrite" if he gave in to his wants.

"Why don't you get back in bed, relax, and I'll see about getting you some food," he said with what he thought was an admirable amount of restraint.

She cocked her head and looked at him with narrowed eyes for a moment, as if she sensed the change in his thoughts. Or maybe his eyes had darkened as he tried to drill some common sense into his thick vampire skull.

She walked to the bed, laughing softly as she tumbled onto the mattress, resting her head on the pillow, her dark hair fanning across the soft white cotton. Her lean body was relaxed, her long legs curled to one side, a hand resting on her stomach.

Aidan's slow-beating heart almost stopped. He wanted that image etched into his brain.

"I'm OK now," she said. "But you don't have to go, do you?"

His heart did a ridiculous flip-flop. "Ahh...sure. I can stay a few minutes." *Such a bad idea.*

Getting closer to her was an even worse idea, but Aidan couldn't enthrall her again if he didn't get close enough to capture her gaze. He sat on the edge of the bed, tamping down the urge to touch her.

"I didn't imagine the evening ending this way, did you?" She smiled. "I don't act like this normally—I really don't. It's just that when I met you...work wasn't what I kept thinking about."

His breath released in a whoosh as she laid a hand on his knee and slid it up to his thigh. *She might want you now, big guy, but wait till she wakes up in the morning and finds herself locked in. She's gonna hate your sorry ass.*

He didn't know Krystal Harris. Did she come on like this to any man she was attracted to? God knows she was pretty enough, but he caught a hint of vulnerability from her, even when she was moving her hand near his point of no return. He believed her when she said she didn't normally act this way, so she must be reacting to their instant chemistry, same as he was. Only difference was, she didn't know that when he left her tonight, her freedom was going with him.

He took her wandering hand, gently removed it from his thigh, and stretched out next to her on the bed, closing his eyes for a moment to take in the scent of her—a sweet, delicate floral overlaying clean skin touched recently by the sun. He took her face between his palms, his eyes seeking to lock with hers so he could enthrall her again before this went any further.

But she was focused on his mouth. "Kiss me," she whispered. "Please."

He was still thinking of excuses when she raised her head and pressed her lips to his, the softest brush that drew his lips down in response. He kissed her top lip, and then nipped at her bottom, keeping his fangs to himself, before covering her mouth with his. Need jolted down his spine and straight into his groin as her tongue sought entrance to his mouth.

No more. He rolled away from her with a groan and sat up. "Krys, we can't do this. Not—"

"Why not?" That laugh again, and he looked back to see her watching him with parted lips, her own hunger naked on her face. Her pulse thudded in his ears, and he knew that if he moved to touch her she would welcome him.

"Aidan, I can already tell you overthink things—just shut up and kiss me again. Unless..." She sat up and looked at him uncertainly. "Unless you don't want me, and that's OK. I know you're probably used to more beautiful women than me and—" She looked down at her hands. "God, I'm just humiliating myself. Maybe you should go after all."

Was she being coy? But no, she was blushing, her skin turning an enticing shade of pink. How the hell could she possibly think she wasn't beautiful, or that he might not want her? Without thinking, he reached out a hand, brushed his fingers lightly across her cheek, and cupped them around the curve between her neck and shoulder. "You shine like the sunlight," he said softly. "Don't ever doubt how beautiful you are."

She leaned into his hand and kissed his palm, then reached down and tugged at the bottom edges of the T-shirt, pulling it over her head. She bit her lip and her blush deepened as she sat holding the shirt, seeming unsure what to do with it.

Aidan wet his lips. Her breasts were small, high, and firm; her mix of courage and vulnerability was about the sexiest thing he'd ever seen. He wanted his mouth on her. Now.

"Hell, woman, you aren't making this easy." Just another kiss. He could kiss her, then enthrall her and walk away. He took the shirt from her and threw it aside, his heart speeding to keep time with hers as he stretched out beside her again. He gathered her into his arms, his kiss harder than before. Reckless. A fang brushed her lower lip, and his breath grew uneven as he watched the tiny drop of blood form, its sweet perfume enveloping him. Gently, he covered her mouth with his again and groaned as the blood hit his tongue, destroying his last shreds of conscience.

"I want you." Her fingers found the bottom edge of his sweater and slipped underneath, raking nails up his spine as he moved his mouth to the sweet spot underneath her ear. That did it. He ripped the damned sweater off, and then lowered his lips back to her neck. He bit gently, pulling the skin between his teeth hard enough to feel her pulse speed and bring a soft gasp, but not enough to break skin. He would not drink, damn it, and he wouldn't—

All thought retreated as her hand slid between their bodies and splayed out on his chest, running the length of his torso down to his hard length, stroking gently till he thought he'd come in his pants like the teenager he hadn't been in four hundred years.

With a deep, rumbling groan, he edged a knee between her legs, and she rolled to her back to accommodate him, cradling him between her thighs.

"Yes," she breathed, closing her eyes. He rolled his hips, pressing himself against her, using the rough denim of his jeans for friction.

He pulled back to frame her face in his hands, and her eyes met his.

Holy hell.

A chill ran through him as Krys reached up to plant small kisses against his neck. She sensed his stillness and stopped. "What's wrong?"

"Look at me," he whispered, and she raised her eyes to his again. In the center of those deep brown irises, her pupils were dilated, black pools he hadn't seen in the soft light of the lamp. She might be walking and talking and setting off his freakin' vampire radar, but she was stoned. It had to be some weird after-effect of the enthrallment, something he'd never encountered.

"What's wrong?" she repeated, frowning, her voice stronger.

"Krys, I—" What the hell was he supposed to say? *Sorry, I was an asshole who took advantage of you? Sorry, I'm just a predator? Sorry, I got carried away?*

He'd have to try to enthrall her again, take her under deep, and hope to God she didn't remember any of this when she woke. Yeah, chickenshit.

"Look at me again." He kissed her lightly before catching her gaze and rolling his mind over hers with his full force of will, more than he'd ever used on a human before.

"What..." She frowned briefly before her lashes fluttered and she closed her eyes with a soft sigh, her hands sliding from his back.

He gently extricated himself and lifted the quilt over her, his hands shaking as he pulled his sweater back on. What the hell had he done to her? And what the hell had she done to him?

❋CHAPTER 7❋

Krys stretched and yawned, eyes still closed. She hadn't slept this well in a long time, so surely it wouldn't hurt to snuggle under the covers a few more minutes. No one expected her back in Americus, and hotel checkout wasn't till noon. LaFayette's hotel was quiet as a graveyard, the only sound the soft whoosh of forced air coming from a heating vent. Surprising, since it was on a state highway that mostly saw local traffic and long-haul truckers.

Consciousness began to stir, and she groaned and began laughing into her pillow. God, the *dream* she'd had. True, Aidan Murphy was one fine-looking man but surely there was some kind of law against having *that* kind of dream about a potential employer.

She rolled over, trying to remember peeling her clothes off and crawling into bed without her usual oversize Emory T-shirt. Wait. Had she even driven back last night?

Her eyes popped open to an unfamiliar lamp on an unfamiliar wooden nightstand in an unfamiliar room. This wasn't the shabby little single at the LaFayette Motor Inn. Where was she?

She sat up, heart thudding. Wait—the room did look familiar. Soft lamplight cast shadows on pale gold walls and rich brown carpet in a room with no windows. She'd been sleeping on a king-size, four-poster bed with cotton sheets as soft as feathers. A light quilt stretched over her. She rubbed her temples, straining to remember.

Weird, the dream about Aidan Murphy. They'd been in this room. She had to be losing her freaking mind. What had happened last night?

Krys rubbed her eyes, trying to think. She remembered talking to Aidan and getting ready to leave his office, then nothing. She didn't remember him taking her back to get her car. She sure didn't remember coming to this room. Only snatches of the dream.

Had she fainted? Had they taken her to a room somewhere in Penton? That certainly would make the perfect ending to the craziest job interview trip in history. She threw back the quilt and froze, chills racing over her skin not from the cool air but from the small heap of red fabric on the floor next to the bed. The T-shirt she'd been wearing last night in the dream, the one she'd pulled off herself, inviting Aidan to touch her.

Holding her breath, she leaned down and snatched the T-shirt off the floor, lifting it to her face. It smelled of her own floral perfume mixed with an unmistakable trace of the clean, masculine scent Aidan had had in her dream. Krys closed her eyes, heat washing through her as a montage of images flashed across her mind—frantic kisses, silvery blue eyes, her hands in thick, dark hair, his mouth on her...everywhere. She pulled the quilt tightly around her. It hadn't been a dream. The son of a bitch had taken advantage of her. Sort of. Maybe.

Except, other images were there, too, igniting her skin. *Did he take advantage of you, or did you practically attack the man?* She remembered pulling his body against hers, kissing him, urging him to take her, ripping off that stupid red T-shirt. She'd practically begged him, except—damn it—she didn't do stuff like that. She was the one who stayed home on off-rotation nights because she knew she'd never fit in with the other med students or residents. The one whose daddy complex was so screwed up that she'd never enjoyed sex. The one whose idea of a club was a *book* club, for God's sake.

She wasn't sexy enough for the likes of Aidan Murphy, and she'd never have done the things she was remembering. She might want to, but she'd never have the guts.

Scalp-crawling tinges of panic overcame Krys for the first time since she'd left home at eighteen, when the bellow of her father's voice from across the house would bring on the shakes. Her breathing came in short bursts, lack of oxygen making the room spin. *Think, Krys.*

One of the first things she'd learned after leaving home was how to relax into the panic. She took in a lungful of air, released it slowly, repeated the process. So what if she'd thrown herself at a man she barely knew and couldn't quite remember the details? Fainting from hyperventilation wouldn't help.

What would help was a plan. And a quick trip back to Americus—no way Aidan Murphy would want to hire her now. She could never look him in the eye again.

First, clothes. Nobody could think straight sitting naked in a strange room. She'd get dressed and get out of here, go to the LaFayette motel and get her stuff, and then try to piece together what had happened once she got the hell out of Penton, assuming that's where she was.

Krys wrapped the quilt around her like a big, overly padded towel, and looked around the room for her suit—and her purse and briefcase.

And where was her car?

She set aside the alarming idea that the Dinosaur might still be sitting in that Quikmart parking lot. Clothes first.

She spotted the dark brown suit skirt and white blouse thrown across an armchair in the corner of the room. The bedroom alone was the size of her entire apartment in Americus. Not to mention nicer, with better furnishings. Besides the cherry four-poster bed with its carved headboard, there was a matching nightstand, a dresser with a mirror, and two armchairs. There were three cherrywood doors in two of the walls. A flat-screen TV hung over an unlit fireplace filled with gas logs. A sofa, chair, and coffee table faced the fireplace, forming a small sitting area. It looked like the fancy boutique hotel she'd stayed in at her one and only medical conference—when her med school had footed the bill. If Penton had this kind of lodging, why had they stuck her more than ten miles away at the dumpy LaFayette Motor Inn?

Still practicing her deep breathing, Krys spotted her purse on the dresser and her shoes underneath the armchair. She was in business.

Bra. Skirt. Blouse. She felt better with her clothes on, wrinkles and all. She picked the pantyhose up, considering. No, those she'd ripped all by herself. She'd just have to go bare-legged and hope it wasn't too cold.

The wooden door next to the chair didn't have a notice on it like hotel rooms were required to post, so this must be a private guesthouse. She grasped the ornate brass knob and pulled, planning to poke her head out and see if she recognized anything. The door wouldn't budge. She squatted, looking for a thumblatch or keycard slot. Weird. She pulled on the door again, but it was solid and heavy. And locked from the outside with a deadbolt, from the looks of it.

Half-panicked, half-annoyed, Krys rattled the knob a few times and then pounded on a door so solid it absorbed her fist-falls.

"Hello? Anyone? I'm locked in here!" She kicked at what looked like some kind of hinged slot in the bottom of the door, but all that earned her was a throbbing, stubbed toe.

"Damn it." She looked around at the two other doors. Maybe she'd been trying to open one of those adjoining room doors that locked from the other side.

The door on the far side opened into a bathroom, all marble surfaces and antiqued fittings, a walk-in shower and a built-in Jacuzzi in opposite corners. A sharp pain stabbed through Krys's head and she closed her eyes. She remembered this room, getting undressed, finding the red T-shirt and putting it on. And walking out to find Aidan.

Her image in the mirror looked no different than usual. She ran her fingers through her hair and stopped, frowning. Turning to the side, she studied her neck. Just under her right ear, there was a freakin' hickey. What was this, high school? Except, the image that came to her as she ran her fingers over the small bruise was no teen flashback. Aidan's teeth biting, mouth roving over her. God, it really had happened. Dreams didn't leave love bites.

Everything in the bathroom looked new, even smelled new, with underlying odors of fresh concrete and stone and glue.

Wrapped toiletries occupied a corner of the vanity—toothbrush, toothpaste, soap, shampoo, lotion.

A sense of unreality settled over Krys as she walked back into the bedroom and opened the third door. A small closet, with clothes hanging in it. Her breath caught when she saw the cream-colored sweater hanging next to her suede jacket. That sweater had been in the hotel room in LaFayette. She slid the hangers to expose the other clothes hanging beside the jacket. She always packed too much, even for an overnight trip. And the evidence was on display right in front of her.

Hands trembling, she jerked the jacket off its hanger and dug in the pocket for her pistol, but she found only a stick of gum. The bright green wrapper teetered on her shaking palm a moment before toppling off. She retrieved it, wrapping her fingers around its familiar shape, a tiny piece of normal. Then she saw her suitcase on the closet floor.

Her suitcase from the hotel. Someone had definitely gone into her room at the LaFayette Motor Inn and brought all her things here, wherever here might be. Who did stuff like that? Kidnappers. But who'd kidnap a doctor from a poor family with over two hundred grand in college debts? Somebody delusional.

Think, Krys. Phone. She scanned the room again, checking the nightstand and the dresser and the small writing desk. No phone. She grabbed her purse, digging in it, finally dumping the contents on the bed. Fast-food receipts, makeup, pens, and half a Hershey bar wrapped in foil—but no cell phone. Even her iPod was gone.

They'd gone through her purse, too. No point in denial. *They* existed. Had Aidan done this? Halfway seduced her, knocked her out, stolen her stuff, and locked her in? The man obviously had money—look at the car he drove, the way he dressed, the salary the clinic offered. Why would he do this?

Fighting a prickly, panicky feeling, she returned to the closet and fell to her knees in front of the suitcase, unzipping the front compartment where she kept her laptop. She could tell it was empty from the heft of it, but she looked anyway, opening every compartment, the teeth of the zipper ripping through the oppressive silence. It held nothing but her stupid book of crossword puzzles.

She collapsed onto the floor with a thump and drew her knees to her chest, wrapping her arms around them. A bandage on her left forearm caught her eye. Just a Band-Aid, flesh-colored plastic, right over the cephalic vein.

She flicked a fingernail under the edge and peeled it off, unveiling a tiny round bruise. A needle mark. Someone had given her an injection. Had Aidan drugged her? That would certainly explain her uncharacteristic (slutty) behavior. But no, she sort of remembered him *taking* blood, not injecting her. Maybe he wasn't the Godfather. Maybe he was Frankenstein.

Panic faded to numbness. This was rural Alabama, for God's sake, not exactly a hotbed of freaky abductions. Crime here most often involved domestic abuse fueled by a lot of alcohol.

There had to be a rational explanation. Krys stood and pulled a pair of jeans and a sweater from the hangers, then looked around the room, trying to inject a smidgen of logic. She crossed to the dresser, opened the top drawer, and found the rest of her clothes, the neatly folded panties and socks. Great. Someone had handled her underwear.

She changed her clothes in the small bathroom after looking around for video cameras. The idea of cameras was no crazier than waking up in a strange bed, locked up after a night of hot almost-sex with a stranger who'd probably drugged her and left her in this room that was...underground, maybe? No windows, and it had a cool, muffled feel. Now that she thought about it, when she'd shouted and pounded on the door, there had been no echo or vibration. Her voice had been absorbed into the room. Definitely a basement.

Running shoes and clean clothes dulled the fear and made way for anger. It seeped into her muscles like liquid fire, energizing them. Who the hell did Aidan Murphy think he was, anyway? Maybe he *was* a freakin' mob boss. God knew that monster-size Mirren Kincaid would be a good enforcer. She should have run over Aidan last night and kept driving.

Or at least she thought it had been last night. She looked around and spotted her watch on the bedside table. Two p.m. She'd lost almost twelve hours.

Krys paced, trying to turn the anger into something she could use. She walked the edges of the room, looking for vents. Heroines in suspense movies always climbed through vents to escape their kidnappers. But the only vents she could find were the size of a prescription pad and located in the ceiling.

That damned son of a bitch, with his blue freaking eyes and silky, dark hair. She'd like to snatch every strand of it out of his head. And inflict some pain a little lower, too.

While her mind ranted, she kept her hands busy. Put her dirty clothes and dress heels in the empty suitcase. Threw the torn pantyhose in the trash can. (Make that the ornate, expensive-looking trash can.) Stuffed the contents of her purse back into the shoulder bag and hung it off the edge of a chair. Brushed her teeth. Brushed her hair.

Finally, her restless gaze fell on the TV. She punched buttons on the front but nothing happened, so she jerked open the nightstand drawer.

Bingo. No Gideon Bible, but there was a remote.

She aimed it at the TV and flipped channels. Not a big selection. Ellen DeGeneres held court on one channel; a TV judge chastised moronic criminals on another; a soap opera ran on a third. She recognized the show as *General Hospital*, which her coworkers liked to watch in the break room. The main character was a mob boss named Sonny, and he had dark hair and dimples. Krys hoped somebody would shoot him.

Running on the fourth and final channel was what appeared to be local-access footage filmed with someone's flip-cam, complete with bad lighting and uneven sound. The fuzzy picture showed a large room filled with people, all sitting in folding chairs turned toward a dais. Facing them from behind a long table on the raised platform sat three figures.

Krys frowned and moved closer to the screen as she recognized Mirren Kincaid sitting on the left and Aidan in the middle. A striking, black-haired woman sat to Aidan's right.

A man in the audience asked a question, and Krys strained to catch it. She raised the volume as Aidan spoke into a microphone.

"Jerry, I can't tell you how many there are." His voice was deep and masculine, and the sound of it sent a shiver through Krys, the memories of last night replaying—as if she could forget.

Shaking aside the memory, she focused on the video. "My brother Owen or the members of his scathe are the ones who killed Doc," Aidan was saying. "I don't know how many of them there are. They can't feed from you because you're all bonded to one of us, but they're still dangerous. We don't want to start a full-scale war without knowing if Owen's acting alone or if there's someone more powerful backing him. In the meantime, we're setting up security patrols and asking you to not go out alone at night."

Krys frowned, trying to make sense of it. What was a scathe? Feeding, bonding, precautions, war. And Aidan had told her the former doctor, if that's who "Doc" was, died in a hunting accident. She felt like a tourist lost in a foreign country where everyone was chattering in a language she couldn't understand.

The town hall meeting, or at least that's what Krys decided it was, lasted about an hour, then the screen went blank and it started over. Must be playing in a loop, making sure the good people of Penton were warned about...something. She watched it again, but the combination of poor sound quality and unfamiliar subject matter made it impossible to follow.

She turned the volume down but left the set on while she did another futile round of beating on the door. Her throat ached from yelling, and her stomach rumbled from hunger. What the hell was she going to do?

She noticed a brown bag sitting on the floor next to the coffee table and picked it up hesitantly. It didn't tick or explode, so she opened it and found a box of vanilla wafers, a can of nuts, and a six-pack of bottled water. There was also a note, written on a plain square of paper in a small, looping script: *Someone will bring more food soon, and I will be there tonight to explain. I am sorry. —Aidan*

Yeah, he'd think *sorry* once she got her hands on him. Except the thought made her remember where her hands had already *been* on him. Good God in heaven.

She took the nuts and a bottle of water and checked to make sure they hadn't been opened. Who knew—poison wasn't out of the question. *Tonight*, he'd written. Guess a kidnapped doctor wasn't important enough to take up time during his busy workday.

The nuts were too salty, but Krys forced down a handful while she flipped through the TV channels again. Was the reason Aidan couldn't talk to her until tonight the same reason he couldn't interview her during daylight hours? And some interview that had turned out to be.

She crawled back on the bed, staring at the ceiling, trying to construct an explanation that made sense. Sometime later, a sudden rattling woke her from a half doze, and she rolled off the bed so fast that she tripped and fell hard to her knees.

A tray came sliding through the slot at the bottom of the door, and Krys scrambled toward it, yelling. It shut with a clang and the click of a lock, and no amount of pushing would budge it.

"Help me!" Krys scrambled to her feet and pounded on the door. "I know you're out there. Let me out of here, damn it! You can't lock me up like this, Aidan Murphy!"

Nothing. Not a sound.

Her breath came in ragged bursts as she slid to the floor, but she gritted her teeth and swiped away the one stray tear that had escaped down her cheek. She was a survivor. Her first seventeen years had been spent with a father who used ridicule and belittlement, and occasionally his fists, as weapons of control. She'd escaped and made a life for herself, and no small-town psychopath was going to take it away. She was smarter than that. Smarter than he was. She had the bully-survival technique down. She just had to stay calm and let it play out.

He was feeding her, so he wanted her for something and it had to be more than sex. Eventually he would show his hand.

In the meantime she was frustrated as hell and screamed as loud as she could. She hoped Aidan "Godfather" Murphy heard her.

❊ CHAPTER 8 ❊

Aidan's eyes flicked open at sunset, exactly 4:49 p.m., and his first thoughts were of Krys. Whether she was more frightened than angry. How much she remembered. What to make of the hunger she'd raised in him—not just hunger for sex or blood, but a bloody mating call, at least as he'd heard it described. Had to be a fluke.

The room was cool and quiet as he rolled onto his side and reached to click on the bedside lamp. He stretched out muscles tight from too many hours without movement, and ticked through the things that he needed to do before sunrise, trying to push thoughts of Krys to the back burner. Now was no time to get distracted.

First on the agenda: breakfast. He might have shown a little more intestinal fortitude last night if he hadn't neglected his feeding. Instead, he'd acted like an asshole. Lesson learned.

He picked up the cell phone on his nightstand and speed-dialed Will. His lieutenant's clipped blue-blood accent sounded alert as he launched into a spiel before Aidan could utter a word.

"Yes, the doctor's apartment has been vacated. No, I haven't delivered her pathetic belongings to storage—it was almost dawn when I got in. That human needs a serious style makeover, by the way. And yes, I intend to finish getting her affairs in order tonight. Anything else?"

"There's always something else, Sir William."

Accent on the *Sir*. A standing joke between them. Where Aidan had been a dirt-poor Irish farmer, Will was a product of his highbrow Yankee upbringing. He'd been turned in his early twenties by his father, Matthias, to ensure him an eternal acolyte. Will had the expensive tastes of early New York high society, but he didn't share his father's taste for power and manipulation. He'd thumbed his nose at Matthias and wandered the world until finally joining up with Aidan five years ago.

"This Irish peasant needs a donor," Aidan said. "Got somebody you can assign me for a few days? Mark needs to heal, and I want Melissa free to take care of him."

Will snorted. "Please. Women will be opening their veins outside my front door when they learn the great Aidan Murphy needs sustenance. Hold on."

Grimacing, Aidan heard the click of computer keys and waited. The last thing he had time for was a woman with social ambitions, especially a human.

While Will looked through the possibilities, Aidan slid out of bed and ran his hands through his hair.

The gesture brought the image of Krys back to him, the way she'd looked at him with that mixture of vulnerability and desire. Back burner. Right.

He realized now that her inhibitions had been lowered by the enthrallment, but it wouldn't have changed her basic personality. She was both fiery and vulnerable, a combination that intrigued him and brought back memories that he hadn't indulged in for a long time. Since Abby died all those years ago, he'd kept his relationships simple: blood from humans, friendship from his fams and lieutenants, and sex that scratched an itch—vampires only. Love was a distraction that ended up hurting everyone.

"I have a possibility here, sister of a familiar." Will clicked more keys, jarring Aidan back to the present. "She's here with her husband. I assume you want a donor already in a relationship so you don't have to disappoint some poor girl deluded enough to think she can make you love her. Or I could send you a guy."

Aidan grunted. "Somebody in a relationship is good. I have enough drama from my psychotic brother. Last thing I need is a woman who thinks she can save me from myself. And no guys." He might not have sex with his fams, but some intimacy was unavoidable and guys just didn't do it for him. He'd fed from Mark a couple of times in an emergency, but it hadn't been comfortable for either one of them.

He took a quick shower and dressed in a pair of black wool pants and a pale blue cashmere sweater he'd never have picked for himself—he didn't much care what he wore, so he let Melissa shop for him. He wasn't sure exactly what she meant by calling him a "vampire Ken doll," but it had to be bad because it amused her so much.

By the time Aidan made his way through the drafty parlor of the 1930s mansion, he sensed the human at the door—pulse too fast, adrenaline pumping. The young woman gave him a tentative smile when he greeted her, and he pretended not to notice when she tripped on the threshold and blushed.

He remembered interviewing the woman, Jessie, when she and her husband requested permission to move to Penton. One of his scathe members had taken both of them through drug detox by keeping them enthralled, then went through counseling with them to make sure they knew what was expected of them in Penton and that they understood that a drug or alcohol relapse would mean a wiped memory bank and a short drive back to the streets of Atlanta.

In other words, standard operating procedure for Penton. Except for bonding to the scathe, she'd never fed anyone.

He considered enthralling her, but decided against it. She needed to see firsthand what feeding was like. Until she and her husband became fams, which would put them off-limits to other vampires, she was expected to feed any scathe member who needed it.

He raised her arm to his lips and licked gently along her inner wrist to anesthetize it, then kissed it, an acknowledgment of the gift she gave him. Her body tensed and jerked as he bit down, but within moments she sighed and relaxed. He closed his eyes at the pleasure of sinking fangs into flesh, at the deep rush of salty-sweet sustenance, and the gentle rhythm of feeding as he drew from her vein. He'd fed for a few moments before realizing it was Krys's face looking back at him in his mind, her vein he wanted, and her body his hard-on wanted to visit.

Not happening.

Jessie sagged against the sofa back, relaxing into a feeder's high. Aidan swallowed a groan of frustration even as the energy of new blood coursed through him, warming his body and speeding up his sluggish heart. Jessie wasn't the one he wanted.

A half hour later, Aidan climbed into his car and headed toward the clinic. Next order of tonight's business: talking to Mark.

After that, damage control with Krys, and God help him with that.

Finally, he needed to have that chat with Lucy about being more careful. If his own lieutenants didn't follow the rules and keep their spaces safe, how could he expect anyone else to?

He slammed the car door harder than he'd intended.

He entered the hospital room and saw Mark sitting up in bed, propped against a pile of pillows. Melissa had gotten him into a pair of old-fashioned plaid pj's that Aidan would give him hell about once this mess was behind him. She'd made some attempt at combing his hair, and he looked a lot better than he had twelve hours ago. Only the clenched jaw and lowered brows gave away how far from OK everything was.

Melissa lay curled on the small sofa against the wall, sleeping. Aidan glanced at her and quietly pulled a chair close to Mark's bed. "How you doing?"

"OK for a damn-fool idiot." His voice sounded stronger.

Aidan studied his coloring and frowned. He looked flushed. "Make sure Mel gives you the antibiotics the doctor prescribed."

"You seen the doctor yet tonight? Mel told me you had to keep her against her will because of me." Mark struggled to slide farther up in his bed and winced as Aidan leaned over to pull him upright. "I'm sorry, A."

Melissa stirred but didn't wake, and they lowered their voices.

"She's in one of the sub rooms," Aidan said, shaking his head. "Seriously freaked out and scared, I'm guessing." Especially if she remembered their time together, but he wasn't volunteering that info. "What the hell happened? Give me one good reason for you to be out alone at night."

Mark settled back on the pillows. "I was stupid. I was late coming back from that business meeting in Birmingham, and just pulled off at the Quikmart to clean fast-food crap out of the car and throw it in the Dumpster. Owen was there before I heard anything."

Aidan thumped him on the uninjured side of his head. "We're vampires. The whole idea is for our prey not to hear us coming."

"I know, damn it. I've been with you long enough to know better. Mel says there's a word cut into me here." He touched the bandages plastered across his stomach. "What's it mean?"

Aidan shook his head. "It's Gaelic for 'food.'"

Mark stared at him a moment, burst into laughter, then collapsed in pain. "God, that's just...funny. Sorry."

Aidan raised his eyebrows. Mark would wear that label for the rest of his life. Nothing funny about it. "Tell me what Owen said."

Mark wiped his eyes, still on the verge of losing it. "He knew I was bonded to you. Called me your little pet—probably thought I was your fam."

He coughed and sipped from the cup of water that Aidan handed to him. "Said if he couldn't feed off your people, he could at least bleed us out. That if he got enough of us, you'd feel so guilty you'd either let him join you or kill you, and he didn't care which."

As strategies went, it wasn't bad. Owen was immoral, not stupid. "Mel said he wanted a meeting?"

"Three a.m., behind the mill," Mark said. "He didn't say anything except come alone. You know it's a setup."

Aidan looked at his watch. "Knowing my brother, no doubt about it. Don't worry. I have plenty of time to get ready." He could be better prepared if he knew whether anyone was backing Owen. He'd have to call Mirren and be ready for a double cross. Maybe Lucy, as well.

He stood and glanced back at Melissa. "She doing OK?"

"Can't get her to go home. But you know Mel—she's worried about you."

Aidan smiled at her sleeping form. "I'm good. But I think I'll bring the doctor back up here and make sure you don't have a fever. I'm on my way to see her anyway."

A prospect that both excited and terrified him.

❊ C H A P T E R   9 ❊

When the dead bolt clicked, Krys wasn't sure she'd really
heard it. The TV had been an endless drone in the background but its noise made her feel less alone. When a late-night
talkfest followed a morning game show and some programs ran
without commercials, she realized it was taped programming—
probably some closed-circuit local system. She'd watched the
minutes pass on her watch, counting the time until dusk. The
onset of night. When Aidan said he'd come back.

She needed answers.

Finally, she'd curled up on the floor in front of the door. If
they fed her once, they'd do it again. Next time, she'd make
them hear her—whoever *they* were.

She'd dozed off by the time the dead bolt released with a
solid click, and she sat up, groggy, wondering if she'd dreamed
it. Then the door swung in and she scrambled out of its way, her
eyes following the long line of black-clad legs and blue sweater
up to Aidan Murphy's face. He stared down at her, wearing a

look of concern that made her want to scratch those pretty eyes out of their sockets.

No hysterics, though. She'd wait and see what he wanted.

Like hell. Her internal alarm screamed, *Run.*

She scrambled toward the door on all fours and got past his legs, glimpsing a carpeted hallway before he reached down, hooked one arm around her waist, and hauled her to her feet as if she weighed nothing.

She went for his eyes, as she'd been taught in self-defense classes. Eyes and throats were the quickest way to disable an attacker.

He caught a wrist in each hand and held her flexing fingers away from his face. "Krys—"

"You son of a bitch, you let me out of here *now*." Her voice came out in strained whisper.

His hands were like steel manacles on her wrists. Strong SOB.

"Krys, stop it. Let me explain." His deep voice was smooth, calm, while her breath came in gasps from the exertion. She might as well have been chained to a wall.

Krys relaxed her arms, and as soon as his grip loosened, she kicked his kneecap, hoping to knock it out of place or at least throw him off balance. Her anger burned red and hot inside her head, and the adrenaline gave her enough strength to dislodge him a few inches. She wasn't a scared teenager anymore, trying to be small and invisible. She might not be strong enough to get away from Aidan Murphy, but by God, she could at least *hurt* him.

Her back hit the wall with a thud that knocked the breath out of her. She hadn't even registered his movement before he'd pinned her against the drywall next to the door, his hard body holding her in place. Strong hands clamped her wrists to the wall on either side of her head.

She fought for breath, and closed her eyes as her expanding lungs brought her body tighter against his, her skin heating as if remembering his touch. She became aware of his scent, of every point at which their bodies met, of her chin pressed into his broad shoulder, his big hands—calloused, strong hands that looked as if they'd done manual labor—circling her wrists. All the images of last night ran through her mind like a silent movie. What he'd done with that body, those hands. What she'd wanted him to do. Maybe she *had* gone crazy.

"Why have you done this to me?" Even to Krys, her voice sounded breathy and high-pitched, like a child's.

"Let's sit down and talk." Aidan spoke softly, his mouth near her ear, the light scent of sandalwood bringing back more sensory memories. He brushed his lips across her neck where he'd left his mark, the lightest of touches, and an involuntary moan escaped her before she could clamp down on it. She gritted her teeth, anger pushing away fear or embarrassment at the way he affected her.

"What did you do to me last night?" She pushed the words out through clenched teeth "Why am I here? You drugged me. What else?"

"Will you sit down? Let me talk to you—just talk?" His voice was low and calming, and her shoulders relaxed a little, her fists unclenching even as her wrists remained imprisoned by his hands. Damned traitorous body shouldn't be responding to him.

"Stop touching me and I'll talk." She quit struggling and managed to get some measure of control back in her voice.

He took a step backward, and only then did she realize how shallow her breathing had been. Her right hand shook as he took it in his and tried to lead her to the sofa.

She jerked it away. Somehow, his touch made her feel better. That was wrong. He should frighten her, not soothe her. She eyed the door, wondering if there was any way to outrun him if she managed to slip past. Doubtful. He was seriously strong, and he'd just moved so fast she hadn't been able to track him.

She walked stiffly to the far end of the sofa and wedged herself into the corner, hugging a wine-colored throw pillow to her midsection with both arms.

Aidan returned to the door, closed and locked it, and slid the key into his pocket before sitting in the chair adjacent to the far end of the sofa. Not getting too close. That was good.

Krys ventured a quick look at him before staring back at the coffee table. His posture was casual, hands dangling off the front of the chair arms, muscular thighs relaxed. But his expression was piercing.

"I can't tell you everything, but I'll answer some of your questions," he finally said. "And, for what it's worth, I apologize for last night. I mean, I don't regret, uh…I realized too late that you…weren't yourself." He stumbled over his words, and she risked another quick look at him. OK, she'd give him credit for having perfected a contrite expression. "I had no right to take advantage of you. You were just so beautiful, and…" He shrugged.

Her voice was ragged. "I know I'm no great beauty, so just forget the pretty words." *Built like a board, or a boy.* That's what her dad always said. *You'll never catch a man when you look like that.* "What drug did you give me?"

"No drugs." He paused and studied her, frowning. "And whoever made you believe you aren't beautiful was a liar."

Right, because Aidan Murphy didn't lie. And she wasn't buying the no-drugs bit—she'd acted too out of character. *He gave you exactly what you wanted.*

She shook off the thought. Half of her brain had obviously been abducted by aliens. She sneaked a glance at him. Nah, he probably wasn't an alien. "I remember you having a syringe."

He raised his eyebrows, and for a second she thought he was going to laugh. And if he did, she was going to gouge out his eyes with her fingernails even if he killed her for it.

"I didn't give you any drugs. I used"—he fumbled for words again—"a kind of mesmerism to get you down here, and I swear to God I thought you were over it or I wouldn't have... we wouldn't..." He finally ran out of words and shrugged.

She put the pillow down and stared at him. "Mesmerism?" *What bullshit.* "You're saying you *hypnotized* me? That's ridiculous. I can't be hypnotized." They'd tried it in psych classes, and she never went under. Never.

He gave her a tight smile. "Whether you believe it or not, it's the truth."

Fine. Nothing she could do about it now. If she'd been the type of person to dwell on the past, she'd still be sitting in a rundown house outside Birmingham, uneducated and waiting hand and foot on her father until she'd succumbed to either alcohol or his fists, or both. Last night was done. She was a fighter, and needed to fight smart.

"What do you want with me? Why are you keeping me locked up?"

Aidan shifted, leaning forward in his chair and propping his elbows on his knees. His mouth was set tightly, and she could see the muscles in his jaw working. Screw him. He should try walking in her shoes if he wanted to know stress. Nobody had *him* locked up in a windowless room.

"I need you to stay here a while. At the end of your time here, if you still want to leave, I'll take you home myself. We won't hurt you."

Effing amazing. Krys's skin flushed as anger filled her body again, which at least wiped out any lingering attraction. "At the end of my time here? What the hell does that mean? And who is *we?*"

She stood, frowning down at him for a split second before walking to the door and shaking the knob angrily. She knew he'd locked it but she needed to do *something.*

She leaned against the door, pressing her cheek against the wood, its surface smooth and cool with a faint smell of varnish. "So how long is my *time here* supposed to last? Until Mark Calvert has recovered? I told you last night he doesn't need full-time care." She turned to look at him again, pressing her back against the door.

Aidan stood as well, and he stared down at his hands for a moment, flexing them, seeming to measure his words. In Krys's experience, that meant he was deciding on what lie to tell. "We need a doctor here for a while, not just for Mark. Our people are under attack, and we need someone who knows how to treat them in case something else happens. It won't be forever. And by *our* and *we,* I mean the people of Penton."

"Attack?" Krys struggled to make sense of his words. "We're in Alabama, not Afghanistan. What kind of attack?"

She began pacing and could feel him tracking her movement, like a big, patient cat watching a mouse run through a maze, knowing that all the exits led right back to him. "You're not telling me a big chunk of this, buddy. I saw the town hall meeting or whatever it is." She gestured toward the TV.

His gaze flicked to the set for the first time and he froze. She'd turned off the sound, but the meeting footage continued to play. Krys didn't know what was going through his head, but she'd swear that his eyes, already that unusual color of light blue, had grown icier. The TV had surprised him, and by the look on his face, Aidan Murphy did not like surprises.

"Why did you take me? Not just anyone, but *me?*" She didn't have the physical strength to overpower him but there was nothing wrong with her brain. "You came looking for *me* for some reason. Why not some other gullible, idiotic doctor who was interested in rural medicine? There are lots of medical residents looking for jobs right now, especially for the salary you were dangling."

Aidan walked to the nightstand, picked up the remote, and punched the off button. When he turned back to her, his voice was flat. "We looked for a doctor who'd never had the pandemic vaccine. We found you."

Krys blinked, surprise deflating some of her anger. Her allergy to sorbitol had kept her from getting the shots to prevent a virus pandemic that had freaked everybody out and killed thousands. She'd lucked out. By the time the CDC released a sorbitol-free vaccine, she'd already had a mild case of the virus and managed to fight it off. She'd never taken the shots. But the virus had taken a heavy toll on the very young, the very old, and the very ill. The isolation wards, the protective suiting, the fear...it had been a horrible time.

She returned to sit at the far end of the sofa, anger giving way to grudging curiosity. "I don't understand. Why did you need a doctor who didn't get vaccinated?" Wait. There was a bigger question. "How did you *know* I hadn't been vaccinated?"

Aidan gave her an appraising look. He remained standing at the other end of the sofa, but Krys thought that if she reached for him, she could almost take hold of the coiled energy coming off him. He seemed used to giving orders and being in control, and her questions—and that video—made him uncomfortable. Too bad.

He sat heavily in the armchair and ran his hands through his hair. Her eyes followed the movement, and a memory of her own fingers twined through those soft waves flashed into her mind so strongly that she had to force her attention back on his words.

"Everyone who lives in Penton is so allergic to the vaccine that even a blood transfusion from a vaccinated person would be lethal," he said. "Most of the property in this little ghost town was for sale, so I bought it all up. About a hundred of us moved here from Atlanta and began repopulating it. We only allow unvaccinated people to live here."

Krys narrowed her eyes. How stupid did he think she was—to believe he managed to round up a hundred unvaccinated people with allergies and bought a town for them to live in? Seriously? Fine, she'd roll with it for now; see where he was going with this ludicrous story. If she kept him talking, maybe some kernel of truth would slip through the nonsense.

But that damned syringe. She leaned back, setting the throw pillow aside and shifting on the sofa to face him. "You took my blood and tested it last night when you..." *When you put your hands and your mouth all over me.* "When you knocked me out or hypnotized me or whatever, didn't you?"

"I did—or, actually, Melissa did." His face remained expressionless.

She stared at the coffee table. His story had enough holes in it to pass for Swiss cheese. "Why would it matter whether your doctor had the vaccine or not? And why keep me here by force?"

He gave her a rueful smile that dropped about ten years off his face and underscored what she'd thought before—he was under a lot of stress from whatever was really going on. "I was naïve. I hoped you'd want to stay once you got to know us, and since no one in Penton has had the vaccine, we want to keep it that way."

Maybe she could bargain with him. "I watched that town meeting video, you know." She made her tone conversational. "You said your doctor had been murdered. Not exactly a hunting accident, so you lied about that, too. And some guy named Owen is hurting people. And...stuff that didn't make sense. I might consider staying long enough to take care of Mark if you'd tell me what's really going on."

Aidan glanced back at the TV, and Krys saw a hard pulse of anger cross his face again. "If you decide to stay here, I'll explain," he said softly. "Otherwise, it's really none of your business."

Of all the boneheaded, arrogant... "And how long do you intend to keep me here by force, helping you take care of things that are *none of my business?*"

He reached into his pocket, ignoring the question, and Krys instinctively curled into the corner of the sofa again, wrapping her arms around her knees. She expected a gun—maybe her gun—or a bottle of chloroform or another needle. Instead, he pulled out a length of black fabric and unrolled it to reveal her iPod and earbuds, which he tossed to her. He didn't seem any more anxious to get close to her than she to him, which made her strangely disappointed. Sneaky bastard. "What about my phone? My computer?" *My gun.*

He shook his head. "Not yet."

She looked at her watch. Six fifteen. "Why do you only want to talk at night? What do you have going on during the day—a war?"

"Something like that," he said, standing. "Someone will bring your dinner soon. Leave any clothing you want washed by the door. First, though, I need you to go with me and check on Mark. He looks flushed."

He was offering to have her laundry done? This just kept getting weirder. Still, if he took her to the clinic, she might find a chance to run. She followed him to the door. "Of course. Infection is his biggest risk."

"Turn around." He held out the strip of black cloth. "I'm sorry, but I need to cover your eyes. It's for your safety as well as ours."

Krys backed away from him, anger and panic stealing her breath. "No. Damn. Way. You will not lead me around blindfolded." She'd stay in this room and let Mark rot with infection first.

Aidan looked annoyed. What a pity. "I promised I wouldn't hurt you."

"Guess what? Your credibility isn't worth much. I will not be blindfolded unless you hold me down and force me. Give Mark an antibiotic—you can do that as well as I."

Aidan paused for a moment, then folded the cloth and returned it to his pocket. "Fair enough." He stepped closer, putting his hands on her upper arms to keep her from backing away. "No blindfold."

Krys struggled against him as he held her arm firmly with his left hand and cradled her face with his right. This is what he'd done last night. She remembered that now. If he thought he could really hypnotize her...

She found herself studying his strong cheekbones and the dark hair falling around his face. His presence enveloped her, and she raised her mouth as he brushed his lips against hers. *"Ní bheidh mé tú a ghortú,"* he whispered.

The strangeness of the words jolted her out of the trance and she jerked away from him—or tried.

"Look at me, Krys." His voice was soft, and she met his eyes. A wave of warm energy rolled over her like a blast from opening an oven door, and she fought it for as long as she could before finally crumbling beneath the weight of it.

❋CHAPTER 10❋

So damned hungry. Owen eyed the young woman crouched in the kitchen corner of the old mill village house. Thin and dark-haired, wearing jeans a size too large and a sweater a size too small, she knelt in shadows. They didn't dare light more than a couple of candles lest Aidan or his people come to investigate.

Still, he could see the fine pulse in her neck, the subtle rush of blood as her heart pumped it through her body. Her scent fueled the hunger churning through him, enough to make him tremble. The few homeless humans they'd enthralled and abducted in Atlanta barely fed his scathe of eight. He hadn't been able to round up any more vampires on short notice—only these desperate few who hoped to feed on some of Aidan's humans once they managed to kill him. And if things got too hard, they'd scatter. Under other circumstances, Owen might have admired his little brother's ability to keep so many vampires and humans loyal to him.

"What's the plan?" Anders sat against the wall opposite the girl, his fingers tapping a nervous rhythm on the linoleum.

Owen closed his eyes briefly, swallowing the hunger. Even though he'd turned Anders a century ago, he hadn't been able to break the guy of his human fidgeting. He was the only one of the scathe who'd come with him from Ireland, except for Sherry. Anders had turned that useless teenage girl six months ago and dragged her everywhere. "We take Aidan out tonight. That's the plan."

Anders increased his finger tapping. "He'll bring backup, you think?"

Owen glared at him. "If you don't stop that infernal drumming, I'll bloody well butcher you before I kill Aidan."

Anders giggled and quit tapping on the floor. In a few seconds, he began cracking his knuckles.

"*Eejit.*" Owen closed his eyes and leaned against the kitchen counter. He considered getting the chair out of the front room, decided it wasn't worth the trouble, and slid heavily to the floor. Soon enough, they wouldn't have to live like paupers. Matthias Ludlam would see to that. He'd already sent a human courier with a small package containing his mysterious "secret weapon." Once he'd seen it, Owen had had to admit it was pure genius. There wasn't much, so he'd have to use it sparingly. Maybe he'd luck out and tag Aidan on the first try.

Pity, that. Truth was, he'd have been happy to stay in Dublin forever and let Aidan live in peace if Matthias and his cronies on the Tribunal's Justice Council hadn't decided to make an example of him. A death sentence just for draining a few hookers was bollocks. If Matthias hadn't wanted to break up Aidan's power base, Owen would already be dead. If the only way he could go free was to off Aidan, so be it.

"Here's how it goes down," he told Anders. "We use Aidan's self-righteousness against him and issue a formal challenge, which he'll be honor-bound to accept."

Anders rubbed a hand across his shaved head. "You sure he'll go for it?"

"Oh, yeah. He'll be jacked by the idea of using the old vampire battle accords. I'll insist on proxies, and then you'll come out." Aidan was a better fighter, but Anders wouldn't let a little thing like fair play bother him. "He's wicked strong, but he doesn't use his left hand as well as his right. Force him to his weak side."

Owen thought a moment, envisioning how he wanted the scene to unfold. "We'll need another proxy, too. Someone Aidan would never pick. A woman or a kid."

Another annoying giggle. "How about Sherry?"

Anders had a taste for the young ones, and that girl had been nothing but useless baggage and another pair of fangs to feed. Not to mention that it had been illegal to turn new vampires since the pandemic. Something else the Tribunal would hang on him if they found out. Still, she was only thirteen. Aidan would never fight anyone that young, so she could finally make herself useful.

"Yeah, have Sherry here by two thirty."

Anders bobbed his head to some personal rhythm and began drumming his fingers again.

"Get out of here and find her—both of you need to feed. I'll take this girl." Owen got to his feet and snuffed one of the candles.

Anders paused on the back stoop. "We really going to follow the accords?"

Owen grinned. "Of course not." If Aidan came alone, he'd use the Tribunal's weapon on him. If he brought the Slayer, well, good-bye Slayer. He'd kill the big guy and take Aidan out another night. Matthias might want to reel Mirren Kincaid back to the Tribunal but if Owen had a chance to take him out, he would.

"What if Aidan wants to do mental battle?" Anders asked, the unaccustomed exercise of thought wrinkling his brow. "I ain't done that in donkey's years."

"My brother's a brawler. Likes a good fistfight, he does— don't worry yourself."

He watched until Anders's form bled into the dark outline of the woods behind the house, then turned back to the girl hunkered on the cracked linoleum, her back against the scarred wood cabinets.

"What's your name, darlin'?"

She blinked, her eyes unfocused. She'd been enthralled so many times that she'd never completely recovered. He'd seen quite a few like her, especially since the pandemic. Too many vampires feeding from too few unvaccinated humans. "I'm Cathy," she said, frowning as if she had to think about it. "Catherine."

"Catherine, you don't have much bloom left, do you? Come to me." Owen held out a hand, and she let him pull her to her feet. With his index finger, he lifted her chin so she looked into his eyes, and then tilted her head to the right.

"Someone's been careless with you, my little Catherine," he said, running his fingers lightly over the mass of scar tissue on her neck. She moaned and slid her arms around his waist.

He turned her head to the left. "Much better here. Doesn't really matter to you, does it, love?"

He kissed her, and she whimpered. Pain or pleasure. Whatever.

"Shh," he said. "You're going to have a special evening. I need to be well fed tonight, and you're going to do that for me. Doesn't that please you?"

"Yes," she whispered, a tear sliding down her cheek.

When he left the house an hour later, heading through the woods to meet Anders behind the mill, he dumped her body in a thick stand of pines. He hadn't fed so well in months.

❀ C H A P T E R 1 1 ❀

Plain, long-sleeved navy T-shirt under a Kevlar vest. Shoulder holster with Colt .45. Guns weren't the weapon of choice for vampires, but Aidan and some version of this pistol had been together a hundred years.

Big and heavy, the Colt fit his hand. Annoying but light-weight, the vest protected his vulnerable chest area. Basic lessons from Mirren 101.

Aidan slipped a kukri knife into a custom-made sheath on his right thigh, its curved steel blade coated in silver. He picked up his leather jacket, reconsidered, and threw it back on the chair. Let Owen see that he was armed.

Acoustic Celtic music—or what modern musicians thought of as Celtic music—played on the sound system in his private living room, which took up most of his home's original base-ment. He'd just pulled his hair into a ponytail and closed the hatch into his subbasement bedroom suite when the intercom on the wall buzzed.

Grabbing his cell phone and sliding it into his pocket, Aidan ignored the intercom, jerked down the ladder, and climbed into the kitchen, making sure the intricate pattern of slate tile that camouflaged the opening slid back into place.

He opened the door as Lucy leaned on the buzzer again. Annoyed as he was with her, he had to grin at her choice of combat attire. Petite and curvy, she wore a feral smile and a skimpy red leather dress. Red pumps with ridiculous heels. This was the Lucy he'd known when she first joined his scathe. They'd been lovers for a while, but their temperaments clashed. She was impulsive, dramatic, and adventurous, and considered him a tense, moody bastard. Imagine that.

Lucy had become almost domesticated since meeting and bonding with Doc as her mate. Aidan wasn't sure her reversion to her old type was a good thing.

"Nice shoes. Let me guess—you're going to seduce my brother and lead him out of town by the balls." He stood aside to let her in, glad she'd gotten his message to get there early. They needed to talk before meeting Owen.

Aidan had chosen his four lieutenants not only for their loyalty but also for their individual strengths. All four were blood-bound to him, and every other vampire in Penton was bound to one of them. Once a vampire was bound, no betrayal could go undetected.

Mirren was a tactician and a brutal fighter if he needed to be. Will's tech skills matched his ability as a lateral thinker—if he ran up against a brick wall, he'd find a way around it to get things done. Hannah's psychic abilities and Native American magic guided them in making decisions. And Lucy—well, until recently, Lucy had been his most well-rounded lieutenant. She had the social skills to troubleshoot any problems in town

and the fighting skills to take on opponents like Owen if necessary—if he could get her to focus.

"Have you missed me?" She wrapped an arm around Aidan's
neck and pulled him close enough to nip his chin with her
fangs, then licked the dot of pale blood that welled up. "Yum.
You've fed tonight. I'm surprised your little Melissa would leave
Mark long enough. Or maybe you tasted our new doctor? Will
says she's *hawt*."

"I have a substitute feeder for a few days." He led her into
the living room, where she settled into one of the brown leather
armchairs. Krys was not a subject he planned to discuss with
Lucy—ever. Even after she'd mated with Doc, she took way too
much interest in Aidan's love life. Besides, Krys was a prisoner,
not a lover. Something he needed to remember.

Lucy crossed her legs and stared at him, waiting. He recognized the stubborn look. She'd shown up when she was told
to, but that would be the end of her accommodation. He'd
already cut her more slack than anyone else would have gotten,
as Mirren was fond of reminding him.

"Oh, you've gone all gloomy and brooding." Lucy narrowed
her eyes at him. "Get it over with. Let me have it. What did I do?"

"Damn it, Lucy, you're being careless." Aidan shook his
head and sat in the armchair facing her. No point in sugarcoat-
ing it. "Every time you're careless with securing one of our safe
rooms or flout a rule, you jeopardize all of us."

He crossed his arms and leaned back in his chair. "You
left the town hall meeting footage looping through the TV in
the sub-suite you got ready for Krys Harris. It makes easing
her into this community that much harder. She's asking about
things she shouldn't know."

Lucy met his gaze with stubborn silence.

"The Tribunal's watching what we do here," he said, getting up to look out the window. "We have one chance to prove that this type of community will work. Otherwise, they're liable to consider this scathe a threat because of its size. They won't only shut us down. They'll make sure no one else can build a place like this again."

He turned and gave her a sharp look. "You want to go back to the way we lived before, sneaking around on the fringes of society? Especially now, when there's such a shortage of humans to feed from?"

Lucy stared at him, green eyes burning in her pale face. "Sorry."

She didn't look it.

"Look." Aidan sat back down, his tone softer. "I know how hard it's been for you since Doc was killed."

Lucy's jaw tightened as she stared at him, but finally her gaze broke and she dropped her eyes, hiding her face behind a curtain of shiny hair. She and Doc had been together a decade, and his death had taken her edge just when Aidan needed her to be sharp.

"You don't know a damned thing, Aidan," she said, eyes still downcast. "You keep everyone in your life stuffed into neat little boxes. You don't ever let it get messy by caring too much."

He glanced at the antique gold band with Abby's name inscribed inside that he wore around his left wrist. He knew more than she thought. About self-hatred, about blame, about emptiness.

"Lucy, in a lot of ways you're my best fighter," he said. Mirren was stronger and more ruthless, but nobody ever underestimated him. Lucy surprised her opponents with speed and strength and smarts. "I need your head in the game."

She nodded and looked up. "I chose a new familiar this week. That will help. New guy you brought in from Atlanta last month named Daniel."

Aidan remembered him. A baby-faced architect in his forties whose taste for alcohol had stripped away his job, family, and his life savings. He'd been too tanked to worry about getting the pandemic vaccine. "How's he doing?"

"Good. He's gotten past that depressed stage where he only thinks about the life he's left behind, and he's starting to see how good life can be here. I think he can help me do the same thing." Lucy uncrossed her legs and leaned forward. "I really am sorry. I'll pull it together. I promise."

Aidan wanted to believe her, but he'd asked Mirren to keep an eye on her anyway. This was no time to take chances. "OK then. Ready to meet my brother?"

She grinned. "I can't wait."

Aidan stepped into the clearing in the woods behind the old mill, getting a close look at his brother for the first time in a couple of months. A light frost had settled on the ground, and the cold wind rattled the pine branches around them.

An unexpected stab of pity struck him. Owen's skin had the flush of a recent feed but he'd clearly been starving. He was three years older than Aidan was, and once he'd only been twenty pounds lighter. Now it looked more like fifty or sixty pounds. He was even thinner than when they'd met in Atlanta. He'd cut his reddish-blond hair short and spiky, accentuating prominent cheekbones that made him look gaunt in the shadows cast by the mill parking lot lights behind them.

The brothers met in the middle of the clearing, a cleft chin and pale eyes the only evidence of shared blood.

"You're looking prosperous and well-fed, little brother." Owen's accent was only two months removed from the Dublin slums if Will's research could be relied on, and it usually could.

"Really, Owen? You want to make small talk?" Aidan's senses revved. The frigid air played across his skin, and he smelled the rotting layer of fall leaves beneath the frost and the musky odor of small animals trailing through the woods.

"Tsk tsk." Owen grinned, looking more like the carefree brother Aidan had once idolized. "You weren't always so impatient, Áodhán. Were you keen on the message I sent last night with your handsome little human? Didn't think you liked boys, but I guess even old vampires can form new habits."

"How are we going to resolve this?" Aidan kept his voice controlled, his expression bland. The days when Owen could intimidate him were long past. "What will it take for you to get the hell out of here? There are plenty of rural areas in this country where your scathe can find unvaccinated people to feed from without bothering mine."

Owen stopped a few inches away. "Still and all, why should I have to round up a herd of stray cattle when you have a ranch here for the taking?"

Aidan slipped a hand to his thigh and fingered the handle of the curved blade. "You can't feed from my people. They're all bonded to a scathe member and here by choice. They're of no use to you."

"Only while you're alive. Besides, you're splitting hairs, Brother." Owen looked past the clearing toward the mill. "You think your little lambs are here by choice? It's all the same, whether you bind them in chains, screw with their minds, or keep them because of some feckin' form of hero worship. You always were a bloody idiot when it came to humans."

"My people know they can leave whenever they want." An image of Krys popped into his mind, but he waved it aside. Plenty of time later to focus on his own hypocrisy.

"Our *people* are vampires." Owen stuffed his hands in his pockets and took another step toward Aidan. "The humans are dinner. At best, pets. If your asinine little experiment works here, we'll all have to live like farmers. Some of us love the hunt—it's what we were made for."

He was fighting for the good old vampire lifestyle? Not likely. "What are you really after, Owen?" Aidan searched again for that glimpse of the brother he remembered, the one he'd idolized as a boy. "Why after all these years? We've hurt each other enough."

Owen looked at the ground. "You think anything's ever enough to make up for Abby?" He raised his head, his eyes like pale marbles in his gaunt face, his voice soft. "You might have been married to her, but I was the one who loved her. In the end, it was me."

Aidan's fury swelled like a rogue wave and crashed through his body, red-hot and explosive. His voice cut like steel through the night air. "Don't even say her name after what you did. You set things in motion, and it cost me everything. Every goddamn thing that mattered."

Why had he ever thought Owen would be open to reason? After all these years, Abby's death still ran like a gulf between them, and there was no bridging it.

"Do you consider us to be at an impasse in our negotiations?" Owen said, his speech suddenly formal.

Interesting. Owen was trotting out the formal words of battle. Aidan uttered the reply, established centuries ago and still honored among their kind. He answered in their native Gaelic: "Talk has failed. I declare an impasse broken only by battle."

Owen circled to face him and replied, "I therefore declare a battle to the death—by proxy."

At his words, two figures emerged from the woods and moved into the clearing to stand beside him.

Aidan took stock of the newcomers. One male, one female, both on the scrawny side. None of Owen's scathe had been feeding well. The girl looked no older than twelve or thirteen and shook with nervous energy. She hadn't been turned long—the stupid, irresponsible bastards. For Aidan, a few things were unforgiveable, and turning a child was one of them. Even the Tribunal didn't allow it.

Aidan stifled his fury and studied Owen's other companion. The man was older than the girl, both in human and in vampire years, and heavily muscled despite his scathe's lack of food. He watched Aidan with a steady gaze and gave off jittery, adrenaline-laced energy. Definitely the fighter. The girl was young, inexperienced, and too weak to be anything more than a sacrificial offering to Owen's arrogance.

"If you have no proxy, you must fight yourself. To the death, of course," Owen said with a smile that didn't touch his eyes. "Pick your opponent, either Anders or Sherry."

So Owen had expected him to come alone, unprepared, and be too honorable to fight a young girl, which meant the guy was a good fighter.

Check and mate.

"Mirren. Lucy." His lieutenants emerged from the thick stand of trees behind him and moved forward. Mirren stood to his right, wearing a rare but chilling smile. On his left, Lucy's leather rustled as she shifted from one red stiletto heel to the other.

"Shite." Anders gaped at Mirren, whose smile broadened.

Aidan shook his head. Had they really thought he'd show up alone? "Rules of battle say you may choose which of my fighters serves as proxy." Owen wouldn't risk letting his man fight Mirren, at least not on even terms. Mirren had eight inches of height and a hundred pounds of muscle on the guy, plus he was a master vampire, which meant he could communicate with and control other vampires mentally.

Sure enough, Owen barely glanced at Mirren before turning his attention to Lucy. He prowled around her, taking in her curves and leather and legs.

"I wouldn't mind a good tussle with you myself, love." He drew in close and spoke in an exaggerated whisper. "As they say in America, you're playing for the wrong team."

Lucy slid green eyes to meet his and curved red lips into a smile. "You want to fight me, you piece of shit?"

Owen stepped closer. "Pity to lose such beauty and a spirit I'd love to break, but I choose you to fight. My brother will choose your adversary." He ran a finger along her collarbone. Her expression didn't change.

"We don't fight children." Aidan nodded at Lucy and she kicked off her heels, bare feet on the frosty ground. She liked fighting in as little as possible.

"Anders then," Owen said, joining the young girl at the edge of the clearing. Aidan and Mirren retreated to stand behind Lucy.

The two fighters circled, each taking the other's measure. Anders flexed long, ropy muscles as he stripped off the baggy sweater, his head clean-shaven. Nothing to grab for an easy hold.

Lucy countered by slipping off her short dress in one fluid motion, and Aidan shook his head at her skimpy black bikini panties and bra. She looked like porcelain under the lights, and Anders wasn't staring at her face anymore.

"Mind or matter?" Owen watched Lucy with hooded eyes.

She flashed a savage smile at him, and then turned to Anders again. "Mind."

Anders clenched and unclenched his fists, flicking a quick glance at Owen as he and Lucy met in the clearing. Her green eyes locked on his brown, and the battle of wills began.

Lucy had argued for the mental battle on the way to the mill, even though Aidan preferred a physical fight. She and Anders would struggle to exert mental dominance, until one's will broke and fell under the other's control. If Lucy lost, she'd be nothing more than a dangerous, mindless shell he'd have to kill himself.

Aidan relaxed, readying for Lucy to connect with his mind when she grew tired. Since all of his lieutenants were blood-bound to him and to each other, Lucy would be able to draw strength from both him and Mirren, even Will and Hannah, if needed. Owen had probably done the same with his people.

Lucy's gaze remained solid, but her shoulders bunched as she fought the fatigue of trying to gain mental control over Anders. As they'd agreed beforehand, Aidan stepped in front of Mirren, keeping his focus on Lucy, while Mirren kept watch for signs of a double cross.

Owen shuddered; Anders had begun to draw on his strength.

Aidan met his brother's gaze and opened his mind to Lucy. Her will pulled at him immediately, and both she and Anders steadied themselves. A half hour passed as Aidan struggled to keep his mind clear and his connection to Lucy uncluttered by stray thoughts so she could draw as much strength from him as she needed. He opened his mental connection to Mirren, and a burst of strength flowed through him to Lucy.

A loud boom pierced the quiet of the clearing, and Mirren bellowed somewhere behind him, cutting off the brain feed. Aidan fought the urge to look around, unwilling to break his connection to Lucy just yet. What the hell had happened?

A smile spread across Owen's face, and Anders pulled a knife that flashed silver in the moonlight. Mirren's mental signal returned: *Accords broken.*

Aidan rushed the clearing, knocking Lucy aside as Anders thrust the knife, angling to go in beneath her rib cage. He took the knife in his side, sharp pain lancing through him as he hit the ground, pulling Anders with him. The fighter lost his grip on the knife, and Aidan scrambled for the Colt, pulling it from its shoulder holster and firing point-blank into Anders's chest.

By the time Aidan rolled to his feet, Lucy had planted a bare foot on Anders's throat, her own blade in her hand. She leaned over and sliced open what was left of his chest, then thrust the knife into his heart. The spray of blood was pink. Anders had been very, very hungry.

Aidan looked around the edges of the clearing for Mirren as Lucy worked to remove the heart from Anders's body. Short of a shot to the brain or fire or exposure to sunlight, it was the only way to make sure he didn't heal. Owen had disappeared, along with the girl. The wet, sloppy sounds of Lucy's work filled the clearing, followed by a thump as the heart hit the ground.

"Where'd everybody go?" Lucy plucked Anders's shirt off the ground and wiped the blood off her hands. She walked across the clearing and found her dress, slipping it back over her head before wedging her feet into the heels.

"Owen's escaped. Bloody coward won't fight unless he has to. I'm more concerned about Mirren." There was no sign of the big guy.

They tensed at the sound of a snapping branch, and Lucy took a side step to give them fighting room.

Mirren walked slowly from behind a stand of trees. "Damned little girl shot me in the back. Not a bullet, though. Look at it and see what the hell it was." He sat on the ground with a grunt and tossed a shotgun at Aidan. "She used this."

"Is the girl dead?" Aidan laid the gun on the ground, knelt next to Mirren, and helped him peel off the leather jacket. The back of it was peppered with small holes.

"No, she fired, threw the gun down, and ran." He flinched as Aidan ripped his sweater to bare his back. "Three centuries as a vampire and I get suckered by a pansy-ass little girl who hasn't been turned for a year."

Aidan frowned as he studied the wounds. Looked like buckshot. He picked up the shotgun and held the barrel to his nose. "Reeks of the pandemic vaccine. Damn it—they must have gotten their hands on some vaccinated blood and coated buckshot in it. We've got to get you to the clinic." How the hell had Owen gotten his hands on vaccinated blood?

Lucy stood next to them, watching. "Need me to help or stay here and do cleanup?"

"Come with us," Aidan said. "Call Will to bury Anders and see if there's any sign of where Owen and the kid went. Tell him I want intel only, and he needs to stay out of sight."

He paused and thought for a moment. Dawn would come soon, so Krys could help them treat Mirren faster, even if it meant an early intro to vampire society. "And call Hannah. Tell her to get Krys Harris up to the clinic."

❋CHAPTER 12❋

Krys awoke with a start. A girl stood near the foot of the bed, staring at her with big, solemn eyes the color of midnight.

"I'm Hannah." Her voice was sweet and pure, caught between childhood and puberty. She brushed back the hood of her pink-and-white paisley parka, unzipped it, and shrugged it off.

"How did you get in here?" Krys slid out of bed, glad she'd been sleeping in her clothes every night. She had no delusions of privacy since everyone but she obviously had a key to this place, and one never knew when a chance to escape might pop up. Like now.

The girl, who looked to be ten or twelve, sat on the sofa and beckoned Krys to join her. First, Krys took a detour to check the door in case the child hadn't locked it behind her. She had.

"I'm Hannah," the child repeated. "I've been dreaming of you."

Krys frowned and looked at her watch. "It's after three a.m., Hannah. Why are you here? You should be in bed."

The girl's black eyes brightened and a broad smile crossed her caramel-colored face. She tucked a strand of straight black hair behind her ear. "There's a lot you don't know about us, but you'll have to know soon," she said. "I've dreamed of you and Aidan, and my dreams aren't ever wrong."

This kid is seriously creeping me out. Part of Krys wanted to ask what she'd dreamed and what Aidan had to do with it—and shouldn't this child be calling him Mr. Murphy? Another, desperate, part of her wanted to try to bully the girl into unlocking the door or, if necessary, knock her out and rifle through her pockets for a key.

She'd try the responsible, adult approach first. "Hannah, you seem like a nice girl, but I need to get back to my home. Could you unlock the door and let me out?"

Hannah cocked her head. "There's no one there for you, where you live. You're alone. You don't have anyone to care about you except us. We can be your family."

A chill crossed Krys's skin and her creep-out meter rose a few more degrees—plus, those words stung. The truth usually did. Scratch beneath the surface of all the platitudes you tell yourself and the ugly stench of reality is unearthed. What could this child know about her life?

"Hannah, listen to me," she said, trying to keep her voice calm. "I'm the adult here. You need to give me the key, and I'll make sure you don't get in trouble for helping me."

Curling her legs under her on the sofa, Hannah shifted sideways to face Krys, wrapping her long green sweater around her knees. "Aidan wanted to check on you again before dawn but he won't be able to," she said. "He has many burdens, but you can help him." She looked at the floor and nodded, as if listening to voices within herself. "Yes, and he can help you as well. It was right that you came here."

Krys blew out a huff of frustration. "You're talking in riddles. I don't have a clue what you're—" She gasped as the child leaned over and encased her wrist in a strong grip. "What are you doing?"

Hannah's grip finally relaxed, but she didn't let go. "He hurt you, didn't he—your father?" Her eyes closed tightly as she talked. "And your mother, who should have taken care of you, she was afraid of him, too."

Her voice lowered to a whisper. "Your mother took too many pills and she died, and you never went back."

Krys jerked her hand away from Hannah's and stood. "What do you know about that?" Nobody else except the officials who had cleaned up the mess and her sorry excuse for a father knew what had happened to her mother. Nobody.

Hannah looked up with pity in her eyes. "I know things about people. It's how I know you need to stay here, to help Aidan. Penton won't survive without him, and he needs you. He just doesn't know how much yet. And you need him."

"Any trouble Aidan Murphy has, he brought on himself, and whatever he needs, I don't have it. Are you going to help me or not?" If the answer was no, Krys would go through this kid's pockets even if she had to sit on her.

Hannah giggled, and the sound sent shivers across Krys's shoulder blades. "You wouldn't really sit on me, would you?"

OK, the kid was psychic. No other explanation. Just add it to Penton's growing list of weirdness. Krys scanned Hannah's clothing. The jacket she'd shucked off had pockets, and so did her blue jeans. The key was probably in the jeans; she'd just have to wrestle her down—

Hannah stood abruptly. "We need to leave now."

Krys stared at her. Talk about an abrupt change of subject, but she was all for leaving. She looked around for her purse, but Hannah had walked quickly to the door. "You don't need your purse, and we have to hurry."

"Fine, let's go." Krys wasn't going to argue.

Hannah fished a gold key from her pocket, but paused before putting it in the lock. "You didn't want Aidan to blindfold you," she said, looking over her shoulder at Krys. "He enthralled you instead, but I can't do that—only he and Mirren can do that."

Enthrall? Aidan was handsome, but she wouldn't call him enthralling. Krys honestly couldn't remember what he'd done. Everything had fuzzed out after he'd stuck the blindfold back in his pocket.

"I don't know what he did," she said, frowning. "But I won't let you blindfold me, either."

Hannah nodded and unlocked the door, slipping the key back into her pocket. Her right pants pocket, Krys noted.

"This way." The girl headed down the hallway to the left. Deep brown carpet absorbed the sounds of their footsteps, and doors similar to hers were spaced at even intervals. It looked like the corridor of an expensive hotel. Wallpaper with a subtle brown-and-gold pattern was illuminated every few feet by wall sconces that bounced soft arcs of shadow on the floor.

At the end of the hall, Hannah opened a door to a stairwell and motioned for Krys to go ahead. She counted the narrow steps—more like a ladder than stairs—trying to commit each movement to memory and ignore the dark walls that felt like they were pressing in from both sides. If she were ever to escape, it might be important. There were twenty-two steps straight up to what looked like a trapdoor.

At Hannah's urging, Krys pushed open the hatch at the top and climbed into what looked like a large storage area. A concrete floor, support beams, no windows. A basement, maybe, yet it was above the area where she'd been imprisoned. Boxes and crates towered more than head high in all directions, and Krys stopped, not sure which way to go.

"This way," Hannah said, stepping around her and weaving through a maze of crates.

"What is all this?"

"Supplies, in case we have to move underground for a long time," Hannah said, weaving her way deftly in what seemed an indecipherable pattern.

Krys opened her mouth to ask why they would have to move underground, but closed it again. It was more important to remember their curving path.

In a few seconds they came to a cleared section of floor, and Krys tried to pinpoint where they'd come from while Hannah maneuvered a crate beneath another hatch door and climbed atop it to release the folding ladder.

This time the climb through the dark, vertical tunnel ended in a locked hatch that, when opened, released a stream of light.

Hannah clambered up with nimble feet and disappeared from view. Krys followed, finally poking her head through the opening to see a familiar room—the clinic office. She'd been underneath the clinic all along. *Way* underneath it.

She climbed the rest of the way out and watched as Hannah closed the trapdoor, locked it, and slid several pieces of wood flooring over it in a locking system that looked like one of the elaborate wooden puzzle boxes she'd seen in gift shops. Finally, the girl pulled an area rug over the whole thing. Unless someone knew the door was there and had the patience of a saint, it would be impossible to find—or to open even if you found it.

Krys looked at her watch again. A quarter to four. She still didn't understand why this child wasn't in bed, but that was someone else's problem—she was leaving.

While Hannah watched silently from a perch near the office desk, Krys strode to the hallway door, praying it would be unlocked. The knob turned smoothly, and the cool fluorescent lights of the clinic corridor shone harsh and bright in her eyes, which had grown accustomed to the soft indoor lighting of her suite. Her heart pounded. Just a few more feet and she would be out.

She glanced back at Hannah, but the child made no attempt to stop her. She simply smiled.

"Thank you," Krys whispered, and stepped into the hallway. The exit was directly to her right at the end of the corridor, and her pace increased as she got closer.

Damn. A brunette with a painted-on red dress and ridiculous heels glided in the door just before she reached it.

"Good, you're here. I knew Hannah would have perfect timing." She moved Krys aside with one arm and held the door open. "I'm Lucy, by the way."

"Sorry, I was just on my way…" *Out*, Krys was going to say, but the glass doorway was suddenly filled by the massive bulk of Mirren Kincaid. He was pale as death itself, his eyes were half closed, and he leaned heavily on Aidan. A blanket was twined around his shoulders, and Krys thought it looked like the one from his Bronco.

Aidan caught her eye as they passed, and jerked his head toward the hallway on the right, opposite the hall where Mark's room was located. She had an annoying urge to do an about-face and follow him like a panting puppy. Not happening. It was time to get her life back. She caught the door as it was closing and took a step toward freedom.

"Oh, no you don't. You've got work to do." Lucy was suddenly beside her, even though Krys could have sworn she'd just been standing several feet away. The shorter woman placed a hand around her wrist and led her down the hall, resisting Krys's attempts to jerk out of her grasp. Everybody in Penton, even Hannah, was ridiculously strong—what did they put in their Wheaties?

"I'm not sure you're ready for this, Dr. Harris, but welcome to our world." Lucy propelled Krys into the first room off the hallway, where Mirren had collapsed face-first onto an exam table—or at least part of him had. The man was way too tall and almost too broad, and bits and pieces of him hung off all four sides.

Krys stared back at the door, but Lucy blocked her escape route. What if she refused to treat Mirren? Would they let her go, or lock her up again, or decide she had outlived her usefulness?

She glared at Aidan, who was hovering next to his friend and talking too softly for her to hear his words. Mirren wasn't responding.

Krys sighed. As long as she was here, she might as well take a look at him. It just wasn't in her to let someone suffer if she could do something to help. That do-gooder attitude was what had gotten her into this mess in the first place. If she'd sped past Aidan Murphy to begin with, she might be at home, asleep in her own bed.

"If you want me to look at him, step back and give me some space," she told Aidan. Bedside manner be damned.

Lucy retreated to the hallway, but Aidan ignored her. He walked around the table, eased the blanket off Mirren's shoulders, pulled a wicked, curved knife from a sheath on his belt, and began cutting off the remains of the big man's mangled sweater. Aidan was also wearing a shoulder holster with an enormous pistol in it—Krys doubted she could even lift the thing—and, below that, his navy sweater had been torn. No, cut. And the cut was stiff around the edges, as if it had been soaked in blood.

"You've been stabbed." She rounded the table and reached for him, but he stopped her with a big hand on each shoulder. "I'm OK—it's minor. Mirren needs you."

Krys turned to study the big man's exposed back. The intricate tattoos of animals and figures and abstract symbols that she'd seen on Mirren's neck extended down the left side of his back—maybe his chest, too, but she couldn't tell. There also were a dozen or so small wounds that were hard to see amid all the ink on his left side but stood out like blisters on the pale skin of his right side.

"His blood's all wrong. The color's too light," she muttered, pulling on a pair of gloves and leaning over to study the damage. "Tell me what happened."

These were fresh injuries, and they should have been vivid red in the middle, darker red around the edges. Instead, the peppering of wounds had a silvery-black cast and the blood was more cranberry than crimson.

"Buckshot, coated in poison," Aidan said, edging closer to the table. "You have to get it out fast."

She moved to the right in order to get a better look at the wounds, and brushed into Aidan. "Step aside and let me work."

He moved a half inch, maximum. Shaking her head, she touched an antiseptic wipe to the edge of one of the small lesions, and Mirren grunted. More of a growl.

"Shhh. It's OK," she said on instinct. David comforting Goliath.

"What was on those pellets can kill him, quickly." Aidan stood in the vicinity of her elbow.

She twisted to shoot him a sharp look. "I told you to stand back."

"Take out as many as you can, as fast as you can. Cut them out, or I'll do it myself. You have thirty-five minutes, max." Aidan gritted his teeth. "Please."

Thirty-five minutes. Biting back the temptation to ask who'd made him God's official timekeeper, Krys turned back to Mirren. Aidan began plundering the exam room cabinets.

"If poison has already gotten into your bloodstream, I won't be able to tell that," she said to Mirren, leaning over the wounds to get a better look. "You'll have to take an antibiotic, and you'll need to tell me what the poison is, if you know, so I can call the state poison control center and see if there's an antidote."

Mirren mumbled, and Krys leaned over him. "What?"

"Cut the goddamned things out *now*." His eyes were closed, but his mouth worked well enough.

"Let me give you something for pain before—"

"*Now*, Krys." Aidan reached across the exam table and grabbed her wrist. "No painkillers. Just do it. Dig them out."

Looking into Aidan's eyes made her dizzy for a second, and Krys took a step back as he released her and shoved a pair of tweezers at her.

"These aren't sterile. I can't—"

"Now!" She wasn't imagining it. Aidan's eyes had lightened to the shade of an arctic iceberg. It was as if the more his emotions roiled, the lighter his eyes became.

Krys took a deep breath, and then another. How many times had her father shouted at her in anger, berated her, locked her up? She clenched her jaw, grabbed the tweezers, and bent over the wounds. She'd always lost herself in her work, whether it was schoolwork or housework or busywork. *This is no different, Krys. Just concentrate. Block him out.*

"That's weird. I swear these holes are closing up." She jumped, startled, as Aidan thrust a small knife at her, handle first. She bit her tongue to keep from pointing out that it wasn't sterile and grabbed it, slicing a satisfying cut into his hand. She didn't look for his response, just bent over Mirren again and began cutting to expose one of the pellets. She hoped Aidan's hand hurt like hell, though, and maybe got just a tad infected.

"I don't like this. The blood's all wrong," she mumbled under her breath. Throwing the knife on the cart beside the exam table, she picked up the tweezers and began gently moving aside skin and tissue.

"Bingo." She picked the pellet out, clinking it on the table. She reached a quick rhythm, cutting with the knife, exposing the pellet, pulling it out with the tweezers, throwing it on the table. Mirren flinched with each cut but didn't make a sound. He just lay there with his eyes closed. If he hadn't flinched, she'd have thought he was dead.

"I don't see any more. Now I need to disinfect these. Maybe a couple of stitches on the worst ones." She turned aside, opening the drawers and cabinets that stretched along the exam room wall, looking for a suture kit.

"No need," Aidan said, and when Krys turned to protest, he'd already helped Mirren to a sitting position, revealing the tattoos that indeed did cover the left side of his muscular chest. The big man's eyes remained closed but he wasn't wobbling. He still needed stitches, though.

"You can't move him before I..." Krys's voice trailed off as she marched around to look at Mirren's back. The first cuts she'd made had almost closed. She could swear his back was healing in front of her.

Frowning, she circled the exam table again and reached up to feel Mirren's face. Cool and dry. He shouldn't be in such good shape.

He leaned his head into her hand, opening his eyes to look at her.

Her breath stopped. His dark gray eyes had turned silver, and as he leaned into her hand, he curled back his upper lip to reveal the tips of sharp, delicately curved fangs where his canines should have been.

He grasped her wrist before she could pull her hand away and kissed it. She couldn't stop the whimpering noises coming from her throat as she remembered the image of him licking blood off his hand that first night. What the hell was he?

"Mirren, stop." Aidan's voice was low but forceful, and after a few tense seconds, Mirren released her arm.

"Sorry." He closed his eyes and shivered.

Aidan squeezed Mirren's shoulder. "Lucy will take you home now. Will called your fams to meet you there so you can feed. Twenty minutes until sunrise."

Krys barely registered the fact that Mirren had slipped off the table and spoken quietly to Aidan before leaving the room. What had just happened? She'd seen Aidan's hand where she'd

sliced him with the knife—it had already healed. And Mirren...
She couldn't form whole thoughts, only flashing images of silver
eyes, fangs, cuts that disappeared.

She tried to back away as Aidan approached her. "I'm sorry
I don't have time to explain tonight," he said softly, framing
her face with his hands and forcing her gaze to his. She felt the
dizzy, falling sensation again, and then nothing.

"Of all the idiotic, screwed-up shit, this has to rank near the
top." Aidan gathered Krys in his arms after Will lowered her,
unconscious, down the stairwell into the subbasement. He carried her to the suite, laying her gently on the bed and watching
in dismay as she groaned and rolled onto her side.

Will came to stand beside him. "Bloody hell, how's she
coming out of it already? She should be out for hours."

He didn't know the half of it—Aidan hadn't been sure
he could enthrall her again after her resistance last time. "Go
home. I'll stay here with her a few more minutes and crash in
one of the sub-suites."

Staying nearby was just more expedient, given how rapidly
dawn was approaching. It had nothing to do with staying near
Krys as long as he could. Right.

"Whatever, man. I'm gone." Will headed for the door. "You
think Mirren will be OK?"

Aidan rubbed his eyes as the predawn lethargy began to
steal over him. "Hope so. We'll see how he is at nightfall."

As soon as the door closed behind Will, Aidan sat on the
bed next to Krys. He shouldn't have brought her into this mess
tonight. Had he really thought she could help, or did he just

want an excuse to tell her what he was; to drive away any chance that she might accept him and kill the screwed-up mating call that had kept her in his mind all day?

He brushed his fingertips across her cheek, flushed with warmth and life, and thought about Abby. She'd loved him when he was human, then rejected him as a vampire. Maybe he would have won her back eventually, but Owen had taken that chance away. Besides, anyone with the misfortune to love someone like him didn't live too long, did she?

"You look so sad."

Aidan had been staring into the past, unaware that Krys had awakened and was watching him. She obviously didn't remember what had happened with Mirren—not yet anyway— and he found that he didn't want to try erasing her memories. This might be the last chance he had to sit with her, the only chance he had to see her face holding concern for him rather than fear or contempt. Too bad she was still half-buzzed from the enthrallment. He lifted a dark curl away from her face, memorizing her features.

She fingered the tear in his sweater where Anders's knife had gone in. "Are you OK? What happened?"

He slipped his hand around hers and lifted it to his lips, placing a soft kiss on her fingertips. "I'm OK. Just wanted to check on you before I have to leave."

"If you're going to keep me locked up, you should have to stay with me." She laughed softly. "That sounds really warped, doesn't it?"

He smiled at the thought. "I'll be back as soon as I can." His energy was waning with each minute that the clock ticked closer to dawn, and he heaved himself to his feet. He looked down at Krys to say good-bye, but she'd drifted to sleep, her breathing steady and even, her heartbeat a soothing echo in his own chest. He predicted that she wouldn't be nearly as calm the next time he saw her.

CHAPTER 13

A half hour after dusk, Mirren pulled the Bronco into a parking spot a block from the mill and killed the engine. He flexed his shoulders, the rough wool of his sweater aggravating the sore spots on his back. The wounds had healed but the skin remained tender. Last night had been a shit storm from start to finish, but at least Owen had one fewer fighter. Mirren only wished he'd been the one to make the kill.

He slipped from behind the wheel and walked toward the mill, sliding from shadow to shadow so Lucy wouldn't know he was following her. Following *them*. Lucy and the stupid kid who'd shot him last night.

Sherry. He'd heard Owen call the girl Sherry. Her human age couldn't be more than twelve or thirteen. A freakin' humiliation, that's what it was. After three quiet years in Penton, maybe he was getting soft.

He stopped at the corner and risked a quick look around the building. Lucy and the girl stood outside the mill entrance and Sherry was pointing down Cotton Street toward the village.

Lucy would know if Mirren opened his mental connection to her, so he closed his eyes to block his other senses and focused on listening.

"You have to wait here," the girl was saying. God, she even sounded like a kid. Probably wasn't much older than Hannah. One more reason to feed Owen Murphy his own balls.

"Just show me where Owen's living. He'll be glad to see me." Mirren recognized the purr in Lucy's voice, guaranteed to break down the willpower of any human she encountered—or a male of any species.

"Right, then," Sherry said, her accent straight out of Dublin. "But if he's mad, don't you go tellin' him I showed you. He'll be all in my face if he found out you caught me near the mill."

What the hell was Lucy up to? She'd always been a nut job, but since Doc died she'd been as stable as a two-legged table. And Aidan knew it, or he wouldn't have assigned some of the junior scathe members to look for Owen's scathe hideouts while Mirren wasted time on this little spying mission.

Once Lucy and the girl headed down Cotton Street, Mirren followed at a distance, sticking close to the houses.

They stopped just before the dead end. Had Owen been staying in the mill village, right under their noses? Mirren needed to set up a house-to-house search.

After a brief conversation, Sherry turned and headed back toward the mill, but Lucy climbed the stairs to the front porch of the last house on the block and knocked. She waited a few seconds before going inside. Mirren heard the door close behind her.

He slipped between two houses and waited for Sherry to pass, then continued to the end of the block, moving slowly. Everything was quiet.

Mirren crept around the house and saw a dim light underneath the back door. He squatted beneath the window, listening to Lucy's laughter and Owen's brogue as he talked and laughed with her. He strained to decipher their soft words, but the closed windows muffled too much sound.

Mirren's palms itched. It would be easy to rush in and take him, just rip Owen's heart out and be done with it. But Aidan suspected his brother had the backing of some of the Tribunal dickheads and wanted to play it safe till they knew Owen—and not the whole vampire nation—was their only opponent. And Lucy being in Owen's camp wasn't safe. Didn't matter whether she'd flipped sides or was on some half-assed revenge mission. Mirren would have cut her out of the scathe, but Aidan had been soft on her so far.

Mirren crept away from the house and headed back toward downtown. Before he made the turn off Cotton Street, he saw Sherry sitting on the front steps of the mill, looking at the freaking stars. The kid was clueless. How anyone had been stupid enough to turn a new vampire since the pandemic floored him. With vampires starving and fighting over unvaccinated humans, why create more fangs to stress the food supply?

Speaking of little girls, maybe Hannah could tell them what Lucy was up to.

A half-block short of the Bronco, Mirren felt the world waver. He leaned against an empty storefront, waiting for the swimming sensation to level off. He'd been queasy when he rose at sunset, but he had felt better after feeding. It was worse this time. A cramp clenched at his gut, and he doubled over, gagging out a clump of blood.

Damned buckshot pellets. Krys had removed them before the tainted blood was fully absorbed, so he hadn't gotten enough to kill him—just enough to make him feel like shit. He hadn't felt nausea since his human life. And he didn't miss it.

Resuming his walk slowly, he got to the Bronco, climbed in, and tilted his head against the headrest until the dizziness passed.

❋CHAPTER 14❋

"You look like hell."

Aidan poured Mirren a whiskey and handed it to him on the way inside. The man looked strung out and pissed off, which meant he could join the club. Aidan and Will had spent two hours driving around town, looking for signs of Owen's scathe, with no luck. If Owen was smart enough to move before dawn every day—which Aidan remembered him doing in the past—finding him would be hard. There were too many empty buildings to hide in, not to mention the woods and caves in the area. They were going to have to lure him out, or wait for him to make another overture.

Aidan's mood hadn't improved when he'd come home to find Melissa waiting for him. The woman kept up a running commentary about Krys while he fed: he needed to talk to her; he needed to explain everything so she'd understand why they needed her; he needed to let Melissa talk to her. As if he didn't think about Krys enough already without Melissa's input. He and his fam were going to have to set some boundaries.

Aidan sat heavily on the sofa. "Hope you found more than I did."

Mirren snorted. "Yeah, I found something, all right. Did you send Lucy out tonight?"

Aidan stared at the pasty mess that was Mirren's face. "No. You feed yet? You look even worse than usual."

Mirren waved him off. "Little bitch who shot me last night just led our girl Lucy to a house in the mill village. Owen's slipping in and out under our noses, and now our girl Lucy's right there with him."

"Shit." Aidan kicked the edge of the coffee table, taking a perverse pleasure in watching the leg splinter. They were going to have to keep someone watching the mill village every night. It was isolated and unoccupied, which made it too easy for Owen to move around undetected. And Lucy. Damn it. "What does she think she's doing?"

"One way to find out. Let's bring her in." Mirren got up to leave, but Aidan moved quickly between him and the door.

"Not without a plan. We don't know how many people Owen has, or how much of that tainted blood. We need to get the lieutenants together and devise an offensive that won't make the Tribunal think we're declaring all-out war in case some of them are backing him."

Mirren opened his mouth to argue, but Aidan held up a hand. "Look, I'm tired of sitting around waiting for Owen's next move, too, but we don't do anything half-assed." He'd survived this long and built a loyal scathe this big by being careful, whether it was negotiating with the local Native American medicine men to settle in their territory, or picking the right people to populate his scathe, or seeking out the best political allies. And Mirren knew it.

"We meet with everyone except Lucy?" Mirren's eyes silvered with either anger or hunger, although Aidan would wager a case of his finest whiskey on anger.

"Everyone except Lucy." She hadn't left him any choice. "I don't believe she'd throw in with Owen, but she's being stupid. Not to mention jeopardizing us all."

Aidan picked up the mangled table leg and threw it into the fireplace. He seriously needed something to hit. "Get Will to meet us at the clinic office in an hour. I'll track down Hannah."

Before he left, Mirren turned and squinted back at Aidan. "Guess I scared the hell out of the new doctor last night. You gonna talk to her?"

Aidan barked out a bitter laugh. "I'll talk to her after our meeting." He could just imagine what she'd have to say. A normal human would be petrified. He had a feeling that Krys Harris would be practicing her self-defense moves on him again.

He took a closer look at Mirren standing in the doorway. "We still don't know how much of that shit got in your system. You look pale."

"I'm a goddamned vampire. You expect me to have a tan?"

"Let me see your eyes." Aidan grabbed Mirren's arm to pull him into the light, but he jerked away.

"Let it drop, A. I just haven't fed."

Aidan didn't argue, but he'd be watching Mirren during the meeting. They couldn't afford for him to limp around half-sick, and the stubborn SOB would never admit he needed help.

"Oh yeah, those green pigs are *so* dead."

Aidan raised his eyebrows at Will, who lounged in one of the clinic office chairs with his iPad. The man loved his toys.

"What are you doing? Who has pigs?" For Aidan, computers were business tools for making spreadsheets and cruising investment sites, but Will was forever coming up with something new to play with.

"Angry Birds." Will slid his finger across the screen. "Your birds shoot slingshots at green pigs and—"

"Shut it." Mirren stretched a long arm from his spot on the sofa and snatched the tablet, punching the off button.

Will trained golden-brown eyes on him. They crinkled at the corners as he grinned.

"Heard you got taken down by an itty-bitty girl, big man, and you look like something a dog vomited. Had to have the sexy new doctor pick buckshot out of your ass?"

Aidan watched them from behind the desk, his eyes following the arc as Mirren pelted one of Doc's old paperweights at Will's head with enough force to cause a concussion in the average person.

"I am late." Hannah stood in the doorway, holding the glass paperweight she'd caught midflight. With her fuzzy pink sweater and striped hoodie, she looked as if she should be headed to a playground, not a vampire war council at midnight.

Hannah had been with Aidan for over a century—longer than any of the others had. He'd found her with a scathe of bloodthirsty vamps outside a Muscogee Creek village just south of here in the 1830s. The small scathe had slaughtered her village, but turned Hannah and her medicine man father in order to use their skills. Her father had died, but Hannah had survived. Aidan had killed her vampire maker on principle—for turning a child—and had taken her with him. Still pissed him off.

She closed the door behind her, dragging a chair to sit next to Will. With Aidan at the desk, it put them in a rough circle.

"What can you tell us about Lucy?" Aidan studied Hannah's face, trapped forever in childhood but so often turned solemn with the burden of her second sight.

She closed her eyes, frowning in concentration, and then looked up in surprise. "Mirren's sick." She swiveled to face him. "You're hiding it."

Aidan grimaced. "Damn it. I knew something was wrong. Spill."

Mirren glared at Hannah but couldn't sustain it against the child's concerned scrutiny, so he glared at Aidan instead. "Couple of dizzy spells. Nothing major."

"And you couldn't feed." Hannah's black eyes were steady.

"Could too," Mirren grumbled. "Just didn't keep it down."

Will shed his languor and sat forward in his chair, shoulders tense.

Aidan swore. Damned idiot. Mirren was the color of yesterday's snow, and his pupils looked like saucers. "No point in talking to you, so I'll ask Hannah." He shifted his gaze to the girl. "How bad?"

She slid off the chair and walked to Mirren, who watched her approach with a look of alarm. Aidan and Will exchanged amused looks. Hannah's psychic abilities made them all uncomfortable sometimes, but she scared the hell out of Mirren, and he'd avoid her when he could. Aidan figured the big guy was afraid that Hannah could see into his head and know everything he'd done as the Tribunal's infamous Slayer. Even Aidan didn't know that full story, and Mirren wouldn't talk about it.

She pressed a small palm against the center of Mirren's broad chest and closed her eyes. The silence in the room was heavy.

"You'll be really sick if we don't help you. We can take some of your blood out and people will give you more to put back in. Krys can help because you might wake during daysleep." She nodded and almost skipped back to her armchair, her job done. "Then you'll be well."

The muscles of Mirren's jaw tightened. "Shite. I'll be damned if I—"

"Stuff it." Aidan stared him down and turned to Will. "Set up a little donor party in the sub-suite across from Krys about three. That gives us time before dawn. Make sure both of Mirren's fams are there till he's down for the day, and a couple of other donors are on standby.

"And you"—he pointed at Mirren—"shut the bloody hell up and be there by three."

Mirren slumped back on the sofa while Will called Melissa with instructions.

"Now let's talk about Lucy," Aidan said, turning back to Hannah. "Can you tell us what she's up to?"

Hannah shook her head and looked at the floor. "I tried to see, but I can't. Only that she's in trouble." When the girl raised her eyes again, they shone with unshed tears. Usually only the newest vampires were still able to cry. Aidan didn't know if the rest of them didn't because they were vampires or because they'd just seen too damn much.

"Did Lucy screw us?" Will asked, his voice hard-edged. "Is she helping them?"

Hannah shook her head. "I don't know." Her clear, high voice shook. "Only that in here"—she touched her head, then her chest—"she hurts and she's angry."

Aidan remained silent, the heft of the others' fear and anger an almost physical weight. He remembered a time after Abby died when he'd been so crippled by grief that his body moved around but his brain had shut down. Hell, he'd lost days, gaping chunks of time he couldn't account for. Maybe he'd underestimated how deeply Lucy had loved Doc. Now that Aidan had experienced even a small dose of those mating instincts—if that was really what was going on with Krys—he knew that he probably *had* misjudged Lucy's sense of loss. But he couldn't take chances.

His eyes met Mirren's. "Until we know her intentions, she can no longer be considered scathe."

Mirren examined a spot on the carpet, and Will studied his nails. More tears from Hannah. The five of them were tight. No matter how angry they were at Lucy, removing a lieutenant from the scathe meant cutting her bonds to all of them. He'd help her if he could, but he had to put the town first.

"Close the circle, then shut down all your bonds, not only to Lucy but to your fams and scathe members," Aidan told them. "We've got major shit to discuss."

Mirren and Will stilled while Hannah walked the four walls, trailing a small hand on the chair rail and chanting softly. The air pressure rose as her psychic wards tightened around the room like a cinched belt.

Her job completed, she perched on the sofa and looked at Aidan with bright eyes.

He smiled at her. She knew exactly what he planned to say, of course. "I had Mark working on some land acquisitions last year. Picked up a lot of acreage twenty miles east of town, right on the Georgia line. It's mostly wooded except for a big, abandoned factory."

Will retrieved his iPad from the coffee table and called up a map, settling himself on the sofa between Mirren and Hannah so they could both see it. "It's out by that old textile plant," he said, holding the screen out so everyone could see.

"Right," Aidan said. "Will has been sending crews in for several months now to excavate new safe rooms beneath the largest warehouse. Their memories are erased at night—with their permission, of course."

Will zoomed in on the site. "It's a big space, and the excavation is almost done but nothing is filled in except rudimentary structural supports." He pointed to a satellite image of the metal warehouse, surrounded by dense woods. "There's nothing around it for miles. Once we get the spaces ready and don't need to get in and out as often, we'll remove the access roads and move enough plants and trees in for camouflage. No one will be able to tell there was ever a road. You'll only be able to see it from the air."

Mirren leaned back on the sofa, and Aidan saw him wince as his back hit the cushion. They couldn't take action against Owen till the big guy was a hundred percent.

"Does Lucy know about this?" Mirren asked.

"No," Aidan said. "We've been taking our time until now, but with Lucy out of control, we need to ramp it up. I'd like to have at least a large basement-level safe room finished and fitted within three weeks, plus a sizable storage area. Then start individual suites in the subbasement the following week. Is that doable?"

Will thought for a moment. "Yeah, I think so. Depends on how many suites you want to have ready and how finished you want them."

Aidan hesitated. He was tempted to soft-pedal this "shelter of last resort," but these were the people who'd have to help run it. "We need to house all of the scathe members, plus as many of our familiars as are willing to go. Assume no one will be able to go topside for six months, maybe longer."

Will settled the iPad back on his lap. They all stared at Aidan.

"Omega," Hannah said softly. "That's what you call it."

"It's Plan Z, only for those who want to stay in this scathe if the Tribunal moves against us," Aidan said.

"How long you been thinking about this?" Mirren asked. "Has it ever been done before?"

Aidan shook his head. "No, but vampire society's never been in this position before. Near as I can tell, human doctors think the blood anomaly caused by the vaccine will disappear with the next generation, and things will get back to normal. But that could be too late for our kind."

Will moved back to his armchair, shaking his head. "There's already been rumors of black market auctions in some of the bigger cities, with vampires selling unvaccinated humans to the highest bidder. It's just gonna get worse."

Aidan looked at Hannah. "I don't know," she said. "I can't see if we will need Omega for certain, but I can't see that we *won't* need it, either."

"We have more than a hundred unvaccinated humans here in Penton, and these are people we care about." Aidan leaned forward in his desk chair. "At some point, even if it isn't Owen or the Tribunal, some group is going to try making a move on us. We either break up the town, or we figure out a way to keep all our people safe—even if it means going underground for a while."

The room was silent for a few moments, the ticking of the wall clock abnormally loud in the stillness. Finally, Will spoke. "What else will we need?"

"If we have to take the whole town underground into Omega, it could be for a long time," Aidan said. "We'll need plenty of storage for food, and facilities for air circulation and waste disposal—anything our fams require. And medical facilities for both us and our people."

And a doctor. His mind flashed to Krys, and he pushed aside a wild desire for her to be the one. He was a selfish bastard even to wish that kind of existence for her, not that he'd really wish it for any of them.

Will chewed his lip and stared at Mirren. Finally, he nodded. "OK, we can do it. But what you're talking about is going to take at least five or six months, even with double crews and bare-bones facilities. Can we sit here that long, letting Owen pick us off like bloody sitting ducks?"

Aidan gave him a grim smile. "No. That's our next order of business—what to do about my brother."

❋CHAPTER 15❋

She needed a hiding place. Krys couldn't believe she'd slept till almost four in the afternoon, but then again, she'd had a little help getting to sleep, hadn't she?

For once, she wished her memory weren't quite so sharp. In fact, a case of amnesia would have been fabulous. But there was no mistaking recollection for dreams this time. Mirren had bared fangs at her—fangs! His wounds had healed as she watched. His eyes had lightened from gray to silver. And then Aidan had put her in another trance, she guessed, because everything went blank, at least until she'd awakened to find him sitting beside her, promising to come back tonight. And tonight was almost here.

One part of Krys's mind kept putting a word out there for her to gnaw on—*vampire*—but the other part, the scientist, knew vampires were horror tales, fantasies. She hadn't been allowed to go to movies when she was a teen, but she'd sneaked in her share of Anne Rice and Laurell K. Hamilton novels. That was fiction. Obviously she'd had some kind of psychotic break, and it was no wonder. She'd been kidnapped, after all.

She ignored the dinner tray someone (*a vampire?*) had slid through the slot about five, and didn't bother to pound on the door or yell. She wanted them to ignore her. And in case they didn't, in case Aidan came tonight, she needed to be ready to hide—or to fight.

She eyed the closet door, wondering if crawling inside would trigger a panic attack. Nerves skittering, she crossed the room and pulled the door open, only to have her sense of reality slip again. Her heart skipped at the sight of the clothes hung neatly on the rod—her clothes from Georgia. She'd been alternating the same two outfits for days now. Had it been four days? Five? Six? Now *all* of her clothes appeared to be here, as if they expected her to stay forever.

She fingered the sleeve of her favorite sweater, ran shaky hands along the rough denim of her jeans and skirts, skimmed her eyes over the shoes lined neatly along the closet floor. She looked at the dresser with trepidation, walked to it, and pulled the top drawer out an inch. Folded sweaters. The other drawers were filled with socks or underwear or T-shirts, all neatly folded.

Someone had cleaned out her apartment, or at least all the clothes. Someone who didn't plan to let her go home ever, despite his charm and phony sincerity and beautiful blue eyes. *Eyes that lighten just like Mirren's did.*

Forget the closet—she couldn't hide there. The bed was high, but crawling underneath it was out of the question. She'd seen too many movies where people hid under beds and were dragged out by their hair. It never ended well. She wanted her back against something solid.

Which left the bathroom and its doorknob with the standard push-and-twist lock. Krys closed the door behind her, locked it, and crouched in the corner walk-in shower. If Aidan broke in, he would scan the room in front of him before looking to his left, and that would give her a few seconds' advantage. A few seconds to do what, she wasn't sure. He'd already shown her how strong he was. *Strong like a vampire.*

After she'd been pressed against the shower wall for what seemed like an eternity, her stomach growled. Ten p.m. Aidan usually visited her early—he'd never come this late. Maybe he wasn't coming. Maybe Mirren (*the vampire*) had killed him.

But I haven't ever seen Aidan during the daytime, either. Even the job interview had to be at night. His eyes change color like Mirren's do. Whatever Mirren is, Aidan is one too.

Her stomach growled again, louder this time. Scrambling out of the shower, she quickly slipped back into the bedroom, grabbed some clean clothes, and snagged a sandwich off the dinner tray, leaving the salad.

Then she spied the fork. She'd had spoons with her meals, but never forks or knives. You could stab a person with a fork. Finally someone had screwed up. She grabbed it and retreated to the bathroom, locking the door again. She ate, changed quickly, shoved her dirty clothes underneath the vanity, and crouched back in the shower, weapon in hand.

She stayed like that forever, seemed like, till her thighs cramped and she had to alternate standing and kneeling. She knew he'd come; the only question was when. *Before dawn.*

The sound of the knob turning, the door shaking, almost startled the fork out of her hand. She hadn't heard anyone open the door from the hallway. Had she dozed off? Her watch read two a.m. She'd definitely dozed.

"Krystal. Open up." Aidan's smooth baritone sounded calm, not angry like last night.

She stayed silent but for the pounding of her heart. It was so loud he could probably hear it. *Especially if he's a vampire.*

"Don't make me break through the door, Krys. At least say something and let me know you're OK."

She backed as far into the corner of the shower as she could, pressed against the cold tile, fork tight in her grip, teeth clenched. She couldn't stop a high-pitched squeak from escaping at the sound of splintering wood.

The door flew open, sending a spray of wood fragments from the mangled door facing in its wake. Aidan walked in slowly and, as she'd anticipated, was looking straight ahead.

This was her only chance. Taking a deep breath, she willed her feet to move, rushing at him before he saw her. She'd decided to go for his neck—not quite as vulnerable as the eyes but easier to reach. And a fork in the neck would hurt, by God.

But she hadn't taken his lightning reflexes into account. By the time her fork got near his neck, he'd thrown up his left arm. The tines stabbed deep into the meaty part of his palm and hung there a moment before he slung it away, its clatter against the shower tiles echoing through the bathroom. She took advantage of the seconds he took to examine his hand and punched at his Adam's apple with her fist, which earned her a satisfying cough.

"What the hell are you?" She scratched his cheeks with her nails, drawing blood again, and kicked at his shins, hoping he would move away from the door so she could run. He didn't say anything, just planted a hand on each of her shoulders and watched impassively while she fought and scratched.

Finally, when she thrust a knee into his crotch as hard as she could, he reacted, grunting and twirling her around till her back was pressed against him. He had one arm clenched around her waist and the other across her shoulders as she continued to fight. "It's OK," he said. "Fight it out. You've earned it."

Insufferable, condescending bastard. She kicked backward at him, which dislodged him a fraction, but not enough to make him release her.

She couldn't do it. No matter how hard she struggled, his grip remained tight. Finally she accepted that her struggle was futile. He'd won. Her shoulders slumped in defeat, her breath as ragged as if she'd run a marathon. Her fight drained away and the tears started. Damn it—she did not want to give him the satisfaction of making her cry.

He continued to hold her against him, lowering his head to tuck his cheek against her hair, swaying slightly and talking softly in a language she didn't recognize except in its tone—the one used to soothe a child. It shouldn't have calmed her, but her heartbeat slowed.

Her tears stopped, too, though her face and neck were wet from them.

His breath was warm in her ear. "Will you let me explain?" Vampire breath wouldn't be warm, would it?

She nodded, and he released her. Swiping her palms across her wet cheeks, she edged past him out of the bathroom and folded herself into a corner of the sofa.

He followed, flipping the switch that controlled the gas-log fireplace. After adjusting the flames to a low blue-and-orange flicker, he sat on the opposite end of the sofa and shifted around to face her.

She stared at the flames. God, she was so tired of being angry and afraid. Seemed like she'd spent her whole life being one or the other, and she was sick of it. All she had left was numbness.

"Are you ready to talk? I'll tell you everything now."

She turned to look at him. Such a beautiful man, with his chestnut hair, pale eyes, high cheekbones. She flinched and clenched her fists in her lap as he moved closer and reached out to stroke a thumb along her cheek.

Cheek. Her heart woke from its stupor and began pounding as she stared at his face. She'd scratched him, but his face was smooth now. Her gaze shifted to his hand and he held it out for her to see, palm up. The tines of the fork had gone in deep; she'd seen the blood. Now his hand was unmarked.

"We heal quickly," he said. "The only reason Mirren needed help last night was the poison on the buckshot. Otherwise, he'd have healed and the plugs would have worked their way out. Plus, it was almost dawn so we were running out of time."

Krys stared at him. She wanted to slap him, or run from him, or just call him a big fat liar. Slapping wouldn't hurt him and there was nowhere to run. That left talking.

"You're trying to tell me you're a vampire? Well, guess what? I don't believe in vampires. I'm a scientist, remember? I believe in logic. I believe in things I can prove."

The corners of his mouth twitched. "You've seen the proof, whether it's logical or not."

Absurd. Krys went through a mental litany of pop culture vampire clichés, and wondered if any of them were true. Did he drink blood? Sleep in a coffin? Burn up if sunlight hit him? Avoid crosses and garlic?

Good Lord. "So, if I'd stabbed you with a silver fork instead of stainless steel, you'd be dead?"

Aidan grinned at her, and she saw the tips of fangs flash against his lower lip. She clutched a throw pillow to keep her hands from shaking. Had he ever smiled at her broadly enough for her to see that before? Hell, she'd never even noticed if the man had teeth—she'd been too busy ogling his eyes and the deep dimple that formed on the left side of his face when he smiled.

Her eyes remained riveted on his mouth as she waited for another glimpse. That mouth she had kissed with such abandon and thought about way too much.

"You're thinking about werewolves," he said, and she saw no evidence of fangs as he talked. He knew how to hide them. "Silver zaps our strength to human levels, but it won't kill us. I also wouldn't dry up or burst into flames if you threw a garlic clove at me, or touched me with a cross, or poured a gallon of holy water over my head. I'm not even sure I understand all the changes we go through when we're turned, but Hollywood's come up with its own nonsense." His mouth quirked again. "Tearing out my heart would do the trick, although I probably shouldn't be telling you how to kill me."

Krys hugged the pillow more tightly and tried to think. He obviously didn't intend to hurt her, so the question was, what *did* he want? What would get her out of here? "Just tell me the whole story."

He stared at the fire a moment before talking. "The pandemic vaccine—you know it changed the blood chemistry of those who took it?"

Krys frowned. "Yes, but it was a minute change—no one had any side effects from it."

Aidan chuckled. "Oh, there were side effects, all right. To vampires. We do feed from humans." He paused when she gasped. "We don't take much, and it doesn't hurt anyone. But we learned quickly that the blood of anyone who'd had the vaccine was poison to us."

He talked on. About forming his scathe in Atlanta and moving it here. About the humans who lived in Penton willingly with them, as familiars or feeders. It was clear he cared about the people here, vampire and human alike.

"What about this war you talked about? The attack on Mark?" If she set aside her gut-reaction disbelief, the whole story made a kind of warped sense.

"My brother, Owen, is behind the attacks."

"Wait...your brother is a vampire? Don't you have to be turned into one?" She hoped it wasn't contagious.

"We were turned at the same time, by the same vampire," he said. "There's...let's just say there's bad blood between us, and he's trying to destroy me—destroy Penton. He killed our doctor; he attacked Mark; one of his people shot Mirren."

Even with this explanation, Krys kept coming back to one question. "Why me, Aidan? How did you know I didn't have the vaccine?"

He at least had the good grace to look sheepish. "Will's a computer savant—he can hack into anything. Including medical records. What I told you earlier was true. I knew you didn't have family you were close to, and hoped you might want to stay here if you took the job and got to know us."

Goose bumps spread over Krys's skin. They'd seen her medical records, which meant they probably knew the litany of broken bones she'd suffered at her father's hands. She must have looked pathetic enough that they thought she'd welcome living in a town full of vampires—or sociopaths. The jury was still out on that one.

An image of dark, somber eyes and oddly formal language came to her. "What about Hannah? How does that child fit into your vampire town?"

Aidan cocked his head, a half smile raising the side of his mouth and creating that way-too-sexy crease. "Hannah is one of us."

Forget sexy; talk about sick. "You turned a little girl into a vampire?"

"God, no." Krys flinched when Aidan reached for her, and he pulled his hand back. "I took her in a long time ago—she'd already been turned."

Krys threw the pillow down and stood up, pacing behind the sofa, aware of Aidan watching her. Somehow, of all the things he'd told her, Hannah's story rang true. She'd been wandering around at three a.m. without an adult. She'd moved crates around that storage area as though they'd weighed nothing. "She's a psychic, isn't she?"

Aidan laughed. "Definitely. She was the daughter of a powerful Creek medicine man—a witch. She has some native magic, but was turned so young she was never trained to use it."

Krys nodded. Hannah had known things about Krys's childhood that nothing other than psychic ability could explain.

Aidan's voice grew hard. "I killed her maker. No one in Penton would ever be allowed to even feed from a child, much less turn one. Hannah's true name is Hvresse—she chose her English name— and she lives with her adult familiars, who serve as parents."

Krys thought of Hannah and her ancient eyes that seemed so at odds with her pink clothes. She wanted to cry for the little girl who would never get to grow up.

"That first night, did you feed from me?" She sat on the sofa again, facing the fire, not wanting to meet his eyes. "Did you do something to make me want to..." She ran out of words, or at least words that weren't too humiliating to say.

He slid closer and caught her hand in his before she could move away. "You mean did I do something that made you want me?" His thumb soothed small, warm circles on her wrist. "I feel your pulse speed up when I touch you."

Krys swallowed, trying to will her galloping heart to slow. "How do you know it's not because I'm afraid of you?"

"Because I would be able to sense your fear. You aren't afraid of me, even though you probably should be." He unbuttoned the top few buttons of his shirt and drew her hand inside it. His chest was hard and warm, and she could feel his heart beating beneath her fingertips. "Feel that?"

She nodded and jerked her hand away, liking the feel of it way too much.

"That's what you do to me." He slid even closer, till his thigh touched hers, and her heart almost stopped. "I wanted you as much as you wanted me, and it didn't have a damned thing to do with me enthralling you. All it did was give you the nerve to act on your feelings."

He slid an arm around her shoulders and leaned in to graze his lips across her neck. Was he going to bite her? Was he going to kiss her? Was she going to let him? "I thought vampires were not really alive. You know," she said, her voice shaky. "Undead."

He kissed her neck and trailed his warm breath till his mouth hovered just above hers. "We don't die, we evolve." He kissed her softly. "Don't I feel alive?"

Oh no. This wasn't going to happen again. She shoved him away and stood up, putting a few feet between them. His eyes were lighter than before, and he watched her with a look she could only describe as feral. He suddenly didn't seem human at all, just beautiful and *other*.

"Why do your eyes change color?"

He leaned back on the sofa, his look intense. "Our eyes lighten when we're agitated, or hungry—or aroused."

Krys paced the length of the room. She needed to stop thinking about Aidan as a man—well, a male—and start thinking of him as a kidnapper. "Why are you telling me all this? How do you know I won't escape and tell everyone about you?"

He laughed, flashing a hint of fangs again. "Who would believe you?"

That was the God's honest truth. As crazy as it all sounded, Krys's mind begin to crack open under the weight of so much revelation. *My God, everything people believe is wrong.* "So, what now? Are you ever going to let me go?" Would they just kill her when the need for a doctor was past?

Aidan studied her. "Stay here for a month. Help at the clinic until we get past this crisis—I mean help us without me having to enthrall you or force you. Then, if you still want to leave, I'll make sure you get back to Georgia or wherever you want to go. While you're here, I'll pay you well for your time."

Krys thought of Mark, lying on the ground outside the Quikmart. If she hadn't shown up, he might have bled out because none of them would have risked taking him to a hospital. And she'd thought Mirren had been afraid of blood. What a joke.

"If I agree to stay here a month, will you let me out of this room?"

"When I'm sure you won't disappear on me," he said. "I'm sorry, but it would be dangerous for you to wander off with Owen on the loose, and I don't know how many vampires he has with him."

It had been worth a try. Krys nodded, resigned to the room. She'd stayed in worse places. Heck, she *lived* in a worse place, except it had windows. Besides, what choice did she really have? She could be uncooperative and have him keep her enthralled, or hypnotized, or whatever it was, or she could make the best of it. Sad thing was, no one would miss her.

"OK, one month. And I have one more question." She raised her eyes to look in his, waiting for the familiar dizzy sensation. It didn't come.

"Why can I look in your eyes right now and nothing happens, and yet sometimes you can hypnotize me?"

"Because I'm not trying to enthrall you now." He smiled. "That was the question?"

"No!" Krys sounded more strident than she'd intended.

"Then the answer is yes, I'll have someone come tomorrow and repair your bathroom door," he said, smiling.

"That wasn't the question, either."

He looked at her, one eyebrow raised.

"Can I see your fangs?" She couldn't help it. The scientist in her had to check it out, see if they were real. She had so many questions, about what role the blood played in their systems, whether they ate or drank, how the fast healing worked, and whether their secrets could be adapted for humans...If she could learn something in her month that might help her understand medicine better, then it would be worth it.

Aidan laughed and pulled himself off the sofa, coming to stand in front of her. Her pulse sped at his nearness, and she wondered if she had the same effect on him—probably not. No matter what he said about wanting her, she didn't have the looks for somebody like him. She looked like a flat-chested geek next to that woman Lucy. That vampire Lucy.

He bared his fangs slightly, and she reached out and touched an index finger to the tip of one canine. It was razor sharp but delicate, extending about a quarter-inch longer that of a human, and it was slightly curved. She tugged on it, but it felt real and didn't give. It was a damned fang.

As she pulled her hand away, she felt a sting and saw blood well up on her finger where she'd nicked the tip. She raised her eyes to Aidan's. He'd grown still, his irises a wintry blue, his pupils dilated. On his face was an expression of stark hunger.

———•———

Damned if this woman wasn't going to be the death of him. He'd fought a raging hard-on since he got to the suite, and now Krys stood there with her finger in the air, blood trickling slowly from the cut, studying his face as if he was a specimen under a microscope.

Aidan reached for her hand and lifted her finger to his mouth. She didn't pull away, so he slid his lips around her fingertip, sucking out a tiny extra measure of her sweet, rich taste before caressing the cut with his tongue.

"Oh." She gasped and pulled her hand away from him.

"You OK?" He stroked a hand down her arm, wanting to hold her but not daring to move too fast. He'd come here tonight expecting her to be overcome with fear and revulsion. Instead, after the shock of it, she'd been more curious than frightened.

And, by some miracle, she still wanted him, even knowing what he was. He could tell from her heartbeat and the heat wafting off her skin. So much for thinking that the truth would drive her away and let him bury his asinine mating instincts six feet under. They'd not only dug their way out; they were building a damned pyramid.

She stared at her fingertip. "It's healed. How did you do that?"

"We're predators, Krys." He needed to keep reminding her, as well as himself. He wasn't just a man with fangs. "One way we survive is that our saliva contains a chemical that can produce pleasure in those we feed from, and then heal them quickly."

She shook her head. "So you make it feel good when you feed, and you don't kill the people you feed from?" She continued to watch her finger, pressing on it, looking for any sign of the wound.

Time for a dose of reality. "A lot of vampires kill their victims. They enjoy it, even make a sport of the hunt and capture. But we're trying to make a different kind of life here, one where we can remember at least a little of what it felt like to be human. Where the people who keep us alive are treated with respect and friendship. Believe me, keeping you here against your will goes against everything I believe in."

Krys gave him a doubting look. "Sorry, but you sound naïve."

Aidan smiled. "You're not the first—"

The sounds of movement from the hallway caught his attention. Time for her to see another reality. "We may need you tonight," he said, opening the door. Melissa stood in the hallway, giving them a tentative smile.

Krys frowned. "Mark should be recovered by now."

"The patient isn't Mark," Aidan said. "It's Mirren. Will you help us?"

Several emotions played across Krys's face at once—at least one of which, he was sure, was a curse. But after a pause, she nodded and followed him across the hall.

She was treated to the sight of Mirren Kincaid, all six-foot-monstrous of him, sitting on the sofa in a room just like hers. He looked even worse than he had at the meeting two hours ago.

Mirren glanced up at Krys with misery-filled eyes and nodded, then turned a hard glare on Aidan. "I'll be damned if I'll let you use these." He picked up what looked like a pile of silver-linked chains and threw them with enough force that Aidan had to take a step back to avoid being clocked.

"Then you are damned, my friend, because you *will* use them." Aidan picked the chains up and advanced toward the sofa. "Nobody's self-control is that good."

Melissa moved around Aidan to stand beside Krys.

Aidan looked back at them. "Mirren absorbed more of that vaccinated blood last night than we thought. So we're going to drain out the bad stuff and replace it with fresh blood." He turned back to his lieutenant. "And he's going to let us use the silver chain on him so he doesn't get all nasty and hurt somebody, isn't he?"

Mirren's jaw tightened. "Fuck you."

Aidan took a length of chain and wrapped it around Mirren's right wrist, then stretched it to a rear sofa leg and fastened it with a padlock. "Sorry, *mo chara*," he said softly, repeating the action with the right wrist. With his arms secured, Mirren's mobility was limited. He slouched further on the sofa and glared at anyone who'd make eye contact.

Aidan glanced at Krys to see if she was frightened, but she and Melissa were whispering. Melissa was explaining how silver reduced a vampire's strength to that of a human, and Krys was asking about Mirren's symptoms.

He fought back a smile. "What would you guess is wrong with him if he were human?"

Krys looked shocked till Melissa said drily, "Something you should probably know—they hear everything. There's really no point in whispering around them."

"Ah. Well." She turned a sexy-as-hell shade of pink. "Clammy skin, pallor, tremors." She frowned as her eyes scanned Mirren's face. "Have you been nauseated? Vomiting?"

Everyone stared at her except Mirren, who propped his head on the back of the sofa and closed his eyes.

"He has," Aidan said. "What would your diagnosis be?"

"Probably food poisoning." As soon as the words were out, she groaned. "I mean, I don't know if you eat. Well, I guess you don't eat. You drink, or—something." She shrugged and blushed furiously.

Mirren started laughing, a low rumble at first, and then a choking, gasping sound. Aidan stared at him. Mirren never laughed. He might smile every once in a while, but laugh?

Aidan grinned at Krys. "I'd say you're a pretty good doctor." In more ways than one. She'd defused the tension in the room without realizing it.

"How far off was I?" she asked.

"I told you the pandemic vaccine turned human blood poisonous to us." Aidan looked down at Mirren. "Our enemies have gotten a supply of vaccinated blood. The buckshot that caught him last night had been scored and then soaked in it. He didn't get enough to kill him, thanks to you, but he got enough to make him sick."

Krys looked worried. "I don't know what to do for that."

"All you have to do is hit a vein," Aidan said, nodding at Melissa. She handed over a needle, an IV line, some empty bags, and other supplies.

"Explain it," Krys said. "What am I giving him?"

"You're not giving, darlin'. You're taking," Mirren answered. He was still slumped against the sofa back, but he watched her through hooded eyes. "You have to bleed me out."

"Oh, no." Krys thrust the needle back at Melissa, who shook her head and retreated, hands up.

"It's the quickest way for him to get better," Aidan said, wishing he'd spent more time preparing her for this and less time acting like a love-starved idiot. "If we wait for the poison to work its way out of his system, he'll be out of commission for at least a week. I really need you to do this." He paused for a beat. "Please."

She squared her shoulders and nodded, then took the IV bag from Melissa and walked to the sofa. Mirren had closed his eyes again but she talked to him softly as she worked. "Are you sure this won't kill you?"

Mirren grunted. "No, I'll just wish I was dead."

"Once you've drained him enough, we'll feed him," Aidan said. "The chains are for your safety, not his."

Krys blinked but didn't respond. She tied off Mirren's arm, found a good vein, and deftly slid the needle in and taped it in place. Other than a slight flare of his nostrils, Mirren didn't react as the blood raced through the tube and began dripping into the bag.

"Is that color normal? It's more magenta than crimson."

Aidan stood next to her. "Yeah, that's about right." He was still amazed at her calm. She was clearly in her element around medicine, even if it involved vampires.

"How much blood do I take?"

He shook his head. "I've only seen this done once before. Keep draining till the bloodlust starts. You'll know when you've taken out so much he can't stand it and he's trying to break the chains. Then he'll have to feed."

"Oh, my God." Krys and Melissa looked at each other, one horrified expression mirroring the other.

Mirren cracked one eye open. "You better have plenty of donors on hand, A. Otherwise I'm coming after your ass."

"Tim and Jennifer are on their way," Melissa said, and turned to Krys. "They're Mirren's familiars."

"Check with Will," Aidan told her. "He was rounding up a couple of others as well."

After Melissa left to track down Will, Aidan took Krys's hand and gave it a squeeze. "You cool with this? Melissa can probably handle it if you want her to."

Krys looked at Mirren a few moments, and then shook her head. "I'm OK. Tell me exactly what I need to do."

He admired her courage—whatever core of steel was inside her that made her look squarely at what frightened her and confront it. Maybe he'd be able to handle Owen better if he had a big dose of it himself.

"Change out the bags when they need it. When he really starts struggling, let his fams take over. They know what to do."

"Won't you be here?"

He'd like nothing more than to take his daysleep in her room, in her bed. But that would require a trust he didn't have, a trust no vampire gave easily. He'd never met daybreak any place that wasn't his alone and completely secure—or at least not since the early days with Owen.

"Dawn will come before long—that part of the vampire legends is true. Mirren will probably stay awake because of the procedure, but as soon as he feeds, he'll be out for the day. He can just stay here and one of his fams will stay with him."

She frowned as she switched out IV bags, looked up at Mirren, and found him watching her with intense eyes that were already beginning to silver with hunger. "Probably not what you had in mind when you came to town, is it, darlin'?"

"Uh, no. It's..." She jumped when Aidan rested a hand on her shoulder. He might have exaggerated how calm she was.

Mirren closed his eyes and clenched his fists, straining slightly against the silver chains as blood began filling the second IV bag.

"I'll tell you what it is," he said, his voice rough. "It's un-freakin'-believable."

❋CHAPTER 16❋

This was a life he could get used to. Owen rolled onto his side and curled his body around the soft curves of the woman lying next to him, pulling her close and running kisses along one silky shoulder.

"Aren't you the early riser." Lucy rolled into his embrace and pulled his mouth to hers.

He broke the kiss first, smoothing the thick, dark hair away from her face.

"Let's feed, then I'll show you how much of an early riser I am, love."

She laughed and imitated his brogue. "Fine Irishman that you are. Your brother and Mirren don't have much of an accent left unless they're turning it on for effect."

He collapsed on the pillow and stared at the ceiling. "Aidan left Ireland and everything in it a long time ago."

"What happened back then, to make you two hate each other so much?"

Owen threw back the blanket on the old mattress they'd dragged into the middle of the floor in a windowless back room of a deserted house on the outskirts of Penton—supplies Lucy had helped dredge up so they wouldn't have to rut on the floor like bloody beasts. Lighting a candle, he walked to the living room and pulled the blinds apart slightly. All quiet. A light snow fell in the illumination of the streetlight.

He lit a second candle and returned to the bedroom with both of them. "My brother is a bloody hypocrite. He hates that he's a killer, like all of us are. Don't buy his noble act, girl. He's done worse than me."

Lucy sat up, letting the blanket fall to her waist, and Owen's eyes took in the full breasts and slim waist. She was a fine-looking woman, no doubt about that. Trustworthy? Not in a million moons.

"I'll agree that Aidan has a bad case of holier-than-thou," she said, crawling from the bed and coming to stand beside him. "What did he do that was so awful?"

Owen slid an arm around her and pulled her to him again, burying his face in her hair. She smelled like lilacs, and his fingers felt rough as they played over her skin. "I'm bored with talk of my boring brother."

Lucy moaned as he nipped her shoulder with his fangs and sucked on the wound. "God, that feels good—I've missed having someone touch me."

He raised his head and cupped her jaw in his palm. "I'm sorry I killed your mate. If I'd known you, I wouldn't have gone after him. Just wanted to get Aidan's attention, that's all." He shrugged. It hadn't mattered to him who he'd used to make his arrival known—Lucy's mate had been in the wrong place at the wrong time.

She rested her head against his chest. "I loved Doc. I won't deny that. But you exposed Aidan's weakness. He didn't act."

Owen laughed softly. "So you wish he'd hunted me down and killed me then and there, do you?"

Lucy pulled away from him and dug around the pile of clothes on the floor till she found the black dress she'd worn before their daysleep. She slipped it over her head. "When it first happened, yeah, I wanted him to kill you," she said, handing his clothes to him. "Better put these on—it's cold enough to freeze a dead man."

Owen tugged on his pants and sweater, wishing like hell Lucy was for real. But he knew more about her than she realized. "So, if you wanted me dead, why haven't you done the deed yourself? Afraid Saint Aidan will be mad at his lieutenant?"

Good. She'd blanched at the reference. She hadn't told him how highly placed she was in Penton's organization. He wanted her to know that he'd done his homework.

"I left Aidan because he didn't kill you," she said, turning hard green eyes on him. "I realized then how weak he was, that he couldn't lead Penton and deliver on what he promised. In my mind, that makes you a stronger ally."

"Besides," she said, sitting in one of the chairs, "I'm no longer a lieutenant. He cut me off."

"Is that so?" Owen studied her. He'd been alone a long time, and someone like Lucy could make life fun again. Hunting, feeding, seeing new places. He already knew the sex was brilliant. Tempting to try, but a mistake would be lethal. She wouldn't get over the loss of her mate so quickly unless she was one cold-hearted bitch, which was exactly how he had her pegged.

Question was, how far would she take this charade of having ditched Aidan? "What about the humans bonded to you—you have someone?"

Lucy paused before answering. "I just bonded a new one. Daniel. Why?"

"Seems to me as a show of good faith, you could share." Owen leaned against the wall and stuck his hands in his pockets. "Our food supply is thin. Shite, we're all thin."

"That you are, but still sexy as hell." Lucy stopped to kiss him as she walked to the corner and dug a cell phone out of her purse. Punching in a number, she waited for a moment and then spoke briefly, giving someone—Daniel, he hoped—directions to the house, with orders to keep it quiet, come to the back, and make sure he wasn't followed.

They waited in silence for ten or fifteen minutes. Owen tensed at the soft knock on the back door. He didn't follow Lucy as she headed through the kitchen, but he pulled a knife from his jacket on the floor and slipped it into his pocket, waiting to see if she returned with a stake-wielding Aidan or Slayer or a young stud she'd enthralled. Daniel came as a surprise. He was handsome, but at least forty.

He halted when he saw Owen. "I know who you are—you have the same eyes as Aidan." He turned to Lucy. "Why are we here? He's the one we're supposed to stay away from. Does Aidan know he's here?"

Owen scowled. No, and this blighter with his cocky mouth was the reason Penton was such a stupid idea. Sheep needed to know their place.

Daniel stiffened as Owen moved behind him and placed a knife at his throat. He pricked a small cut beneath the man's ear and licked off the blood that welled up. Daniel shivered and looked at Lucy. "Wh-what's going on? You said I'd only have to feed you."

Lucy looked at the floor. "I said you were on the menu tonight. For both of us. I've cut my bonds to you so I can share." She looked up at him. "It'll be OK, Danny."

The man didn't try to pull out of Owen's grasp as he snaked an arm around his waist from behind. "It will be OK, Danny-boy," he repeated, staring over the man's shoulder at Lucy. She met his gaze, bit her lower lip, nodded.

She was handing over her human to gain his trust. Maybe she was on the level. Or maybe he'd been right the first time—she was a coldhearted bitch.

"Join me, love." He reached around Danny and held out a hand. She walked toward them slowly and wrapped her fingers around his, pressing herself against Danny from the front so the man was sandwiched between them. Owen closed his eyes, hearing the thunder of Danny's pulse, feeling the rush of blood from vein to vein, smelling his fear.

He looked over the man's shoulder at Lucy again, and smiled. She angled her head to the right, licked Danny's neck just below his ear, and bit. The man grunted, and then relaxed as she began to feed.

My turn. Danny tilted his head back, eyes closed, as Lucy fed. Owen had clear access to the other side of his neck. He bit without bothering to lick and anesthetize, and held on to Danny's waist as the man jerked and groaned.

Owen felt Lucy pull away, but he had no plans to stop. Would she let him drain her human? He opened his eyes to see if she looked upset, but she'd turned her back and walked to the window. Well, then. She was willing to let him die.

Danny's legs collapsed beneath him, but Owen held him upright, closing his eyes again and feeding deeply. He felt the man's pulse weaken, his heart fluttering like a hummingbird's wings. When he was gone, Owen dropped the body to the floor with a thud and swayed from the rush of being sated for the first time in a while. The girl he'd drained before his meeting with Aidan had been so used up, she'd barely slaked his thirst.

"We'll need to get rid of him," Lucy said, still facing the window. "Somewhere Aidan won't find him. With me cut off from the scathe, they'll just assume he left Penton."

"They'd let him do that? Just leave?" Owen felt drunk with the glut of blood. If he hadn't been starving, he'd never have been able to finish a human male off in one feeding. Even then, he suspected that the guy had some kind of heart problem or he wouldn't have buzzed so fast.

Lucy turned back to him with the face of someone who'd suddenly aged. "He'd been an alcoholic for years. Lost everything he had. We helped him shake the habit, hoping he'd want to stay on with us. But if he wanted to go back to Atlanta, Aidan would let him."

Owen grimaced. "Aidan's too soft."

Lucy didn't answer. Owen still didn't think he could trust her, but he was beginning to really, really wish that he could.

❋CHAPTER 17❋

Krys jammed the iPod buds into her ears and relaxed on the sofa, listening to soft acoustic music with a Celtic lilt, one of Aidan's additions to her song list. It was almost seven, and the hours just after sundown had become her favorite for reasons that she didn't want to examine too closely.

Five nights had passed since the big vampire unveiling. Amazing how fast she'd eased into a routine once she'd agreed to stay for a month. She'd get up at eight, shower and dress, and find her breakfast tray on the floor by the time she'd dried her hair, always with an Atlanta newspaper alongside it. Lunch came at noon, then dinner at six—usually with a fresh flower laid atop the container. Sometimes it was a rose, but more often it was an enticing bloom whose name she didn't know. Somebody had exotic taste in flowers.

She'd go stir-crazy if she had to live this way forever, but she believed Aidan when he said it was only for a month and, truth was, she had nothing to go home to except a lot of debt, a crummy apartment, and an endless parade of nights in whatever emergency room or clinic she eventually landed in.

So in the quiet, empty hours, she read from one of the books Aidan had brought her, worked crosswords, and thought about her life, including a lot of the crap she usually avoided dwelling on for very long. How had she never realized that every goal she'd set for herself, every plan she'd made, had revolved around her father—getting away from him, staying away from him, trying to get past the head games he'd played with her?

The last time she'd lived under his roof, she'd been seventeen and just a few days out of high school. She'd kept her acceptance letter from Auburn University, and her scholarship notification, hidden in her room for months, but somehow graduation had made her feel brave; her impending freedom had brought an unfamiliar happiness.

"I got accepted at Auburn. I start in August," she'd said at the family dinners her dad always insisted on having. "I think I want to major in biology."

Her mother's face had brightened, and Krys had had a fleeting hope that her dad would be happy for her. He didn't say anything except a noncommittal "Hmm," and then ate his dinner in silence. Before the meal ended, he'd risen from the table, gone to the counter to pour himself another drink, and blindsided Krys with a punch to her left jaw. If he'd been sober, he would've broken it. Instead, she'd hit the floor and protected her head against his kicks. All he ever said was, "You ain't going nowhere."

When he'd staggered out of the kitchen, Krys pushed herself to a sitting position and saw her mom still seated at the table. Her voice was soft. "Reckon you better plan on getting a job 'round here."

It had taken seventeen years, but Krys realized then that her mom would never come to her rescue, never defend her, and maybe even needed her to absorb some of her dad's wrath. That night Krys had stuffed the few clothes she owned into a pillow-case, climbed out the window, and found her way to a shelter. The only time she'd seen her dad since then had been after her mother's suicide, at the funeral.

She had let his criticism and bullying define her. Now it felt as if her life had been stripped bare, and she wasn't sure who Krystal Harris was or what she wanted, except that it couldn't be a life defined by another controlling man.

Which made her fixation on her kidnapper—her *vampire* kidnapper—even more ridiculous. She waited for Aidan Murphy to show up every night as if he had been God's chosen, and then practically fell over herself trying to coax a smile or a rare laugh out of him. Somehow she'd gone from being the victim to worrying about the guy who victimized her. Seeing him not as a monster but as a good man who worried about the people for whom he felt responsible. She'd grown able to read his moods, from the tightness around his eyes that meant he was worried about something to the stiff set of his shoulders when he was stressed.

You are a great big cliché, falling for your abductor. Your vampire abductor, who could snap your neck with one hand or drain all the blood from you and make you enjoy it.

Stockholm syndrome, that's what it had to be.

She no longer doubted that he was a vampire. Watching Mirren's procedure had stamped out any misgivings. Medically speaking, he should be dead. He'd been virtually drained of blood, his already slow heartbeat growing erratic. But the loss of the magenta fluid dripping into the bag hadn't made him weak—only stronger and angrier and more desperate.

She hadn't wanted to watch him feed, so she'd left the room. The whole idea gave her the heebie-jeebies. When she had gone back to check on him, he'd dropped into a sleep so deep she couldn't rouse him, then he'd come by at sunset to issue a halting thanks, looking as big and scary as ever. Science—the belief system she'd built her whole worldview around—had failed her. One more gigantic chink in life as she'd planned it.

A haunting song called "The Taming" had ended and another was about to begin when she heard Aidan's knock, even under the earbuds. Her heart sped, and she hated that he'd know it, know how her body reacted to him whether she wanted it to or not. But there was nothing she could do about it, except maybe keep her thoughts on something like chemical equations. But then again, chemistry was part of the problem, wasn't it?

She pulled the door open to find him peering at her from behind an oversize cardboard box. "May I come in?"

She raised an eyebrow. "What if I said no?"

"You'd be really sorry to have missed out on all these books." He wasn't nearly as good at hiding his feelings as he thought he was, and Krys read the strain behind the small smile. Something had happened.

She took the box and set it on the floor beside the coffee table, trying not to grimace at its weight, while Aidan took his usual spot on the sofa. Instead of claiming the armchair or the far end of the couch, she sat next to him. She'd been prepared to be bitchy and *victimlike* tonight, but one look at his face brought out the need to help him instead. "What's wrong? I can tell you're upset."

He grunted, slouched down so that his head was even with the sofa back, and closed his eyes. "Just been a helluva night already."

She wanted to soothe him, so she sat on her hands to keep them to herself. Touching him might be soothing for him but it would take her mind to places it didn't need to go. "Talk to me about it. I mean, really, who am I going to tell?"

He swiveled his head to look at her. She could tell he wanted to talk, was measuring her ability to understand, maybe, or to empathize. At first she thought he wasn't going to answer.

"Mirren and I tried to follow another of my lieutenants tonight—you met Lucy, right?"

Krys nodded.

"She's shacked up with my brother, Owen. They move every day, so we haven't been able to find them. But she's with him. She could've let us know where they are so we could put an end to this, but she hasn't."

Krys struggled to piece together the bits of information she knew or had overheard. "But Lucy was the mate of the doctor Owen killed. It doesn't make sense that she'd join up with him."

Aidan stared at the fire. "I don't think she's sold us out, or Owen would have made a move already. She's just being stupid. But she went too far. She—" He stopped. Krys stared at his profile as he focused on the fire and wanted to smooth away the worry lines. She rested her hand on his arm without thinking, and he reached to twine his fingers through hers.

"What happened?"

His jaw muscles twitched. "She let Owen kill her familiar, a guy named Daniel. Helped him. He'd been fed on by two vampires. Mirren and I found his body in the woods behind the mill village."

"It couldn't have been somebody else? Maybe Lucy wasn't involved."

Aidan shook his head. "It doesn't work that way. He was bonded to Lucy, so the only way another vampire could feed from him is if she broke their bond. She lured him to her and then she and Owen bled him out."

He dropped her hand, got to his feet, and began pacing like a trapped animal. Ironic, since she was the prisoner here—but maybe she wasn't the only one. He seemed caught in a web that she didn't understand.

"I didn't want to move against him until I knew where our Tribunal stood—that's the vampire lawmakers. Now I'm thinking we should take him out—if we can ever find him."

"He's your brother. Could you really kill him?" Krys shuffled the bit about vampire lawmakers aside to ponder later. She hadn't thought about there being such a large vampire population that they needed organized leadership.

Aidan sighed. "He's not leaving me any choice. Plus, he's not really my family, not anymore. Mirren's my family. Will, Mark, and Mel. Hannah."

Krys understood that distinction all too well. Her father was blood but he was not family. She sat in silence while Aidan stared into the fire as if it might have answers.

"You should use your humans to do it," she said, thinking.

He turned from the fire and frowned. "What?"

"Send your humans out to hunt Owen and his vampires during the day—seems to me they're your greatest advantage. They aren't controlled by the sun and can hunt during the day when there's no danger Owen will be skulking around, and could even kill them with very little risk." She couldn't believe she'd advocated murder, but she'd learned a long time ago to look life square on and do what needed to be done. The stakes here were high. "I saw how out of it Mirren was the other day. He was totally vulnerable."

Aidan shook his head. "We can't ask our fams to fight our battles for us."

Being a vampire hasn't kept you from being a stubborn man. "Why not? Listen, you say the people have a good life here. I'd think they would want to protect it—protect you—especially since there's virtually no risk to them. And besides that, they're the ones getting attacked. Owen seems to be afraid to come after you directly. Let them defend themselves."

Aidan stared at her. "But..."

She wanted to laugh at the perplexed look on his face but stifled it, picking up the gold and purple orchid that had been on her dinner tray and cradling its fragile bloom in her hands. "Just think about it. You have to admit it's a good idea if you decide not to wait for your...sheriffs, or senators, or whatever you called them."

He grinned at her. "Tribunal. And yeah, I'll think about it." His gaze slid to the flower and then back to her face. "Let's go for a walk."

Her heart leaped at the idea of leaving this room under her own steam for a change, and she jumped up before he could change his mind. "Where are we going?"

"I want to show you something. You'll need a coat."

Krys pulled her jacket from the closet—the first time she'd used it since her so-called job interview—and slid it on over her sweater. Instead of turning left toward the clinic access tunnel, Aidan headed right, taking her hand in his again, his warm palm against hers, strong fingers enveloping hers like a glove.

"I didn't realize there was an exit on this side."

He glanced down at her, slowing his pace so she didn't have to jog to keep up with him. "Daniel's body is up at the clinic. I don't want to go back in there tonight."

They walked in silence for a moment, and Krys could practically feel the guilt radiating from him. "You aren't responsible for what Lucy did, you know." They'd almost reached the end of the hallway, and she couldn't figure out where they were going—it looked as if it ended in a solid wall.

He gave a bitter chuckle. "Thanks for trying to make me feel better, but I am responsible. I recruited Daniel. I brought him here. I might as well have killed him myself."

Krys tugged him to a stop. "Look, I grew up with this abusive son of a bitch for a father who made me feel like every bad thing that happened was my fault and exactly what I deserved. But you know what I've realized? People make bad choices, and sometimes stuff just happens. You aren't responsible for somebody else's choices or for random acts of the universe. You might be stuck cleaning up the mess, but that doesn't make it your fault."

He stared at her. "That's the first time you've mentioned your father except to say you were estranged."

Krys laughed—her turn to sound bitter. "Yeah, well, he's not worth talking about. I've had a lot of time to think since I've been here and you know what? I've let him define my whole life without realizing it. And I want to be more than that."

Something intense flared in his eyes, and her heart thudded as he slid a palm up her arm. "Do you realize how extraordinary you are? I—" He paused, then shook his head and started back down the hall. "Come on, let's walk."

Damn. She really, really wanted to hear the rest of that sentence. But he'd reached the end of the hallway, pressing a tiny button in the corner of what looked like a dead end. A panel covered in the same design as the wall whirred and slid open wide enough for them to ease through single file.

"What is this?" Krys shivered as they stepped into a concrete tunnel and the panel slid closed behind them with a soft click.

"Escape hatch." He grasped her hand again and they walked along an upward-slanting concrete tunnel with masonry walls and harsh industrial lighting overhead—everything painted gunmetal gray. "Hang around vampires long enough, and you'll learn we're a wee bit obsessive about making spaces where we'll be safe. Like you said, Mirren was vulnerable that day when he was in his daysleep. We're all vulnerable. So we come up with elaborate ways to create safe spaces. Then we devise equally elaborate ways to escape from them."

Krys laughed, and he squeezed her hand.

"You know what that laugh does to me, don't you?" His voice teased, and she felt a wicked stab of need shoot straight through her. He tugged her against him and lightly grasped the back of her neck with his free hand. "It makes me want to do this."

He angled his head for a kiss, but this was no soft brush of lips. His mouth was hard and searching. God, but the man could kiss. She probably shouldn't...*oh, what the hell.*

She snaked her arms around his neck and molded her body against his. His hard arousal, pressing between them, was like an electrical jolt to her brain. "Wait." She stepped away from him. God, his eyes were almost white. "I'm not—I don't think—"

"Shit." He closed his eyes and took a deep breath and chuckled. "Sorry about that. You test all my control, you know?"

She couldn't speak for his control, but he sure tested hers. *He's a vampire. He's your kidnapper. He is not long-term relationship material.* She needed to keep reminding herself of that.

Aidan's thoughts were tangled as he and Krys climbed the stairs out of the sub-suite tunnel into an abandoned house on the eastern edge of Penton. Her common sense and quick grasp of the situation with Owen (and hardheaded assessment of how to take care of it) had bulldozed him. Hell, just being within three feet of the woman bulldozed him.

His body ached when he was with her, ached with the need to touch her and be touched by her. He knew now that his attraction to her wasn't driven by hunger anymore—if it ever really had been. He wanted her, and only her. She wanted him too, but was it real? If she were free to leave tonight, would she stay with him, or would she run away?

He didn't have the guts to find out. Owen's threat made a good excuse for keeping her here, but in truth, he couldn't bear to let her go. Not yet.

"What is this place?" She looked around the darkened room, illuminated only by shards of light coming through the unshuttered windows from the street outside.

"Just an abandoned house we use for the escape hatch." He shifted the floor tiles around to camouflage the opening through which they'd just climbed. "There are lots of empty houses here, so we try to put a few of them to use. Don't want to tear them down in case we need them, although I don't see our population ever getting back to the size Penton was when the mill was active."

They walked into the cold night air, and Krys stopped and took a deep breath, looking up at the stars and around her. Watching her, Aidan felt a stab of guilt. He missed the sunlight so badly, and yet he'd even taken away her freedom to breathe fresh air.

"Come on, I want to show you something." They walked along the empty street, crossed a couple of backyards, and finally edged a wooded area that led into his own yard.

"Nice digs," she said, taking in the cul-de-sac surrounded by the early-twentieth-century houses.

He laughed. "Yeah, they are. I live here"—he pointed at the nearest house—"and Mark and Melissa live next door." Lights shone behind the Calverts' curtains, and both cars were in the drive.

Krys glanced at their house briefly before turning to study his. He tried to see it from her viewpoint. "It's over-the-top, isn't it? I don't know how I let Mark talk me into it."

"It's perfect," she said. "You need something that shows you're the guy in charge. People put stock in things like the size of a house or the kind of car someone drives." She'd noticed the BMW. "Where *do* you get your money?"

"Well, some vampires earn their living enthralling rich humans and clearing out their accounts," he said, smiling at her look of alarm. "Most run nightclubs or other evening-hour businesses in the larger cities. I turned out to be pretty good at playing the stock market and making investments, plus Mark's a great business manager."

"Were you a businessman before you were, uh..."

He knew she'd accepted that he was a vampire, but she still had trouble using the words. He couldn't blame her. Her worldview had done a one-eighty in the last week. That she was even standing here with him was a bloody miracle, and if he wanted her to become more at ease around him, he needed no repeats of the scene in the tunnel. He stuck his hands in his pockets, where he wouldn't have to worry about them straying in her vicinity. Nothing he could do about the raging hard-on.

"Never a businessman. Come on. I'll show you what I was, sort of." He led her across the side lawn to his pride and joy. He'd actually chosen the house on Mill Trace not because it fit his status as the head of Penton but because it had a large enough yard for him to grade it level and add a freestanding greenhouse. Bronze frame with a redbrick base, bronze-tinted glass, and thermostatic roof vents. His most peaceful moments were spent here, where he could work with the soil.

He juggled his key ring, shaking loose the key for the greenhouse door, then unlocked it and turned on the lights as Krys entered.

"Oh my God." She stopped inside the arched entrance. "You grew these?"

These were his night-bloomers, pulsing with color and vibrancy under the soft lights. Showy white moonflowers, brilliant gold lemon lilies, rich purple evening irises, and his favorites, the red night-blooming hibiscus.

"I was a farmer before I was turned," he said, walking down the aisles, pinching off a faded bloom, shifting a pot to equalize the light source, turning off a sprayer. "This has been my way of staying close to it. I swear when I come here early in the evening, I still smell the sunlight on them."

God, she must think him the world's biggest whiner. Mirren always told him he was a moody bastard but at least he used to keep it to himself. He held his breath as she came to stand behind him and slipped her arms around his waist. "That's got to be awful, to love something so much and lose it."

He didn't trust himself to answer, or he'd be pouring out the whole sorry story of Abby and Owen and how they had all ended up in this shit to begin with. Instead, he gave her the greenhouse tour. When they came to the orchids, she stopped. "You grow the flowers that someone brings to my room every night?"

Now he felt stupid in addition to pathetic. Trouble was, the more he knew Krys, the more his heart and brain got in sync with his screwed-up mating instincts. He was freaking *wooing* the woman he'd kidnapped.

He turned to face her, pretending to shrug it off. "I pick one for you and give it to Melissa."

"You pick it yourself?" She blushed. He loved the sweetness beneath her practical exterior, her utter lack of guile—even though he realized a lot of her self-consciousness stemmed from the doubts inflicted by her warped upbringing. She had no idea how lovely she was.

He leaned over and snapped off a ruby-throated hibiscus and tucked its stem behind her ear. "Beautiful. And I mean you, not the flower."

Before she could protest—because she *would* protest—he caught her face in his hands and bent his head to hers again, his mouth taking possession, trying to show her through his kisses how much he wanted her, wanted her to be a part of him. So much for not repeating the tunnel scene.

The flash between them sparked deep and hot, her breasts pressed tight to his chest. "Ouch!" She pulled away from him, breathless, and touched a finger to her lips. It came away bloody. "How do you control those things?"

Shit, he'd nicked her. "Occupational hazard," he said, and she laughed a little, her fingers plucking at the buttons of her jacket. He could feel her nervous energy, and God knew scaring her was the last thing he wanted. "Krys, nothing happens unless you want it, you got that? You say walk away, and I'll take you back to your room and that will be the end of it, even though that's sure as hell not what I want."

She looked up at him, and he could practically see her gathering her courage. "It's not what I want, either. I'm just afraid that I won't—" Another laugh. "Maybe you need to enthrall me again so I can get out of my own head."

He ran a hand through her thick, silky hair, tucking a strand of it over her shoulder. "No, we just go slowly." He'd need to, because she wasn't ready for him to feed from her. The vocabulary word for everyone today was *slow*.

He stepped closer again, and she backed up till she bumped one of the potting tables. Another kiss, soft at first, till she deepened it herself and he followed her lead. "Don't be afraid of me," he whispered, placing his hand between them, over her heart, his fingers splayed so that her heart thudded as if he were holding it in his hand.

His mouth took hers again, and she moaned softly as his hands cupped her breasts, his thumbs circling the hard peaks through the soft sweater. Her tongue made a tentative inroad into his mouth, and he groaned, pulling her in, tasting her.

She pulled away from the kiss, but kept her arms around him. Kneading her fingers into his back, she burrowed her face against his chest.

Her shoulders shook and at first he thought she was crying, at least till she burst out with that husky laugh that drove him crazy. "I think we need to get a room."

Aidan laughed and hugged her, memorizing the feel of her in his arms to carry with him into his daysleep. When was the last time he'd laughed this much with anyone? Rhetorical question, because he didn't know the answer.

Krys pulled away from his embrace. "I think we should go back to my room."

Aidan couldn't help the pang of disappointment, but what did he expect? That she'd drag him to the dirt floor of the greenhouse and beg him to take her? *Man, you are one delusional vampire.*

They retraced their steps to the suite. When she reentered her room, he paused at the door. It seemed wrong to kiss her and then lock her in. But if he didn't, and she tried to run, and something happened to her, he couldn't live with that.

"Are you just going to stand there?"

She stood next to the sofa, hands on her hips, a quizzical look on her face.

"I wasn't sure if—"

She laughed, low and soft. "I said we needed to get a room." She looked around. "This is a room, Aidan."

Holy hell. She didn't have to tell him twice.

CHAPTER 18

Was she really doing this? Krys watched Aidan push himself off the doorjamb where he'd been leaning, close the door behind him, and reach her in two strides.

His mouth covered hers in a hungry kiss, and she gave in to the sensations as his hands pulled her against him. "Wait, wait." He stepped back. "Are you sure?"

She wasn't sure of anything, except that she wanted him. Maybe if she made love to him she could sort her feelings out better, to know if what she had begun feeling for him was real, or if it was just sexual frustration. Because he definitely made her feel frustrated.

Krys took his hand and pulled him toward the bed. "Is there anything I need to know? I mean, uh, is..." *God, what an idiot.* She felt her skin heating and knew she was turning that particular shade of pink that clashed with her hair.

Aidan's laugh was soft and low and made the muscles in her pelvis clench and throb. "You can't get pregnant. You can't catch a disease. And as much as I'd like to taste you, I can keep my fangs to myself if that's what you want."

Damn, she hadn't even thought about that. "I'm sorry, I'm not ready for that. If—"

"Shhh. No apologies." He brushed his lips across hers and lowered his mouth to her chin, planting soft kisses around to her neck. He kissed her lightly underneath her ear, and she felt her pulse against his lips. "See?" He smiled. "No fangs."

Krys laughed. She shouldn't want him but, damn it, she did. Reaching up to smooth a lock of chestnut hair away from his cheek, she covered his mouth with hers and pushed him toward the bed. When he hit the edge of the mattress and tumbled backward, she followed him, resting her body atop his. She shifted her hips to bring that hardness she felt in line with her restless heat, and he groaned.

"You're killing me, woman." He flipped them, settling himself to align his body with hers, and shifted his hips until she gasped.

Krys felt as if she'd catch flame if he didn't move faster, but he took his time. His tongue pulsed against hers, matching the rhythm of his hips. When his hands snaked underneath her sweater, she grabbed the hem impatiently and tore it over her head, then got to work on his. "Get this thing off."

"Yes, ma'am." Laughing, he finished ripping his sweater off and threw it aside, pausing to look at her lacy black bra. "Sexy... too bad I'm about to tear it up."

She giggled until he proved he wasn't kidding. "Hey, that was my favorite—oh." Her protest died on her lips as flicked his thumb across one nipple while taking the other in his mouth. She arched into him with a moan. God, he had a talented mouth.

"You are so beautiful." He propped himself on his elbows, looking at her with eyes the color of arctic ice.

"No, I'm n—"

He covered her mouth with his again, stopping her protests. Krys had never thought of herself as beautiful—just the opposite. But damned if he didn't make her feel that way. She closed her mind to the nagging doubts about the rightness or wrongness of being with him, of giving him more control over her than he already had. How could something that made her feel this way be wrong?

She stroked her fingers down the bunched muscles of his back and slid a tentative hand to the front of his jeans. He was hard and hot, and she wanted to feel him in her hand. She unzipped the jeans and closed her fist around him.

"Holy hell," he gasped, burying his face in her hair. "You're killing me."

Krys knew she wasn't the most experienced lover. She'd had a few flings but nothing serious. What if he was disappointed? *Stay out of your head. Just feel.*

He rolled away from her, jerking the jeans off and throwing them on the floor with his sweater. She shed her own slacks, then followed him, wrapping her body around his like a cloak, her heart pounding against his chest, her hair a waterfall over his skin as she nibbled at his neck.

"I love the feel of your hands on me." His breath grew ragged as she sat astride him, raking her hands down his chest and reaching behind herself to sheath his silky heat in her fingers. He rocked against her hand, and then rolled her over fast enough to make her squeal.

Holy cow, had she actually giggled? He was turning her into one of those silly girls at whom she'd always rolled her eyes.

Aidan smiled as his lips hovered over hers. "You sure about this, Krys?"

She didn't answer, but kissed him with a fury that left no question, and finally lost herself in his mouth, his scent, the tightening and release of muscle under skin. She hadn't realized how close to the edge she was, but when he slipped one finger inside her, then two, it didn't take long before she felt the pressure growing, wiping out all thought as she came, tightening her arms around him like a band.

"I want you inside me," Krys whispered. "Please."

Aidan moved above her, and she felt him, hard and ready as she wrapped her legs around his hips. He entered her slowly, filling her with heat and restrained tension. Krys made a noise deep in her throat when he circled his hips and pushed harder, each thrust slow and controlled.

They moved together in perfect sync until her breath hitched and she fractured again, pulling him with her. He groaned, pulsing inside of her, losing his rhythm, his body shuddering with release. She wanted to hold him inside her forever, to stay this close.

He closed his eyes and rested his weight on her gently as they caught their breath, and they both laughed. "You're bloody amazing. You OK?"

Krys twined her fingers through his thick hair. "You have to ask?" She'd never really understood what all the fuss over sex was about before. Now she knew. Her muscles felt like melted wax, the restless buzz of her brain had calmed. For the moment she felt content, and even though part of her knew it was only for a moment, she didn't care.

Aidan shifted inside her. "Because if you need me to try again, I could probably—" A generic cell ring tone sounded from somewhere in the vicinity of the floor. "Damn."

He ignored the phone and kissed her again. It fell silent for a few moments, and then started again. "You better answer it," Krys gasped, pushing him away. "It might be...important." She'd almost said, "It might be something to do with Owen." But she really hoped it wasn't something ugly that would spoil tonight.

Aidan groaned, rolled off her, and scrambled for his jeans, digging his phone out of the pocket. From his end of the conversation, Krys couldn't tell what was happening, but when he ended the call, he began pulling on his clothes. "That was Mark. There's a strange car parked outside my house, so I better go and check on it." He sat on the bed and leaned over to kiss her. "Sorry."

She smiled. "You think it has anything to do with Owen?"

He dug under the bed and fished out a boot. "Don't think so—Mark said it was a sedan with dark-tinted windows. That's not Owen's style, plus he's more of an attack-from-the-shadows type than a pull-into-your-driveway type."

Krys leaned against the headboard and pulled the quilt up to cover herself as she watched him leave. The bed already felt cold and empty.

❊CHAPTER 19❊

Aidan let his car idle for a few moments at the end of the block with the headlights off, studying the sedan parked in front of his house. After a few seconds, a slender, dark-haired man emerged from the backseat and stood next to the car, lifting his face to the night air and snapping his head around to look at Aidan.

It was Lorenzo Caias, Aidan's biggest ally on the Vampire Tribunal. His muscles relaxed, and he drove the rest of the way toward his house, parking in the drive.

By the time he got out of his car, Renz had climbed the front steps and waited on the porch. Aidan passed him without speaking and led the way inside, throwing his coat over the back of the armchair and lighting the kindling in the fireplace.

"I'm surprised to see you so far north this time of year, Renz," he said, poking at the sticks to spread the flames. "You usually stay in Buenos Aires in the winter. You always say your place in New York's too cold."

"It is frigid and miserable," Renz said. "But this is no time to be out of the States, not with Europe in such disarray and vampires flocking here under the delusion that there are more unvaccinated humans to feed from."

The "vampire pandemic," as their people only half jokingly called the vaccine crisis, had driven many city dwellers into rural places they never would have gone normally. But the last Aidan had heard, Renz and a couple of fams had moved into an Upper East Side apartment. He'd bet that one of them was driving the car outside.

"Nice to see you," Renz said, shrugging off his jacket and tossing it on the chair next to Aidan's. "Before we talk business, can you put us up? Got my fam in the car so I don't need anything but daysleep space. One room is fine."

"No problem." Aidan placed a couple of logs on the fire, and then called Will to get one of the sub-suites ready.

By the time Aidan finished the call, Renz had emerged from the kitchen with a bottle of whiskey and two glasses.

"Made myself at home, obviously." He laughed, opening the bottle.

"So what's prompting the personal visit, Renz? Or do I already know?" Aidan filled one of the tumblers and set it on the end table next to his chair. Tribunal members—even old friends—didn't normally make house calls.

Renz lounged on the sofa, legs stretched out and crossed at the ankles. He ran a hand through spiky black hair sprinkled with a trace of silver at the temples. He was always as tightly wound as a coiled spring, but his nervous energy was more palpable than usual tonight. "You know I'm here about Owen, speaking of riffraff coming over from Europe."

Aidan rubbed his temples. "I wondered if the Tribunal was aware of his attacks on our humans—he's killed one so far and injured another. So far, I've hedged on fighting Owen too openly because I was afraid the Tribunal might be supporting him. I can't hold out much longer, though. Matthias Ludlam and his lot—are they openly backing Owen? Who exactly am I fighting here?"

Renz shrugged. "Matthias is too smart to back Owen publicly. But privately? You better believe it. He's had a Tribunal detective moonlighting for him to track down his son William. Unhappily, that led him right to your door. That's all we were able to get out of the detective before he was found drained—probably at Matthias's hand."

Shit. Part of Aidan had always known that taking Will in and making him part of Penton's power structure could attract the wrong kind of attention from Matthias, but it wasn't Will's fault—a person can't choose the family he is born into. "How does Owen fit into this?"

Renz sipped his drink and rattled the ice. "Did you know that the Tribunal Justice Council issued a death warrant for Owen a few months ago for a stunt he pulled in Dublin? Drained several women and left them poorly hidden, causing the human authorities to get involved."

Sounded like Owen. Arrogant and sadistic. "Obviously, he isn't dead."

"The council rescinded the death sentence in November—shortly before Owen surfaced in Atlanta. Matthias is head of the Justice Council. Come to your own conclusions, my friend."

Damn. Now it made sense. Owen wouldn't come after him to defend something as tenuous as the vampire way of life. But he *would* do it to save his own hide.

"What about you?" Aidan asked, studying Renz's face. The man had taken Aidan in when he'd first fled Ireland centuries ago. Renz had given him a home, shown him how to survive in what was just a wild colonial outpost of England. That was long before Renz had risen to Tribunal status and Aidan drifted south and began building his own scathe.

"I think the type of thing you're doing here is the only hope we have of surviving this crisis without going public and throwing ourselves on the mercy of humans." Renz took a sip of whiskey and stared at the reflections of light on the amber liquid. "Nobody wants that."

Of all the crazy ideas. "Is going public really being considered? It would be a bloody disaster."

Renz nodded. "I agree, which is why I'm here. I want Penton to succeed. I can't back you openly by sending people to help. I'll be honest—there are more on the Tribunal against you than for you. Not because of Penton per se, but because you have bonded your entire scathe to yourself and no one is sure how big that scathe is. Anyone outside the Tribunal who has too much power makes them twitch. But given my political straitjacket, tell me what I can do to help."

Aidan had an easy answer for that one. "Find out who's supplying Owen with vaccinated human blood, for one thing."

Renz choked on his drink. *"Mierda.* How do you know?"

Aidan shared Mirren's adventure with the buckshot. "I don't know how much of that stuff Owen has, but I doubt he used all of it. It's a damned effective weapon."

Renz looked thoughtful. "I heard a rumor that Kincaid had joined you. I don't have to tell you his presence will enrage those who see you as a threat. His years as the Tribunal's executioner left him with quite the reputation. Has the Slayer recovered from his injuries?"

"Don't let him hear you use that name unless you want to see how recovered he is." Aidan finished off his whiskey. "I won't throw Will to his father, and Mirren's not going anywhere. We'll fight whomever we have to—but don't share that with any of your Tribunal cronies."

Renz nodded. "Let's hope it doesn't come to that. You have, what, about twenty-five scathe members?"

Aidan hesitated. He wasn't inclined to trust any outsider these days, even Renz. He didn't doubt his support, but the man was also a political shark who could flip sides if his survival depended on it. The Penton scathe numbered more than fifty now, but he decided to keep that figure to himself. "Yes, about that. All the humans are fams or mates, except a few bonded extras—mostly relatives."

"What about kids?"

He shook his head. "None. Anyone who wants kids or gets pregnant moves out. Maybe one day, but it's doubtful. This is just not the kind of lifestyle kids need to be in—we aren't exactly set up for education and day care." Not to mention that children would be the first targets for someone like Owen. Aidan knew that from experience, but he pushed thoughts of his son, Cavan, from his mind. All it did was make him angrier.

They sat in silence for a few minutes, and Aidan pondered the pros and cons of telling Renz about Krys. He might not trust the man with the whole future of the Penton scathe, but he did value his opinion.

"I have one other thing to tell you," he said. "We have a new doctor—our original doc was the first one Owen killed. This new one, a woman, was able to get the vaccine-laced pellets out of Mirren just before dawn and helped us do a drain-and-fill on him. Otherwise he'd have been out of commission for weeks."

Renz poured more whiskey. "I can't believe you found another one so fast. Is she human or vampire?"

Aidan got up and stood with his back to Renz, facing the fire. "Unvaccinated human. We didn't just stumble across her. We researched till we found her, and when my business manager was attacked by Owen and needed treatment, I kept her here against her will." The words sounded as callous as the act itself, and he found it hard to reconcile them with his feelings for the woman he'd just held in his arms.

He remained still, watching the fire and waiting for Renz's reaction. If the man told him to get rid of Krys to keep from attracting Tribunal attention, he'd consider taking her back to Atlanta and letting her go—if he could squelch that selfish part of himself that wanted her with him. What he'd never do was kill her, even if Renz ordered it.

The older man surprised him.

"Given what's happening, it was a smart move. Penton needs to survive this, and if it means taking one person's freedom to save the whole, then it's worth it. How's she handling it? How much does she know?"

"Everything. Even handled the drain-and-fill on Mirren without a meltdown. She's bloody amazing."

When Renz didn't respond, Aidan looked back at him. His friend was eyeing him with amusement.

"What?"

Renz opened his mouth and then closed it. "Nothing." He finished his drink. "You're handling this right. Don't let Owen pull you into an all-out war that will draw human attention to Penton or give the hotheads on the Tribunal a reason to target you. Right now it's just Matthias trying to stir things up and get his hands on William. Play it low-key, and take Owen out when you can. Chances are, his people will scatter once he's gone—I doubt he has many. The important thing is to have this town of yours survive."

Aidan cracked his neck. He'd been almost relaxed around Krys and now that seemed like a week ago instead of an hour. "You think what we're doing here is that important?"

He'd like to have said that he had come up with the idea of Penton as a template for vampire society in a post-pandemic world. Really, though, he'd just wanted a place where he and others like him could hold on to the shreds of their humanity and live in peace. No prey. No politics.

Renz got up and set his glass on the coffee table. "Yes, I do think it's important. Many of our people in Europe and North America are starving. Hunger is causing them to be indiscreet, and a black market for unvaccinated humans is springing up. It's only a matter of time till someone gets caught and we're forced to either go public or exile everyone to some Third World jungle to live on animals. It's a damned nightmare."

He picked up their coats. "We have a few hours till sunrise. Show me your town, and introduce me to the Slayer."

———— • • ————

If anyone ever made a vampire sitcom, the meeting between Renz and Mirren would be an episode all by itself. Aidan chuckled as he walked home through the sub-suite tunnel at about three a.m. He'd dropped Renz and his fam off at one of the clinic sub-suites, down the hall from Krys.

He'd warned Mirren that they were coming, but it hadn't helped. The big guy sat through the twenty-minute ordeal wearing his stone-gargoyle face, arms crossed over his chest, answering Renz's questions with a full repertoire of grunts and vague, monosyllabic replies. Thank God Renz had a good sense of humor.

"You don't like to talk about your past, do you, Mr. Kincaid?" he'd finally asked.

Mirren fixed him with a look that would freeze icebergs. "You think?"

It had been his longest sentence of the night.

Aidan emerged from the tunnel into his greenhouse and stopped to pick one of the hibiscus blooms. They'd forever remind him of Krys.

She'd brought two emotions to life in him: wonderment and loneliness. The first was a new one for him; the second hadn't tormented him in so long that it had taken him a while to recognize the empty, longing feeling.

Krys was at the crux of everything. When he was with her, he couldn't imagine letting her go, even if he had to keep her locked up for the rest of her life. Screw the guilt, as long as he got to be with her, talk to her—hell, even listen to her advice, for God's sake.

Once he was away from her, as now, his brain would start working instead of his dick. Listening to her talk about her father earlier this evening, and piecing that together with some of the things he knew from her school records, he wondered why he'd been so arrogant as to think he could uproot her life, lock her up, and make her want to stay in Penton. She'd worked hard to stand on her own and escape being under a man's control.

The great Aidan Murphy, savior of abused and addicted humans. Arrogant ass with a God complex, Owen had called him. It awed him that Krys not only had survived what he'd done to her, but also seemed to have become stronger through it. He could just as easily have broken her spirit so badly she'd never have recovered.

He should take her home, but he couldn't. And not just because of Owen, but because, at heart, he was a selfish prick. He hadn't felt happy in so long that those minutes with her, the feel of her desire, was something he didn't have the courage to give up.

He left the greenhouse and approached the front of his house, growing still as he picked up subtle movement in the dense row of ligustrum in front of his porch. A figure moved slightly away from the shadows, enough for him to get a clear look.

Lucy.

He sniffed the heavy night air, making sure that she hadn't led Owen here, intentionally or not. He also wanted a few seconds to dampen the anger that threatened to obliterate all reason when he thought of how she'd sacrificed Daniel.

Finally he moved fast, grabbing her arm on his way to the door and shoving her inside ahead of him.

"Ouch. Shit, Aidan. You don't have to pull my arm out of joint." Lucy jerked away from him once they'd cleared the threshold and put some distance between them. He slammed the door hard enough to jar the front windows.

"What the *hell* do you think you're doing, killing one of our fams? And what did you tell my brother once you finished screwing him? How much of Penton have you given up?" Aidan advanced on her, fists clenched.

Her nostrils flared, and he smelled the fear on her as she backed up against the wall, holding her hands in front of her. "I didn't betray you. You know me better than that. I'm trying to find out as much as I can about Owen and his scathe."

Aidan veered away from her and threw his car keys on the sofa table. "You stink. You smell of Owen."

He pointed her to one of the armchairs in front of the window. He sat in the other, crossed his legs, and watched her.

Lucy looked tired. She wore her usual provocative garb— leather skirt and tight sweater and boots—but her eyes lacked the old Lucy Sinclair spark. She looked a helluva lot healthier than her fam, though.

"You might be interested to know we're having Daniel's body embalmed and sent back to his family in South Carolina, along with a big load of bullshit about how he died."

Lucy flinched and looked at the floor. "I needed to gain Owen's trust."

Damn her to hell and back. "Was it worth it? Owen isn't stupid, Lucy. He's good at playing the fool, and he knows how to charm the ladies."

"Runs in the family then, doesn't it?" she snapped, glaring at him. "Want to know how you compare in the sack? I'm probably the only woman who's screwed both of you—or did you share back in the good old days?"

It took all his strength to keep him from breaking something, like her pretty little neck. "Don't try to make this about us, or about sex. Owen killed Doc, a man that I know damn well you loved. How can you stand for him to touch you?"

Lucy deflated, her shoulders slumping. "Because I want him dead, Aidan, and the quickest way for me to get him there without jeopardizing Penton is to gain his trust. You might be willing to sit around and play cat-and-mouse games with him, but I want that son of a bitch gone. First I'm going to find out how much power he's got behind him, and then I want him to know that what he did to Doc mattered."

Aidan wanted to point out that she'd treated Daniel's death as lightly as Owen had treated Doc's, but she wouldn't have heard it. She was too lost.

Her voice softened to little more than a whisper. "You don't know what it's like to lose someone like that. I've told you before. You keep people in neat little compartments— lieutenants, familiars, scathe, Mirren. He gets his own category. You don't allow messy things like love to make you vulnerable."

Aidan closed his eyes. She had no idea. "There are too many people, vampires and humans alike, whose lives depend on how this plays out," he said, the anger draining from his voice. "I won't run after Owen without knowing how big his scathe is, where they're hiding, how many humans are with them, how many on the Tribunal are backing him—because there are some. Can you answer any of those questions?"

Lucy looked at the floor. "Not yet. He wants to screw me, but he doesn't want to have pillow talk. All I know is what little I've overheard. He does have someone he's in contact with by cell phone—he changes phones constantly so no one can track him, and he makes sure no one can hear those conversations. He moves every day, and has someone going to Atlanta every couple of days to pick up new phones and supplies."

Aidan pondered the information. "What kind of supplies?"

She shook her head. "Food for their humans, since they can't store anything. I don't know what else."

"You still don't know how many vampires he has with him?"

"They're scattered in caves back in the hills and take their daysleep in the basements of some of the abandoned houses. They move constantly. He'd be suspicious if I asked him out-right—maybe after I've had a while longer to work on him."

Aidan studied her, weighing the trust he had left. Not much. But he'd at least try to keep her safe. "Stay away from the mill village for a couple of days."

She arched an eyebrow. "Why?"

"Just do it. And if you can leave Owen there without you, all the better." He was sure he'd feel a few regrets about hearing that his brother had died in a mill village fire. They could join all the other regrets that he bundled around with him.

She gave him an amused look. "Just listen to you. I thought Owen was the bigger hard-ass among the Murphy brothers. Exactly what happened between the two of you back in the olden days? He won't tell me." Lucy relaxed in the chair and leaned back against the cushion, obviously having decided that the physical threat from Aidan had passed.

His eyes rested on the half-burned chunks of wood in the cold fireplace and let his mind go to a place he seldom visited anymore.

"Owen was responsible for the death of my wife," he said, as flatly as he might have told her the weather forecast. "My son, Cavan, was six years old at the time, but I was able to save him from Owen. He was raised by a neighboring farmer as an indentured field hand, but he ended up happy. Will tracked down his descendants in Ireland. He lived long." It was the only consolation in the whole sorry tale—that, and hoping Cavan hadn't remembered what had happened to his parents.

Lucy's eyes widened. She'd been a member of Aidan's scathe for almost twenty-five years, since he'd found her in Atlanta.

188 | SUSANNAH SANDLIN

But he'd buried the memories of Abby and Cavan deeply. Only Mirren and Hannah knew the story, and he hadn't told Hannah. She'd just known.

"I never knew you were married." She sounded shocked. "So you *did* know how I felt when Doc died. She was your wife when you were made vampire? Did Owen turn you?"

"No, he didn't turn me." Aidan's mind had conjured a beautiful, laughing girl with hair the color of honey and a small, dark-haired boy with his father's quiet, serious way of looking at the world. "Owen and I were turned by the same vampire." His laugh was bitter. "He thought being turned was the best thing that ever happened to him. He's a much better vampire than I am, as I'm sure he's told you."

Aidan's fingers picked at the seam on the arm of his chair. He wouldn't talk to her about this anymore, wouldn't have told her this much if Krys hadn't stirred up so many memories. The woman was distracting him, and he couldn't afford it.

Lucy leaned forward. "Owen's jealous, you know. That people follow you, trust you. He leads by fear and he knows you don't have to. That's why he wants whatever you have."

Aidan turned from the fireplace and looked at her. She obviously didn't know that Owen was doing this to save his own life, so she hadn't gotten as close to him as she thought. "Jealous or not, he won't get Penton. Kill him if you get the chance, or don't. Regardless, watch your back. He won't ever fully trust you, no matter what he tells you."

He paused, hating that she'd set this plan in motion. "You know, after what happened with Daniel, I can't bond you back into the scathe. No human would ever agree to be your fam, and I wouldn't ask anyone to."

Lucy stood up and pulled the front window drape aside about a quarter-inch, looking for movement. "I understand that. I knew the cost of what I did, and I'll live with it."

She dropped the shade and headed for the door. "And just so you won't be surprised, Mirren's been standing outside the window waiting to rip my heart out if I made a move against you. Tell him he's not nearly as stealthy as he thinks."

Aidan gave her a grim smile as he got up to see her out. "Tell him yourself."

Pausing in the doorway, she turned and placed her hands on either side of his face, and then kissed his cheek. "Good-bye, Aidan." As he watched her stride across the yard and disappear into the shadows, he thought of their years together, her spirit and humor and love, and it felt as if part of him were walking away with her.

Mirren cursed as he climbed the front steps and paused on the stoop to look into the darkness between the Calverts' house and Aidan's. "How'd she know I was here?"

"It's a talent." Aidan led him into the house and poured them each a glass of whiskey. They had some planning to do in the final hour before dawn.

"Have those talents helped her learn anything more useful than how well Owen can fuck?"

"Don't even go there." Aidan posed Krys's idea of using the fams to hunt during the day and filled Mirren in on Lucy's situation. "I think, to be safe, we have to assume this phone contact of Owen's is someone on the Tribunal, maybe even Matthias Ludlam himself. That complicates things for us. And they know you're with me now, as well as Will. So it makes us an even bigger target."

Mirren found a few choice names for Matthias and the Tribunal. "So we have to sit back and wait for Owen to hit us again?"

Aidan took a sip of whiskey and watched the golden liquid swirl around the glass as he twirled it between his fingers. "Hell no. No waiting. We need to make some phone calls before dawn. Our scathe might not have enough information to attack Owen's people directly, but even the Tribunal can't complain if we have our humans burn the rodent infestation out of the mill village tomorrow."

❋CHAPTER 20❋

A rap at the door jolted Krys awake, and she sat up, heart pounding. A second knock sent her fumbling for the bedside clock. Just after four thirty a.m. Something must be wrong. What if Aidan had been hurt?

"Just a minute." Wait—was the door locked? She tried to remember whether she'd heard the click of the deadbolt when Aidan left her, but couldn't. Either he'd forgotten, or he couldn't make love to her and then lock her up. She hoped it was the latter, a sign of trust. If it was unlocked, why didn't the person come in instead of knocking?

She scrambled out of bed and pulled on jeans and a sweater, tossing her nightgown on the chair. She looked at her shoes for a moment, considering, but a third round of knocks sent her to the door in bare feet.

Pathetic how she'd gotten so used to being locked in that answering the door was a novelty. She looked blankly at the smiling man in the hallway. He was about her height—maybe an inch shorter, with graying hair, olive skin, and soulful brown eyes. Human or vampire? She'd guess the latter, based on the utter stillness with which he regarded her.

"Uh, can I help you? Are you supposed to be down here?"

He upped the wattage of his smile, making no attempt to hide his fangs. "I'm Lorenzo Caias, a member of the Vampire Tribunal visiting Aidan. My familiar and I are staying down the hall. May I come in?"

As if she could keep him out if he wanted in badly enough. She stepped aside and shivered as he passed. He seemed to exude an energy that was almost electric in its power, as if she might feel a charge shoot through her fingertips if she touched him.

"Isn't it close to dawn for you to be out visiting, Mr. Caias?" What the hell would a member of the Vampire Tribunal want with her? Till a few hours ago, she hadn't even known it existed.

"Call me Renz." He took a seat on the end of the sofa and crossed his legs, looking as if he was settling in for a long chat. She hoped he didn't keel over into his daysleep here in her room. What would she do with him if that happened? "I thought I might be able to answer some questions for you."

His voice carried the trace of an accent, but it was different from the faint lilt of Aidan and Mirren, more as if his native language might be Spanish, which jibed with his dark good looks.

She sat tentatively in the armchair near the other end of the sofa. She'd learned enough about vampire strength to know that she would be out of her league if he came after her, but there was no point making it easy on him by sitting within reach.

Not only did he exude that sense of power, but once he settled, he was utterly still in a way she hadn't seen with Aidan or Mirren. They still fidgeted like humans most of the time, but not this guy. Either he was more vampy than they were, or they practiced acting like humans.

"Don't you need to go..." She waved a hand in the air. "Sleep? Pass out? Whatever?"

Renz laughed, and she got another glimpse of fangs. The Penton crew was used to dealing with humans and knew how to smile without looking all fangy. She got the impression that Lorenzo didn't get out much.

"I am very old," he said. "And one of the benefits of age is that we are less prisoners of the night. I can't go outside, of course, and my strength is diminished during daylight hours, but I don't have to take a full daysleep. Besides, it's safe enough down here."

Krys pondered this information. Renz looked to be in his midforties, which wasn't exactly *very old*. She'd never asked Aidan his age. It had never occurred to her that he was other than what he looked, late twenties or early thirties. That had been stupid. She should have it tattooed on her forehead: *human rules no longer apply*.

"Exactly how old are you? And why would you tell me any more than Aidan would?"

"Because he's let himself get too close to you, whether he'll admit it or not," Renz said, laughing. "He gets a protective, mated-male look on his face when he speaks of you, so he'll try to keep you as far removed from his problems as he can."

Krys struggled to keep a composed look on her face while she digested that bit of information. Actually, Aidan had been discussing his problems openly with her, but she didn't plan to share what she did and didn't know.

Besides, something else he had said was more intriguing. "What, exactly, is a mated-male look?"

Renz lifted an eyebrow. "Male vampires have an instinctive reaction when they encounter a female who would make an ideal mate—it's quite overwhelming, I'm told. Some of us never find the right one. After what happened with Aidan's human wife and child, I expected him to remain an old bachelor like me."

Krys wasn't sure how to respond to that. She wanted to ask about Aidan's wife and child—sounded as if they weren't around anymore. As for the mated-male bit...she and Aidan shared some pretty wild chemistry, but *mating* sounded kind of permanent. Renz was obviously nuts. "You're wrong about that. Sorry. Aidan feels guilty for taking me because it goes against what he believes in. I'm only here for a month."

Renz's eyes roamed the length of her body, sending goose bumps racing along her arms. She felt like a dinner steak on the butcher's cart. "Oh, he feels guilty about taking you, but more guilty about how he's begun to want you. Not that I blame him, but I don't want your charms to make him lose sight of why he brought you here. He can't afford the distraction."

If she were smart she'd keep her mouth shut, but his arrogance was sucking all the air out of the room.

"My *charms?*" The heat rose in Krys's face, and she sat on her hands to avoid slapping him, which, even in her anger, she recognized as a bad idea. "Look. I'm not relaxing in this underground spa using my *charms* to distract the man who *kidnapped* me. I'm the victim here, got it?" OK, so she hadn't acted very victimlike tonight, but still.

His laughter made her fume more, and she ground her teeth as he slapped his knee in amusement.

"I see why he admires you," he said, finally getting himself under control.

Krys narrowed her eyes and clamped her lips shut.

He gave her an approving look, not that she cared. "The vampires are loosely governed by a group called the Tribunal, of which I am a member. He's told you this much, yes?"

She gave him her best arrogant doctor look but didn't answer, which seemed to amuse him even more.

"Some of us are very supportive of Aidan's little social experiment here because it might give us a blueprint for how to survive this pandemic crisis—at least until the next generation of unvaccinated humans reaches adulthood." Renz uncrossed his legs and smoothed out his gray slacks. "Aidan's also an old friend, and I want him to succeed."

"And you're telling me this why?"

"I know you aren't here by choice, but I ask you to help Aidan where you can. What he's doing here is important."

Krys gave him a thin-lipped smile. She knew guys like this. The medical profession was rife with them. Ambitious. Self-righteous. Never did anything without an agenda. "So you're here because you want me to think well of you? Understand the plight of the poor vampires?"

Renz laughed. "Fine, it was a poor ruse, I admit. I'm here to see who's captivated Aidan after all these many years alone." He slid to the end of the sofa nearest her, watching her intently and trying to capture her gaze.

Now that she knew what enthrallment was, she knew how to avoid it. No prolonged eye contact. She propelled herself toward the door, thinking that she might be able to lock herself in one of the other suites. She'd bet Aidan didn't know this guy had stopped by for a chat.

Suddenly, he was standing between her and the door. He grasped her shoulders with strong hands as her forward momentum propelled her into him. She flipping hated it when they moved like that.

She shoved both hands against his chest to push herself away, and then stilled as she saw his eyes turn a tawny, silvery brown. He buried his face in her neck, inhaling deeply. "You were with him tonight," he whispered. "And yet he hasn't bonded you to him. Such temptation."

Krys wished she could slow her jackrabbit heart rate. She remembered a brindle pit bull their neighbor, Mr. Nelson, used to have. It had cornered her in the Nelsons' yard one day when she'd run out of the house to escape one of her father's tirades. "If yeh run from him, he'll eat yeh," the old man had told her. "Don't throw the evil eye at him, just set still and he'll leave yeh alone quick enough."

Vampire. Pit bull. Same principle. She remained still as Renz inhaled her scent, trailed his lips along the curve between her neck and shoulder.

Finally, he raised his head and released his grip. She stumbled away from him and backed toward the fireplace. Just when she started feeling safe and thought she was going to survive this whole ridiculous experience, something would happen to remind her how utterly not in control she was.

Renz smiled as he opened the door to leave. "You should tell Aidan to bond you, doctor. It would protect you from wily old vampires who are up past their bedtime."

Krys stepped into the shower, letting the hot water beat into her muscles. She'd finally managed to get to sleep well after daylight, but had been restless, afraid that Renz would return.

Now it was two p.m. and she'd just gotten up. Pretty soon she'd be keeping vampire hours. *Funny. And pathetic.*

But the older vampire hadn't come back, and she had awakened convinced of two things. First, Aidan was one of the good guys, as far as vampires were concerned. Renz? Not so much. If Aidan was putting a lot of faith in his Tribunal, he was going to get hurt. She might not know vampires, but they'd been human once, and she was a good judge of character. Renz Caias would back Aidan as long as it was convenient.

And second, despite the elder vampire's belief that she was too busy playing the vixen to understand how serious the situation was, she knew she could help Aidan. If nothing else, she could be a sounding board, someone with a little distance who didn't give a rat's ass about the Tribunal and its politics.

As for the rest of Renz's claims—all that nonsense about Aidan and mating? Sheesh. They could set the house afire with chemistry, but they weren't ready to pick out china. Wouldn't ever be. He drank blood, for God's sake, and from Melissa. Wonder how Mark felt about that?

She worked sweet-smelling shampoo into her hair, then closed her eyes and stepped under the cascade of water, letting the warmth drain the tension away. Ironic. Except for the little detail about not being able to come and go as she pleased, her standard of living had really improved. She'd always had to hurry through showers at her little apartment in Americus, rushing to finish before the hot water ran out.

She also hadn't had any more near-panic attacks. After all the years she'd spent managing them, maybe the answer all along had been to find something that scared her so badly that there was no energy left for fake fear.

She dried her hair and had just finished dressing when she heard the outer door open and footsteps enter the room. Her muscles tensed. Nobody came in during the day, and she was sure she'd locked the door.

"Dr. Harris? Krys? I knocked but you didn't answer. It's Mark Calvert."

A boyish face framed by disheveled blond hair appeared through the hole in the splintered door. He looked a lot better than when she'd last seen him a couple of weeks ago—it seemed like years.

Mark whistled and gave her a lopsided smile, running his hand around the jagged wood. "Did you do this?"

Krys raised an eyebrow. "Not me. That would be the work of your lord and master."

The smile faded, and Mark's expression grew guarded. "I know Aidan told you about everything. He didn't mention turning the door into kindling. Maybe you can tell me about it on our way to the clinic. We've had a couple of people injured."

Krys followed him into the outer room. "What happened? It's still daytime, so I assume these are human injuries?" She hoped so. She'd had about all the vampire blood-draining she could handle.

He nodded. "A couple of volunteer firefighters—just minor injuries, but I thought you should look at them. We burned the mill village. Flattened the whole thing." He paused and added, "Rat infestation."

She felt a surge of triumph. Rats, indeed. Aidan had listened to her and had ordered the humans to burn the village to try to flush out his brother. "And you're actually trusting me to go to the clinic alone?"

He looked sheepish. "Well, I'll be there."

"To guard me?" She grinned at his discomfort.

He shrugged. "Yeah. Sorry. But when Aidan is down for the day, I'm in charge."

She followed him through the hallway toward the stairwell. She wanted to ask what they'd decided to do about Lucy's dead fam, but figured that Mark wouldn't tell her. He was the business manager, not the undertaker.

When he reached up to extract the ladder, though, light flashed off the steel grip of a gun in a shoulder holster under his jacket. Maybe he handled more kinds of business than she thought.

She just couldn't understand why the humans stayed here, and this might be her only chance to find out. "So when Aidan's asleep...out...whatever, you're in charge. And the rest of the time, you're a blood donor? What's in it for you?"

Mark didn't respond. They climbed the ladder from the subbasement into the storage room below the clinic and began weaving their way through the maze of crates.

"You know where I was when I met Aidan?" He didn't wait for her to answer. "I was dodging the cops and hanging out at a homeless shelter in Atlanta, strung out on heroin. That was what I turned to when I couldn't find the painkillers I'd been hooked on after a back injury."

Krys followed him in silence for a couple of heartbeats, thinking about the track marks she'd seen on his arms that first night. "Why were the cops after you?"

"Burglary, petty stuff. I'd just graduated to my first robbery. Anything to get money."

Krys stared at his back as he lugged a crate underneath the fold-down door—he had to expend a lot more energy than Hannah had—and climbed up to unlock it, holding on to his stomach. He was probably still sore from the attack. She had trouble reconciling the image of the man he described with the healthy one in front of her.

"Where does Aidan fit in?"

"He's friends with Hank, the night manager at the shelter. Hank doesn't know what Aidan is, of course. Just that he has a good track record rehabbing hopeless causes like me. Drugs, alcohol, some minor mental-health problems. The vamps can keep us out of it through detox, and then they make sure we have a lot of counseling. No one comes to Penton till they're clean. No one comes against their will. And no one stays here if they relapse."

Mark pulled down the ladder into the clinic office and turned back to Krys. "Aidan saved me. I'd be dead in some back alley if not for him, or so screwed up I might as well be dead. He kept me enthralled until that shit was out of my system, helped get my head on straight, and then gave me the choice of starting over in Penton or going back to Atlanta. I decided to come here, and never regretted it."

He climbed out of view into the dark tunnel. Krys paused for a moment, and then followed him up to the clinic office. She blinked at the sunlight visible through the blinds, and stopped short.

Mark had already reached the door into the hall, and turned to look at her. "What's wrong?"

She couldn't stop tears from welling up, and wiped them away impatiently. "It's just…I haven't seen sunlight in a while."

He winced. "It made Aidan sick to bring you here like this. No one knows about it except the lieutenants, me and Melissa, and Mirren's fams, since you were there for the drain-and-fill last week. Most people think you just moved here and are getting settled in before you start seeing patients."

Mark motioned her to follow him. "Of course, I'd probably be dead if you hadn't come along when you did, so I can't say I'm too sorry."

Krys didn't have a chance to answer. As soon as she entered the hallway, she recognized Tim, one of Mirren's familiars, standing near the front door. His tall frame was draped across the reception desk as he talked to Melissa.

"Tim was injured?"

"No, he's the city's construction manager and heads up our volunteer fire department. Neither one's a full-time job here."

Tim greeted them and Melissa left the desk and headed toward the exam rooms. "They're in here," she said over her shoulder, waving at Krys.

In the room on the right, where she'd had her shocker of a night with Mirren, a young man lay on the exam table and an older guy in a John Deere hat sat on a nearby stool. Both wore oxygen masks hooked up to portable tanks, the mechanical release and pause of air filling the silence.

"Tell me what happened." Krys switched into doctor mode, pulling her stethoscope off the rolling table where she'd left it the night Mirren came in, and listening to the supine man's lungs.

"Mill village burned," Tim said. He and Mark had followed her into the room. "Guy on the table is Eric. Jerry's on the stool, there." Jerry, an older man with a bit of a beer overhang, nodded at her.

The exam room was crowded, but Krys decided to let everyone stay. Mark had to play watchdog, and Tim could tell her what she needed to know. She took pulses, listened to lungs, treated cuts, and wrapped a wrenched knee while she listened. Luckily no one had suffered burns.

"One of the floors of the older houses caved while they were inside. It took us a while to get the fire under control and pull 'em out." Krys glanced up and noticed Tim had been talking more to Mark than to her.

"Nobody else was inside?" Mark asked.

"Nope. The houses were all empty." Tim sounded disappointed.

———•———

Two hours later Krys relaxed in the waiting area with Melissa while Mark paced the hallways. The two guys had suffered minor smoke inhalation and she'd sent them home with instructions to take it easy for a day or two. Eric had been a nice, almost shy guy while Jerry was a bombastic know-it-all. Krys had been glad to see him leave. To hear him tell it, he'd handled the mill village burning almost single-handedly, and would wipe out the bad vampires in a heartbeat if Aidan would just give him the go-ahead.

Krys wasn't volunteering to go back to her dungeon. Mark would have to force her, and so far he hadn't mentioned it. She studied him as he looked out the front window, hands in his jeans pockets, the gun out of sight under his jacket. Surely the whole town couldn't be full of people who'd been addicts, who fed vampires out of some warped sense of obligation. What was somebody like Jerry Know-It-All doing here?

Melissa broke the silence. "Want me to run that last blood work? I can come back tonight and do it when I bring your dinner."

"It can wait till tomorrow—the guys weren't hurt that badly and their oxygen levels were OK." Krys shifted her gaze from Mark to Melissa. "I'm sorry. Taking those trays down to the suites three times a day must get old."

What the hell was she apologizing for? Idiot. Make Aidan apologize.

Melissa laughed. "I volunteered. I had hoped..." She paused and looked back at Mark, who remained standing with his back to them.

"You hoped what?"

Melissa shrugged. "I guess it sounds stupid, given the way you came here, but I hoped we might become friends."

Friends. Krys hadn't had many of those, not close ones. She hadn't been allowed to have friends over as a kid, or to visit other children's houses. Finally they had quit asking. For a flash she wished Melissa's wish could come true. "Well, we can be friends even though I'm only here temporarily." She laughed. "I always thought you put the flowers on the tray till I saw Aidan's greenhouse."

Melissa broke into a grin. "He showed it to you? Be honored—he doesn't let just anybody in there. Afraid they'll break a leaf or something."

A flush of heat gathered in her gut at the memory of that night—they'd done a lot more than see the greenhouse. She didn't regret it, even though she knew she should.

"Do you want to go back downstairs?" Mark had made his way to the waiting area and stood in front of them. Melissa got up, put her arms around his waist, and stood on tiptoe to kiss his chin. Krys envied their easy affection.

"You go on home, honey," Melissa said. "Aidan will be here in a few minutes anyway. Krys and I can get better acquainted. It'll be fine."

He kissed her again, and then headed back to his spot by the door. "Nice try, but I'll hang out here a while longer."

"Sorry," Melissa told Krys, returning to the adjoining seat. "He's cautious. It's what Aidan pays him for."

Krys rolled down the sleeves of her brown sweater. The waiting room had to be at least ten degrees colder than the exam rooms. "It's OK. I know what Aidan pays him for," she said. "I know he's a…"

She couldn't bring herself to say *familiar*. It sounded too stupid. "I know you're both blood donors."

Melissa gave her a steady look and leaned back in her chair. "I can tell by your voice you don't approve. But don't judge what you don't understand. I know how it must look, but you're wrong."

Krys hated to admit how much the blood thing bothered her. She'd managed to ignore it when she was with Aidan, but even he'd told her he wasn't just a man with fangs. "Explain it to me. I don't understand why you stay if you're really given the choice of leaving." She swiveled sideways in her chair, facing Melissa. "Mark told me about his background. I mean, the drugs and all. I get it that Aidan helped him, but letting one of them…" She waved her hand in the air, not sure what to say. *Suck your blood* sounded too Bela Lugosi.

"Feed?" Melissa said, laughing. "You can say it. Mark's a substitute feeder, just when he's needed. But I'm Aidan's familiar. Think of it this way—he has to feed to stay alive, just like the rest of us. Just a different diet, that's all."

She looked at the floor, brows drawn together. "How to explain…I care about Aidan and want to do that for him, and it's pleasurable for me. In return, Mark and I have good jobs, good lives. We don't have to worry about money or insurance or anything except living our lives and being happy."

"But what about kids? Don't you and Mark want children?"

"Mel can't have children." Krys jumped at the deep voice that seemed to come out of nowhere, and her heart rate kicked up a gear. Aidan stood behind her, wearing a black sweater that made him look downright ethereal. His eyes were an icier shade of blue than usual. "But if she and Mark decide they want to adopt a child and move somewhere else, I wouldn't stop them. I'd really miss them, though."

"We don't want to go anywhere." Melissa smiled at him. "And you look like you need some breakfast."

Krys shook her head. She understood the attraction to this place, the sense of belonging, maybe even the feeling of being needed. But to trade your freedom for security, to wonder always if you were only here because your blood had the right components or you'd been brainwashed...

"Earth to Krys."

She blinked at Melissa.

"Come on, I want you to see something."

Krys frowned and followed Melissa out of the waiting area and down the hallway to a room she hadn't noticed on her clinic tour. It was the size of an exam room, but instead of the steel table and small writing desk and cabinet, there was an overstuffed leather love seat, an armchair, a couple of fluffy rugs. It looked more like a small living room.

"What is it?"

Aidan had followed them into the room and closed the door behind him. He sat on the love seat next to Melissa. He motioned Krys toward the facing chair. "I'm not sure this is a good idea, but Mel does, so I'll play along." His expression was indecipherable, but he'd tensed his shoulders and was drumming his fingers on the arm of the love seat. Humanlike fidgeting he didn't seem to be aware of.

With her eyes on Krys, Melissa pushed up the right sleeve of her scrubs, and then held her arm out in front of Aidan. He gripped her wrist loosely with one hand and placed the other at her elbow.

Oh. My. God. He's going to... "Oh no," Krys said, standing. "I don't want to watch this."

"Sit down." Melissa's sharp voice and defiant expression stopped her. "If you're going to judge us, at least see what you're judging."

Krys wrapped her arms around her middle and looked at Melissa, who'd been nothing but kind to her, and who seemed to think this was important. She slowly lowered herself back into the chair.

Aidan watched the exchange in silence, still holding Melissa's arm. Now he raised it to his lips and kissed the inside of her wrist, his eyes on Krys.

He's so damned beautiful. She chastised herself for the thought as he closed his eyes, slowly running his lips from Melissa's wrist to the bend in her arm. There, over the big vein, he licked once and sank his fangs into the delicate skin.

Melissa flinched, then relaxed against Aidan's shoulder as he pulled at her arm. Was he drawing blood through the fangs or just sucking on the wounds they'd made? Krys thought the latter.

Suddenly, his eyes opened to watch her. As he continued to feed, his gaze softened and his irises deepened from arctic ice to a clear, rich blue. Melissa leaned into his shoulder and watched her as well, a lazy smile on her face.

That should be me. Krys took a gulp of air and clutched the arms of the chair. She closed her eyes, fighting the urge to tell him to stop. She should be afraid or grossed out, damn it, but she wasn't. She was jealous. She wanted to be the one who brought that look to his face. She also wanted to jerk those thoughts out of her head like so many strains of bacteria, throw them on a slide, and figure out where they came from. Of all the things she could be feeling now, jealousy was the most wrongheaded.

It seemed like forever before Aidan withdrew, pulling Melissa into a hug. She leaned against his shoulder for a few moments and he relaxed against the back of the loveseat, both of them looking satiated. What had Melissa gotten out of it? It was one of the most sensual things Krys had ever seen, but would it be the same if he fed from *her*? And didn't Mark resent Melissa's experiencing this kind of intimacy with another man?

"Well, you haven't run screaming from the room." Aidan watched her from beneath lowered lids. His voice sounded rougher and his skin had lost its pallor.

They continued to look at each other, him silent and calm, her mind swirling. How could she want that to be her? Why had he never tried to feed from her? Did he not want her?

"Oh boy, I feel like a third wheel," Melissa laughed, looking from Aidan to Krys and back. She stretched and stood, pulling the sleeve of her scrubs down and heading for the door. "I'll call the two guys who were hurt tonight, just to see if they're OK."

She turned back to Krys, who couldn't seem to find her tongue. "I'll find you if they seem to be having any problems."

Krys nodded, still mute.

❋CHAPTER 21❋

Aidan continued to study Krys as Melissa's footsteps faded. She'd surprised him by sitting there quietly and watching him feed, but then again, the woman constantly surprised him. He'd felt the flare of heat between them, too. Did that mean she'd let him feed from her? He shifted in his seat. Just the idea of it made him hard, and he ached to be inside her wet heat again. To claim her.

But he had to do this right. He had to get a grip, keep his distance, and give her some space.

"You hungry?" he asked on impulse. *Yeah, that's keeping your distance.*

Krys's eyes widened, and he chuckled.

"Don't worry. I was thinking about something like barbecue."

She covered her face with her hands and shook her head. "I thought you...God, how silly. You mean I can actually go somewhere besides my little cell and eat?"

She hadn't said it in a sarcastic way, which made it sting all the more. But as long as he kept her in a locked basement, calling it a suite was like putting lipstick on a pig, as Mirren would say. You could doll it up, but it was still a pig.

He got to his feet. "Let's go to dinner, then."

"But you don't eat, do you? Food, I mean?" She looked sexy as hell when she was trying to figure him out, her dark eyes warm, a tiny wrinkle of a frown between her brows that sent an ache straight through him.

"I don't eat solid food anymore, but I can watch you eat and have a glass of wine. I do drink occasionally." He paused for a couple of beats. "I prefer red wine, of course."

Krys began laughing. The sound was full-throated, strong, and infectious. Unafraid.

He inhaled the scent of her hair, the rhythm of her heartbeat, the heat of her.

She took his outstretched hand and let him pull her from the chair, but she eased her hand away as they reentered the hospital corridor.

Mark was leaning on the front counter talking to Melissa, and they turned as Aidan and Krys approached.

Mark cocked an eyebrow. "Ready for a report on the fire, boss?"

"I got the highlights from Will already. We're going down to Clyde's. Meet the lieutenants at Mirren's about three and we'll strategize." He narrowed his eyes at Mark, daring him to comment.

Mark grinned. "You kids have fun."

Aidan shook his head as he held the front door open for Krys and she walked outside ahead of him. "Mark's a funny guy."

He'd walked past her and taken the first two steps before realizing that she wasn't following. She remained just outside the clinic door with her eyes closed, breathing deeply, the way she'd done when she finally hit fresh air the night before.

He wanted to comfort her, to wrap his arms around her, and tell her he'd take her home, that he was sorry he'd kept her cooped up. But the fire today showed once again how much his people needed her, and he didn't trust her to stay on her own. She was too confused about how she felt. He was pretty damned confused himself.

Aidan and Krys entered Clyde's shortly after six, prime dining hour for Penton's humans. Most tables were full. The smell of smoked meats hit them in a wave at the door, and Krys groaned in appreciation. He could still enjoy the aroma, himself: the smoky richness of the charred pork, the vinegar-laced tang of the barbecue sauce, the onions. But the undercurrents of blood and pheromones were even more enticing. And riding over it all, the delicate floral scent of the woman beside him.

The clatter of the crowd dimmed when they entered. Aidan grimaced. Penton's busybodies would be getting enough fodder to keep them buzzing for days.

Behind the grill, up to his neck in pork ribs, sauce, and smoke, even old Clyde—one of the few remaining original Penton residents, who'd been surprisingly circumspect about the existence of vampires—paused to give Krys a careful once-over.

She smoothed her hair, tugged on the hem of her sweater, turned an enticing shade of pink.

"They just want a look at you," he murmured as they crossed the dining room to claim a table against the far wall. "We don't get that many new people here."

Red oilcloth topped the random scattering of wooden tables. Most seated four or eight but Aidan picked one of the two-seaters along the dark-paneled wall. Small punched-tin containers on each table held votives that gave the room an intimate ambience.

"They aren't looking at me because I'm the new doctor," Krys hissed, jerking out a chair and sitting down even as he reached to pull it out for her. "They're looking at me because I came in here with you, their..."

She ran out of words and frowned at him as he sat opposite her. "What do they call you? Mayor? King? Dictator? Vampire Lord? Most eligible bachelor?" She looked part amused, part exasperated, a smile turning up one corner of her mouth.

Aidan laughed, pulled a menu from its spot behind the napkin holder, and handed it to her. "I probably don't want to know what they call me. Mirren and I are the strongest here, although not the oldest. A vampire community is called a *scathe*, and I'm the master of the scathe. But as to what the people call me?" He shrugged. "I'm listed as mayor in the official directories and any kind of paperwork that has to be filed with the state. Guess that works as well as anything."

A plump young woman with bright red hair and a face full of freckles bounded up with a small notepad. "Hi, Mr. Murphy," she said, green eyes shiny. "And you're Dr. Harris? Everyone's been wondering when we'd get to meet you. Welcome to Penton."

Krys nodded, smiling. No harm in letting them think she'd come here on her own.

Aidan took over the introductions. "Krys, this is Kathleen. She's been in Penton, what, about six months now?"

The girl beamed. "Wow, I mean, I can't believe you remember me."

"Of course I do." He made a point to know everyone, or at least to which of his scathe members each human was bonded or related. He remembered Kathleen because, at twenty-one, she was at the cusp of what he considered too young to join the community, and he was keeping an eye on how well she assimilated. Her older sister was the mate of a scathe member, however, and they had made a case to bring her with them to Penton. She'd been hanging with a bad crowd and headed for trouble, and there were no other family members.

Aidan ordered a glass of whiskey from Kathleen and wished she weren't acting so damned giddy. It made him feel like a jerk—or a mob boss.

Krys picked out a beer and a plate of chopped pork barbecue. "Does it bother you to be around food?" she asked. "It smells amazing in here, and you can't have any. Or can you?"

He smiled. "No, our systems won't tolerate solid food, but the smells don't bother me anymore," he said. "A lot of my kind can't tolerate them, but those of us who've chosen to live among humans instead of isolated in our own society still enjoy them. And when we feed, we get a hint of whatever our fam has eaten."

Kathleen brought their drinks, and Krys took a sip of her beer. "You said you and Mirren were the strongest but not the oldest. How old are you? I asked the man who came by early this morning but he never answered me."

Bloody hell. Aidan returned his glass to the table with a thump. "What man?"

"Lorenzo something? He said he was with the council...no, that wasn't it. Tribunal." Krys opened her mouth to say something else but seemed to change her mind. She studiously began peeling the label off her bottle of Corona.

She was hiding something. Aidan's skin crawled at the thought of Renz alone with her.

He watched her a few seconds. "What aren't you telling me? Did he touch you?"

She glanced up at him quickly. "He didn't hurt me. He said he might be able to explain better why you brought me here."

Damn it. He should have considered this possibility and stuck Renz somewhere else, but, honestly, he hadn't expected Renz to have much interest in a human. Aidan clenched his jaw. "What did he say?"

Krys paused for a moment too long. "Nothing, really."

Reaching across the table, Aidan rested his hand on hers, stopping her paper-shredding. "What did he do to you?"

She stared at his hand on hers, and then took a deep breath. "It was nothing. I don't want to cause any problems."

"Answer me." The words came out harsher than he'd intended, so he softened his voice. "Tell me, Krys."

She looked up at him, her dark eyes wary. "He just scared me a little. He...I thought for a minute he was about to, well, uh..." She blushed, formed her fingers into a V and stabbed them into her neck, mimicking fangs. "But he just got really close for a few seconds, and then said you should bond me to protect me from people like him. What does that mean, exactly?"

Aidan forced himself to pick up his glass, take a sip of whiskey, and get a grip on his anger. Renz should never have touched her.

"Aidan?" Krys's eyebrows knit in a look of worry. "I'm sorry. I shouldn't have mentioned it. He didn't hurt me, really."

He struggled to make his voice sound light, unconcerned, when he really wanted to bond her immediately so no one else could go near her. "You have nothing to apologize for. Renz had no business in your room, much less getting that close. I'd never have put him in one of the suites if I thought it would put you in danger. If anything, I owe *you* an apology." The apologies he owed her were stacking up fast.

Krys narrowed her eyes, studying him. "What does bonding mean, exactly? How would it have made a difference?"

Kathleen arrived with the food, and Aidan waited till she'd weaved her way between the tables to take another order before he answered. "It's a small blood exchange, basically, with me or one of my scathe. Every human in Penton is bonded to a member of the scathe. If you're bonded, no vampire outside the scathe can feed from you—I've never heard a good explanation as to why. Some metaphysical vampire shit."

"Blood *exchange?* No thanks." Krys wrinkled her nose. "I don't have to, do I?"

Aidan laughed. "Don't worry. Renz has gone back to New York. Left just after sunset."

Krys picked at her barbecue, shoving the coleslaw off to the side. "Sometimes when you talk, I hear a trace of an accent... British, maybe?"

Aidan feigned a look of horror and fell easily into a heavy Irish brogue. "My ancestors would be hanging you from the nearest tree should they hear you sayin' that, they would." He smiled. "I grew up in Ireland. County Cork. But I haven't lived there in many, many years."

How much information should he give her? She'd surprised him with her adaptability so far. "As for one of your earlier questions, I was turned vampire during the Siege of Kinsale. Do you know it?"

She frowned and shook her head. "Sorry, I think I've heard of it but..." She stabbed a bite of pork with her fork and popped it into her mouth. "So, a vampire...one of them attacked you?" She paused and put her fork down. "I'm sorry. Maybe it's rude to ask that."

He shook his head. "Don't feel awkward about it. We are what we are, and it's been a long time. Go ahead and eat, and I'll bore you with my history."

He watched her till she took another bite, and then continued. "Kinsale was Ireland's last gasp at independence for many years before England took us over and stole our lands. Not that I'm biased."

"What year was that?" Krys asked.

"It was 1601. My brother Owen and I were in the infantry—really a fancy name for a bunch of ragtag farmers engaged in a winter march. Half of us were sick, and we all were starving. One night he and I left camp to forage for food. A stupid thing to do. We were attacked by a vampire whose scathe had come over from Spain with the soldiers sent to help the mighty cause of Irish independence. They'd been living in the countryside and preying on farmers and soldiers."

Aidan had been toying with his glass as he talked, but finally realized that Krys had quit eating and was staring at him, round-eyed.

"What?"

"You're telling me you're four hundred years old?"

"Four hundred and change, actually." Aidan laughed. "But—"

Something was wrong. He suddenly smelled hot electrical wiring, gasoline, and underneath that, Owen.

He stood quickly, knocking the chair over behind him, only vaguely aware of Krys's startled expression. "Everybody get out of here now!" he shouted. "Krys—door. Now!"

Puzzled faces turned toward him. Used to following his instructions, people began rising from their chairs. He grabbed the shoulders of the man at the next table and shoved him toward the exit, then turned to Krys, holding out his hand.

An explosion sent the front of the building flying outward and plumes of smoke into the room. Within seconds, the roof caved in, raining smoking wood, embers, and chaos.

Aidan had fallen beneath a piece of plaster from the ceiling. He shoved a big chunk of it away and struggled to his feet, looking around for Krys. He'd lost track of her, and visibility had dwindled to a couple of feet. Closing his eyes, he sent a quick mental call to Mirren and Will, and started scrabbling through the smoke and rubble, shouting for her. He unearthed the table where they'd been sitting. Its legs had collapsed, and he looked around frantically. Where the hell was she?

CHAPTER 22

One second, Krys had been trying to wrap her brain around anyone—or anything—being over four hundred years old. The next, she was surrounded by hell, or at least some Dickensian vision of hell, complete with smoke and sparks and the screams of the dying.

Her own clumsiness had saved her, at least so far. When Aidan jumped up and the first impact of the explosion hit, she'd moved her chair back too quickly and toppled over.

Then the ceiling caved, and she couldn't see anymore. The smoke and dust clogged her lungs, and every breath set off a spate of coughing. God, how many people had been in there? Could vampires be burned or crushed? Maybe not, but the humans could. She needed to find Aidan and get outside.

She dropped to her knees and scrambled in what she thought was the last direction she'd seen him. Someone tripped over her, and she backed against an overturned table as another chunk of debris fell. She had to get out of here.

She screamed as someone else stumbled over her, his white shirt and black pants barely identifiable beneath a layer of gray ash. The man turned to her and she froze at the pale, silvery brown eyes. She'd met him that first night—Will something.

"Where's Aidan?" he shouted. She shook her head.

"Shit. Come on." Will grabbed her arm and jerked her to her feet, hauling her through the scorched beams and falling soot faster than she would have thought possible. She tripped every few steps, and only his grip on her upper arm kept her upright and moving. She couldn't see a thing as she squinted against the smoke and pulled the neck of her sweater over her nose and mouth as a makeshift air filter.

Finally, they reached the front of the building, or what was left of it. People milled on the sidewalk, coughing, vomiting, lying on the pavement with injuries, sitting dazed and staring in shock.

"Are you all right?" Will still had a strong grip on her upper arm.

She rubbed grit from her eyes with her free hand, trying to clear her vision. "I lost track of Aidan when the ceiling caved in," she shouted over the din. "You have to find him."

Mark made his way through the crowd in time to hear her. "Aidan's still in there?"

"I'm going after him," Will said. "Maybe you and the doc can get things organized out here." Without waiting for an answer, he disappeared into the smoke.

Mark pulled out his cell phone and punched a number. "Aidan's cell is ringing but he isn't answering."

Krys looked through the haze at the restaurant. What would happen to them all if Aidan had been killed? She didn't know much about their organization, but it all seemed to revolve around him. She felt panic rising at the thought of losing him—not just for all of them but also for herself.

A familiar voice rumbled behind them, and Krys turned to find Mirren with storm clouds on his face.

"What the hell happened?" he bellowed. "Got a mental call from Aidan. Where is he? Where's Will?"

Mark was still on the phone, so Krys answered. "The restaurant exploded, and the ceiling caved." She tried to keep the panic out of her voice. "We can't find Aidan. Will's gone back in to look for him."

"Shite. Bloody effing hell." Mirren stalked through the smoke until she lost sight of him near the entrance.

She felt a hand on her shoulder, squeezing. "Will and Mirren will find him," Mark said. "Aidan's probably just trying to track down who did it."

Krys felt better knowing that Mirren was there. She didn't know much about Will, but she knew Mirren and Aidan were like family. The only thing she could do was help their people.

She took stock of the injuries, and saw Tim organizing volunteers to go into the building and bring out the injured. Just like triage drill. She could do this.

"We've got to get organized," she told Mark. "Is Melissa at the clinic?"

"She's at home since—"

"Call her," Krys interrupted. "Tell her to gather anything she can find that's easy to bring here. Portable oxygen tanks and masks, portable stretcher if you have one, blankets, sterile wipes, bandages..." She looked back at the building. A light, misty rain was dampening the fire, but she could see Will inside the door, shoving people out, and none too gently. The heavy, cold air smelled of wood smoke and burned wiring. Where was Aidan?

Mark had been talking to Melissa, but looked up when a flash of light from a snapping electrical line cut through the mist. "Just get here," he said, and ended the call. "I've got to make sure someone cuts power to this block before another fire starts, then I'm going to the old armory to get some generators and portable lights. When Mel gets here, let her know where I am." Within seconds he'd disappeared into the mist.

Krys shivered in the cold rain, staring after him, then she began wending her way through the dead and injured, pulling a jacket over someone, trying to ease panic, answering questions. All the while, she kept an eye on the entrance to the building.

Aidan had described his brother Owen as brutal. Was he the one behind this? Had he taken Aidan? Killed him? Her heart ached at the idea, and tears threatened to mingle with the rain wetting her cheeks.

Two figures lurched out of the building, and Krys squinted through the smoke and mist. Mirren and—she felt her breath whoosh out of her—Aidan was next to him, covered in soot and carrying someone.

Mirren pointed toward her, and Aidan changed directions, carrying the man she now recognized as Clyde, the owner of the restaurant. Clyde was dead. She could tell by the way his head and arms hung limply in Aidan's grip.

He laid the old man's body on a clear spot of ground in front of her, and she knelt and felt for a pulse, knowing there wasn't one.

"He's gone," Aidan said, his tone clipped and angry. "Are you OK?"

She nodded. "Mel is on her way with supplies. We'll treat whoever we can here and send the rest to the clinic." They stared at each other for a moment, just long enough for her to want to wrap her arms around him and calm the anger she felt radiating from his clenched fists and squared shoulders. She thought she saw longing flicker across his face before he looked away, toward the landscape of horror. "Do what you can for them."

"I will." She paused. "Aidan, are you OK?"

"No, but it's nothing a run-in with my brother won't cure." His eyes were hard when they turned back to look at her. "Stick with Mark and Mel—they'll take you back to the clinic. I'll try to see you before dawn."

Then he was gone again.

———

Four hours later Krys sat on the fender of a pickup parked across Main Street from what was left of Clyde's BBQ. She didn't remember the last time she'd been so tired. Her brown sweater was coated with equal parts blood and soot, and her hair hung in clumps from the misty rain. She fumbled in her jeans pockets for an elastic band to tie it back, but found only a napkin from the restaurant. She wiped her face with it and stuck it back in her pocket.

The street was empty now, and mostly dark. Only one portable light running on a generator remained, and Mark would be back to take that one away soon.

It was bad, but it could have been worse. She'd bandaged most of the injured and sent them home with minor wounds. Melissa had run a couple over to the clinic, and together they planned to spend the night keeping an eye on them. Fifteen were dead, all human. Three vampires had been badly burned, but Will had them taken to the sub-suites near Krys's room and would take care of them. Apparently they'd be in pain but would heal on their own given a little time.

She put her hands on her hips and stretched her back, trying to ease some of the tension. She knew she needed to get out of the damp cold, but she couldn't seem to drag herself to her feet.

A familiar voice cut through the mist and Krys searched out Mirren. He stood near the front of what was left of the restaurant, along with Aidan and Will. They were deep in conversation and hadn't spotted her.

Realization struck suddenly. She could leave. She was outside and alone for the first time since she'd been taken. What was she thinking?

Adrenaline energized her limbs. She *should* leave, shouldn't she? The patients at the hospital weren't in imminent danger and she was finally on her own. Her hesitation convinced her to go— she shouldn't *feel* any hesitation. If she got sucked into this place any deeper, came to care about these people any more, she'd never go. She'd never have her life back. Not that it was such a great life, but it was *hers*. Her choices, her decisions, her control.

Krys kept her eyes on Aidan and his guys as she slowly rose from the truck bumper and circled behind the vehicle. She edged in the opposite direction from them, crouching from shadow to shadow until she hit a side street, when she broke into a run for a few moments before spying the solid mass of the old mill a few blocks in front of her. If she could get behind the building she might find a place to get out of the rain and hide until daylight. It was only a few hours away now. The vampires would be down for the day, and she doubted any of the humans would care enough to look for her, especially after the explosion. She'd find her way to the state highway and hitch a ride. At least the temperature wasn't so low tonight. Forties, maybe.

Her slick-soled boots skidded on the wet sidewalk, but she managed to stay upright as she ran across the street that fronted the mill. To the left she could see what remained of the burned mill village houses silhouetted in the streetlights.

Aidan's face kept coming back to her. He'd be upset that she had run after promising to stay with them for a month, but he didn't understand how easy it would be for her to fall into life here, to be sucked into everything he offered. Or maybe he did understand, and that's why he wanted her to stay. But it wasn't right, was it?

As soon as she rounded the side of the mill, a hand clamped over her mouth and jerked her into the shadows against the brick wall. She struggled, but her head was pinned so tightly she couldn't move it, and the man's right arm slipped around her waist. Everything above the waist was immobilized. Not man. Vampire. No one else was this strong.

"One of Áodhán's little lambs has strayed from the fold." The man's voice was soft, right in her ear. She couldn't see his face, but he spoke in a heavy Irish accent. Aidan's brother, then. Had to be.

He slid his hand away from her mouth and down her neck. Scream or try to talk to him? She didn't want his hand over her mouth again, so she struggled to keep her voice even. "You're Owen?"

"I am, and if you know my name, then you do indeed know my brother." He lowered his mouth to her neck and inhaled, licked the skin below her ear, nuzzling her hair out of the way.

"Maybe not one of Áodhán's, after all. Could he really have let such a morsel go unbonded?" He laughed softly, and the coldness of it drove icicles of fear up Krys's back. "My little brother is getting careless. Or are you vaccinated?"

He wouldn't feed on her if she'd been vaccinated. "Yes," she whispered. "I got the pandemic vaccine."

"Yes? Well, let us check it out." He dipped his head and grazed a fang across the curve between her neck and shoulder, just enough to draw blood. She felt the roughness of his tongue as he licked the cut, then a groan of pleasure. "Such a pretty liar. Your blood is pure."

He twisted her around to face him, and she gasped at his eyes. Exactly like Aidan's, only so pale they were almost white. He was really hungry.

She thought of her experience with Renz. Stay calm. "I know you're angry at Aidan, but you did a lot of damage tonight already, and I'm of no importance to him. It won't gain you anything to hurt me." God, she had to keep breathing. Not show fear. How could she, though, when her heart was racing and she knew he could feel it?

Owen chuckled and ran a finger along her cheek, lowering his mouth to hers. "Oh, I wouldn't say you were unimportant, darlin'. Every unvaccinated human is important." She let him kiss her. Opened her mouth to his, trying to redirect his hunger. A fang pierced her lower lip and she flinched when he licked the blood.

"It would be a shame, really, not to take you back with me and enjoy your company a while. Our women are all used up." He smoothed her wet hair away from her face and then gripped her chin in one strong hand. She tried to look away but he caught her gaze. "You want to come with me, don't you?"

Part of her brain fought, but it was like a moth beating its wings against a gale. "Yes," she breathed. "I want to go with you. Please take me with you."

On some level, she knew she should be running from him, screaming—*something*. But she let him lead her along beside the dark mill and into the parking lot. The farther they walked, however, the more her brain broke through her mental fog and was able to send commands to her limbs. She eased a hand in her pocket and pulled out the napkin. One-handed, she ripped off bits of paper and dropped them along the way. If she could leave a trail for Aidan, maybe he'd find her. If he even realized that she was gone.

She struggled again as Owen pulled her into the woods behind the mill. "Coming out of it already? You must have a strong mind, love."

The beginnings of a scream were cut short when he back-handed her, and she felt her own teeth dig into her lip, drawing blood. He dragged her to her feet and pulled her deeper into the woods and into a clearing.

Fear made her heartbeat stutter and start, and she fought to slow her breathing and pull her panicking thoughts into a plan.

"I'm beginning to think you aren't worth the trouble, love." Owen jerked her against himself again. "I first thought I'd keep you for leverage, or for a more leisurely feed, or at least a good lay. But not if I have to enthrall you every five minutes."

She struggled to get out of his grasp, and got out a scream before he clamped a hand over her mouth again. "But I'm very hungry, and you're a pain in the arse," he said. "Your heart is sending all that sweet blood dancing through your veins, and I want it."

Krys couldn't gain purchase. He was too strong, one arm around her waist, the other forcing her head to the side and exposing her neck. All those veins and arteries. If he hit her carotid, she'd be dead in two minutes.

As he laid a line of kisses along her jawbone, tears mingled with the mist on her face and she cursed God and wondered why he'd even bothered to put her on this earth. She'd always been fighting to get away from something. From her dad, her hometown, and now from vampires, for pity's sake. She'd never found a place just to *be*. Maybe that's all life was, in the end—a struggle to run somewhere better until time ran out. But damn it, she wasn't ready to stop running.

Owen pulled back and caught her gaze, and she felt that familiar falling motion. "See, I'm being generous, love. I could've let you suffer," he whispered. "This way you'll enjoy it. Well, most of it."

He replaced his lips with his tongue, licking a long swath from ear to shoulder, and then he bit.

Krys's eyes watered at the sharp stab of pain. Then she felt waves of pleasure that caused her knees to buckle. *Oh my God.* She'd never felt anything like this mindless, blinding ecstasy. She didn't want it to stop. She hoped it never would.

She felt the pull of his mouth at her neck as if from a distance, and time became irrelevant. No past, no future. Only now, and him.

She didn't know how much time passed before alertness began seeping back in, before the pleasure morphed into pain, gradual at first, and then sharp. She felt her skin tear, felt teeth and tongue and sticky wetness. A rich smell laced with iron... then blackness.

CHAPTER 23

"We have thirty scathe members ready to search. You need more, we got more." Mirren paced the same square of sidewalk back and forth, one big study in walking anger.

"Should be enough," Aidan said. "Take half of them and comb the woods behind the mill. Make sure everyone's armed. Kill any of Owen's people you see. If you find him, bring him to me." He'd snap Owen's neck with his bare hands—shooting him would be too kind. Then he'd rip out his black heart, and the Tribunal could screw itself.

He turned to Will as Mirren headed out. "You take the other half and scatter them around town. Same instructions. I'm not worried about you being recognized because you're going to take out anyone who sees you. I want to talk to Hannah, and then I'm going to search the mill itself. What about our injured?"

"Fifteen humans dead. Only three of the scathe besides you were in the restaurant when it blew," Will said, wiping grime off his face with his sleeve. "I've got them on ice in one of the subrooms. Couple of days, they'll be fine. Your girl Krystal took care of the humans. She's still over—"

He looked down the block to where Clyde's old pickup was parked, across the street from the restaurant. "She was down there not long ago. Don't see her now."

"Shit." Aidan turned, scanning both sides of the street for any sign of Krys. He'd been frantic when the ceiling collapsed, torn between finding her, getting everybody out, and going after Owen. As soon as he'd seen Will push her out of the building, he'd decided to see how many he could rescue. His soon-to-be-dead brother had escaped.

He flipped open his cell, spoke quietly, closed it again.

"She's not at the clinic. How long since you saw her?"

"No more than ten minutes," Will said. "Think she ran?"

Would Krys leave? Hell, probably. Aidan was torn between fear for her and anger. He'd told her how dangerous it was. She'd seen what Owen had done to Mark. And she knew his brother was out there tonight. Even his own scathe members were pissed-off jumpy—they didn't know her yet and would assume that any unbonded female was Owen's.

"Get some feet on the streets," he told Will, checking the ammunition in the Colt that Mark had brought from the house. "I'll find Krys."

Damn it, he should have bonded her from the beginning. He'd been so consumed by his own guilt and lust that he had put her in danger.

He strode to Clyde's truck and stopped to see if he could scent which way she'd gone, but the wet streets and overwhelming odor of charred wood drowned out any clues. Where would she go?

Away from you. He looked back to where he'd been standing with Will and Mirren, and imagined her watching them, thinking about running. She'd head in the opposite direction. Toward the mill. Probably straight toward Owen.

He set out walking, but broke into a run as he rounded the corner and raced toward the mill. He thought he scented her once, but lost the trail. A cursory search of the mill's interior turned up nothing, and he walked out the back door. He stopped when he heard a noise. A scream? The sound had come from the woods, back in the area where Mirren had encountered the buckshot.

Halfway across the parking lot, he began seeing scraps of soggy paper on the ground. A line of them, leading toward the woods. *Good girl.*

He scented the blood, and began to run again. A rage he hadn't felt in centuries—since Abby—almost blinded him when he saw them. Owen feeding, Krys hanging in his arms like a bundle of rags.

A growl built in Aidan's throat and Owen raised his head, eyes at half-mast, blood covering his mouth and chin. His voice was raspy with it. "Want to share, Brother? There's still a bit left."

Aidan took a step closer, and Owen let Krys go. She crumpled in a heap on the ground, and Owen shoved her out of the way with his boot. "You want to fight over an unbonded human, Áodhán?" He unsheathed a short-handled knife from his belt.

"I don't have time for your shit." As much as he'd have liked the satisfaction of hearing Owen's neck snap, Krys had to come first. Aidan pulled the Colt from its shoulder holster and fired, aiming for Owen's heart.

"Fu—" Owen reacted quickly, the first bullet plowing into his shoulder as he dived for the ground, the second hitting a tree. He rolled to his feet and blended into the woods.

Aidan kept the gun aimed at the shadows, but the sounds of his brother's retreating footsteps had already grown faint.

He holstered the gun and knelt next to Krys, gathering her in his arms. When he stood, the sight of her ravaged neck and the scent of blood threw him off balance, and he swayed. He knew what he needed to do. Question was, did he have the strength?

"Owen has two fewer scathe members, thanks to...shite." Mirren emerged from the direction of the parking lot, a cut on one cheek starting to heal and knuckles that looked as if they'd just beaten the hell out of somebody who probably wasn't alive to tell about it. "Need help?"

Aidan had to choke out the words, his throat was so tight. "Have to stop the bleeding, but you've got to make sure I don't finish what Owen started." He had to lick the wound to close it, and do it without feeding. Otherwise she'd bleed out before they could get her to the clinic.

"I've got you. Do it."

He sat cross-legged on the ground, holding Krys in his arms. He tried not to look at her face as he turned her head to expose the neck and tried to find the source of the heaviest bleeding. God, the pig had *chewed* on her.

"Move faster. Here." Mirren handed him a fistful of balled-up flannel—his shirt.

Aidan nodded, took the soft fabric, and pressed it against Krys's neck, blotting away the heaviest blood. He could see the wounds better, the original punctures and then the vertical gashes.

He closed his eyes and prayed for strength. He didn't know if vampires were damned, as the legends claimed, or if they were just a peculiar abomination of God's greatest creation. *But if there's anyone listening, I could use some help here.*

He lowered his mouth to the wounds, and began to lap at them lightly with his tongue, hoping his saliva would stanch the bleeding and buy her some time. He shuddered at the sweetness of it, of her, and fought the desire to drink. His head ached with the hunger it awakened.

"Aidan." Mirren touched his shoulder after a few moments too long. Then he grabbed a handful of his hair and jerked his head back. "Aidan!"

He closed his eyes and rolled his head to face the night sky. "Take her."

❋CHAPTER 24❋

Melissa had been pacing the clinic lobby for forty-five minutes, since Aidan's call. Krys had run. Melissa wasn't surprised; she'd watched Krys's face earlier tonight as Aidan fed, and had seen the shock register as the woman acknowledged her own jealousy.

Krys wasn't running from them, or even from Aidan. She was running from her own feelings. Melissa recognized the symptoms; she'd trotted down that road a few times herself.

Mirren's big Bronco lurched to a halt outside the front entrance, and Melissa pulled the door open as he barreled through, carrying Krys. Aidan trailed close behind, looking pale and shaky.

"We need blood," Aidan said as they passed her. "At least a couple of pints, to start. Bring it to the small office."

Melissa hurried for the blood and IV equipment, and ran into Mark leaving one of the patient rooms. He joined her as they rushed back to the smaller clinic office where Krys had watched Aidan feed a few hours earlier.

By the time they got there, Mirren had laid Krys on the sofa, and both he and Aidan were staring at her, immobile.

"Make yourselves useful," Melissa snapped. "Mirren, bring me some blankets from the supply room—she's freezing. Aidan, go down to her suite and bring up dry clothes. Something loose and warm." She turned to Mark. "Run to the house, heat up some soup or broth, and bring it back. We've got to warm her up."

Melissa readied the IV with the first pint of O negative and inserted the needle into Krys's vein. The tube from bag to arm streaked from clear to red as the transfusion began. The guys remained planted where they were, watching like oafs. She didn't think she'd ever seen the vampires look more human.

"Go!" she shouted, and their paralysis finally broke. Aidan headed toward the stairs to the sub-suites, and Mark and Mirren disappeared into the hallway.

Checking on Krys every few seconds, Melissa went into the office bathroom, got the hand towel off the rack, and soaked it with water as hot as the old plumbing could manage. When she went back into the office, Mirren stood next to the sofa with an armload of blankets. If he piled all those on Krys, she'd suffocate.

"Let's start with a couple of the thermals," Melissa said, pulling two gold waffle-weaves from the stack. Mirren set the others on the desk as Aidan's head poked through the hatch and he climbed out with an enormous pile of clothing.

Honestly—men. Especially vampire males. Useless except when it came to political maneuvering and muscle. Well, and sex, or so she'd heard.

"OK, thanks. Now, get out of here," she said. "Go catch whoever caused this."

Mirren grunted and went for the door, looking relieved.

Aidan folded his arms and gave her an obstinate glare. His pigheaded Irish farmer stare, as she called it behind his back. He couldn't be bullied when he got that look on his face, but he could be managed.

"Aidan," she said calmly, resting the hot towel on Krys's face and being rewarded with a moan and a stirring of limbs. Krys should be coming around soon, which meant they'd gotten to her in time. "I'm about to take the scissors on that desk and cut off her wet clothes. Do you want me to tell her you refused to leave the room and give her even that much privacy?"

Pigheaded and practical battled on his face for a few moments before practical won—as she had known it would.

He stopped to look down at Krys on his way to the door. She could read his face: anger, sadness, and—to her satisfaction—longing. If she could bring Krys around to admitting her feelings and keep Aidan from drowning in guilt, those two might have a chance. He'd deny it, but she knew that Aidan was lonely and she sensed the same from Krys. Plus, she'd seen them together, and Melissa wasn't above a little matchmaking.

———•———

Two hours before dawn, Aidan slumped in an armchair in Krys's room, where he'd been parked for the past four hours, cell phone to his ear. Damned thing might as well have been attached.

"No signs of Owen, but Will and I caught a couple of his scathe behind the mill," Mirren said. "I used some friendly persuasion on them, but they didn't give up anything we could use."

Aidan couldn't imagine his brother earning enough loyalty from his scathe members for them to withstand Mirren's persuasion. In his days as the Slayer, he'd specialized in slow dismemberment. Or so he'd heard.

He doubted Owen had told his makeshift scathe members that Matthias was behind him—the promise of feeding on Penton's humans would have been enough to keep them around these days.

So Owen had lost at least four scathe members tonight. How many could he have left?

"How's Krys?" Mirren asked. "Mel thought we got to her in time."

Aidan looked at her still form, dark hair spread over the pillow. Still pale, but looking a hell of a lot better than she had four hours ago. "Took more than two pints of blood, but she finally came 'round. She's sleeping now." He'd been tempted to erase her memories, fill her head with the suggestion that she'd had an accident. That skill was one of the perks of being a master vampire. But he was pretty sure that she'd rather remember what happened, no matter how ugly, than have him mess with her mind.

Mirren's voice jarred him back to business. "Tim says the fams want to take action. They're ready to go all vigilante and do a serious suntime hunt for Owen's scathe—they'll comb the whole county. You just need to say the word."

Fifty vampires, most of whom had joined his scathe precisely because they didn't want to spend their lives fighting and hunting prey. One hundred and twenty-five humans. The numbers were on his side if the fams hunted in daylight—Krys had been right about that. Owen couldn't have that many with him and keep them hidden this well, especially after tonight.

If something went wrong, though, none of the scathe would be around to help. But he had to be practical.

"OK, put together a plan for the day after tomorrow. I don't want them going out half-cocked and unorganized, and it's too close to dawn to plan tonight. Get the lieutenants together tomorrow after rising. Seven o'clock. My house."

Krys groaned and moved restlessly under the heavy quilts, riveting Aidan's attention back to her. He ended the call with Mirren and stuck the phone in his pocket. She'd begun moving an hour ago, which Melissa seemed to think was a good sign.

Melissa had been amazing. After she'd thrown them out of the room, she'd gotten Krys out of her wet clothes and into a sweater and flannel sweatpants before having him take her downstairs. Now Krys's color had returned, but she still looked so fragile lying there with the thick swathe of bandages on her neck.

He walked around the bed and eased himself down next to her, where he'd spent most of the last two hours. She was less restless when he held her, or at least he told himself so as he carefully stretched an arm across her and pulled her close. He'd done the one thing that he'd vowed never to do again. Make that two things. He'd let himself care too much, and he'd let her get hurt because of him.

He buried his face in her tangle of hair. He could still smell the rain, the blood, even goddamned Owen. But underneath it was Krys, and he would rip apart anyone who came near her again.

"Aidan?" Krys's voice was no more than a hint of a whisper.

"It's OK, *grádhág*. You're OK." *Beloved*. Where had that come from? He stroked her shoulder, and she turned to look at him through shuttered lids.

She blinked at him sleepily, and her voice sounded as if it had been mixed with gravel. "What happened?" Her eyes grew round as she remembered, and she tried to sit up. "Oh my God. Owen."

She reached for her throat and ran her hand along the thick layer of bandages.

"It's OK," he repeated, rubbing her arm and easing her back onto the pillow. "You're going to be fine. We found you in time and gave you a transfusion."

He waited for her to chastise him for not taking her to a hospital, but her mouth quirked. "You gave *me* blood?"

Smiling, he smoothed a curl away from her face as she closed her eyes. She was a freakin' miracle—making a joke when most people would be hysterical. "Yeah, imagine that."

He thought she'd gone back to sleep, but she spoke again. "I'm sorry I ran."

The words pierced him, and he buried his face in her hair again, his hand atop hers. She was apologizing? "I should have warned you about Owen more, made you understand how dangerous it is out there. You're more vulnerable than our people because you aren't bonded to any of us."

"I'm like a free-range chicken."

He pulled her closer to him and she settled against him with a sigh. How the hell could she joke? She was too good for him, for any of them, and he needed to get her out of here.

"It's almost dawn," he said. "I'll take you out of Penton tomorrow night, I promise. Back to Americus. Wherever you want to go."

He looked down to see her reaction but she'd fallen asleep. He kissed her cheek and pulled away from her. Could he do it?

Let her go, try to wipe her memories clean of him, and never see her again?

"Don't do it, Aidan." Melissa stood in the door—and obviously had been eavesdropping. "I've never seen you like this around anyone, and she feels the same way. If you take her back to Georgia, you're a damned fool."

"It's almost dawn. I'm out of here." Aidan looked at his fam sharply as he brushed past her. "Stay out of this, Mel. It's none of your business."

He stomped into the clinic parking lot and came up short. His car was still at the restaurant; he'd ridden here with Mirren. He pulled the phone from his pocket, and then shoved it back in. The walk might do him good; help flatten this screwed-up swirl of feelings.

His anger at Owen had lain dormant a long time. Out of sight, out of mind. Turned out it had just been festering. Seeing his brother with Krys had brought back all the old nightmares: Owen with Abby, her blood on his face, Aidan holding her while she died.

He'd reached the edge of his yard and circled to the greenhouse. Faint light from the street filtered through its retractable glass, illuminating the neat aisles and giving the flowers a luminescent glow.

What a joke. Another place for him to play at being human, when he'd seen the truth tonight. He wasn't any better than Owen was. He'd wanted to hold Krys in his arms and drain every bit of blood from her. Would he have been able to stop had Mirren not been there? Now she was going to pull through and he wanted to lock her up where no one but him could ever touch her again. The only way he knew to keep her safe was to get her away from Penton, and away from him. If he loved her—and after tonight, he realized that he did love her, God help him—he'd do that for her.

He ran his hand along the smooth wooden shelves that held the plants, stopping at the night-blooming hibiscus, the deep burgundy throats of the blooms paling to almost white at the edges. Like the eyes of a hungry vampire. He plucked a bloom from the plant and crushed it in his fist, and then toppled the whole shelf with a satisfying crash of broken glass and bent metal shelving.

"Make you feel better, did it?"

Aidan whirled to see Mirren's bulk shadowed in the green-house door.

"Yeah, as a matter of fact. It did."

He reached for another shelf and sent pots and plants into a heap of blooms and dirt, and reached for another, then another.

The world spun, and he found himself on his belly, one of Mirren's big boots on the small of his back, a hand the size of a dinner plate clamped on the back of his head, pressing his face into the dirt.

"I don't like where you're headed, A. I'm not letting you go there. You hear me?"

Aidan pushed himself up with his hands, only to have Mirren put more weight on the foot and shove him back down.

"Remember where and when you met the famous Slayer?"

Aidan tried to shut him out, but couldn't help remembering Mirren thinner even than Owen's skinny wraiths, starving him-self, making himself too weak to be the Tribunal's paid killer after he decided that the people he worked for were bigger mon-sters than the ones he was being told to kill. Aidan had heard tall tales of a fanged man living in the woods outside Atlanta during the Civil War, daring soldiers to shoot him, occasionally killing one. He'd managed to track him down, helped him fake his death, and kept him off the Tribunal's radar. Until now.

The hand on his head pressed harder, and Aidan had to clamp his lips shut to avoid eating dirt.

"Tell me you remember."

"Mmmph."

The pressure on his neck and back disappeared, and Aidan sat up, spitting soil. "Not the same, Mirren. I'm not suicidal."

"The hell you're not. You've built Penton into somewhere we can all have a life, not just an eternity of the same old empty shit. You get your ass killed, that's fine, my friend. But stop and think what's going to happen to everybody else who's here."

"You could run the town."

"You're right, Aidan. I could." He turned and walked toward the door. "But I won't."

CHAPTER 25

K rys burrowed under the quilts and cracked one eye open. She pulled her wrist in front of her face to check the time but her watch was gone. Had she forgotten to put it on?

She fought off a panic attack as it all came back to her. Taking deep breaths, she reached a tentative hand to her neck and flinched at the shot of pain when she touched the bandages. She hadn't dreamed it. Aidan's brother had attacked her. A vampire had attacked her. *And another one saved me.*

She vaguely remembered Owen dropping her on the ground, then Aidan lying on the bed next to her before she'd fallen asleep. Everything else was a blur.

The bed creaked as she threw the covers back and sat up, bracing herself with her hands until her head quit spinning. She felt fuzzy and heavy-limbed. How much blood had she lost? A bandage circled her forearm, and she pulled it off to see the needle mark. She vaguely remembered Melissa giving her blood.

Holding onto the furniture for balance, Krys beat a slow path to the bathroom. A digital clock had been placed on the dresser since the last time she'd been here. Three p.m. Holy cow. She'd been out at least fourteen hours.

She used the bathroom, and then stopped in front of the dressing table mirror. Framed by her dark hair, her face looked almost translucent. *I look more like a vampire than the vampires do.*

Splashing her face with warm water helped. Her brain started working better, and she felt as though she'd only had a few beers instead of a case of Irish whiskey.

She took a shower, careful to keep the bandages on her neck dry and still wash her hair—no easy task. Bits of dried blood were caked in her scalp, smeared across her shoulders, even on her hands. She scrubbed so hard her skin burned under the water, but she wanted all traces of Owen gone.

She pulled on a loose sweatshirt and jeans, brushed the tangles from her hair, and went back to wait for Aidan. She started the fire and sank into the sofa, leaning against the back cushions and concentrating on her breathing. No thoughts of Owen—her only focus was on the one decision she'd come to during her periods of waking and sleeping. Aidan wouldn't like it, but she would insist.

At six, the knock at her door set her heart racing, but her first thought when she opened the door was how exhausted he looked. She wanted to help him but his problems were far beyond her abilities. She'd been naïve to think she could do anything more than be there for him.

His expression brightened as he scanned her face. "You're looking really good after what you went through last night. You scared me." He sat beside her on the sofa and pulled the bandage away from her neck, wincing at her hiss of pain. "Sorry. It's healing fast, though. It'll heal better without the bandage."

"Uh, doctor here. Remember?"

He smiled. "Right. You would know that."

She finished pulling the bandage off and tossed it on the coffee table, running her fingers along the wounds that had begun to scab. "It's healing a lot faster than it should, actually. Did you do something? Your saliva has a clotting agent in it, right? My memories are fuzzy."

He nodded. "I got the bleeding stopped till we could get you to the clinic. You remember getting blood?"

She squinted. "Sorta. How much did I need?"

He held up two fingers. "Mel's going to take a look at your neck in a little while."

Krys had vague memories of Melissa helping clean her up and get her undressed. "I like Melissa," she said. "She's lonely, you know."

"I know." Aidan fidgeted with the cuff of his shirt, and Krys had the feeling he was trying to scrounge up the courage to say something.

"What is it?"

He leaned back on the sofa and looked at her. "Do you remember what I told you this morning before I left? That I'd take you home tonight?"

Krys stared at him. "Home?" Her heart starting doing that thumpy thing again and she wasn't sure if it was out of fear or happiness or sadness. *Not true. Own your feelings. Admit what it is.*

"Back to Georgia, or wherever you want to go." His jaw tightened and he looked at the fire. "I shouldn't have kept you here. I can't stand it that Owen got within a mile of you."

Hands splayed on her knees, Krys frowned and nodded. Now that he'd said it, she wasn't surprised. She should have realized he'd find a way to blame himself. Well, she didn't want his guilt, and she didn't want to leave him. There. She'd owned it.

She put a hand on his arm. "Look, I'm not stupid. If I'd thought about it instead of bolting, I'd have realized it wasn't safe. For God's sake, Owen had just burned down the restaurant and killed all those people. Don't hold yourself responsible because I acted like a fool."

He shook his head and started to speak, but she put her fingers over his lips. "Let me say this before I lose my nerve. I ran because I was afraid, because I realized I didn't *want* to leave, and it scared the crap out of me." She looked at the floor, afraid to see his expression.

"You didn't want to leave?" His voice was incredulous.

She shook her head and finally got the courage to look at him. "I want to stay here a while, like we agreed, only longer, maybe. I don't want to go home—I don't even know what home is anymore. Let me show Melissa how to run the clinic better and we'll see how things go." She held her breath, waiting for his reaction. But she'd made her decision. If he drove her away, she'd just come back.

Aidan was quiet for a long time, and she steeled herself for him to tell her to pack her bags. The irony of the whole situation wasn't lost on her.

"You've surprised me," he said finally. "I don't get surprised very often."

"Well, I'm going to surprise you again." OK, this was it. "I promise to be careful, but if Owen grabs me again, I don't want him being able to feed from me and make me think I want it."

Aidan frowned. "I don't understand."

Damn if he wasn't going to make her ask for it. "When he was feeding from me at first, all I could think was how good it felt, how I didn't want him to stop, even though another part of my mind realized that he was going to kill me. I didn't *care* if he killed me, as long as he didn't stop." Krys crossed her arms, anger flaring at the memory. "If someone kills me, fine. But I'll be damned if they should make me think I want it. You need to bond me."

Aidan grew very still, very vampirelike.

When he didn't say anything, she gritted her teeth and slid closer to him. "Look, I want to stay here a while, and this is the best way to keep me safe. It's not that big a deal, right? I want this."

Still he didn't answer, and she shivered at the icy cast that had come over his eyes.

"You're hungry," she said. "Your eyes always turn light like that when you're hungry."

He gave her a small smile, a slight up-curve of the edges of his mouth. "There are all types of hunger, Krys."

Heat crept up her face, and she tried to slow her racing heartbeat without much success. She cleared her throat, determined to plow through this awkwardness that she'd started. "Bonding," she said. "Does it involve, uh, you know." She waved her hands in the air. "Sex?" She kind of hoped it did.

Again that hint of a smile. "Not unless we want it to," he said, his eyes still more icy than blue. "A regular bonding between a vampire and a familiar is a simple blood exchange. I take yours, and you take mine."

Before she could catch herself, Krys wrinkled her nose at the words *blood exchange.*

Aidan smiled. "You probably won't find it as horrible as you think, or so I'm told. But I'm not sure it's a good idea."

He might as well have slapped her.

"If you find it objectionable, then get someone else to bond me to. If you want me to stay here, you'll do this." The longer he remained quiet, the more stupid she felt.

Aidan stood up and reached out a hand. She looked at it for a few seconds and then stood on her own. She didn't need his help. "Never mind. I'll talk to Mirren." Like Mirren was going to do anything without Aidan's OK.

He made an exasperated noise that sounded like an honest-to-God growl. "No one else is going to touch you—*ever*. You got that?"

Her heart flip-flopped at the caveman thing. Who knew? After spending a lifetime trying not to be controlled by anyone, that little sound of possessiveness filled her with a desire so fierce that she clenched her fists to keep her hands from touching him.

He stroked a thumb over her cheek, and then slipped an arm around her waist, pulling her body against his. She thought he was going to bite her, and steeled herself for the stab of pain. Instead, he brushed his lips over hers, bringing a flash of memory, of pale blue eyes and lighter hair. She willed Owen's face out of her mind.

Aidan's kiss was gentle, tentative at first. He nipped lightly at her lower lip, and she opened her mouth to him, then slid her arms around his neck and grabbed a handful of that beautiful, thick hair.

He pulled away from the kiss, smoothing her damp curls away from her face. "Are you sure about this?"

She nodded, and he pulled her toward the sofa.

"No." She walked toward the bed instead, trying not to think about what she was about to do, and she didn't just mean the blood exchange. "Let's do the bonding here. I want you to replace the memories of him in my head, to remind me what it really feels like to want someone."

Aidan's eyes paled again as he stretched out beside her on top of the quilt. She reached for him, pulling him into another kiss. He ran a hand down her arm and then pulled it to his lips, kissing the back of her wrist and turning it over to expose the smooth skin of her forearm.

"No," she said again, and turned her head to expose the other side of her neck, opposite where Owen had fed. Aidan paused, and she thought he was going to refuse. But finally, slowly, he smoothed her hair away, running his lips from her mouth to her jawline and down to her neck.

She closed her eyes and bathed in the softness of it; his hands roaming over her stomach, her breasts; the soft fall of his hair on her cheek; the smell of sandalwood; and the heat of his mouth on her. His tongue swiped a spot below her ear and the sharp prick of his fangs caused her to flinch momentarily, but the pain was quickly replaced by an overwhelming pleasure and heat building in a spot nowhere near her neck. She was floating, tethered to earth only by the soft pull of his mouth, and she wasn't sure if she'd moaned aloud or only in her head.

It seemed no time had elapsed before he withdrew, leaving her empty and wanting. He rolled to his back, pulling her with him with one hand and reaching into his pocket with the other to pull out a small knife. Watching her with slightly unfocused eyes, he flicked it open and drew a short cut across the side of his own neck.

"Taste me." His whisper sent shivers dancing over her skin, and Krys tried not to think about what she was doing as she stretched her body across his and laid her lips lightly to the cut. The taste was sweet, salty, warm—not the hard metallic tang she expected. She drew on the cut and felt a sigh shudder through Aidan's body. She continued until he stopped her a minute later.

"I can't stop the bleeding like you can," she murmured. She felt drunk, in a good kind of way.

"Watch the cut." Even as he said the words, it slowly closed.

Krys began to move away, but Aidan held her next to him and turned his head to kiss her again. She didn't have to see the color of his eyes. She could feel his desire pressing against her. She'd never known one person could want another so badly. She had his blood in her veins; now she wanted that velvet hardness inside her as well.

He groaned and wrenched away from her suddenly. The band tying back his hair had gotten lost somewhere along the way, and as he sat up, he gazed back at her through a tangle of chestnut waves. She shivered at the feral look of need on his face.

"It's all right," she said, reaching for him. "I want you to stay."

He shook his head. "You don't understand. I can't make love to you again without it meaning something I can't ask of you. God, I know that doesn't make sense, but I can't...I have to go." He got up and walked to the door. He didn't look back.

What the hell had just happened?

Aidan heard Mark open the back door a half hour before dawn. He'd been holed up in his basement den, thinking. Melissa would have called it brooding.

He had plenty to brood about. After he'd left Krys, the lieutenants had gathered and decided to use her idea. Their fams would hunt during daylight hours, looking for Owen's hiding places—but only those who volunteered.

Most of his brooding was about Krys, though. Whatever screwed-up DNA formed the vampire bonding mind-set, it was screaming at him. And even if he wanted what it was selling, Krys had almost died last night. She might want to have sex with him, but mating was part of the deal for him now that he'd had her blood, and she had no idea what she'd be signing on for. To her it was as simple as making love or voicing a commitment. How did he explain that he couldn't touch her without wanting her, and that he couldn't have her without its being long-term? Really long-term. There were no one-night stands or short-term affairs for mated males.

As soon as she realized what it meant, she'd reject him the way Abby had. He couldn't do it again.

Head resting on the back of the sofa, Aidan shifted his gaze to the drop-staircase when it lowered and Mark's boots clattered downward.

Mark collapsed in a nearby recliner, pulling a beer from each pocket, tossing one to Aidan and popping the tab on his own. "So, guess you know Melissa made me come over here."

"Mel needs to get a hobby—one besides me." Aidan popped his own beer and took a sip. "Man, this stuff's foul."

"Whiskey snob."

They sat in silence, listening to the music.

"You need a happy meal before you go down for the day? I'm offering up a vein."

A pillow went flying at Mark's head hard enough to get an *oof* when it hit him, and Aidan laughed. Mark was a good friend. Smart, good instincts, and able to pull him out of his moods. "No, I'm good."

"Is Krys going to stay?"

Aidan took the pillow back and stuck it behind his head. Wasn't that the million-dollar question. "For a while, anyway. Says she wants to help Mel get the clinic up and running again. Make a database of treatments, shit like that. Good idea."

Mark nodded. "Yeah, Mel could handle a lot of the stuff we're likely to get, at least after this Owen problem goes away. She likes Krys, though. She'd really like her to stay."

Aidan didn't answer. They sat in silence for a few more minutes, till it was time for Aidan to crash.

"Find her a house," he said, getting to his feet and opening the hatch to his subbasement suite.

Mark blinked. "You serious?"

Aidan pulled the sweater over his head and threw it across the sofa arm. "She's bonded to me now, and God knows she gets what a mean-assed bastard Owen is. She might or might not stay, but it's gotta be her choice. Get her wheels back, too."

"Where you want her?"

Aidan shrugged. "Get the list of the renovated properties from Tim and find something she'd like. Better, take her to a few and let her pick."

He wanted her with a desperation that scared him. But not by force. Either she'd stay and accept this life, or she'd decide that it was too much and leave him. And he'd have to live with it.

❊ CHAPTER 26 ❊

Piss and dirt, sex and blood. Live in the first, pray for the
second. Life was turning out to be one cold bitch.

Owen leaned against the dirt wall in the underground
storm shelter. The remnants of his scathe—two older vampires
plus the girl, Sherry, and four half-used humans—had been living here since the mill village burned and Aidan's people had
begun combing through the caves. Hell, *live* was an exaggera-
tion, and calling this glorified bog hole a shelter was too kind.

Still, for all of his brother's dotted i's and crossed t's, Aidan
had missed this little corner of Penton. All it had taken was
tracking down a former resident, applying a little fangular pressure, and the sorry old redneck had spilled his guts. Some cotton mill boss had gotten all antsy about tornadoes and dug a
hidey-hole under the mill, complete with an entrance tunnel
from outside. Smelled like mud and mold, but at least it had a
couple of rooms in which they could spread out. Well, he could
spread out in one, and the rest could cram their sorry asses in
another.

A groan from the shadows made him smile. "Ready for another go-round, love?"

Lucy stared at him from the corner, her sweater in rags, arms and legs wrapped in silver chains. She shook a strand of hair out of her hunger-lightened eyes, which reflected equal parts fear and hatred in the light of the battery-operated lanterns.

He'd caught her leaving Aidan's house, the stupid bitch. Thought she could be a hero. Although she'd end up being more useful to him this way.

"You should've taken me out at the start, Lucy, or joined me for true. Now we're going to keep playing till you tell me something useful."

Owen picked up the silver dagger from the dirt floor and wiped the blade on his thigh with exaggerated slowness.

"You're going to kill me anyway." Lucy's voice sounded flat, but her eyes were riveted on the knife. "What's in it for me if I tell you anything?"

"There are worse things than death, love. For example, what would happen if I left you in this hole, wrapped in silver so you couldn't escape? You'd starve, of course, but you wouldn't die. You'd grow thin and shriveled till you were nothing but a pile of bones and a pair of hungry fangs. Helluva way to spend eternity, darlin'."

He'd spent two days carving into her skin with the silver blade, cutting figures and words in blood and letting her suffer till she healed. Hours of breaking fingers and letting her writhe till the bones knitted themselves. He'd borrowed the technique from the rumors about how bloody Mirren Kincaid used to work, before he got soft and joined the Penton fun house. Had to admit, it worked. Lucy finally looked worn out and scared.

He laughed at her wide-eyed stare. "Hadn't thought of that, had you? So tell me who I can get to sell Aidan out from the inside, and I can at least promise you'll really and truly die."

Sullen silence.

"Suit yourself, then." He twirled the knife so its silver blade reflected the light in flashes. "Shall we spell again? Maybe on that pretty face this time?"

She leaned against the dirt wall, sending a clump of damp earth rolling. "I still don't understand why you're so hell-bent on killing Aidan. I mean, why go to so much trouble after all these years?"

Owen pricked his palm with the tip of the knife, watching it heal, and then repeated the action. "Well, love, it's a matter of survival. I don't give a shit about Aidan, personally. In truth, he probably hates me worse than I hate him." Flick, bleed, heal.

"Then for God's sake, why?"

"Because I'm not ready to die at the hands of whoever's playing executioner for the Tribunal now. Got in a bit of trouble back in Dublin, enough for a death sentence—unless I get rid of Aidan. Then my death warrant disappears. It's quite the incentive."

"Oh my God." Lucy's eyes widened. "Aidan wondered if the Tribunal was backing you but he didn't think they'd actually do it. Why don't you just kill him if that's the whole point? I mean, you followed me to his house. You know where he lives."

"And what would be the fun of that, now?" Owen wiped his knife on his pants leg again. "Of course, now that I've told you all my secrets, you don't ever get to leave me, sweetheart." Pity he couldn't take her with him, keep her in silver chains for his own amusement. But it was another mouth to feed, and he was tired of playing the provider.

Lucy eyed the knife, and wet her lips with the tip of her tongue. "None of his lieutenants will flip on him, Owen. Doesn't matter what you do to me. I was your only shot."

He cocked his head. "Doesn't have to be a lieutenant, Lucy. Actually, the lowest of the low is better, less likely to be detected. Give me a human."

Lucy hung her head and mumbled something.

He crawled toward her, lifting her chin with the point of his knife and sending a trickle of pale blood dripping. "What did you say?"

She repeated a name.

❋CHAPTER 27❋

Mark showed up in place of the breakfast tray, all dressed up in a navy suit and striped tie. His unruly blond hair was even combed and in place.

Krys gave him a once-over. "Nice. Special occasion?"

"I have meetings for Aidan today, so I'm in business-manager mode," he said, grinning. "I clean up good, though, don't I? Just wanted to see if you'd join me for breakfast."

Breakfast? As in going out? Hell yes, although there had to be an agenda. "What's the catch?"

"No catch. I have a surprise for you."

Krys looked at him suspiciously, but grabbed her shoulder bag off the chair and followed him into the hallway. They made the trek from the subbasement to the basement, through the maze of crates, and climbed the vertical tunnel into the clinic administrative office without talking.

Krys clambered into the office and stopped at the sight of Tim, the volunteer fire chief and Mirren's fam, sitting at the desk. He was working on a laptop, his broad frame and big hands overpowering the small keyboard.

"Hi. There's not another fire, is there?"

He laughed. "No, I'm building the town today, not burning it down."

"And is there a lot of construction in Penton?" Krys thought she'd like Tim if she got to know him better—he was open and friendly, and seemed like a nice guy. She wondered why Mirren had both Tim and his wife as fams while Aidan only had Melissa.

Tim raised his eyebrows and grinned. "You'd be surprised."

Interesting. Krys knew she wasn't in the inner circle, and there was no reason for them to tell her things that she didn't need to know. *Shouldn't* know. The more she got involved in the goings-on of Penton, the more likely she'd do something stupid like sign on as a permanent resident. She'd been overcome with Aidan-itis last night, ready to hang her doctor's shingle and put up a picket fence. The morning had brought with it some common sense. She needed to go slowly and think about what she really wanted.

"You got a few minutes to look at some stuff I've pulled together for tonight?" Tim picked up a stack of papers and waved them at Mark.

He shook his head. "We're going for breakfast and then over to Mill Trace. But I'll stop by after that."

It was Tim's turn to look surprised. "Mill Trace, huh? Well, OK then." He studied Krys curiously. "Don't forget to come back for these."

They walked down the hallway toward the sunlight pouring through the glass front doors. It was so bright that Krys had to shield her eyes from it. She felt like a mole digging out of its hole into blinding, dazzling daylight. "So, what's at Mill Trace?"

Mark laughed. "Food first. Then the surprise."

Breakfast turned out to be a monstrous spread at the Penton Café, and Mill Trace a shady street full of early-twentieth-century houses, many with wraparound porches and balconies off their second floors. Very old South, with big yards and lots of mature shade trees. It would probably be beautiful in the summer with the green lawns and leafed-out branches.

"What do you think?" Mark maneuvered his silver Toyota along the street, finally ending in a cul-de-sac with three houses situated around the circle.

"I think it looks familiar." Krys looked around. "Wait, that's Aidan's house, isn't it? I recognize the greenhouse. And you live next door."

"Right—last time you came in the back way, from the clinic escape tunnel."

Krys took a better look at Aidan's house. She hadn't been able to tell much at night, plus they'd gotten distracted. Boy, had they ever.

It was a grand two-story home, painted a pristine white and fronted by tall shrubs that sheltered most of the columned porch from view. At least a dozen garden gnomes kept watch over the flower beds.

She looked at Mark, eyebrows raised. "He has garden gnomes?"

"He thinks they're funny. Buys them when he travels." Mark shrugged. "Vampires have really warped senses of humor."

Mark pointed past her out the passenger window at a neat house with a broad screened-in porch. "Mel and I live there. 'Course, she's at the clinic right now."

He pulled the car to a stop just past his house, killed the engine, and took the key from the ignition.

Krys glanced at the third house, a square white one-story with a pretty, arched entry leading onto the small porch. "Who lives—" She did a double take at the car in the driveway. The Dinosaur sat there, complete with its Georgia license plates and the small dent in the right rear bumper. She'd backed into an SUV in the Trader Joe's parking lot in Atlanta a week after she'd bought the thing and could never afford to get it fixed.

She turned to Mark, her mind full of questions. Had they given her car to someone? Were they letting her go? Why did letting her go feel more like sending her away, and how stupid was that?

Mark held out a key. "Your new house, or at least your house for as long as you want it. I'm having the rest of your stuff brought over this afternoon. Aidan wanted you to have the pick of a couple of places, so if you don't like it I can let you see more. But this really is the nicest one."

Krys stared at him for a split second before snatching the key out of his hand. She opened the car door but stopped as soon as she got out. She didn't know how to act, what to feel. Elation, fear, disbelief—they all scrambled for room in her brain. She wondered if people who'd been in prison felt this way when they finally were released and the prison doors closed behind them, nothing but freedom and an uncertain future on the horizon. Mark came up behind her, slipped an arm around her shoulders, and squeezed. "It's OK. Take your time."

This was silly. It was just a house, temporary quarters. The front door wasn't locked, and she stepped inside. Shining hardwood floors graced a large open space furnished as a combination living and dining area. A brick fireplace took up the right wall, and a door in the back led to a small hallway linking a kitchen, bathroom, and two well-furnished bedrooms. It was nicer than any place she'd ever lived. Ever. Her parents had lived on the poor side of Birmingham, and she'd been a broke student since leaving home. The sub-suite didn't count.

When Krys finished her tour of the house and returned to the living room, Mark had taken his suit jacket off and sat in one of the armchairs.

"Why?" she asked. "I mean, why do this?"

Mark looked at her for a few seconds before answering. "Sit down a minute."

He remained silent as she perched on the end of the sofa nearest him. "Aidan asked me to find you a house. I think he really cares about you and wants you to see what it's like to live here without being locked away. If you want to get in that ugly-ass green car and drive back to Americus, a lot of people will be disappointed, including me and Mel. And especially Aidan. But no one will stop you. All we ask is that you leave during day-light hours because it's safer right now, and let someone know you're going so we don't worry."

Wasn't this what she'd waited for, wanted? To be free? To go home?

Crappy apartment, a hospital job with long hours, pecking away at her debts for the next ten years or more, all the backbit-ing and status-climbing that went on in medicine.

As she was faced with the reality, her life back in Georgia looked sterile and empty and she desperately didn't want it any-more. No doubt about it; she'd become Patty Hearst.

✾CHAPTER 28✾

By twos and threes, the people of Penton gathered in the small community center auditorium filled with rows of folding chairs. Aidan sat on the edge of the dais while one of the fams adjusted the microphones.

He watched as Will and Mirren and Hannah worked the room, chatting with the other vamps and their friends. Creating community. It's why he and his scathe were there.

He nodded at Mark and Melissa as they entered the back door, then his eyes fixed on Krys. He hadn't thought what letting her live among the townspeople would mean, that he could just run into her anywhere.

Their eyes met for a few moments before she smiled and gave a sheepish wave. He had to stop himself from grinning. Damned mating instincts had his normally sluggish heart thumping as if he were human again. *What an idiot.*

"Got that mic ready?" He turned to Will, who handed him a live one. He took it and stood in the center of the dais, waiting a few seconds for the chatter to die down.

"Let's go ahead and get started," he said. "We have a few things the whole town needs to decide on, and this seemed the easiest way to get everybody together."

"You shoulda offered us a midnight snack," shouted a man in the back, and everyone laughed. Aidan squinted against the lights. It was Jerry Caden, the brother-in-law of a scathe member. He wore jeans that tucked under his substantial belly and a plaid flannel shirt that gapped to reveal a white undershirt. Jerry had been injured slightly in the mill village fire, and Aidan had been surprised he was participating. He'd never gotten involved in Penton society before, and Aidan had half expected him to leave town. Maybe he was finally settling in.

"Sorry about the snacks, but I don't think you're going to dry up and waste away anytime soon, Jerry," he said, and a wave of laughter rolled through the crowd.

Jerry tipped his baseball cap at Aidan, who held up his hands for everyone to stop the chatter.

"I don't have to tell you the situation with my brother's scathe has escalated." At his words, the whispers and fidgeting stilled. "Tim and his crew burned the mill village, as many of you know, but we came up empty. We got a few the night of the explosion at Clyde's. They're still out there, though, and we honestly don't know how many there are or where they are."

A young woman in the second row of chairs waved her arm—one of the scathe members. "Is it true Lucy went to their side, that they're going to know all our daysleep places?" A rustle went through the crowd like a breeze over a wheat field.

Aidan grimaced. He should have known that the rumor mill would be hard at work.

"I'll tell you what I know," he said, and waited for the noise to die down again. "Lucy has been seen with them. But the day before, she'd helped me fight them. I think she's trying to help us and won't give up our secrets, but we're working on a backup plan in case we're compromised. I can't say any more about that plan yet but I will as soon as I have specifics." If information about Omega got out too early, it would cause a panic, vampire and human alike.

He sat on the edge of the dais and went through the options. No one wanted to leave, and all the humans raised their hands and said they were willing to hunt.

He turned the mic over to Will, who began talking logistics—how many should hunt together, where they should go. Aidan scanned the room, gauging reactions. He saw creased brows, nervous foot-tapping, general restlessness—but no fear. Maybe this would work.

Then again, maybe not. His gaze came to rest on Hannah, who was sitting with her fam parents but staring into space, eyes wide and unseeing. She looked to be in a trance, which was when the visions came. Shit. He needed to get her out of there.

Aidan sent mental alerts to Mirren while Will continued to take questions. *Check out Hannah.*

Mirren leaned back in his seat, looking casually around the room until his eyes came to rest on the girl. *Bloody hell. Something's going down.*

Get her out of here and take her to my house. I'll break things up as soon as I can.

Mirren nodded, and then waited a few seconds before heading toward the back of the auditorium with his hands in his pockets. He skirted the room and reached Hannah, whose eyes were unfocused and wild. She jumped when he touched her on the shoulder. Then she nodded and took his hand. They exited the back door, arousing a few curious stares but nothing Aidan had to handle. Most Pentonites thought Hannah was just a cute kid who'd had the misfortune to be turned vampire at an early age.

The questions from the crowd were fizzling out, so Will handed the mic back to Aidan. "It sounds pretty clear that most of you favor a few daytime hunts before members of the scathe go in for a fight. Right?"

Scattered applause and shouts of agreement met his question. "You'll start tomorrow, then. Groups of three or more only. No solos. Stick together. See Tim to sign up on the schedule of places to look." Aidan paused as Mirren stepped inside the back door and nodded. His face was grim.

"Everybody head home now and stay in for the night," he said, keeping his expression neutral. "Don't go anywhere at night if you don't have to till this is over."

He was beginning to wonder if it would ever *be* over.

———•———

Krys followed Mark and Melissa to their car as everyone filed out of the community center. Signs for quilting classes, art projects, and community gardens covered the cinder-block walls. Typical small-town stuff. Well, except for the vampires. The only differences were a lack of kids and probably a dearth of red blood cells.

Mark had cranked the engine before she and Melissa got their doors closed. "Something's wrong," he said, peeling out of the lot and attracting a few curious glances.

"I know, but slow down," Melissa said, putting a hand on his arm. "Aidan won't want anybody following us."

Aidan's expression had changed during the meeting, and Krys knew it had something to do with Hannah. She'd been watching the girl during the meeting and she had looked one step short of a seizure.

"What do you think happened? Hannah got a vision or something?" she asked.

Melissa glanced back at her and nodded. "Aidan had Mirren take her out of there. They probably went to his house."

Krys saw Aidan as soon as Mark stopped the car in their driveway at Mill Trace. He was on his porch talking to Mirren, while Hannah sat on the front steps with her head on her knees. She and the Calverts walked over, with Mark charging ahead.

"You guys might not want to see this," Aidan said, not looking up.

They approached the porch anyway, until Melissa saw something that made her cry out and turn back to Mark. He took one step closer, and then he turned away, too, cursing.

Her doctor's instincts kicking in, Krys pushed past them, touching Hannah's bent head gently as she climbed the steps. A woman lay on the porch, and Krys fought an urge to avert her own gaze. Instead, she tried to absorb it from a clinical point of view.

The woman had been bound in a silver chain. A crazy road map of bloody cuts stretched across her face and chest, and a splintered femur burst through the black fabric of one pant leg. Definitely vampire—delicate fangs showed below her lips, which had been peeled back in obvious pain.

"Is she still alive?" Krys knelt next to the woman.

Aidan's face was grim. "Depends on what you consider alive. Technically. She'd eventually heal from all the physical damage but the mental..." He shook his head, jaw clenched.

The cuts looked odd, and Krys leaned over for a better look. Something granular glistened on the ribbons of red crisscrossing the woman's face. Krys stuck out a finger to pinch a bit in her fingers, but Mirren grabbed her arm.

"Some kind of acid," he said. "To make sure her face is scarred. We can't heal that."

Krys felt a chill run through her. What kind of monster would do this? In her head she heard the soft voice and Irish brogue of Owen Murphy. That's who'd do this.

"Her name is Lucy, isn't it?" She looked up at Aidan, and he nodded. The woman had been beautiful. Krys reached out and touched her face, avoiding the acid-laced cuts. "How do you know she's mentally damaged?"

"She was talking crazy when I got here," Mirren said. "Wild. Aidan did his trance number on her when he got here, till we decide what to do."

"There's no deciding. We know what we have to do." Aidan planted his back against the door facing and stared into the night. Krys wished she could comfort him.

"Well, shit." Boots thumped up the stairs and everyone moved back a step to make way for Will. "That's what Hannah saw tonight? I knew something was up." He knelt next to Lucy, looking at her with a detachment that the rest of them couldn't manage. Krys wondered at his background.

Aidan walked to the edge of the porch, looking out at the night, seemingly unaffected by the cold that had Krys shivering and Mark and Melissa huddled together. Krys moved to sit on the steps next to Hannah, instinctively putting an arm around the girl's thin shoulders. Hannah leaned into her, and Krys rested her chin on the girl's head, stroking her hair.

"Hannah, did you touch her to see if you could tell anything?" Aidan asked. "Is there any way you can find out if she told Owen about our safe spaces? Do you know if her mind will heal?"

The girl shook her head. "I'll try it now."

Krys frowned and tightened her arm around Hannah. Every instinct left over from her childhood screamed at her to protect the girl. "She's been through enough. Don't make her do this."

"She's a vampire, Krys, not a child," Aidan said, his voice soft. "Don't ever forget that. In some ways she's the most powerful of all of us."

Hannah pulled herself away from Krys and turned to look up the steps. Moving slowly, she climbed onto the porch and knelt next to Lucy, then took the woman's hand in hers and closed her eyes. She whimpered once and went still. Krys could see her eyes moving behind her closed lids.

They waited in silence. After a while Hannah removed her hand. "There's guilt inside her, but I can't tell why. Her mind is hard for me to read."

"Has her mind been broken?" Aidan looked at Hannah.

"I don't know."

Aidan closed his eyes and leaned against one of the porch columns. "If she's been mentally broken, she'll never come out of it. It'll never be safe for her to live here again. Plus, she's already been cut from the scathe. If we let her loose in another city, she could kill aimlessly or even lead problems back to Penton."

"I'll take care of it," Mirren said. He lifted Lucy, chains and all, and left the porch.

"Wait." Krys jumped up. "What do you mean you'll take care of it? You're not going to kill her before we know for sure she's not going to recover."

Mirren paused and looked at Aidan.

Krys appealed to him. "Please. Let me try to treat her. You can keep her in the chains until you know for sure." Krys saw his resolve waiver, and pressed. "Please."

She couldn't stand to see them put Lucy down like a rabid dog. Not without trying everything.

Hannah slipped one of her slender hands into Aidan's and leaned against him. He looked down at her and she nodded. "Fine. We'll try it for a couple of days. But not in one of our regular rooms and not at her house—she's too dangerous. Put her in one of the secure rooms beneath city hall. A scathe member needs to be with her all the time at night, and a human during daylight hours."

Will followed Mirren toward the cars, and then turned back to Aidan. "You realize they knew where to leave the body. Be careful."

Aidan nodded, and then looked at Krys. "Where are you living? Did Mark find you a place?"

She pointed to the house across the street. He blinked, gave Mark and Melissa a pointed look, and broke into a weary smile.

"Welcome to the neighborhood."

❋CHAPTER 29❋

*H*ome. Well, house, anyway. Krys sat in the middle of the living room floor of the house on Mill Trace and stared at the sunlight streaming through the plantation shutters. When she'd come in three hours ago, all her stuff from the room beneath the clinic had been packed in cardboard boxes and delivered, along with boxes of books and personal items from her apartment in Americus. Her two lives had merged, at least physically.

She'd been too overwhelmed by the night's events to think much about this new house of hers, but now she sat on the floor and pulled a box open. Who had touched her things, meager though they were? From what she knew of Aidan's power structure, she'd guess the job had fallen to Will or one of his fams. He seemed to be the all-around go-to guy in the organization, but Krys just couldn't get a feel for him. He'd been downright calculating when he looked at Lucy last night, but maybe they didn't like each other. He did seem devoted to Aidan.

Boy, he must think your life is pathetic. All she'd managed to accumulate since college was a little bit of cheap furniture, a few clothes, the Dinosaur, and a lot of debt. Now she had the clothes and the Dinosaur, and wasn't too worried about the debt. She'd gone way off the student-loan collectors' grid.

A knock at the front door jolted her out of her brain fog. She could see Melissa through the sidelight window, and smiled as she welcomed her neighbor. No, her friend. She liked the sound of that.

"Want to go for breakfast before we head to the clinic?" Melissa already wore her Auburn scrubs.

"Sure." Krys grabbed her bag and followed Melissa to her car. "Like your scrubs—I went to school at Auburn. Did you? Or are you just a football fan?"

"I was in the nursing program there." Melissa cranked the engine and pulled out of the driveway. "Well, at least I was until I got mixed up with an abusive guy. I'm not proud of this, but you might as well know. I struggled with depression and tried to kill myself before I met Aidan at the free clinic in Atlanta."

Krys had trouble imagining Melissa in that life, but she herself was walking proof that grim things often hid behind smiling facades.

The spiky-haired waitress at the cafe, Laurel, recognized Krys. "Here with Mark's better half this morning?" She laughed and showed them to the same booth. Melissa pulled laminated menus from behind the napkin dispenser and handed one to Krys. "Did Mark make you eat the monster meat meal?"

Krys nodded. "I swear, a whole herd of animals died for that platter. You know, you really won't get anemic from Aidan feeding every other day."

Melissa rolled her eyes. "Mark just uses that as an excuse to eat bacon."

Krys looked over the menu and was glad to see items that didn't oink, moo, or cluck. "I'm thinking oatmeal sounds good."

Their orders came quickly, and Melissa proved to be a nonstop conversationalist, which gave Krys a chance to ask questions about her new neighbors.

"So you were already with Aidan when you met Mark?"

Melissa crunched her cereal. "Yep. Been with Aidan five years, and Mark and I have been married almost four. Aidan introduced me to his new business manager, and that was it for me. Knew he was the one."

Krys ran her spoon in circles through her bowl of oatmeal. "I hope this isn't too personal, but I've been wondering. Doesn't it bother Mark that you and Aidan…" If she was going to stay here, she had to get over this aversion to the lingo. "Does it bother him that Aidan feeds from you? I mean, it's really intimate." Not to mention that it had made her ridiculously jealous.

Melissa laughed. "No, it's intimate but…Aidan's a good friend. I think he considers me a good friend. That's all there is, and Mark knows that. He's been around the vamps enough to know that unless one of them is mated, they really can separate sex and feeding. We're happy here—or we will be when this Owen situation gets taken care of."

There was that word again: *happy.*

"While I'm being nosy, can I ask you something else?" Krys fidgeted with the pink and blue sweetener packets on the table, not wanting to look Melissa in the eyes.

"Shoot."

"I still don't understand why you stay. I mean, at first, yeah. You owe Aidan and all. And you like him. But this"—she looked around—"it's not real life. I mean, it's like hiding out, living in your own little country unplugged from everything outside."

Melissa was silent so long that Krys finally looked up, afraid she'd made her angry. Instead she looked thoughtful.

"Let me ask *you* a question," Melissa said. "What takes more courage—doing what's normal and being miserable, or admitting what you need in order to be happy? Here's the problem. You have feelings for Aidan and don't want to admit it because he's a vampire and he kidnapped you and you think you should be scared. Well, guess what? Screw what you *should* feel." Melissa took a sip of her coffee. "Sorry, Mark says my brain-mouth filter gets turned off sometimes. I've been wanting to give Aidan the same lecture about you but haven't gotten up the nerve."

Krys looked at the pink and blue packets stacked in neat piles across the table and realized that she'd emptied the container. She started putting them back in the plastic holder before Laurel came back.

"Why would Aidan need that lecture?" She couldn't deny that she had needed it. Melissa had nailed her whole dilemma in three or four sentences, and now Krys's doubts seemed stupid.

"Because Aidan's a brooder, if you haven't noticed." Melissa giggled. "Don't tell him I said that, either. He's a good man, but he'll think things to death and back. He's so convinced you won't want to be with him because of the kidnapping and the blood-drinking and all that crap that he won't even give you a chance to turn him down."

Krys leaned back in her chair and stared out the window. People walked past the café, stopping occasionally to look in the window of the little clothing store across the street. All so normal. What Melissa said made sense. If she stripped away what she thought she *should* feel and what she *should* do, if she ignored what society would *expect* her to feel or do, what was left? Aidan and her feelings for him.

"You were right earlier," she said, looking back at Melissa. "When I ran away, I wasn't running from Aidan or even from Penton. I was afraid of what I was feeling. It still scares the hell out of me."

Melissa reached across the table and patted her hand. "We all went through that same thing, Krys. It's hard to throw out what you're conditioned to believe or how you're conditioned to react. But weigh that against what you have and see what sticks."

When Aidan practically ran out of her room after bonding her, Krys had thought he hadn't wanted her. But maybe he was just afraid she'd push him away.

"Still friends? You're not talking to me." Worry creased a line between Melissa's eyebrows.

Krys smiled. "Friends. Definitely friends. You've given me a lot to think about."

After breakfast, as Melissa drove to the clinic, she grew quiet.

"Something wrong?"

Melissa shook her head. "Just wishing Mark hadn't insisted on going on the hunt today. I know Owen's vampires are down during daylight but it still scares me."

"I didn't know Mark had gone with them," Krys said as they turned in to the clinic lot and parked near the front entrance. "What time are they supposed to be back?"

"Three, at the latest," Melissa said. "He'll come by here and stay till I get off, then we'll swing by Aidan's for a few minutes before dinner." She grinned. "I would invite you to dinner with us, but it's date night."

"No problem. I'm going to start keeping clinic hours every day while I'm here, and this afternoon I'll just unpack and explore." Krys stopped as she opened the car door. "Wait. You're going by Aidan's because..." She kept tripping over the words. *Stupid, Krys. If you're going to admit how you feel, you need to be able to say it.* "Because he needs to feed?"

"Yeah, he likes to feed as soon as he gets up for the night. You don't have to be squeamish about it. It's just the way things are."

Krys laughed and hoped her voice was loud enough to camouflage her pounding heart. "I know. I was going to tell you and Mark to go ahead on your date night. I'll go to Aidan instead and you can both have the night off. I need to be there about five?"

Melissa's eyes widened. "Four thirty's better. Are you sure about that?"

"Really, I want to." Krys felt her face grow hot. She wanted *him,* was more like it. One of them was going to have to finally admit it and take a chance on being rejected.

Looks like it's going to be me.

❊CHAPTER 30❊

S he was here. Aidan knew before his eyes opened. He didn't sense Melissa or Mark. Just Krys. Something must be wrong.

He slid out of bed, pulled on a pair of jeans, and jerked down the ladder in the sitting area outside his bedroom. He climbed both sets of stairs in a rush and lifted the latch into the kitchen, pausing only long enough to sense her in the living room, alone.

He padded in on bare feet and there she was, standing with her back to him, jabbing at the fireplace with a poker. She'd started a fire, and it was already crackling, sending out warmth that felt like a caress. Aidan didn't use the fireplace often, but he liked the feel and smell of it. *Especially with her in front of it.*

"Krys?"

She whirled, her hand to her chest, and burst into the throaty laugh that got its usual reaction from his dick. It did its best to stand at attention.

"God, you scared me. You should be required to wear bells or something so you don't sneak up on people."

He smiled. "Vampires like sneaking up on people. It's what we do. Where's Mel? Is something wrong?" Krys was tightly wound, heart pumping color into her face, the heat on her skin infusing the air around her with her light, sweet scent.

She twisted her hands together. "I told Melissa I wanted to come instead, that you could feed from me. Is that OK?"

She looked so damned beautiful. Her dark hair fell below her shoulders in loose curls, and she wore a red sweater that tested every bit of his self-control.

Krys backed up as Aidan prowled toward her. He looked at her intently, knowing how his eyes had paled and, OK, trying to scare her a little. *If she's going run from me, she needs to do it now.*

Finally he had her backed against the wall next to the fireplace, and he pinned her there with his body.

Last time they'd been in this position, she'd struggled against him. Not today. Her breath was uneven, and he knew she saw the hunger in his face and felt it in his body. "Be sure about what you want, Krys," he whispered. "Be sure you really understand who and what I am."

He felt her heart racing beneath his chest and the pulse in her throat visibly quickened. He traced a finger over her neck. "Do you want to leave?"

Her voice surprised him, strong and a little husky. "No. I'm exactly where I want to be."

"Do you understand that I can't just feed from you? It won't be the same as it is with Melissa. I have to be inside you, to have you inside me. Another blood exchange, except this one mates us."

She swallowed hard and he sensed her arousal. Her nipples pebbled beneath her sweater as he pressed his hips against the juncture of her thighs. Her voice was shaky. "I understand."

He circled his hips against her and ran his tongue up the side of her neck. "It means you're mine, Krys." He kissed her deeply, rocking against her, slow and insistent.

"I want to be yours." Her words broke off in a moan.

His shoulders shook with the effort of getting himself under control. Slowly he pulled away from her and took her hand. "Come on, then."

She followed him, not speaking until they climbed down the ladder into the basement and resealed the hatch.

"This is the real mother ship?" She laughed, her voice still a little shaky, and wandered around the room, picking up books, a knife, even one of his hand weights. He leaned against the doorway and watched her explore, his resolve wearing thin around the edges.

She paused in front of his bookcases, trailing her hands across his collection of CDs. "You have really eclectic taste," she said, smiling back at him.

"I've had a lot of time to broaden my horizons," he said drily, and she laughed again.

Finally, she came back and stood in front of him. "Let me see the lower level."

"Think about this, Krys. You don't—"

She covered his mouth with her hand. "I don't want to think anymore, Aidan. Here's the deal. If I can admit I want you despite the fact that you're a vampire and you freaking kidnapped me, surely you can admit how you feel. Unless I'm reading you wrong and you don't want me—in which case, just say so. I'll be embarrassed, but you know what? One of us has to get this train moving."

Moving? Good God. She didn't realize it, but the train was on the verge of running off the tracks.

He knelt and released the hatch into his subbasement bedroom. He gestured to it and she didn't hesitate. She just climbed down and waited for him at the bottom.

She took in the polished mahogany and deep colors of his sitting room as he descended the last step and raised the ladder behind him.

"It's really beauti—"

He covered her mouth with his, and after a second of surprise, she leaned into him, wrapping her arms around his neck, making his body ache for her.

She pulled away and opened the door to the bedroom, giving his brain a second to reengage. *Holy hell.* He closed his eyes and took a deep breath. He had to make her understand what she was committing to before this went any further.

When he opened his eyes, she'd already gone inside. He found her sitting on his bed. The woman was going to kill him.

He took a deep breath. "Krys, you don't know what this means in my world. If we—"

"We're mated. It's a long-term deal. I know." She crossed her arms and gave him a steady look. "I told you that's what I want. Are you telling me you don't?"

He could reach her in three steps, undress her in two, be inside her in under a minute. "Of course I do." He gritted his teeth. "I just want to make sure you understand what it means."

"So tell me."

"We become a part of each other. I'll always know where you are. If I'm hurt, I can draw strength from you. Your life span will be longer—"

"Aidan, shut up."

He blinked at her, caught off guard. Had she changed her mind?

"I'm tired of talking." She stood, closed the gap between them, hooked two fingers in the top of his jeans, pulled him to her. His mind started to protest, then shut down on him altogether.

"I'm tired of thinking." She slid both hands up his chest and rested them on his collarbone, easing him away from the door. Her hand slipped away for a second, flicking the switch on the wall, and all the light fled the room except the soft illumination from the bedside lamp.

"I'm tired of being scared." She stood on tiptoe and kissed him, reaching for his hand and pulling him toward the bed.

He took two steps before he looked down, saw the band on his wrist, and froze.

———•———

She'd noticed the bracelet before, but thought it was just jewelry. Should have realized that a seventeenth-century Irish farmer wouldn't be a "just jewelry" kind of guy. Now he pulled away from her and sat on the edge of the bed, staring at it. Were all vampire males this complicated?

She sat beside him and took his hand in hers, studying the simple gold bangle. There were figures etched into it, in a language she didn't recognize. "What does it say?"

He flexed his hand. "Abigail, in Gaelic. I put it on a long, long time ago, after my wife died. To remind myself of what I am and what I can't ever be again."

Krys knew he'd been married, and that he carried scars from whatever had happened. She'd thought his hesitation with her was a commitment phobia, that he thought a mate would be a distraction. Instead she'd been competing with the past.

"Tell me about Abby. You were married before you were turned, right?"

He fingered the band. "Yes. I held the family farm because Owen, as the eldest, hadn't wanted it. We had a son, Cavan, who'd just turned five when I left to fight. Owen and I traveled for a while after we'd been turned, but then I was a selfish bastard and decided to go home. I thought we could still have some kind of a life. But Abby was afraid of me. She saw me as the monster I was. Still am."

Krys bit her tongue. She could hear the rest of the story later. Right now she either had to exorcise Abby or walk away from Aidan. And she didn't want to walk away.

She gently grasped the bracelet and tried to slide it off his hand. Finally, after a few tugs, he compressed his palm enough for her to remove it. She held it in front of him. "Here are some facts. You're not a monster. You could be, but you're not."

His focus remained fixed on the bracelet in her right hand, so she reached up with her left and turned his face toward hers. "Look at me, Aidan. I am not afraid of you. You can try all you want, but you can't scare me off." She took a deep breath. "I love you, OK? You. Now. Just like you are."

She caught her breath as a tear slipped down his cheek. He opened his mouth to talk but couldn't, and he turned his face away. She laid the bracelet on the nightstand and slipped her arms around his shoulders. *All that strength camouflaging such a wounded heart.* He'd told her once that vampires couldn't cry. He'd been wrong.

She felt him bury his face in her hair, and gripped him harder, her heart full and aching at the same time. How long they sat that way she wasn't sure, but finally he pulled away, reaching across her to pick up the bracelet. He looked at it for a moment before walking to his desk and taking a wooden box from a bottom drawer. He fumbled with the latch and finally got it open, laying the bracelet inside and snapping the box shut again.

He put the box away, closed the drawer, and stared at it a moment before turning to face her with an expression she couldn't interpret.

She smiled at him and was relieved when he smiled back. She stood up and began pushing up the sleeve of her sweater. "OK then, you still need to feed. We'll take the rest slowly if it's what you decide you want." She edged past him toward the sofa, figuring he'd rather go to a more neutral spot. He grasped her arm as she passed. "That's how I feed from a fam, not from a mate. And I decided a long time ago—I was just too thick-headed to realize it." His voice was soft, and when she looked up at him, his eyes had grown pale with need. For her. Heat flashed across her body, and he knew it. His nostrils flared as he leaned over to kiss her, slipping his hands over her backside and pulling her against him.

She thought about stopping him, asking him if he was sure. But they'd talked enough. She didn't want him to think with anything except his hands and his mouth and the hard core of him that was pressing against her.

His fingers caught the hem of her sweater and he eased it over her head. She reached up to unhook her bra, but his hands covered hers. "Mine." He lowered the straps, slowly, following the line of exposed skin on her shoulders before unhooking the clasp and letting it drop to the floor between them.

Krys held her breath as he pulled her against him and recaptured her lips, his hand working at the button of her jeans and then sliding them down her hips. She stepped out of them and returned to splay her hands across his broad chest, its planes and ridges moving under her touch.

She dropped her head to slide her lips across the smooth muscles of his pecs and take a hard nipple between her teeth, biting down with a slight pressure at his sharp intake of breath. Good, he liked that. She paused over a scar on his stomach.

"What happened here?" she murmured, running her tongue along the lightened skin.

His breathing was jagged. "I was learning to use a scythe, when I was fifteen," he said. "Ah, holy hell."

His words became jumbled as she unbuttoned his jeans and slipped a hand inside to cup him while her tongue traced the indentation over his hip bone. She thought that dimple of skin was the sexiest part of a man, and took care to let him know she appreciated it.

Aidan growled and leaned over, picking her up and carrying her to the bed. He laid her on the mattress and looked at her with utter possessiveness as he ran his hands down her sides, hooked her panties and pulled them off with a flick that sent them flying.

"I'll never find my clothes again." She laughed as he ripped off all she had left—her socks—and threw them over his shoulder with a grin.

"Good. I like you this way."

He skimmed off his jeans, all toned muscle and slim hips, his erection heavy and thick. Suddenly she felt self-conscious. She was so plain—how could he want her? She reached over to turn off the lamp.

"No you don't. You're beautiful, and I want to see you." He sat beside her and pulled her hand away from the lamp, bringing it to rest on him. "Feel what you do to me."

She stroked him, silk over iron, and watched his face as he threw his head back with a groan. She saw his fangs and her heart sped up. He was so used to playing human that it was easy to forget that he wasn't.

As if he'd heard her, Aidan growled and rolled her onto her back, sliding his body atop hers and burying his face against her neck. "I love the feel of you," he whispered, his breath hot in her ear. She gasped as his hand slid down to caress the ache between her legs. His fingers plunged and scissored and his mouth slowly moved from her neck to her breast, causing her to arch underneath him.

She grabbed a handful of hair and pulled him back within kissing range, nibbling along the edge of his jaw until she reached his lips. His big hand between her legs was making her crazy, and she writhed under his touch. "You have some really talented fingers but I want you inside me," she said, gasping for breath. "Please."

He laughed, dark and wicked, the sound of a man who knew exactly what he was doing. Then he disappeared and she struggled up on her elbows to find him grinning at her from between her thighs. Oh no, he wouldn't...

A quick swipe of his tongue sent her over the top. "You... oh..." She closed her eyes and lost the ability to form words as he used his hands to spread her legs farther and poise himself at her entrance.

"Krys, keep looking at me." His voice was resonant and she opened her eyes, looking into his as he hovered above her then began entering her slowly, the thick heat of him stretching her, pushing deeper, his eyes locked on hers.

His hips surged and he stilled, deep inside her. "*Is tú mo maité*," he whispered. "*Tá tú mianach.* You are my mate. You are mine. Is this true?"

Hot tears blurred her vision but she didn't take her gaze from his. She'd spent her whole life trying to not belong to one man, and now she wanted nothing more than to belong to this one. "I am your mate," she answered. "I am yours."

He smiled and kissed her as he began to move in long, slow strokes that sent sparks through every nerve ending. Those first gentle strokes became harder, faster—a pounding rhythm that took her breath away and sent her soaring again.

"Don't come yet," he said, his voice rough from the exertion of trying to slow his own rhythm. He fumbled for something on the bedside table, a small knife whose blade he drew in a small cut beneath his collarbone. The blood welled up and dripped onto her shoulder as he began to move again, resuming a frantic rhythm that brought her back to the edge.

She felt her muscles gathering energy, the white-hot tension coiling inside her, and as she went over, she latched onto the wound, taking his sweet, hot lifeblood into her. Her orgasm tightened around him, and she felt his bite on the side of her neck as his body stiffened and he jerked inside her.

The sound of their breathing filled the room as Aidan collapsed on top of her, holding her tight. "You are my mate."

Krys couldn't keep the grin off her face. "I am."

Krys lay with her back to Aidan as he kissed her shoulder. He nestled against her, tracing his fingers across the small puncture wounds beneath her ear that had almost healed. That would be the third set. Or was it the fourth? He felt at peace—an emotion he wasn't well acquainted with. He felt really, really good for a change.

He growled when his cell phone rang on the nightstand. He wasn't ready for reality yet, but Krys grabbed it and handed it to him.

"Bad timing," he snapped into the phone.

"Where the hell are you?" Mirren snapped back at him. "We're sitting in your living room waiting to talk about what our people found today and you up and disappear on us. Gave me a bloody heart attack, already."

"You're a vampire," Aidan said. "You can't have a heart attack."

Krys stifled a snort in her pillow.

"Who was that? What is *wrong* with you?"

"Never mind. I'm on my way." Aidan clicked the phone shut and kissed Krys until she quit laughing.

"I don't have time for a shower right now, but you're welcome to stay. Or are you ready for your debut?" He crawled out of bed and jerked on a clean pair of jeans, then began digging in the dresser for a sweater.

She began dressing as well, coming up with everything but one sock. "I'm afraid to ask, but what do you mean by debut?"

He laughed and ran his hands through his hair, pulling it back with one of the elastic bands that seemed to be scattered over every surface. "Well, put it this way. I can either go upstairs and talk to my lieutenants, who are all in my living room—and they'll know you're down here because your scent is all over me. Or you can go up with me and admit you distracted me enough to forget I had a meeting about our hunt, which only impacts the whole future of the town."

Krys hid her face in her hands. "Oh my God. Isn't there a third choice, like dying of humiliation?"

"No, that's about it."

She sighed. "I'd rather have Mirren mock me to my face than behind my back, so I'll take the second option." She leaned over and finger-combed her hair so that it shimmered around her shoulders when she straightened up. Aidan was tempted to let the lieutenants wait a little longer.

They climbed the ladders, emerging into the kitchen. "They're in the living room," he said. "They've already realized you're here."

"I hate that about you guys," Krys muttered. "Can't hear you sneaking up on me, and you know way too much about each other's business."

Aidan took her hand as they walked into the living room. Mirren sprawled over most of the sofa, while Will sat in one armchair and Hannah in another. They all stared at Aidan, and then at Krys, with varying degrees of raised eyebrows and smug expressions. Hannah put her hands over her mouth and giggled.

Will was the only one who looked surprised. "Damn. I was going to ask her out."

Mirren cleared his throat.

"Nice seeing you all. Gotta go." Krys edged toward the door, her face bright pink. Aidan didn't know whether to laugh or feel sorry for her.

"I'll talk to you before sunrise," he whispered after her.

She grumbled on her way out, "Might as well not whisper. They can hear you, remember?"

Aidan watched till she opened her front door and waved at him, then turned back to the room. "OK, get it out of your systems."

Mirren twisted on the sofa. "Hell no. As long as it's you and not me doing the mate thing, I say go for it. You brood too much anyway. In fact, you're a walking, talking vampire cliché."

Aidan ignored the others' laughter, shoved Mirren's feet off the sofa, and sat down. "Tell me what happened today."

Mirren grabbed a clipboard off the coffee table and sat up, rifling through sheets.

"We didn't get every place covered, but a lot." He handed the clipboard to Aidan. "A team found one member of Owen's scathe in one of the caves out near the hiking trail—pulled him out in the sunshine and fried his ass. Found one more guy in one of the burned-out mill village basements that still had enough structure to keep him protected. Dragged him out, too."

"That's just two," Aidan said. "Surely they're not all scattered around like that."

Mirren shook his head. "Look on the last page, at Jerry's report."

Aidan flipped to the last sheet in the clipboard. "So, one of them said that Owen's been chaining his humans up in the old mill? And nobody's found this till now?" Hell, he'd been out there himself and hadn't seen anything.

Mirren nodded. "Yep. I'm wondering if there's some kind of basement space in the mill that isn't on the original blueprints—something underneath or on the other side of that collapsed basement we know about—and maybe that's where they've been hiding."

The clipboard hit the coffee table with a clatter as Aidan threw it aside. "Under our noses, damn it. If it exists, there must be outside access or we'd have seen it."

"How about we burn the mill? It might run 'em out."

Aidan frowned, thinking. "We don't want to burn out the humans, so we'd have to move them or let them go. Any idea how loyal they are?"

"Can't be that loyal if the man keeps them chained up all day," Will said. "Maybe we can just go in and release them if we can find them. They'd probably run like hell if we popped their chains."

Aidan pondered the options. He hated sending the Penton humans out to clean house again, but if they wanted to release Owen's humans with as little violence as possible, they needed to do it while Owen and his scathe couldn't fight. Will was right: Owen wouldn't have earned his humans' loyalty unless he'd kept them enthralled for so long that he'd fried their brains.

"Let's send a couple of extra teams into the mill tomorrow," he told Mirren. "See if we can find them, how many people we're talking about, and how loyal they are—or aren't. Let the rest of the searches go on as they did today."

"What should our humans do with theirs? Just let them go?" Will asked.

Aidan thought for a moment. "Have our people take them to the secure rooms at city hall and lock them up till tonight. Then we'll scrub their memories, drive them to Atlanta, and release them. We don't want them coming back here for any reason."

Mirren headed for the door. "I'll find Tim and let him pick who goes in with him. He knows the mill building best." He looked back at Aidan. "Then we burn it?"

His brother might be in there. Aidan clenched his jaw and nodded.

"Then we burn it."

CHAPTER 31

Snow flurries had already dusted the ground with a light layer of white by the time Krys scurried to the Dinosaur and drove to the clinic.

She had asked Mark to buy a new computer and a pile of medical software, and they had arrived. The boxes sat in the lobby—turned out Penton had UPS service just like anywhere else, but she bet none of the vampires signed for their packages.

She had dragged the computer box to the reception desk and was digging the monitor from its Styrofoam packing when Melissa came in, stomping snow off her shoes.

"So, tell." She grinned and threw her purse behind the desk.

Krys had been expecting this conversation. Aidan had come to get her as soon as the lieutenants left, and they'd spent a long night in his suite. She'd run into Mark when she slipped out just before dawn. She knew that he'd blab.

"I have no idea what you mean," she said, smothering a yawn as she crawled under the desk to plug in the computer.

When she pulled her head back out, Melissa stood with arms crossed, waiting.

She laughed. "I am *not* going into details, so forget it."

"But you're on the permanent menu? Every other day? Or do you want me to go on the sub list? I mean, I'd miss Aidan like crazy but I'd understand."

Krys stopped in the middle of finding a spare USB cable. She hadn't thought about it. As much as she liked Melissa, she didn't want to see that blissed-out look on the woman's face while Aidan fed from her. There was no point in being ridiculous about it, though. He'd have to make that call. If he wanted to keep feeding from Melissa, Krys would just have to get over it.

"That's Aidan's decision." She plugged the cable into the back of the monitor.

"Uh-oh, girl's jealous." Melissa piled pieces of Styrofoam into the computer box, laughing. She picked up the last bit of packaging, stuffed it into the carton, and closed the flaps.

Krys had never felt happier, but she wasn't going to share that, either.

They spent the rest of the day installing software and playing around with ways to log patients, inventory drug stock, and set up appointments. At four they shut down the computer and got ready to go home.

Krys wondered if she should go to Aidan's or her own house. *Her house.* She liked the sound of that.

Mark's car careened into the lot just as they got to the door. He rushed in, melted snow pooling on the shoulders of his leather jacket. "Take your coats off. We've had some folks hurt—they're on their way."

"Who is it?" Melissa asked.

Before he could answer, Krys held up a hand. "Wait. First, tell me what kind of injuries so we can get ready."

"Tim got shot, close range, and it looks pretty bad. Couple of others with minor stab wounds."

Krys left Mark and Melissa at the front desk and went into the exam rooms one at a time, making sure she had what she needed. In a few minutes, Melissa joined her in the larger room, pulling out tape and sutures, bandages and antiseptic.

"Mark OK?"

Melissa nodded. "He's gone to leave a note for Mirren, although there's no point. He'll know something's wrong with Tim as soon as he wakes."

"What happened?"

Melissa didn't get a chance to answer. A couple of men Krys had seen at the town hall meeting opened the door to a swirl of cold air, while two more brought in Tim. She recognized the older man as Jerry, the one who'd been hurt in the mill village fire. He'd been a joker at the meeting, but his expression was grim now.

"Put him in Exam Two," she told them. "How far behind are the others?"

"Couple of minutes," Jerry said. "They ain't hurt as bad."

Krys pulled out the extension on the exam table, lifting one end to keep the head higher than the feet, and Jerry and the other man laid Tim down gently. His ruddy complexion had turned pale and clammy, and his breathing was ragged. But he was alive.

The facial wounds were all surface stuff. Bruises and cuts, nothing too deep or serious. Pulling on gloves, Krys turned to the gunshot wound, which had turned his chest to a sickening mix of sweatshirt fabric and raw hamburger. She said a quick prayer and steadied her breathing. This was very, very bad.

Using a pair of long-bladed scissors from the exam tray, she cut up the middle of his sweatshirt and pulled the shreds away, then blew out a frustrated breath. He needed an emergency room with a full setup and medical team and an OR, and he needed them a half hour ago.

Melissa appeared at her shoulder. "The other two guys are in Exam One. I bandaged them up and told them to wait. Nothing life-threatening. They'll just need stitch—oh God." She finally got a look at Tim and swallowed hard. "What do you need me to do?"

"The best thing we can do is try to stabilize him enough to get him to the hospital in Opelika—and if he survives that, they'll send him to Birmingham or Atlanta," Krys said, removing the blood-soaked packing and replacing it quickly. "Call an ambulance, then look in the supply room and find something to stop the bleeding." At Melissa's deer-in-headlights look, she added, "Should have a name like Celox or QuikClot. And a couple of units of blood."

Melissa disappeared, and Krys finally noticed Jerry and the other men who'd brought Tim in standing against the wall, watching. Jerry looked scared. "You guys get out of here. Go home or wait in the lobby," she said. "If you leave, keep your phones handy. Aidan will want to talk to you." She glanced at her watch. He should be up in a half hour.

Melissa returned with a couple of envelopes and a small cooler. "These boxes say Celox. Is this what you wanted?"

Krys nodded and grabbed one, ripped off the top, and uncovered Tim's wound. She poured granules in and quickly replaced the packing. Once the bleeding stopped, she could get a better idea of what she was dealing with, but the biggest thing she needed was an ambulance. "Did you call nine-one-one?"

Melissa shook her head. "We can't." Her hands shook as she took a wet cloth and began wiping the blood and dirt off Tim's face. "We have to wait on Aidan."

Krys glanced at Tim to make sure he was still unconscious. "We can't wait on Aidan or he's not going to make it," she hissed. "Call them."

Krys hooked Tim up to a heart monitor and blood pressure gauge. She set up an IV and ran a bag of blood to one port and a line of morphine to another. She didn't know what else to do for him.

His eyes cracked open, aimed at the ceiling.

"Tim? You're at the clinic. Can you talk to me?"

No reaction. He was in shock; not surprising, given the trauma and blood loss. The man was conscious in name only.

Melissa stood in the doorway. She hadn't called for help, damn it. Krys turned back to look at Tim. *Shit. Time for a reality check.*

She hung her head in defeat. Even if the ambulance was here now, even if they had a freaking helipad, they couldn't reach an ER in less than a half hour, minimum. No way he'd survive the trip, and she'd be endangering Penton's secrets for nothing.

"Mel." Krys motioned her to one side. "You need to get in touch with Tim's wife."

Melissa closed her eyes and nodded. "Oh God. Jennifer. She works down at the Superette."

"Call her, then come sit with Tim a few minutes. I'll take a quick look at the other guys, then you can suture them." Melissa had been practicing stitches on a dummy with Krys watching. Now she could try the real thing.

Melissa nodded and swiped a tear from her cheek, pulling her cell phone from her pocket and returning to the hallway.

Krys pulled a stool over and tried in vain to get a response from Tim, talking to him, stroking his hand, while she watched his vitals. He wasn't stable enough for surgery, even if they had been set up for it. Krys had seen enough gunshot wounds when she'd done her ER rotation. This was unfixable.

Melissa returned from the hallway. "Jennifer's on her way. I didn't tell her how bad it was. Want me to stay with him?"

Krys nodded. "Keep trying to get any kind of reaction from him, and call me if you do. We got any blankets?" She opened cabinets along the wall until she found some, and handed Melissa a couple of thermals. "Cover him up. Keep him warm. The longer we can keep him alive, the better chance he has. Call me the *second* anything changes."

Melissa wiped away more tears with the back of her hand and climbed on the stool. Krys could hear her talking softly to Tim as she headed into the adjacent exam room.

"Sorry it took me so long," she told the men. One sat on the exam table, the other in a chair. Melissa had been right. Both had knife cuts that would need stitches and minor scrapes a simple antiseptic would handle.

"What happened out there?" Damned if Penton wasn't getting to be a dangerous place. But she couldn't see herself anywhere else now.

The older man, Michael, shifted on the exam table, wincing as Krys examined his injury. "We'd gone to the old mill, trying to run off the humans Owen's scathe was keeping tied up," he said, his heavy Southern accent sounding more local than most Krys had heard there. "There was only four of them, all dogs."

"Dogs?" Krys frowned at him.

"Humans who've been enthralled so many times they can't do much besides follow orders," the other man said, introducing himself as Gary. He was younger, and Krys remembered seeing him with Will at the town hall meeting. A fam, maybe? "They were armed and waiting for us. It was FUBAR start to finish."

"How's Tim?" Michael asked.

Krys shook her head. "Not good. Next hour is going to be touch-and-go."

"Mirren's gonna do some damage," Gary said. "I don't want to be here when the big guy finds out somebody put a hole in his fam. Can we leave?"

"I guess, soon as Melissa stitches you up. Keep your phones on you, though."

She called Melissa in to do the suturing, and glanced at her watch again on her way back into Tim's room. Four forty. She, too, kind of wished she could be somewhere else when Mirren heard what had happened, but she figured she'd have a front-row seat.

Krys was adjusting the fluids feeding into Tim's IV when Jennifer arrived, a petite blonde who looked scared and half in shock herself. She caught the distraught woman's arm before she got to Tim. "Take a deep breath," she said softly. "Calm yourself down. Then sit with him, talk to him quietly, try to get him to respond to you. Don't let him see you're afraid."

"Is he going to make it?"

Krys hesitated and Jennifer covered her mouth with her hand. "Oh, God. Oh, God."

"What you can do for him is to not let him see how scared you are. Talk to him. Can you do that?"

Jennifer swallowed hard, wiped her eyes, and nodded. She took a couple of deep breaths and walked to the stool next to Tim. As soon as she said his name and took his hand, his eyes shifted and latched onto her.

At least he won't die alone. Krys squeezed her shoulder. "He sees you. Keep talking to him."

She slipped into the hall and leaned against the wall, exhausted, closing her eyes and beating her head gently against the painted paneling. There were still two patients in the clinic who'd been injured in the restaurant explosion, and now Tim. How was Aidan going to fix this? In her visions Hannah had seen Krys helping him, but how? She could treat the injured but that wasn't going to solve the problem.

After checking on Tim again, she walked to the front reception desk, leaning against it and waiting for Mirren or Aidan. She wasn't sure who would get there first. Tim was Mirren's fam, so he'd know something was wrong as soon as he woke. But Mirren and Aidan were bonded as well, so it was a toss-up as to who'd get where, and when.

Turned out to be Aidan. She'd barely registered his car pulling into the lot before he strode through the doors, his eyes pale and angry. If she'd had an ounce of sense, she'd have avoided him when he looked like that—very predatory and not so human, despite his iron self-control. But she hurt for him. This was one more thing he'd blame on himself.

"How is he?" Aidan put a hand on Krys's elbow and headed toward the exam rooms.

With him she had to be straight up. She stopped outside the door and kept her voice low. "Honest answer? I've done all I can. It'll be a miracle if he makes it—I'm surprised he's still alive."

She stopped him on his way into Exam One. "Not that one, next one. You had two guys stabbed but the wounds were minor. Mel's stitching them up, and I told them they could go home but stay by the phone in case you wanted to talk to them."

He nodded. "Names?"

"Gary Thomas and Michael something."

Aidan nodded again and eased into the second room. Krys followed close behind in case he tried to talk to Tim, but he stopped just inside the door, watching Jennifer as she continued to chatter in the face of Tim's unblinking stare.

Aidan looked devastated.

A minute later, Tim flatlined. Krys had already moved the clinic's portable defibrillator into the room, so she ordered everyone but Melissa outside and used the paddles. His heartbeat bounced erratically for a few seconds, then flatlined again. Krys knew it was hopeless but she worked on him for another ten minutes before calling time of death. Even Penton would have to file reports, but she'd figure out the paperwork later.

She turned off the monitors and unhooked them before nodding to a tearful Melissa to open the doors again. Jennifer could be as hysterical as she wanted to be now.

Mirren stood motionless in the hallway, and when Krys shook her head, he clenched his jaw and followed Jennifer into the room, closing the door softly behind him.

"I'm sorry." Krys took Aidan's hand.

"This has to stop," he said, his voice so quiet she strained to hear. "It ends tonight."

✤ CHAPTER 32 ✤

G un: check.
Knives: check.

Extra bullets: check.

Pissed-off, righteous fury: check.

Aidan slipped into his Kevlar vest and jerked the straps tight.

Mark handed him a jacket, but he shook his head. "It'll slow me down." He'd fed from Mark at his insistence, since Krys and Melissa were busy at the clinic, but now it was time to go.

Mark pulled a pistol from his jacket pocket and checked the clip.

"Go home," Aidan said. "This is my job."

"Listen, Ai—"

"No. I won't have Mel go through the shit Jennifer's dealing with tonight. Besides, I need you to contact Will and Hannah and the other scathe leaders. They know the chain of command if something happens to me. I'm shutting down the bonds between me and everyone except Mirren. Tell him if that bond gets cut, he's in charge." He paused. "Mating bonds can't be cut, so keep an eye on Krys." That was a factor he hadn't dealt with before.

He didn't give Mark a chance to answer, brushing past him to the porch, down the steps and to his car. He cranked it and was backing out of the driveway when a figure behind him gave him no option but to slam on the brakes.

Mirren got into the passenger seat, sliding it back to accommodate his long legs. His voice was quiet. "You aren't taking this one by yourself. That son of a bitch is mine, and I want his human shooter too."

Aidan nodded. He didn't like it, but a man had a right to avenge his own. He backed his car out of the drive and headed toward downtown.

"What's the plan?" Mirren checked the clip in his gun.

"Kill Owen," Aidan said. "I haven't thought much beyond that."

"Works for me."

They drove in silence to a side street a block from the mill. It was still early evening, and Aidan thought chances were good that if the scathe had found day spaces nearby, the vamps might not have gone far.

He parked the car in an alley between a closed-down feed store and the old Greyhound station, and they sat for a few seconds, listening, scanning the area for movement.

"Let's go." Aidan exited the car and eased the doors closed, Mirren behind him. They stayed in shadows, moving in silence toward the mill.

The rectangular two-story building rose like a tombstone of Southern industry—Aidan's first purchase in his systematic acquisition of Penton. His plan had been simple: buy all the land, period. Nobody outside the scathe could move in because he controlled the real estate. But he hadn't done more than a cursory walk-through of the mill. He should've been paying more attention.

He visualized the interior as nearly as he could remember it: large, cavernous factory floor where the remnants of a few behemoths lay scattered: roller combs with needle-sharp steel teeth, spinning machines, and, along one end, the remains of a weaving room containing the skeletons of a couple of massive early-twentieth-century machines.

Offices and smaller rooms were upstairs and in poor repair, thanks to a crumbling, leaky roof. Aidan doubted they'd improved since his walk-through. The partial basement had collapsed around the stairway.

They circled the building and approached the rear entry. Aidan shut down his mental bonds to Will and Hannah, and mentally told Mirren to do the same. If they both went down, Will would take charge. Damn...they really could have used Lucy.

They stood outside the entry and listened. *Humans inside,* Aidan said. *No vampires. Secure any humans unless you find Tim's shooter; do what you want to him. I'll flush Owen out, but I'll need to cut our bond temporarily to lure him.*

Mirren nodded and moved away, dark, fast, lethal.

Aidan leaned against the brick wall, turning his mind to his brother. Once, he'd known Owen better than anyone, could have predicted his moves. Maybe he still could. Time had passed, but he doubted Owen had changed any more than Aidan had. Vampires didn't do personality changes—they kept whatever shitload of baggage they'd had when they were turned.

A leopard might change its spots, but even if it put on a zebra suit, it would still be a leopard. And Owen would still be charismatic and funny and able to charm the horns off a devil. He'd also still be an arrogant bastard, a show-off, and, at heart, a coward.

Aidan walked into the center of the mill's empty rear parking lot and stood beneath the light, his back to the tall wooden pole still crowded with staples from handbills advertising garage sales and bake-offs and fairs long past. He waited.

Occasionally his senses alerted him to vampires in the vicinity, and even to a couple of humans. Gunshots rang from the front of the mill, tingeing the cold air with the acrid odor of spent bullets and human blood. Whatever it was, Mirren could handle it.

It took an hour for Owen to get close enough for Aidan to sense him, approaching from behind. He slowed, no doubt wondering where the cavalry was hidden. Aidan didn't move.

Finally boot heels clicked on the pavement behind him. "Áodhán. You've come to turn over the keys to your fair city?" Owen walked around to face his brother. He'd just fed; his skin was flushed and his blue eyes darker than usual. Aidan wondered if the human donor had survived. Owen didn't have any weapons visible but for a knife strapped to one thigh and a long silver blade—a sword—strapped across his back, hilt-up for an easy cross-draw.

He searched Owen's face for the boy he'd idolized when he was young, hoping he wouldn't find a trace of him. It would make killing him harder. But the brothers locked gazes and Owen smiled—the same smile he'd used on their *máthair* to get out of milking; the one with which he'd charmed the girls while Aidan didn't have the nerve even to speak to them. It lit up his face, and for a second he was *Eógan* again.

But memories were a trapdoor through which Aidan couldn't afford to fall. "You know why I'm here. It's time this ends." He slid into the formal tongue. "I declare an impasse broken only by battle." He didn't move as Owen prowled around him, but his nerves were sharp, his fingers ready to react.

"By proxy again, is it? I agree." Owen held up a hand toward the woods behind them. The same young girl he'd used to ambush Mirren emerged from them. "You remember Sherry?"

Aidan looked at the young girl, who licked her lips and fidgeted with the buttons of her coat. Nervous.

Interesting that he'd brought the girl—could she be the only scathe member he had left? "No proxy. You've made it clear you don't honor the accords, *Eógan.*" Aidan spat his brother's name in the old language, the sight of the child wiping out the sentimental crap and replacing it with icy rage.

Owen laughed and nodded at Sherry, who circled behind Aidan and out of his view. He could hear the girl's shoes making soft thuds on the pavement before stopping directly behind him.

"You must think I'm a fool, Brother. I know the way you bond your people and how big your scathe is. You think I'm stupid enough to go against you one-on-one?"

"I know you aren't stupid." Aidan held his hands out, palms up. "I have severed the bonds to my lieutenants. It's just us."

Owen's mouth pulled up in a slight smile. "Even you wouldn't be that big an *eejit.*" He walked to within a few inches of Aidan and raised his eyes slightly to look at him. "I always forget you grew taller than me, little brother."

He leaned in, his face next to Aidan's, and inhaled deeply. "You are that big a fool," he laughed softly. "Except—" He grabbed Aidan's shoulders and inhaled deeply again. Aidan stiffened but didn't push him away.

"*Amrae n-amrae*," he exhaled. *Wonder of wonders.* "I sense one or two bonds remaining, and you have taken a mate. My congratulations to you, Brother. Maybe we can share again."

Aidan clenched his jaw but kept his expression bland. He hadn't expected Owen to be able to tell that his bond with Krys was different. Wrong, obviously.

He sensed, rather than heard, movement at his back, and he suddenly dropped to a crouch as Sherry rushed him from behind, knife flashing in his peripheral vision. She was no fighter. He easily grabbed her arm and pulled the knife from her grip, shoving it into her abdomen and angling it upward. She fell to the ground with a whimper. The girl would survive, but Owen wouldn't be sending her in to fight for a few days.

As Aidan spun to face his brother, a sharp pain shot through his leg. He'd left Owen unwatched too long, and his knife blade sank into the large muscle of Aidan's right thigh.

"Lucky move. Silver blade, Brother." Owen pulled the knife free with a wet, sticky sound as Aidan shoved him away. "It won't kill you but it will hurt like hell."

The brothers circled slowly, each searching for an advantage. Aidan pushed past the pain, snaking his right index finger behind the Kevlar vest and gripping the Colt. Like most vampires, he'd resisted firearms for a long time. When he killed, he thought it should be for food or revenge. Either way, his victim deserved to look him in the eye. But guns were expedient, and he slipped the pistol next to his leg, holding it flush.

Owen spotted the movement, and lunged as Aidan fired. The bullet opened a hole in Owen's hip that bloomed dark red under the streetlight, but his forward momentum took them both to the pavement, with Owen on top.

Aidan gathered his strength to push Owen off, and then hissed as a spike of fire went through the heavy muscle below his shoulder. He bared his fangs at Owen, who rolled off him with a laugh.

Aidan glanced down at the long silver blade, which had gone all the way through his deltoid muscle, hard enough to pierce through his back and embed in the asphalt beneath him. He felt the pain—hot at the core, cold radiating outward—as he closed his eyes and tried to find the threads of his bonds with Mirren.

The pain sharpened. Owen had crawled back to him and twisted the blade, digging it farther into the blacktop, increasing the damage. Aidan threw a punch with his right hand and connected enough to send Owen back a couple of feet.

He had to unpin himself from the pavement before Owen healed enough for the hip to hold his weight. The bond to Mirren hadn't reconnected, but he found another one open and waiting for him: his connection to Krys. He pulled strength from her, just enough to pitch himself forward, shoulder fighting pavement for the right to see which one tore open first.

Finally the asphalt gave up the blade. Aidan's momentum threw Owen back, but he took the fall in a roll and hobbled into the woods.

Damn it. Aidan started after him, but fell on his ass before he reached the edge of the parking lot. His thigh was soaked in blood and the long blade still pierced his shoulder. He collapsed on the ground, reset his bond to Mirren and waited for help to arrive.

"Shite, he skewered you like a hog at a luau." Mirren grasped the end of the knife and jerked it out.

Aidan cursed at the pale blood pulsing from the wound and pulled his keys from his pocket, handing them to Mirren. "Get me back to the clinic. I had to draw power off Krys and I'm not sure how much I took."

Mirren was still giving him the once-over. "How's the leg?"

"He used silver, but it'll heal." He threw an arm around Mirren's shoulder and the big man pulled him to his feet, helping him limp toward the car. "Bastard got away again, but the girl who pelted you is on the other side of the lot, wounded. Get Will to pick her up and put her in a secure cell. Then tell me what you ran into."

Mirren opened the passenger door, and Aidan half sat, half fell inside. Mirren grabbed Aidan's cell phone off the console.

"You got Mark on speed-dial?"

Aidan held up three fingers, and Mirren punched it in as he climbed into the driver's side and adjusted the seat.

Mirren's end of the call wasn't illuminating: "Yeah. No. How long? Where? On our way. Call Will and get him to pick up some trash in the mill parking lot—secure it next door to Lucy."

He threw the phone back on the console. "Krys is OK. Mel was with her when you pulled from her, and Mark's gonna take her to your house. You heard the rest." He turned away from downtown and headed toward Mill Trace.

"What happened with Owen's humans?"

"Two are dead." Mirren paused for a few seconds, staring at the road ahead. "Both of the ones I found fought me, but one had a lot to say before I put him down. They knew we were coming today, knew to have armed fams on guard at the mill. Even knew what time our people would get there. Tim walked right into a trap."

Aidan gripped the door handle hard enough to dent it.
"Shit. One of our people talked, then. Who gave us up?"

"He didn't know, just that it was a human male. The one
who met with our rat died in the fight."

"You're sure he wasn't lying?"

Mirren's smile was chilling. "Oh yeah, I'm sure."

This complicated things. Aidan looked at the clock. Three
a.m. "We're going to have to question everybody. Divide the list
between the lieutenants."

"Even Hannah?"

Aidan thought. "Actually, we should talk to Hannah first
and see if she can help us narrow it down. Get a list of everyone
who went out today." He paused. "No, get her the full list of
male humans. It could be anyone, whether they hunted today
or not."

Damn it, he'd been so careful about screening people to live
here. Who had sold them out? He opened his mental bonds to
Will and Hannah again, and sent an SOS to Hannah. No need
to tell her why.

He heard her clear, high voice in his head: *I know. Daddy
Ray is taking me to your house. Krys is good.*

Relaxing against the leather seat, Aidan closed his eyes and
felt his shoulder wound slowly reknitting. He wouldn't be fight-
worthy for at least a day.

He felt the car turn and opened his eyes to see the lights of
his porch shining at the foot of the cul-de-sac. Hannah stood
at the top of the steps, and standing next to her was Krys. That
the light shone around her head like some angelic vision wasn't
lost on him. She'd saved him tonight without even knowing it.

❋ CHAPTER 33 ❋

As soon as Aidan's car turned the corner onto Mill Trace, Krys took the first deep breath in what seemed like hours since she'd had a sudden, sharp image of a sword and then keeled over in a dead faint. Thank God, Melissa had been there, although neither of them knew what had happened until Mark rushed in and told them that Aidan was hurt.

She still wasn't clear on how the strength-sharing thing worked. One more vampire mystery to add to the thousands of questions she had piling up. Well, 112 questions, to be precise. Now 113. She was literally making a list.

The BMW pulled into the drive, and Krys's heart sank when she saw Mirren driving. She tried to run down the stairs but lost her balance; only Mark's quick reflexes kept her from tumbling over. "Stay here." His voice was sharp. "If you fall and break your neck, Aidan will kill me."

"I'm not the one hurt." She tried to pull away but he kept a hand clamped around each shoulder.

"Aidan wasn't the only one fighting tonight—you just did it without being there."

She didn't care about her headache or balance problems or even the nosebleed she'd had when she regained consciousness. All she could see was Aidan needing to lean on Mirren to get out of the car, and the blood soaking his right pant leg and his chest. Good God, she'd thought vampires were invulnerable to just about everything except pandemic vaccines.

She tried to wrestle out of Mark's grasp without success. Melissa grabbed her hand. "Mirren's going to bring him inside—let's get things ready for them."

She let Melissa pull her into the house and followed her to a small bedroom in the back, off the central hallway. Krys had never seen it before.

"Nobody ever uses this room, but it'll be too hard to get him down the ladders into his safe space till he's healed a little. I think there are towels and stuff in the bathroom."

While Melissa pulled back the bedding, Krys explored the small bathroom, finding a stack of towels with the price tags still on them, along with some washcloths. "Do you know if there are any bandages here?"

"He probably has stuff downstairs but I wouldn't know where to look," Melissa said, coming to stand in the doorway. "I'll run over to the clinic. What else will you need?"

"Just go out to my car." She pulled the key from her jeans pocket. "There's a first-aid kit in the trunk. Do they get infections like humans?"

"Don't think so."

"The kit should have everything I need for bandaging and suturing, then." She'd know more once she got a look at the wounds.

Mirren's rumble preceded him down the hall, and Krys held on to the door facing to steady herself as she pushed past Melissa. Aidan hobbled into the room, mostly under his own steam. His face was the color of snow, but he stopped, looking for Krys, before Mirren could hustle him to the bed.

His eyes were scary pale, and she knew he needed to feed. "Are you OK, *mo rún?*"

My beloved. He'd told her what it meant after he'd used it on her a few times. It sounded so much like "moron" that she'd had to make sure it wasn't an insult. "I'm well enough to take care of you."

He finally let Mirren help him into bed and began barking orders. "Mirren, get Will over here. Mark, get Hannah. We need to figure out what happened today. Krys can take care of me." Being hurt hadn't made him less bossy. That was probably a good sign.

By the time they got him settled on the bed, Melissa had returned with the oversize first-aid kit. "You want me to stay or go?" she asked Aidan.

Aidan's voice was curt. "Go home."

"Ignore him." Krys shook her head. "You need to stay a few minutes."

Melissa laughed. "And let me present Aidan Murphy, giving you his pigheaded Irish farmer look."

Krys bit back a laugh. He was up on his elbows, glaring at both of them, and she could tell that he was not going to be an easy patient. As much as she'd like to be the be-all and end-all for Aidan, she might faint again if he fed from her.

"Which is the worse injury—the leg or the shoulder?" she asked. In her world, it would be the leg, but who knew what healed fastest in vampires.

He flopped back on the pillow. "Take your pick—silver blade. They'll both heal but slower than normal."

She assessed what she could of the two injuries. "Clothes need to come off."

He propped himself on his elbows again. "Good-bye, Mel."

Good Lord. "If you're going to kick her out, feed first," Krys said. She turned to Melissa. "That OK with you?"

Melissa nodded, and Krys piled up enough pillows to get him in a semi-reclining position, and then elevated his leg. Melissa sat next to him, pushed up the sleeve of her sweater, and held out her arm. He bit fast, and pulled hard on Melissa's arm, holding it tight enough to pucker her skin. She closed her eyes and clenched her jaw.

Krys stretched out beside him and propped herself on her elbow. With her free hand she swept his hair away from his forehead and stroked his face. "Slow down a little," she murmured. "You're hurting her."

It took a couple of seconds for him to respond, but he gradually loosened his grip on Melissa's arm, his feeding taking on more of its normal rhythm.

Melissa sighed, and her shoulders relaxed. Krys smiled at her as Aidan finished, licking the wound to heal it and releasing her arm. "Sorry about that," he said, dropping his head back on the pillow. "You OK?"

"You bet." Melissa checked the supplies she'd pulled from the first-aid kit and spread atop the small dresser. "You sure you don't need me?" she asked Krys. "You still dizzy? Nosebleed stopped?"

Jeez, but the woman had a big mouth. "We're fine. I'll call if we run into problems," Krys said before walking her to the door. She then returned to Aidan, who was trying to pull his bloody sweater off without much luck.

"Here." She helped him shed the sweater and got light-headed when she saw the bloody mess over his left deltoid muscle. "You sure this will heal?" She wet a cloth with warm water and drew it gently across the wounds in front and back. He watched every move. "You're making me nervous."

"I bet you give good sponge baths, Dr. Harris."

"You're flirting with me?" She laughed, and was so happy to see his grin that she set aside her bandages and gave him a thorough kiss before resting her forehead against his. "You scared the hell out of me tonight."

She bandaged his chest and shoulder, and then went into the bathroom to wet another cloth. When she returned, he was fumbling with his jeans button and zipper.

"Raise your hips and let me do the rest." She eased the denim over his thighs, ignoring the urge to remove the little red briefs along with the jeans. The urge disappeared as soon as she saw the deep gash, which glowed an angry red. "Damn, Aidan. At least tell me Owen looks worse."

He chuckled. "He's not dead but he's hurting. And his doctor isn't nearly as sexy as mine." The crease in his cheek disappeared. "Truth now. Still dizzy? How bad was the nosebleed?"

He hissed as Krys cleaned the wound in the meaty part of his thigh. She didn't want him feeling guilty. "If you were a normal patient, I'd stitch this up, but you tell me—will you heal better with or without stitches?"

He propped himself up on his elbows and looked at the wound. "Without. It's not as bad as it looks. Silver fries our skin a little. And you didn't answer my question about the dizziness."

Melissa and her big mouth. "It comes and goes. Nosebleed lasted about ten minutes and then it was over. It feels sort of like getting over the flu. I'm just kind of tired." She finished the cleaning and bandaging, and stretched out beside him. "If it helped you, it was worth it."

He wrapped his good arm around her, and she settled against him under the sheet. "I hate it that you were hurt. The mating bonds can't be severed the way I can cut off the lieutenants or the fams."

She thought about that for a few moments. "I'm glad you can't cut our bond. If you need to pull energy from me, I want you to be able to do that."

He pulled her more tightly against him. "We need to practice communicating mentally. It's something Mirren, Will, Hannah, and I can do, and now that we're mated, it should work with you. Just takes concentration—"

A knock on the door interrupted him, and Will stuck his head in. "We're here—you ready to talk?"

"Yeah. Just sit wherever." Aidan eased himself up till he was propped against the headboard, and Krys stuffed a couple of pillows behind him.

Will took an armchair beside the bed. "Krys, love, maybe you could go downstairs, make sure everything's ready when Mirren takes Aidan down later."

She was being dismissed so that the big bad vampires could have their secret meeting? She nodded and tried to get up, but Aidan held her in place. "Stay. You need to be up to speed on whatever we decide to do." He closed his eyes and waited while Mirren and Hannah came in and found places to perch.

Krys met Will's eyes. They were golden brown, steady, serious, and doubtful. If Aidan wanted her here, she was staying, and if Will wanted a pissing match, she'd give it to him.

Finally, he nodded. "Sorry. You're Aidan's mate—gotta remember that. Just whack me upside the head if I forget again."

❋CHAPTER 34❋

Krys traced her fingers across Aidan's face: the contours of his cheekbones, the crease in his left cheek that turned into sexy personified when he smiled, the long lashes for which any woman she knew would kill.

He lay on his back, his legs tangled in the soft white sheets, his upper body bare. She traced her fingers along the smooth, strong chest, then reached over and lifted the bandage off his left shoulder. The skin beneath it was unmarked. He'd said it would heal as soon as he slept, and it had. She'd already checked his thigh, and it was almost healed, only a scabbed-over cut remaining.

Only this wasn't sleep, really, was it?

She settled back in bed next to him, keeping a hand on the cool skin of his chest. Not cold like a corpse, but not warm like a living human, either. Mirren had helped him down to his safe suite after the lieutenants' meeting, and when she'd climbed into bed with him, he'd been warm. She grinned. Well, more than warm.

Not that she got tired of looking at him, but she was bored. He'd made her promise to stay in his quarters throughout his daysleep. She loved going to sleep in his arms, but she had to admit that it was beyond weird to wake up next to him while he was...down. Out. Unconscious. Day-tripping. Even he couldn't tell her where he went during daylight hours.

Wherever it was, he had healed. Krys kissed his shoulder and slid out of bed, grabbing yesterday's clothes and heading for the bathroom. She looked at her watch, and then did a double take. Past noon already.

She looked back at Aidan, then at her clothes. She needed to move some stuff over here since it seemed she'd be waking up here a lot. Pulling on her jeans and sweater and tugging on her boots, she slipped out of the bedroom and closed the door softly behind her, not that Aidan would hear a bomb detonate during his daysleep.

She would take shower at home and get clean clothes. Then she'd run by the clinic and check on the patients who were still there. She'd be back long before Aidan awoke. Plus, she was hungry.

Krys climbed the ladders into Aidan's kitchen and replaced the locking mechanism the way he'd shown her. She paused to look out the kitchen window. The day was overcast and looked cold and damp. Bare branches of oak trees along the street rustled in the wind, and tall loblolly pines swayed like giant rubber straws.

She didn't have her coat with her, so she grabbed Aidan's leather jacket off the sofa and enveloped herself with his scent. It made her smile as she left his house, locking the door behind her and running next door to her own house. Hers. She'd already begun to think of it that way, although she guessed that eventually she'd move in with Aidan. Whatever he wanted. Boy, had her tune changed in the last month.

As she went into the tiny foyer of her house and closed the door, she glanced out the sidelight at Mark and Melissa's. Both cars were gone. Mark was probably trying to follow up on some of the people Hannah hadn't been able to eliminate from the list of possible traitors, and Melissa was already at the clinic.

Fifteen names. The girl had gone through the entire list, saying each name aloud and closing her eyes, seeing God only knew what. Then she'd either pronounce them faithful or say she couldn't be sure. There were fifteen "not sures," four of them fams; the rest, relatives of fams. She'd bet it was one of the relatives—fewer personal connections.

Krys sighed and went through the house to her bedroom, opening the closet and dresser and pulling out clothes. She paused, listening. Had that been the door? She waited a few seconds and then shook her head. *Get a grip, woman. These vampires are making you jumpy.*

She took the pile of clothes with her into the hallway and made a left toward the small bathroom, then heard it again. Someone *had* been at the door.

She laughed at her jitters and peeked through the window again. It was Jerry, the guy from the town meeting who'd joked with Aidan and been injured in the mill village fire. Probably wanted to know how the injured guys were doing.

She smiled and pulled the door open.

Jerry took off his baseball cap. "Hi Dr. Krys. Can I come in?" He kept talking as Krys moved aside for him to enter. "I just wanted to thank you for all you did for the guys yesterday, and for Tim. We're just torn up about what happened to Tim." He twisted the cap in his meaty hands.

Krys nodded. "It's OK. I wish I could have done more for him. He seemed like a really nice guy."

"He was the best." Jerry took a seat but seemed nervous, fidgety.

"Was there something else you needed?" Krys asked.

"Uh, well." He straightened out his Braves cap and settled it back on his head. "Aidan's, uh, asleep?"

Krys frowned at him. "You can talk to him about five, but you know that. What's up?" She wondered if he had a medical problem that he didn't want anyone to know about.

"I need you to come with me." He stood up and faced her, his fists clenching and unclenching.

"What?" Krys smiled. "To the clinic? Is somebody hurt?"

Even as she asked the question, her internal alarms finally rang. She should have been more wary. Jerry was on that list of fifteen don't-knows, and he was jittery. She began edging toward the front door.

"Gotta take you to the mill," he said. "He promised he wouldn't hurt you if you don't give him trouble. He just wants Aidan."

A rivulet of sweat ran down Jerry's forehead as he adjusted his cap again. Krys felt the familiar slide of fear, and took another step toward the door.

"Why would you help him? Isn't your sister one of the fams here?"

Jerry moved quickly between Krys and the door, his beefy face red and twisting in anger. "She's brainwashed, like all of you damned fools. You're a doctor, for God's sake. You should know better than to drink their Kool-Aid. She had some problems before she came here, but at least she had a life."

Krys made a run for the door, but Jerry grabbed her arm and jerked her around to face him. She kicked him in the knee—hard—and he let her go. She scrambled away again, heading toward the back door this time. If she could get into the woods, she could get away from him. No way she'd lead him into Aidan's house.

"You bitch. Think you're too damned good for a human man, don't you?" He tackled her around the waist before she cleared the living room door, and she landed on her stomach hard, with Jerry on top of her. As Krys struggled to get away, she felt a hot jolt shoot through her hip, sending pain down her leg and numbing the right side of her body.

It took a few seconds for her brain to reconnect and figure out what was happening. Taser. She felt another zap on her belly, and her arms drew in, the muscles in her shoulders and neck tightening. She couldn't control them. She couldn't do anything but lie on the floor and try to remember to breathe. How the hell was she going to get away from him?

A ripping sound drew her attention, and she shifted her eyes to see Jerry pulling a long length of silver duct tape off the roll. She tried to will her legs to move, and they did. Just a little. Just enough to make her muscles burn and itch.

"Yeah, you stupid bitches want your vampire lovers to just suck the life out of you, don't you? Don't want a real man. Don't want a real life."

While he ranted, Jerry wrapped tape around her ankles several times before pulling a penknife from his pocket and slicing through the end of the tape. Her wrists followed, and a length across her mouth, as if she could utter more than a moan anyway.

"You like damn bloodsuckers so much, I'm gonna take you to a new one. I don't like Aidan's brother any more than him, but at least the SOB wants to break up this zoo, and I can get my sister out of here."

He grunted as he hauled her over his shoulder like a sack of trash, walked out the front door, and threw her in the back of his pickup. She landed hard on her side, and her head thumped on the truck bed hard enough to send shards of bright light behind her eyeballs.

Then she was bouncing through the cold day, watching a wrench slide around in a puddle of damp leaves in front of her face. She tried to look above her for landmarks, till finally the red brick of the old cotton mill's second story rose above the side of the truck, filling her limited horizon. Jerry had brought her to Owen, and in a few hours he'd be awake.

———•———

Krys kept her eyes closed until the sounds around her died down and she thought she was alone. Jerry had hauled her into the main factory space of the mill at first, leaving her on the concrete floor surrounded by dust and cotton lint and the accumulated grime of a century of mill workers and machinery.

With her were two women bound and gagged, dirty and ragged. Probably some of the human fams Aidan's people hadn't been able to free. They watched her with dead eyes and weren't in any position to help her even if they'd wanted to. She tried to relax her muscles to ease the pull of the tape, and focused on her breathing. She had to play this smart, if she got a chance to play at all.

She cracked open an eye at the sound of movement nearby and came eye-to-toe with Jerry Caden's boots.

"Your new master'll be up soon, Doc. Gotta get you ready." He grabbed a handful of her hair in his meaty fist and pulled her to her feet before remembering that her legs were still taped together. Cursing, he hefted her up again, his shoulder slamming into her gut and making her gag.

His breathing grew ragged as he slowly shuffled up a long flight of wide concrete stairs, and Krys hoped he didn't have a heart attack. If he'd remove the tape on her wrists and ankles, she'd have a better chance of escaping Jerry than any of the vampires. If Owen got her again, he'd hold her as bait for Aidan, and God knew what he could do to her before help arrived.

Jerry finally heaved himself to the top stair and shuffled her across a narrow hallway, dropping her to the floor with a thud that sent sharp pain shooting through her hip and shoulder as she tried to keep her head from bouncing off the concrete. He left her there, closing the door behind him.

Krys struggled to a sitting position and looked around. The floor was concrete, the cinder-block walls painted institutional puke green. Probably some midlevel bean counter's office during the mill's glory days. A couple of cracked, grimy windows—the ones that weren't broken—let in a murky bit of light. Looked like late afternoon, but dark would creep in early, urged by heavy clouds and the threat of more snow.

Pushing with her legs, she propelled herself backward until she was wedged into the corner of the room farthest from the door, her back against the wall. The pain and heat and itch of the Taser had worn off, leaving her with only a dull ache in her muscles and the threat of cramps where the tape had caught her arms and legs in an unyielding, unnatural position for so long.

Aidan. Krys closed her eyes and wondered how soon he would awaken, and whether he'd know what had happened to her. She thought about what he'd said about concentrating and communicating mentally. She didn't know if he could hear her in his daysleep, or if he could hear her at all, but she began a mantra. *Jerry is traitor. I'm at the mill. Second floor. It's a trap. Don't come alone. Jerry is traitor. I'm at the mill...*

She might die tonight. The odds were pretty good, her scientist's brain told her. She just hoped that somehow, some way, she'd get a chance to take Owen with her. Killing his brother might bother Aidan more than he'd admit. To her own surprise, she realized it wouldn't bother her at all. She just had to be vigilant and smart and look for an opening.

The room grew darker. Krys could barely make out the outline of the door, and what light did filter through the window was coming from the streetlight.

She shivered, not from the cold of the room but from the sound of footsteps on the stairs.

CHAPTER 35

In the hour before twilight, Aidan dreamed for the first time in four hundred years.

He sat at a rough-hewn wooden table across from Abby, at their little farmhouse outside Kinsale where he worked fourteen-hour days to scratch out enough food to feed them and five-year-old Cavan. Owen had joined them, as he often did, regaling them with stories of his adventures.

"It's soldiers we need," Owen said as Abby cleaned off the table. Cavan had finally nodded off, and Aidan had deposited him in the small corner bed.

Owen was fired up. "Red Hugh is marching Ulstermen to meet the Spaniards. They're coming to help us. You're the best blade fighter in the county, Áodhán. Help us kill the English, and you won't have to waste away on this cursed farm."

"It's only cursed to you." As the eldest, Owen had inherited the small family farm. He hadn't wanted it, but to Aidan it was everything. His own land to work. His own home.

Owen was insistent. "Look at your son. He deserves better than having his *da* slave under the bonds of an Englishman."

The boy's dark hair, so much like his father's, reflected light from the hearth fire. Aidan couldn't help but agree: his son did deserve better.

———•·———

Aidan pulled his wool cloak tighter around himself and huddled closer to his fellow soldiers. January had blown in cold and wet. Hunger gnawed at his guts, and today's march had seen a rough pebble finally work its way into the sole of his boot. He'd torn off part of his long, filthy shirt to wrap his feet, but he couldn't feel them anymore.

Next to him, Owen stirred. "A hunt. It's what we need, Brother. We must find something to eat. Otherwise we're going to die out here."

And then where would Cavan and Abby be, if I let myself die of hunger out here in the countryside while the Spaniards wait in Kinsale?

He nodded and unwedged himself from the cluster of men around him, the *kern*, the foot soldiers. "Keep your arse still," the man next to him mumbled. He never opened his eyes, and Aidan and Owen slipped out of the pile and into the dense woods behind the small clearing.

The rest of Red Hugh's men were scattered, sick, hungry, freezing. Every day they came across the bodies of those who had died along the way and been left to feed the buzzards.

Aidan felt inside his cloak for his skean, its blade sharpened, and he and Owen slipped silently across a broad field toward another wooded area. Moving helped warm him, and even if they didn't find food, he was glad they'd left the huddle of their defeated countrymen.

Kinsale lay less than a day's ride southeast, and Aidan imagined he could smell the sea from here as he and Owen headed for the trees near the river. Animals would come to the river to drink, and then they would eat.

The brush ahead of them stirred, and they locked gazes before moving ahead quietly across the wet ground.

Three figures emerged from the brush, and the brothers froze. "Friend or foe?" Aidan asked.

A woman's voice: "Neither friend nor foe, and yet both." Aidan and Owen looked at each other. A woman, out here? And a Spaniard, from the sound of her.

Then the strangers were on them. Aidan heard Owen hit the snow-packed ground a second before he did. Then a sharp pain at his throat wiped out everything but the lethargy that held his limbs to the ground, the pull at his neck and another at his arm, the fire of pain through his veins, and the sound of his heart hammering in his ears. Then blackness, then awakening to a thirst like he'd never known.

———•———

Aidan stared from the back of the cave where he'd recently awakened for the night, sensing the rising moon. He ached with hunger. He rolled off the flat rock on which he'd rested, crouching near the rear wall and moving a small rock away from its resting place.

He added a mark to the series of scratches in the rocky dust of the cave's floor. His calendar. He'd been gone from Abby and Cavan for a year now, as near as he could tell.

They lived by night, this small scathe led by Daire and the Spaniards. Vampires. They fed on soldiers and prostitutes and unwitting passersby in the nighttime alleys of nearby Cork. Owen thrived on the hunt, the power, and the blood. Aidan wanted to go home. What would happen if he returned now? Would Abby help him learn to live with this curse, find as normal a life as he could? Or was it too great a risk?

He slipped outside under the moonlight, drinking in its shadows and illumination.

"Time to hunt, Brother." Owen stood behind him, throwing his cloak over his shoulders—a much finer cloak than any Murphy had ever owned. He'd learned to pick his targets among the wealthier patrons of the Cork brothels, and had amassed a fine wardrobe. Aidan still wore the rough wool cloak that Abby had made for him when he joined the ragtag army, her touch woven through every fiber.

"I think I'll try a new district tonight," Aidan said. "I'll let you know if it's worthwhile."

Owen laughed. "Suit yourself, Brother. I like a bit of fun with my food."

A bit of rape before murder, more like. Aidan left his brother behind and headed for the farm.

———•—•———

Abby cried when he arrived, and even though Aidan had fed from a drunkard at a pub not far to the north, he fought the hunger when he looked at her. Hunger to feed and hunger for sex.

Cavan had grown inches. Aidan could tell by looking at his small form curled in the same bed as before. He still looked like his *da,* with his dark, tousled hair.

Aidan struggled for the words to tell Abby what had happened, but when he did she laughed at him. "I've missed your jokes," she teased. "But that's more a tall tale worthy of your brother than you."

She'd kissed him then; had cut her lip on his fangs, and had been forced to believe. She'd been afraid, had pushed him away.

"You'll kill us all," she said. "You should have stayed with your new kind. Cavan and me, we've mourned your passing and now we'll have to mourn you again."

He began cleaning out the root cellar to give him a safe day space, sure that he could change her mind when she got used to the idea. He could do farm work at night, could feed from her. They could figure it out.

But Owen had followed him, and he made enough noise to wake Cavan when he swept into the room, just as he'd done so often before. Only this time he was hungry for more than Abby's stew.

"*Da!*" Cavan rushed toward Aidan, who'd followed Owen inside. He knelt and reached for his son, but Owen waylaid him. "No greeting for your uncle, then, Cavan?"

Abby screamed as Owen moved to bite, and Aidan looked from her to Cavan to Owen, frozen. He lunged for his son.

———

He'd done exactly as Owen hoped. He'd saved the boy, thinking his danger the greatest. He'd snatched Cavan away from Owen, taken him outside, and told him to hide. By the time he returned, Owen held Abby's limp form in his arms, his mouth at her throat, and a knife at her breast.

"I'll drain her and you'll turn her," Owen gasped, blood—Abby's blood—dripping from his chin. "She can love both of us now."

Owen had loved Abby first, but Abby had chosen Aidan. He'd always known that his brother was jealous, but he hadn't known how deeply or how far he'd go to have her.

"Let her go, Owen. She wants no part of our kind. We'll both leave her, go back to Dublin." Maybe there was still room to reason with him. Abby might survive if she got help.

Owen gave him a macabre and bloody grin. "She might love me more now, Brother. You might have been a better man; I'll give you that. But I'm a better vampire."

Aidan finally rushed him, lunging to place himself between Abby and the knife, but Owen had easily sidestepped him and plunged the skean hilt-deep into his wife's chest. He lowered Abby, near death, to the floor, and dragged the sharp knife over his own wrist to feed her.

But Aidan had seen the revulsion on her face when she learned what he was. She wouldn't want it for herself, wouldn't want Cavan to grow up among them. He threw himself at Owen and pulled his own skean, holding it to his brother's throat. But he couldn't do it. He remembered the wild, carefree big brother he'd loved, and knew that killing him wouldn't make Abby love a monster.

Owen had run away, leaving Aidan to gather Abby in his arms, touch the face he'd loved so much, smell the hay and the wildflowers and the earth that made up her world. He could have tried to turn her and hoped she'd accept it. Instead, he let her die.

He found Cavan hiding in the barn, erased his memories of the night, and took the child to a nearby farm, where he left him an hour before sunrise. He buried his wife and set his torch to the little farmhouse. The next morning he made his way to Ulster and stowed belowdecks on a ship heading for the colonies, leaving his brother and Ireland behind.

———•———

Aidan sat up, disoriented by the dreams. Then he knew. Krys had been trying to talk to him, to warn him. He rubbed his eyes and tried to shake off the fog of daysleep.

"Owen has her," Mark said. He and Melissa sat on the sofa in Aidan's suite. Melissa's eyes were red-rimmed.

"Shit." Fighting off panic, Aidan shook off the last of the dream and grabbed the clothes Mark handed him, dressing quickly and heading for the hatch. Mark grabbed his arm.

"Feed first," Mark said. "While you do, I'll fill you in."

Aidan hesitated, and then nodded. He had to be at full strength, especially after all the healing he'd just done. He sat on the edge of the bed again, with Melissa beside him, already rolling up her sleeve. "Talk to me."

"Our traitor is Jerry Caden," Mark said. "I was a half step behind him all morning. When Mel told me Krys hadn't come to the clinic, I went to her house. I figured she was still with you but I wanted to be sure."

Damn it. Jerry had been volunteering for a lot of stuff lately, which was out of character for him. Aidan had thought he was finally settling in. Instead, he was gathering information to sell them out. He was a walking dead man.

"He broke in here?"

Mark shook his head. "She'd gone home—to take a shower, looked like. Her door was unlocked, your coat was on her sofa, stuff overturned. There was a scuffle, but no blood. Truck tires in the driveway slush. It was almost dusk, so we came straight here."

Aidan closed his eyes and concentrated. "She's been trying to communicate with me. I'm pretty sure she's at the mill, on the second floor."

He patted Melissa's leg, and leaned over to grab his boots. "Call Will and have him scatter the scathe around the mill." He thought for a second. "And talk to Hannah, get her to help Mirren any way she can. Tell Mirren to rebond everyone to him as soon as possible."

Mark stopped in midpace and stared at Aidan. "You're turning the scathe over to Mirren?"

Aidan put a hand on his shoulder. "Tell him. If I don't come back, he'll keep everyone safe." Mirren might not want the mantle of leadership, but he'd accept it if there was no other choice.

Owen Murphy was going to meet his final death tonight. And if Aidan went with him, so be it—as long as Krys survived it.

CHAPTER 36

The door opened, light from a bright fluorescent lantern spilling into the room and causing Krys to squint at the man's dark outline. She didn't have to see his face to know it was Owen. Her heart began a steady, hard pounding, as if it remembered him and how close he'd already come to stopping its rhythm forever. She swallowed and took as deep a breath as she could through her nose. She had to stay sharp if she had any hope of living through this.

If Owen was awake, so was Aidan, and he'd said their bonds would always let him know where she was. He'd be here. Her job was to survive till help arrived.

As her eyes adjusted, she noticed the boots first, black leather with a silver buckle, worn but expensive-looking.

"There you are, little lamb." Owen sat cross-legged on the floor in front of her. The lantern cast odd, elongated shadows across the room as he laid a shotgun on the floor next to him.

Krys looked at him and tried to see Aidan. They had the same eyes, strong cheekbones. Owen had blond hair to

Aidan's dark, and the same cleft chin, which should have softened his features but instead gave his mouth a cruel edge. His complexion was slightly flushed, so he'd fed. The less hungry he was, the better for her; except that he couldn't feed from her now because of the bond—at least not as long as Aidan lived.

He smiled and reached for her. "This will hurt. Sorry, love."

She braced for a cut or a blow, but he simply grabbed one edge of the duct tape that crossed her mouth and yanked it off. After all these hours, it felt as though half of her lips went with it, and Krys hated the involuntary gasp it produced. She reached a tongue to touch her bottom lip and tasted blood. Great. Like Owen needed more stimulation.

She worked her jaw back and forth a few times. "Why don't you just leave us alone?" She hated that her voice sounded whiny and scared. He'd broken Lucy, but Krys was determined that he wouldn't break her, no matter what. She wouldn't sell Aidan out. Plus, she had a big advantage over Lucy. If Owen tortured her, it would be easier for her to die.

He pulled a long knife from a sheath on his thigh and leaned over her. She gritted her teeth and waited for the pain, but he wrapped both arms around her, inhaling as he reached around and, she finally realized, used the knife to cut the tape around her wrists.

"There now, love." He pulled her arms in front of her, and she winced as the tight muscles tried to unwind. Gently he pulled the tape off her wrists, and then shifted over to cut and remove the tape from her ankles. She shifted her gaze to the door but it looked impossibly far away.

"Now we can have a proper conversation. We are practically in-laws, after all." Owen settled cross-legged in front of her again and propped his elbows on his knees. "What is your name?"

Krys studied him. Would it be better to engage him in conversation or just push him to do whatever it was he planned? She needed to give Aidan and his lieutenants enough time to get there.

"Krys," she said. "Krystal Harris."

Owen smiled, and Krys could see the resemblance to Aidan more clearly, in the shape of his eyes and the way they crinkled at the corners when he smiled. He'd probably been as beautiful as Aidan was in his own way, before he'd grown so gaunt and desperate.

"You look alike, you and Aidan." She rubbed her wrists, massaging the feeling back into her hands.

Owen began rubbing her ankles, mimicking the motion she made on her wrists. "We look like our ma," he said. "She had the light hair like mine, but we both got her eyes. You surprise me, though. You're nothing like Abigail."

Aidan's wife. She wished she'd asked Aidan more about her now, and wondered what her relationship with Owen had been.

"What was she like?"

Owen leaned back, stretching his long legs out beside Krys and leaning back on his arms. "She was sweet and soft, with golden hair and eyes the color of the sea off Kinsale." He smiled as he spoke. "She laughed a lot, but when she got mad at you she was a fierce one."

"You loved her. All this was about jealousy?" Krys spoke without thinking and as soon as the words were out, she wished she could retract them.

Owen stood quickly, grabbed her wrists, and pulled her to her feet. "I did love her, and your precious, sanctimonious Aidan killed her."

Killed her? Krys shook her head. He must be mistaken. Aidan's tears were etched into her memory. "Abby didn't want him after he'd been turned, but he's mourned her all these years. He wouldn't kill her."

She flinched as Owen stroked her hair. "Oh yes he did, love. My baby brother decided he'd rather her be dead than become one of us, where she might love me better than him. He didn't know I was watching, but I saw him hold her while she died and then set fire to that shitty little farmhouse. Then he left wee Cavan an orphan and sailed off to America."

As he talked, he trailed a finger down Krys's neck, down her chest, and between her breasts. "You're his mate now, Krystal Harris. Would Saint Aidan kill you before he let you become one of us? He thinks we're such monsters."

He leaned in to kiss her. The smart thing would be to go along with it, even encourage him, but Krys couldn't stand the idea of his mouth on her again, not after last time. She quickly slammed a knee into his groin and shot a fist toward his Adam's apple.

She didn't see his reaction coming; only saw the floor and the shadows tilting past as he flung her headfirst across the room. On instinct, she held her arms out to brace herself for the impact against the opposite wall. She hit it with such force that she heard bone snap in her left forearm. Even then, she still hit her head hard enough to blacken her vision.

When consciousness returned, she was curled on the concrete floor, cradling her arm against her. The whole thing flopped—both the radius and ulna had snapped. Everything went gray for a few seconds as she stirred, but the pain brought her around.

Strong fingers grasped her hair and jerked her to her feet.

"Where were we?" Owen asked.

He pulled her against him, pressing the broken arm between their bodies, and Krys fought to remain conscious. She tried to pull herself beyond the pain, away from her physical self. But God, this hurt, and the nausea and dizziness meant she probably had a concussion as well.

"...Of course, my brother has bonded you so I can't feed from you."

He'd been talking all along, but words finally began to filter through the sharp pulses shooting through her head. Her mind started working again, enough to realize that he could beat her to death, but he couldn't drain her life away and make her think she wanted it. Good.

"Since I can't feed from you, Aidan and I will have to play the game a bit differently this time. Perhaps he'll turn you into one of us to keep me from cutting out your heart in front of him." He laughed softly and kissed her cheek.

Owen stilled, becoming so quiet and motionless that Krys could hear her heart pounding. The quiet made her more aware of the pain, and dizziness made the room go gray and tilt again. Finally she heard the sounds that had caught Owen's ear. Noises downstairs, then loud pops that sounded like gunfire, then silence.

The sound of boots on the stairs floated up to them, a steady thump made by someone who wasn't trying to be silent. Owen shoved Krys to the floor in front of the door and backed into the shadows, leaning over to pick up the shotgun. He aimed it at the door, waiting.

Krys opened her mouth to scream, and then closed it. She thought the words instead, over and over. *Shotgun aimed at door. Shotgun.*

❄CHAPTER 37❄

The message came through: *shotgun.* And Krys was hurt. Broken arm. Concussion. She was thinking clearly enough to warn him but he had to move fast.

He sent a message back to her, not knowing if she'd understand: *I'm here.* Then he concentrated on his brother.

Things had gone smoothly so far. Will had taken the two human women to the secure rooms under city hall. Mirren was hunting down Jerry Caden, and God help the man when he caught him.

Aidan stood to the side of the door, grasped it with his right hand, and turned the knob. A shotgun blast flew past him as the door opened. Owen would fire again as soon as he could ready the gun, so Aidan rushed in before the dust settled. Part of his mind registered that Krys was on the floor, but he had to move past her for now.

He charged Owen with a head to his midsection, knocking the gun to the floor. They grappled for a few seconds, grunting and pushing and accomplishing nothing. As far as physical strength, Aidan had a size advantage. But Owen had fed steadily for a couple of weeks now, and was strong enough. Finally, they separated and stared at each other.

Move to the wall, he told Krys, and she heard him. In the periphery, he saw her dragging herself away from them, towing Owen's shotgun with her. Smart girl. He didn't know if she could use a shotgun, or even if she was able to hold it with a broken arm, but at least she was getting it out of Owen's reach.

The sound of the shotgun barrel scraping on the floor distracted Owen briefly, and Aidan pulled the knife he'd been fingering in its sheath and sank it to the hilt in Owen's midsection. Forcing the blade inward and up toward the heart, he shut down the voice in his head that said "brother" and listened to the one that said "mate." This was for Krys.

But he'd hesitated an instant too long, and Owen shoved him away, leaving the knife embedded. He looked down at it for a moment, then grasped the hilt and pulled it out with a sticky, wet sound. "You should use the kukri blade, Brother. Works better." His voice was raspy, his breathing uneven.

Owen staggered toward the corner where Krys had wedged herself, holding the shotgun in her right hand and cradling her left in her lap. "Krystal and I were having a talk, weren't we, love? I was telling her all about how lovely Abigail was, and how you let her die. Of course, she already knows what a selfish, self-righteous bastard you are." He kicked her in the shoulder above her broken arm, and she shrieked as she toppled to her side, but still managed to hold onto the shotgun.

Rage blackened Aidan's vision, but Krys's voice eased through him like cool water. *Don't listen to him. Stay focused.*

She was right. Owen was trying to push his buttons, get him angry enough to make a mistake, and it had almost worked. He sent a thought back to her: *Slide the shotgun to me when I get in front of you.* He moved slowly to his right, two small steps, and as he hit the ground, she shoved the gun toward him.

By the time Owen reacted, Aidan had it aimed.

Owen backed up and held up his hands. "You're no killer, Áodhán. You couldn't kill me in Kinsale, and you can't do it now." He circled the room slowly, away from Krys, edging toward the door.

Aidan's hand was steady. The barrel of the shotgun tracked Owen's progress.

They both stilled at the sound of footsteps on the stairs. Aidan grinned. "Friend or foe, *Eógan?*" he said. "You assumed I cut the bonds to my people again, but are you willing to bet your life on it?"

Owen hissed and bared his fangs, charging as Aidan pulled the trigger. The shot tore through Owen's shoulder and upper chest, splattering blood on the wall but not stopping his forward motion. Too late, Aidan saw the syringe in Owen's hand and heard Krys scream.

The needle entered his belly, and Aidan's thoughts blurred with pain as he hit the concrete floor with Owen's unconscious weight on top of him. He didn't have the strength to move Owen off him, but he squeezed his hand between them to fumble for the syringe. His fingers finally closed on the cylinder and pulled it out, empty but for a coating of red inside. Vaccinated blood. He'd forgotten about the damned blood. How much had he gotten?

Enough that he already felt like someone had doused his guts with gasoline and lit a match.

His mental link to Krys had gone black, and he struggled to push Owen off him.

He'd never been so glad to hear Mirren's gravelly voice. "I got him, A." Then Owen's weight disappeared, and Aidan turned his head in time to see Mirren's big hands clamped on either side of Owen's head. His brother's neck broke with a dull snap.

Aidan tried to sit up. "Krys—gotta check."

Mirren pressed his shoulders to the floor and stuck his face an inch from Aidan's. "I'll check on her, but don't you freaking move, got me?"

Aidan nodded, and Mirren left his field of vision. If anything had happened to her, he couldn't survive it. He didn't want to.

"She's alive." Mirren pulled out his cell phone and punched in a number. "You keep getting in so much trouble, even I have Mark on speed dial now."

Aidan closed his eyes as Mirren barked instructions. Then he opened them again as the big man peeled off his jacket, sat on the floor next to him, and pulled up the sleeve of his own sweater. He jerked a knife from his boot and made a neat incision on his forearm. "Emergency rations," he said, and lifted Aidan's head to help him drink. "Go slow. Then we're going to have a repeat of the drain-and-fill routine you did on me. Payback's a bitch."

Warmth spread through Aidan's system as Mirren's blood revived him a little, and he relaxed, slumping back to the floor. "Nasty stuff. How bad is she hurt?"

A groan from Owen got their attention.

"Shit." Mirren went to stand over Owen while Aidan struggled to his feet, holding onto the wall until the room quit spinning. When his brother had fallen, his head rested at a decidedly odd angle. Now it was beginning to straighten.

"He's healing." Mirren looked at Aidan. "What do you want to do with him?"

Aidan looked at his brother for a few seconds before leaning over to pick up the knife he'd lost earlier in the fight. He dropped to his knees beside him, closing his eyes till another wave of dizziness passed. Owen's face was softer in unconsciousness, more like the carefree boy he'd once been. They'd loved each other then, and Aidan wasn't sure when things had changed, how they'd ended up so far apart. It had started long before Abby. Damned thing was, he'd finally realized tonight that Owen wasn't the only one he hadn't forgiven for Abby's death. He hadn't forgiven himself.

But this wasn't the brother he'd loved. That brother had died in the woods north of Kinsale. "Good-bye, *Eógan*," he whispered. "Be at peace."

Aidan lowered the knife and pierced his brother's heart. Owen never woke.

✳ C H A P T E R 3 8 ✳

Mirren couldn't believe Aidan had done it—just cut the damned heart out and laid it carefully on the floor, then toppled over in a dead faint.

He looked around at the mess. Aidan unconscious, Krys unconscious. Blood all over the room. Owen dead next to his own lump of a heart. What a freaking train wreck.

Where the hell was Will? He heard a noise at the door, but it was Hannah.

She stopped and stared at Aidan for a moment, then walked to Krys and knelt beside her, touching her arm. "Her future is uncertain." The girl frowned. "There are two paths, one that leads into light and one into darkness, and I can't see which one she takes. It will depend on Aidan."

Damn. They were mated, so he could be draining energy from her. Mirren had to get him into a drain-and-feed. He was turning a nasty shade of yellow. There was a reason Mirren didn't want his own scathe, and he was looking around at it. Responsibility.

"Bloody hell. Literally." Will breezed in and stood over Owen. "Please tell me that's the son of a bitch's heart on the floor."

"I'm tellin' you. But he didn't die before he shot Aidan full of vaccinated blood. Get him over to the clinic while we figure out what to do with Krys."

"You called Mark and Mel for the feed?"

Mirren nodded. "Yeah, they'll meet you there. I'll come as soon as I can."

"What's the deal with her?" Will stood over Krys, watching Hannah hold her hand and croon to her in an unintelligible chant.

"Hannah can't tell. We need to get her to a hospital and—"

"Negative." Will grabbed Hannah's shoulders and moved her out of the way, leaned over, and picked up Krys. "No hospitals. No humans involved in this bollocks. I'm taking her to the clinic—you bring Aidan. If she makes it, terrific. If not, so be it."

Mirren had never seen Will look so fierce. Fact was, he'd always wondered what Aidan had seen in the man. Good at organizational shit, but never kept the same fam for very long, never formed any close ties. Didn't seem to like humans for much besides feeding and sex. But Aidan trusted him, and that had always been enough.

"It won't matter if he moves her," Hannah said. "Her future paths remain the same."

Will snorted and left, his boots echoing in the stairwell as he took Krys away.

"Holy mother of God." Mirren looked at Hannah. "Can you tell anything else?"

She shook her head. "Jerry told you something, though?"

Mirren had broken a few strategic bones when he finally caught Jerry Caden outside the mill, but the bastard had spilled it before he died. He didn't know a lot about Owen's backers, but he did remember the name Ludlam: Will's daddy and Mirren's greatest nemesis on the Tribunal. Taking on Matthias Ludlam promised that some major shit was going to fly.

He didn't say it aloud, but Hannah looked at him with those creepy black eyes and said, "Yes, it is."

"Can you do this?" Mirren watched as Melissa pulled the portable IV unit into the sub-suite where they'd done his drain-and-feed earlier. He'd laid Aidan out on the bed. The man was still in coma-land, but Mirren had secured his arms and legs with silver chain just in case and had tied him down at the waist as well.

Melissa's hands shook as she set up the IV bag, and she sniffled. "I can't believe we're having to do this."

"Hold it together, darlin'." He watched her tie off Aidan's arm and insert the needle, watching the pale blood race through the tube and into the bag. "How's Krys?"

Melissa sat beside Aidan and stroked his hair, looking up as Mark arrived. "She's in and out. Wants Aidan. Wants to get up. Talks to her father. Really hates her father."

Hell. Sounded as fruit-loopy as Lucy. She was still restrained in one of the secured suites under city hall, behind silver bars, next door to Owen Murphy's teenage vamp. They were feeding Lucy at knifepoint to keep her from killing the donors, who were scared shitless. They were going to have to put her down eventually, so maybe he should go ahead and just do it while Krys couldn't lay a guilt trip on them about it.

"I think he's coming around." Mark sat on the bed on the other side of Aidan while Melissa switched IV bags. Aidan had begun straining against the chains, although he hadn't opened his eyes. "Where's Will?"

"Playing lookout," Mirren said. "Trying to track down the rest of Owen's wandering scathe members."

Melissa looked up. "Is Hannah still with Krys?"

"Won't leave her." Mirren couldn't believe the way she'd latched on to that human. Maybe because Krys didn't seem nearly as creeped out by Hannah's skills as the rest of them were.

"Uh-oh, showtime." Mark took a step away from the bed. Aidan's eyes popped open, silvery white, and he struggled against the chains. He bared his fangs and jerked toward Melissa, who calmly moved out of reach.

"Suck it up, A." Mirren moved to the foot of the bed where Aidan could see him, and the chains stilled. "I know you can understand me, 'cause Jenn talked my ear off while I was at this party and I heard every word she said. Here's the deal, in case you're fuzzy on the details. Owen's dead. Will's rounding up any of his people who might be hanging around and convincing them it's not in their best interest to stay. You got some vaccinated blood and we're getting it out."

Aidan's voice rasped. "Krys?"

Mirren had hoped he wouldn't ask. She was barely hanging on. "She's across the hall. Hannah's taking care of her."

Aidan closed his eyes, and Mirren was glad he hadn't asked for specifics. On some level, because of their mating bond, A probably knew how bad off Krys was. But he hoped that awareness would stay cloudy a while longer.

"He's getting weaker." Melissa watched the heart monitor, drawing signals from the sensors that she'd stuck on his neck and chest, beeping more slowly. "Mark, you go first so I can keep an eye on him. Remember from when we did this with Mirren—he doesn't know to anesthetize and go slow. It's gonna hurt. I have some bandages over there for afterward."

Mark pulled a small knife from his pocket, scoring his forearm. He stretched out on the bed and held his arm so the blood would drop on Aidan's lips. Aidan stirred and opened eyes that were almost white.

Aidan had better pull through this. Mirren had suspected how unsuited he was to lead a scathe but he hadn't really known till tonight. Aidan could have it. Too many decisions—who got medical care, who was responsible for what job, everybody wanting a piece of you. He'd always known that Aidan was one tough SOB in his own moody way; he had to be, just to hold the same scathe together for so long. Tonight Mirren had had to deal with just a fraction of the focus it must take to keep up with everybody's crap. No thanks.

Aidan pulled against the chains, fangs out, reaching for Mark's wrist. "Here we go," Mark said, and flinched as he lowered his arm and let Aidan bite.

❊ CHAPTER 39 ❊

Before she fell asleep at night, Krys always flew. She'd ease into some twilight half-consciousness where she could soar. She'd fly over foreign landscapes she'd never seen in real life, gliding soundlessly, watching the terrain change below her, feeling the air move out of her way as she traveled.

She felt like that now, only she was awake. And the terrain was a ceiling with crisp edges and crown molding. Her room in the sub-suites.

She was dying. She knew it in the lucid moments, recognizing the physical symptoms. Her hands and feet felt like blocks of ice, telling her the circulation was slowing. Her lungs were full of cotton. She slept most of the time. And the pain seemed distant now, only background noise.

She turned her head and saw Hannah's black eyes on her. The girl had been here whenever she woke. Last time she'd looked, those eyes had been closed in daysleep. So it must be evening again.

Krys needed to know one thing, and she swallowed, trying to pull enough breath to ask.

"Aidan will be well. They are replacing his blood. He'll be here soon."

Right. This was Hannah. She didn't have to ask, because Hannah always knew. "Tell him——"

Hannah placed a small hand over Krys's mouth. "Don't talk. You must make a choice, and I must ask you this before Aidan gets here."

What was she talking about? Krys swallowed and finally gave up, just thinking the question at her: *What choice?*

Tears spilled from the girl's eyes. "You are dying."

Krys tried to smile. "I know," she finally croaked out, then thought: *It's OK. Tell Aidan I wouldn't have changed anything. Make sure he knows that.*

"You could still be with him." Hannah's voice dropped to a whisper. "You can become one of us."

Krys's heart, slowing on its march toward a total stop, caught a burst of adrenaline and fluttered. Could she do that? *Would* she do that, to stay with Aidan?

"It doesn't always work," Hannah said. "And we don't have much time. But decide now. If you wait, it will either be too late or the choice will fall to Aidan."

Krys closed her eyes. She didn't know what came after death. There were the near-death stories of white lights and peace. Once she had thought peace was all she wanted, but not anymore. Aidan hadn't realized it, but he'd shown her how to live. And she wanted to live with him, on whatever terms it had to be.

He was so conflicted about his own nature, would he still want her if she were a vampire? Would he rather have her be like Abby and die whole and human? She started to ask Hannah those questions, but didn't. This wasn't Aidan's decision. It was hers, and she wasn't Abby. She wanted to live.

She opened her eyes and looked at Hannah, choking a little as she swallowed again. "Do it."

Hannah moved to the opposite side of the bed, away from Krys's broken arm, and closed her eyes.

What was she waiting on? If she dragged it out too much, either Krys would lose her nerve or faint again, or Aidan would get here. He might or might not turn her. But he'd flogged himself for centuries over what had happened with Abby. She didn't want him having to decide.

"What is it, darlin'?"

Krys shifted her eyes to the door, where Mirren towered. Had Hannah called him?

"She is dying, and we're going to make her vampire."

Krys felt the room gray and float farther away. "Do it," she whispered. "No time."

Mirren closed the door behind him. "Hannah, the Tribunal's outlawed turning anybody, and last thing we need is more of their shit raining down on us."

Krys was vaguely aware of Hannah moving away from the bed. "Do you care about the Tribunal or do you care about Aidan?"

Somebody had better move. Krys batted her hand on the bed to get their attention, and it wiped out all the strength she had left.

"Shit. Damn it all to hell." Mirren sat on the bed where Hannah had been. "I'll drain her. I can take more blood than you. Then you feed her."

He turned Krys. "You ready for this, darlin'? It's almost like the drain-and-feed, but we take it all the way. You'll die on us, and then we'll bring you back. But you gotta know, it doesn't always work. It's about a fifty-fifty shot."

What difference did it make? She was dying anyway. Krys blinked to show she understood. "S'OK."

He stretched out alongside her. "I need to hit a big vein and do this fast, right?"

She blinked again, and felt his fingers probing for her carotid artery. Her heart suddenly galloping, she swallowed hard and fought the flight urge. Was she really going to do this? God, what if she came out a real monster? What if...

She gasped as his fangs hit the artery. The last thing she saw before the room faded was Aidan standing in the doorway, his face twisted in rage.

CHAPTER 40

Aidan was immobile, eyes frozen on a scene that could have taken place four hundred years earlier. Owen at Abby's neck. Mirren at Krys's.

With a roar he flew at Mirren, whose mouth sucked hungrily at her artery, her blood streaming down her neck onto the pillow. She was the same color as the sheets.

Something tackled him halfway to the bed and he fell, trying to scramble out of the iron grip that dragged him to the floor.

Fangs bared, Aidan looked over his back at Hannah. Her arms were locked around his chest and her legs around his thighs, crippling him. She might have looked like a child, but her physical strength was vampire. He wrestled her beneath him, unwilling to hit her.

"She wants this," Hannah gasped. "She was dying. It's her only way to survive."

Aidan shot an elbow back and heard an *umph* as her grip broke and she fell away from him. He stayed on the floor, staring up at Mirren. His long body stretched beside Krys, a heavily muscled arm thrown across her waist, his mouth at her neck, jaws working. Aidan rose and gave Hannah a warning look that kept her on the floor. God help him, he didn't know what to believe.

"Are you sure?" He swallowed his own hunger as he watched Mirren feed. "Are you sure she was dying? Are you sure this is what she wanted?"

Hannah's voice was steady. "Yes, I saw it from the beginning—that she would have a choice between two paths. I didn't know until today what paths they were. She could die or she could live as one of us. I asked her and she wants to try. She knows it doesn't always work, but she wants you."

Time was running out. She still might not make it. Or she could survive but end up like Lucy, a mad animal that had to be fed and caged. And the Tribunal would have one more reason to come after them, for turning someone during the pandemic crisis. Not to mention that she might not want him anymore afterward, might not love him the way she had as a human.

Krys gasped, and her breathing grew rapid and shallow. She quit breathing for a few seconds entirely before gasping again and falling still.

"It's time," Hannah said quietly. "I will feed her. You are still too weak."

Mirren rolled away and fell heavily to the floor, his face flushed and eyes hooded as he leaned against the side of the bed.

Hannah moved to take his place, but Aidan stopped her. "No. Stay away from her."

She clenched her little fists and stared at him, openmouthed.

Mirren staggered to his feet, blood-drunk. "Listen, A—"

"No," Aidan repeated, his voice low. "Nobody feeds her but me. Nobody else touches her."

He climbed onto the bed beside her, ignoring his fatigue. He heard Mirren on the phone, probably calling Will to find feeders for a new vampire while they were in their daysleep. At least he hoped it would work out that way.

The last time he'd lain beside her, they'd just made love. She'd been so careful of his injuries, had taken care of him in every way. Giving. Always giving. Now it was his turn.

"Knife," he said, his voice hoarse. He held out his wrist. Mirren grasped his arm, and the pain of the knife's edge drawing across his skin helped clear his mind. He trailed a finger across the cut and stuck the finger in her mouth, leaving the blood on her tongue. Repeated the action until he felt her tongue move, seeking more. It seemed to be taking hours. He was vaguely aware of Mirren and Will talking, coming, going, but someone always there to keep his cut open.

"It's working," Hannah finally whispered.

Aidan dropped his wrist to Krys's mouth, and she didn't respond at first. "Come on, drink, damn it." He worked his wrist between her lips so his blood would reach her. Finally he felt her tongue probing at the cut, then a soft pull.

She moaned and tried to curl into a ball as the blood hit her stomach and her still-human system tried to reject it. He remembered the horrible cramps that had lasted for days as the vampire blood kept the body alive while transforming the physical systems.

Then, if she survived, the real hunger would start.

CHAPTER 41

Life had dwindled to states of half waking and pain, with long periods of blackness between. Krys remembered the fight with Owen, but not how it had ended.

Everything hurt. Whenever her mind brought her to the surface, Aidan would be there, holding her, talking to her softly in his native Gaelic as if he knew she needed to hear his voice even if she couldn't understand the words.

Sometimes he'd be in his daysleep but Mark or Melissa would be nearby and would talk to her in words that didn't make any more sense. She must be dying, and wished she'd go ahead and be done with it—for all their sakes.

The last few times she'd stayed awake longer and had been able to lie quietly with her eyes closed and float away from the pain for short periods. She heard snippets of conversation. Aidan talking to Mark and Melissa about feeding schedules. Another time, Mirren talking about a trip. Something about Will's father.

Finally she woke without pain, and its absence made her almost euphoric. She couldn't open her eyes yet, but lay still and thought for the first time that she might live, might *want* to live.

Voices broke through: Will shouting and Aidan shushing him. She tried to open her eyes, to speak, but she couldn't bring herself out of the physical paralysis.

"It's better for all of you if I leave," Will said. "My father knows I'm here and he won't give up just because Owen failed. He'll kill everyone here to get to me."

What was the deal with Will's father? Krys couldn't remember. Aidan's voice was soft, yet she seemed to be able to hear everything with sharp clarity. Will's shouting had been almost painful. She'd had a concussion—she remembered that much. Maybe it had made her hearing hypersensitive.

Aidan was arguing. "Matthias is going to come after us anyway—using Owen was just the opening round. We're already short a lieutenant with Lucy. I need you here. Plus, if we have to fight Matthias, who knows him better than you?"

The voices faded as she drifted again, until Hannah arrived and she heard flashes of frantic talk about Mirren. He was missing? How could someone that big be missing?

Thinking of Mirren and hearing Hannah's high, clear voice evoked odd snippets of memory. Of the child lying beside her on a bed. Of Mirren coming in to help turn her...oh my God, had they backed out? Had she lived, after all? Or had they done it?

Krys fought her way to consciousness, concentrating on opening her eyes, squinting against the light, moving a hand, a foot. She finally focused, dazzled by the brightness, the sharp images, the colors and textures. That must have been some concussion.

Aidan, Will, and Hannah were standing near the foot of the bed, and she caught Will's eye.

He smiled at her and gestured to get Aidan's attention. "I believe someone's awake."

The bed dipped as Aidan stretched out next to her. She tried to reach for him, to brush away that stubborn strand of hair that always fell over one eye, but she couldn't move her arm more than a couple of inches. Either arm. Concentrating, she raised her head a fraction and saw silver chain wrapped around her wrists and ankles. What was going on?

"Hey, shhh...shhh." Aidan turned her face to his, and she was struck again by how different everything looked. Colors shone brighter, contrasts were sharper. She shifted her gaze to the paintings on the walls, to the woodwork, then the sofa, and recognized it as her old room in the sub-suites. Why was she chained to the bed?

"Krys. Look at me." Again Aidan turned her face to his. "Keep your eyes on me. Can you understand me?"

He looked beautiful, but exhausted. Had he fought Owen? It took a couple of tries, but she finally got her tongue to work. Her mouth felt as if it had been glued shut. "What happened?"

"What's the last thing you remember?"

She frowned, sorting through a clutter of images. "Owen hit me?" Talking was easier this time.

Aidan nodded. "And you were badly hurt. Very badly, *mo rún.*"

She stared at him. Could she have been turned? Wouldn't she know? *How* would she know? Finally she whispered, "Am I changed?"

He smiled and smoothed a hand across her cheek. "You made it. How do you feel?"

She felt as if—well, as if she were more alive every minute. "Are you sure?" She explored her mouth with her tongue and flinched as she cut it on a sharp canine that extended below her upper teeth. She had freakin' fangs.

Aidan chuckled. "That's going to happen a lot till you get used to them, but you'll adjust quicker than you think. Are you sure you feel the same?"

She did a mental inventory. "The pain is gone. My vision is sharper. I...well, I feel good. But hungry. I shouldn't feel hungry, should I?" She wasn't sure what she was hungry for, but the more she thought about it, the hungrier she was—almost painfully so.

"New vampires sometimes crave food for a while. Varies from person to person." He slid off the bed and walked to a tray that sat on the dresser. "See what you think of this."

She was aware of Will and Hannah leaving the room as Aidan came back with a small plate containing a sandwich and a piece of fruit. He broke off an edge of the bread crust and held it out to her. At the smell, her stomach reacted with dry heaves, and she cut her lip again on a stupid fang. Tears started to build as her own blood ran down her chin. She was going to be the worst vampire ever.

Aidan laughed. He leaned over and swiped a tongue across her chin, then kissed her. "No problem. Guess you're past people food. Time for a real meal."

"How long have I been like this?" She'd lost all sense of time. It could have been a month since she'd been taken to the mill, or a year. "Where's Jerry? Did Owen escape?"

"Owen's dead. Jerry's dead. All you have to worry about is getting through your transition, and you're almost there."

"Mirren's gone?" Now that she knew the fangs were there, it felt as if she had too many teeth. Not only was she going to walk around bleeding on herself, she was going to lisp.

Anxiety tightened the skin around Aidan's eyes, and his smile disappeared. "Mirren went to South Carolina, to take Jennifer back to her family. She didn't want to stay after Tim died. He was late getting back and he doesn't answer my mental signals. Our bonds are still there, so I know he's alive. He's just off radar for some reason."

"You need to go after him?" She didn't want him to leave her. She didn't know how to be a freakin' vampire without him.

"Not yet. He's probably just taking some R and R."

Right. Mirren was *so* not a rest-and-relaxation kind of guy. She shifted uncomfortably on the bed. "Why am I chained?"

She started as a voice came from the other side of the room. "It's for my benefit."

Mark rose from a chair in the far corner, smiling. "Welcome back."

Had he been here all along? Why would the chains be for his benefit unless...oh God, another chance to be a vampire failure.

As Mark approached the bed, the scent of him hit her like a tire iron, straight in the gut. She sensed his pulse quickening, could almost feel the rush of blood through his body, and her hunger deepened. She was so hungry, and her new fangs ached. His scent was a perfect blend of aftershave and clean skin and man. Warmth and life.

She wanted to taste him, and the thought excited her and shamed her at the same time. She struggled against the chains, not sure if she wanted to grab Mark or run from him. Maybe both. And she couldn't do this in front of Aidan.

"Mark would like to be your fam," Aidan said, stroking her shoulder to calm her. It didn't work. "Mel will stay with me. That OK with you?"

No, it wasn't OK. God, no. "I don't want to do this. I can't—"

Mark lay beside her, sandwiching her between himself and Aidan, and the scent drove all thought from her. She tried to lunge toward him before she could stop herself, but the chains stopped her. Mortified, she felt the tears start. She hadn't expected to feel like such an animal.

Aidan's voice was little more than a murmur. "Use the knife. She's not ready to bite."

She started to look at Aidan, but her attention was riveted—her mind emptied—by Mark's arm in front of her face. He'd cut across his forearm and was holding it toward her. A drop of his blood hit her mouth, and she instinctively touched her tongue to it and a groan escaped her. A voice that sounded like a ragged, frantic version of hers said, "More."

"Lick your tongue across the cut first so you don't hurt him," Aidan said, his voice soft in her ear.

Mark dropped his forearm to her mouth, and she licked across it, then sucked on the wound, and finally bit. He sighed and rested his head next to hers, keeping his arm pressed firmly to her mouth, till Aidan brushed her hair off her forehead and kissed it.

"Stop now, Krys."

She didn't want to. She could've gone on forever, but she remembered Owen's bloodlust and savagery, how the pleasure had turned to agony. She'd never do that to anyone.

———•———

Aidan set the showerhead to pulse and let the hot water beat into his back and shoulders as he poured a few squirts of shampoo into his palm and worked it into his hair.

Krys had made it through the third day of feeding. In fact, she'd taken to the whole vampire shit a helluva lot better than he had. She was going to be fine, Mark and Melissa were working perfectly as fams, and Owen was gone.

But he wasn't exactly basking in Happyland. Mirren had disappeared, and Aidan had a bad feeling about it. It wasn't like the big guy to go off radar for a day, much less a week. Will was ping-ponging among self-pity and anger and hyperactivity, which meant that Omega's progress was slowing down. He and Will were going to have a serious sit-down, and then he was going to have to find Mirren. And get someone to help develop Hannah's skills as a witch, to see if she could create a secure magical border around Penton. And find a couple of new lieutenants.

Aidan switched the water setting to rain and stuck his head under the spray. Those weren't the immediate problems. The damned elephant in the room was Krys, and where they stood. He had wondered if whatever drove his vampire mating instinct would still consider her his mate once she was turned. No problem there. He'd gotten such a raging hard-on watching her feed he'd had to leave the room and put his right hand to work.

What he hadn't considered was that she'd have her own new vampire mating mojo. He didn't know where he stood in that department. What if she wanted Mark? Or Mirren? Even the idea of that made him crazy.

Gutless wonder that he was, he hadn't had the nerve to bring up the subject with Krys, and he'd been afraid to push her toward sex. How long had it been, after he'd been turned, before he'd had any interest in women? A long time, but the situations were different. He'd been all tied in knots about Abby and pissed off about his situation.

He sensed Krys in the room before she spoke.

"Aidan?"

He turned, and damned if she didn't take his breath away. He hadn't thought she could get any more beautiful, but he'd been wrong. Her cheeks were still flushed from a recent feed, her nipples peaked beneath the sweatshirt that looked a helluva lot better on her than on him, and her mile-long legs were crossed at the ankle as she leaned against the door to the step-in shower.

He grew hard at the sight of her, and she grinned as her eyes dipped to take him in. "And here I've been so worried, thinking you didn't want me anymore. Or do you greet every female vampire who walks into your shower this way?"

He grinned. "Well, you might find this hard to believe, doctor, but I don't let just any stray female vampire wander into my shower."

Her husky laugh almost brought a groan from him as she raised her eyes to meet his.

Damn. Her dark-chocolate eyes had turned silvery and pale. She needed to feed again. But at least they'd made it back to the playful-banter stage of their relationship. "Want me to call Mark back? Remember, you have our eyes now. I can tell when you're hungry."

She shucked the sweatshirt over her head and stepped into the shower. "There are all kinds of hunger, Aidan."

❋ACKNOWLEDGMENTS❋

Thanks to agent Marlene Stringer, for being my number-one advocate; editor Eleni Caminis and the rest of the team at Montlake Romance, for all your faith and hard work; editor Melody Guy, for smoothing the rough edges; Dianne, alpha reader extraordinaire (see, the Ludlams are vampires, not aliens); chief brainstormer Susan; super-critters Kat and Amber; and the patient members of the Auburn Writers Circle, who don't always see the allure of fangs but listen anyway: Larry, Pete, Jennifer, Delaine, Matt, Shawn, Mike, and Julia.

❋ABOUT THE AUTHOR❋

Susannah Sandlin is a native of Winfield, Alabama, and has worked as a writer and editor in educational publishing in Alabama, Illinois, Texas, California, and Louisiana. She currently lives in Auburn, Alabama, with two rescue dogs named after professional wrestlers (it was a phase). She has a secret passion for quilting, reality TV, and all things paranormal.